S0-BOB-899

COLD RIVER

Also by CARLA NEGGERS

THE MIST
BETRAYALS
COLD PURSUIT
TEMPTING FATE
THE ANGEL
ABANDON
CUT AND RUN
THE WIDOW
BREAKWATER
DARK SKY
THE RAPIDS
NIGHT'S LANDING
COLD RIDGE
ON THE EDGE
"Shelter Island"
THE HARBOR
STONEBROOK COTTAGE
THE CABIN
THE CARRIAGE HOUSE
THE WATERFALL
ON FIRE
KISS THE MOON
CLAIM THE CROWN

CARLA NEGGERS

COLD RIVER

Doubleday Large Print
Home Library Edition

This Large Print Edition, prepared especially for Doubleday Large Print Home Library, contains the complete, unabridged text of the original Publisher's Edition.

ISBN-13: 978-1-61523-790-6

COLD RIVER

Printed in U.S.A.

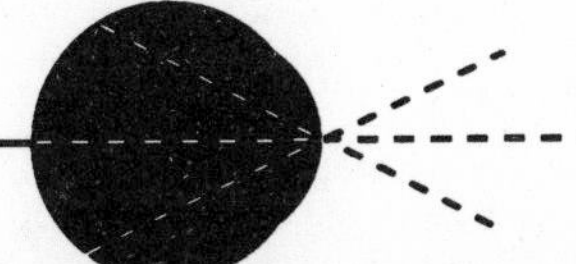

This Large Print Book carries the Seal of Approval of N.A.V.H.

For Aunt Evelyn

One

March 26—nine months ago—Black Falls, Vermont

The Cameron brothers were in town that night. Hannah Shay watched them enter O'Rourke's from her perch on a high stool at the rough-wood bar. She couldn't remember when she'd last seen them together. A.J., the eldest, was down from the mountain lodge the family owned and he ran with his wife. Elijah was home briefly from war. Sean had flown in from Southern California between fighting wildfires and making his fortune.

As they gathered at a table on the far wall, under old black-and-white photographs of their small Vermont town, Hannah doubted they noticed her with the glass of chardonnay she'd been nursing for the past thirty minutes. She had no concerns about being at the bar alone. The owner, Liam O'Rourke, a longtime Cameron friend, had little tolerance for troublemakers—including ones who were blood-related. Everyone in Black Falls knew stepping out of line at O'Rourke's meant a boot out the door or a trip in the back of a police cruiser.

Even Bowie O'Rourke, Liam's cousin, had to know.

Bowie followed the Cameron men into the bar, shutting the door with a hard thud. He didn't take a table but instead stood two stools down from Hannah and ordered a beer. He was a stonemason and, at thirty-four, the same age as Elijah, three years younger than A.J. and a year older than Sean, but Bowie and the Cameron brothers had never gotten along. He was combative and often in trouble. They were rigid and often unforgiving. He'd finally moved away from Black Falls in his early twenties, but he was back now.

Built like an ox, Bowie wore a down vest over an orange hooded sweatshirt, jeans and scuffed work boots. He and Hannah had grown up in a hollow up on the river. Isolated and poor, it was a different Vermont from the one the Camerons and most people in Black Falls had experienced.

Without acknowledging anyone else, Bowie looked up at the basketball game on TV while he waited for his beer.

The Camerons tensed visibly at their table but didn't move to leave.

Hannah considered quietly easing off her stool, paying for her wine and getting out of there. Her younger brothers needed her help with homework, and she had studying of her own to do. She'd turn thirty this year. Time to finish law school and get on with her legal career. She was also part-owner of a breakfast-lunch café just down Main Street from O'Rourke's. The café closed at three o'clock—hours ago—but she kept the books and managed the staff as well as cooked and cleaned, and work could go well into the night. It probably would tonight.

Two more sips, she thought, lifting her glass and trying to stifle a rush of self-consciousness. It was a stubborn demon she thought she'd finally conquered, but with Bowie just down the bar and A.J.,

Elijah and Sean Cameron at their table in their canvas jackets and hiking boots, with their very blue eyes and square jaws and scars from hard work, fighting fires and fighting wars, she found herself wishing she'd stayed away and hadn't taken this time for herself. She hadn't bothered with makeup, and she'd pulled on a long wool skirt, sweater and boots more for comfort and warmth than style. Her blond hair, which she'd hastily tied back at dawn, had to be stringy by now.

But how would she know? She hadn't taken a half second to check herself in the mirror before she'd set out for her hour on her own.

Her sudden self-consciousness had nothing to do with A.J., a happily married father of two young children, or Elijah, a Special Forces soldier who'd left Vermont at nineteen—all but kicked out of town by his own father. No, Hannah thought. Sean was the Cameron who could have her forget she was a top law student and a successful businesswoman.

Nothing new there.

All three were competent, good-looking men anyone would want to have as allies and rescuers and dread to have as enemies. Their sister, Rose, the youngest, one of Hannah's closest friends, was likewise competent and attractive, but she was out of town with Ranger, her search-and-rescue dog.

Sean was considered the charmer of the three brothers, but only in contrast to A.J. and Elijah. Hannah had never been intimidated by any of them, but that didn't mean she didn't wish they hadn't come to town tonight.

As she sipped the last of her wine, Sean seemed just now to see her. He smiled that devastating smile she'd first noticed back in high school Latin class, when she'd been an eager freshman—at thirteen, a year younger than most other freshmen—and he'd been a bored senior, a star athlete who'd had no interest in Latin. He'd just needed a class that fit his schedule and provided the needed credits for him to graduate. She remembered a rainy afternoon when she was the sole student who'd known that *Dido and Aeneas* was a Henry Purcell opera based on the tragic love affair between the queen of Carthage and a Trojan refugee. Proud of her answer,

Hannah had heard laughter behind her. No idea what it was about, she'd turned around and seen Sean Cameron's smile, those blue eyes, and realized he was laughing at *her.*

She hadn't let him see how mortified she was and had redoubled her efforts to maintain an A in class—not that it was much of a victory when Sean was happy to squeak by with a D. What did he care about an A in Latin? He was on to bigger and better things.

She tipped her glass to him now and gave him a warm but reserved smile. She wasn't thirteen anymore, and as sexy and appealing as all the Cameron men were, she'd never had any serious romantic interest in Sean or his brothers. She had plans of her own, ones that wouldn't fit into the life of a driven, blue-eyed Cameron.

Out of the corner of her eye, she watched Bowie O'Rourke raise his beer with a callused, scarred hand. He'd first learned his trade working after school and summers with Hannah's father, Tobias Shay, who'd led his own troubled life before ramming his car into a tree sixteen years ago. She had learned not to speak of her father in

Black Falls. Who remembered him now? Who even wanted to?

"I do," Hannah whispered.

She stared at her chardonnay, wondering where the words had come from. Why was Bowie even back in Black Falls? Short-fused and on the verge of doing time, he had finally figured out that he and his hometown weren't a good mix and moved up to Burlington ten years ago. Last October, he'd purchased his family's old place out on the river. He'd spent the rest of the fall and the winter fixing it up and had moved in a few weeks ago.

Hannah could see her father leading her and Bowie through the woods above the river as they searched for old cellar holes—the foundations of long-abandoned homes. He'd imagine where those early Vermont settlers had ended up. Ohio? Wisconsin? San Francisco? He'd turn to them with a grin and ask why *his* ancestors hadn't cleared out of northern New England.

He and Bowie both had always been at their happiest, their most controlled, in the woods.

Hannah wasn't yet fourteen when her

father died. Her younger brothers didn't remember him at all. Devin was two, Toby just one. Nine years later, they lost their mother to an infection from a tick bite. Hannah had navigated the legal battles to become her brothers' legal guardian. They were eighteen and seventeen now. They'd be out on their own before long.

A loud male voice shouting insults from a table toward the back of the bar drew Hannah's attention. She didn't think the insults were directed at anyone in particular, but she didn't intend to stick around to find out. She eased off the stool and reached for her jacket on the floor. She slipped a ten-dollar bill out of a pocket, tucked it under her glass and turned to leave.

The voice grew louder.

Derek Cutshaw.

Although she couldn't make out what he was saying, Hannah tensed as she started for the door. Derek and his friends Robert Feehan and Brett Griffin had been in O'Rourke's when she'd arrived. They were private ski instructors who didn't live in Black Falls but would sometimes stop at the café on their way to Killington, Okemo or Stratton. They'd struck her as arrogant, but she'd never had serious trouble with them.

She'd never seen them drunk, either.

"I see you took off your apron to sit at the bar and booze it up." Derek chortled, obviously pleased with himself. "Good for you, Hannah. You wouldn't want people to think you were your mother's daughter."

She laid her jacket over one arm. So. His insults *were* directed at her. Her mother had worked at O'Rourke's, making a living for her and her three children. Had she endured comments—however rare—from people who had their own prejudices and fantasies about an attractive young widow of limited means?

Derek didn't relent. "A secondhand jacket for a secondhand girl."

Robert laughed at his friend's awkward insult and gave him a better gibe to try on her, but Derek shifted to bragging about his recent female conquests. Hannah felt her face grow hot. *Do they mean me?* Out of the corner of her eye, she saw the Camerons look over from their table. Would they hear the insults and innuendos and *believe* them?

Embarrassed and angry, she headed for

the door. She didn't care how cold it was outside, she had no intention of spending another second listening to drunken insults.

"Hold on, there," Derek yelled. "You can't leave. Who the hell do you think you are?"

Hannah could see him coming toward her from the back of the bar and jumped back, dropping her jacket. She stepped on the sleeve and slipped just as Derek got to her, swearing, drunkenly slurring the taunts he aimed at her. She tried to find her footing but couldn't. She went down hard, putting out her hands to brace her fall. Pain radiated up both arms, but she immediately got up onto her knees.

Derek and his friend Robert both stood over her now, laughing. Derek bent down and got in her face. He was as fair as she was and very fit, clad in ski clothes, but his face was contorted with anger, entitlement and alcohol. "That's a good position for you," he spat at her. "You can tell your—"

"That's enough."

Bowie. Hannah recognized his voice. "No, don't," she said, grabbing the edge of a table and pulling herself back onto her feet.

Derek and Robert both spun around at Bowie. Brett Griffin was up now, too. One of the men shoved a table into Hannah, pinning her against the wall. Frantic, angry enough now to throw a chair at someone, she pushed the table away from her, striking Derek in the upper legs. He started to leap over the table to her, but Bowie got one of Derek's arms and twisted it behind him. Robert came at him, and Bowie stomped him on the instep. He went down in pain.

Hannah came to her senses. "Bowie, stop." She didn't know if he could hear her. "These bastards aren't worth a jail sentence."

He loosened his grip on Derek, who repaid the favor by lunging for Hannah. She reached for a chair to defend herself, but before he could get to her, a strong male arm clamped her around her waist. She didn't see who it belonged to and jabbed a sharp elbow into an iron abdomen. The man who had her didn't break his stride as he lifted her off her feet and carried her out the door.

Kicking and clawing, Hannah was down the steps and into the March cold before she'd caught her next breath. The man released her, but she was so off balance from fighting him, she almost landed butt-first in a puddle. She managed to stay on her feet and spun around, ready to pound whoever had just hauled her out of O'Rourke's.

"Hold on. I'm on your side." Sean Cameron licked a split knuckle, the steady, cold drizzle already collecting on his dark hair and obviously expensive long black coat. He must have brought it from California with him. He certainly hadn't bought it in Black Falls. He grinned at her. "I never thought I'd be carting Hannah Shay out of a bar brawl."

Anyone else, and Hannah would have pulled herself together and marched home. But Sean? She didn't know whether she was mortified or just really irritated that he'd been the one to get her out of O'Rourke's. She could hear grunts and thuds, breaking glass and swearing, as the fight went on inside.

Police sirens sounded down the street.

She was breathing hard, the insults fresh in her mind. *It wasn't me,* she wanted to scream. *That bastard didn't mean me.*

Hannah adjusted her twisted skirt. "I didn't ask for your help."

"You're welcome," Sean said with a mock bow.

She shivered, wondering how many of the insults he'd heard in the dark, noisy bar. She swallowed, tasting blood. She realized she'd cut the inside of her lip. She managed a smile. "Sorry. Thank you for your help."

A.J. and Elijah came out of the bar. Elijah handed Hannah her jacket without comment. She slipped it on, the cold rain already soaking into her hair. The three Camerons stood in front of her, controlled, steady—she'd been the one out of control.

Of course. She was a Shay.

"Go home, Hannah," A.J. said.

His wife, Lauren, was one of the nicest people in Black Falls. She hadn't grown up there, but she was respected and well-liked for her kindness and her love for A.J. and their two young children. Her husband, however, wasn't known for his patience, especially with Hannah.

The sirens were louder now. She could feel where the table had hit her in the hip. "If the police want to talk to me—"

Elijah stopped her midsentence. "They won't," he said.

Sean's eyes seemed black in the Vermont night. "I'll take you home."

"No," she blurted, panicked at the idea of walking down the street with him, or, worse yet, being in a vehicle with him, but she calmed herself and managed a smile. "Thank you."

A.J., Elijah and Sean paid no attention to the commotion inside O'Rourke's. Shaking with the cold and adrenaline, Hannah tried to make out Bowie's voice. She wanted him to appear in the doorway and say he'd walked away from this fight, as he hadn't so many fights in his past.

But he didn't, and she zipped up her jacket and started for the bar entrance.

Sean touched her shoulder. "You're not going back in there."

She spun around at him. A.J. and Elijah stood next to him. She sighed. "One of you I could take, but all three?" Of course, any one of them out-muscled her, and they all knew it. She gave them a cool smile. "Good night, gentlemen."

She walked past them down Main Street, which formed the heart of the pretty village of Black Falls, located in a narrow river valley in the Green Mountains. The sand and salt that had accumulated on the sidewalk over the long winter handled any of the cold rain that would have otherwise frozen.

None of the Camerons followed her.

A town cruiser passed her on the street, its lights flashing. She didn't look back to see it stop in front of O'Rourke's.

She finally came to the graceful 1835 brick house across from the town green, on the corner of Main and Elm Street, where she'd lived with her brothers for the past seven years. Sean Cameron had inherited them as tenants when he'd bought the house two years ago. Hannah had expected him to kick them out and renovate and sell the place at a tidy profit, but he hadn't. Then she and two friends talked him into letting them create a café on the first floor. They'd scrubbed, sanded, painted, installed a kitchen, brought in tables and chairs and a big glass display case and come up with a name, a logo, a signature color.

As Hannah unlocked the heavy front door, she thought of the family who'd built the house. They'd made a fortune in

Vermont's burgeoning wool business in the early nineteenth century. Then came high tariffs and an economic bust, and they'd cleared out for a new start in Ohio.

Part of her wanted her own fresh start. To just pack up and take off.

But that wouldn't happen. Devin was struggling with his grades and needed her help and support to graduate. Toby had another year of school. She had law school to finish, then the bar exam and hopefully a clerkship and work as a prosecutor. She wasn't going anywhere.

A second cruiser raced down Main Street.

Shivering now, biting back tears, Hannah went inside.

There was nothing she could do to help Bowie O'Rourke.

There never had been.

The three men who'd insulted Hannah came to the café two days later and apologized to her for their behavior that night at O'Rourke's. Derek Cutshaw did most of the talking. Robert Feehan was flushed and clearly embarrassed. Brett Griffin, who hadn't participated in the fight, stayed quiet.

They'd been drunk. They were idiots. They didn't mean what they'd said.

They were so sorry.

"It was all me," Derek said. "Robert and especially Brett didn't do anything."

"Apology accepted," Hannah said.

They all received the legal equivalent of a slap on the wrist.

Bowie, on the other hand, was charged with aggravated assault. His court-appointed lawyer got the charge reduced to simple assault, for which Bowie received a split sentence of sixty days in prison and three years' probation. He'd had too many run-ins with the law. He wouldn't just get a fine and a warning to behave.

The Cameron men went back to their lives. Sean returned to Beverly Hills. Elijah returned to war. A.J., as ever, continued his work at Black Falls Lodge.

Two weeks later, their father shocked his three sons and daughter and everyone in Black Falls when he went missing on Cameron Mountain in a fierce spring snowstorm. Search parties fanned out into the wilderness, but it was Devin Shay, Hannah's eighteen-year-old brother, who found the seventy-seven-year-old Vermonter's body on the remote north side of the mountain. The autopsy indicated that Drew Cameron had died of hypothermia, probably after becoming lost and disoriented in the storm.

The one consolation to A.J., Elijah, Sean and Rose Cameron was that if their father could have chosen where to die, it would have been on the mountain he loved.

But he hadn't chosen.

It wasn't until November—seven months later—that everyone in Black Falls knew the truth.

Drew Cameron had been murdered.

Two

December 28—Black Falls, Vermont

Hannah raised the shade in her bedroom window and looked down at the frozen branch of the Black River that ran through the middle of the village. There were actually two Black rivers in Vermont. The other was farther north. This one originated in the western Green Mountains and flowed south and east, emptying into the Connecticut River on the Vermont–New Hampshire border.

Sunrise wouldn't come for another hour, but she could see white drifts of new snow on the ice and exposed rocks of the shallow river, and, on its banks, the silhouettes of naked trees, dormant for the long, cold northern New England winter.

She'd finally given up on sleep and was dressed and finished with her to-do list for Sean Cameron. She'd itemized everything his house on the town green needed, from painting the woodwork to replacing the gutters and fixing the leak in the cellar. He hadn't asked for a list, but the holidays were over, things needed to be done and he was in town.

Strike while the iron is hot, her mother would say.

As Hannah turned from the window, she admitted to herself that she wasn't ready to crack open her law books and start her marathon of studying for her bar exam in a few months.

She still had too many images of the past five weeks to keep at bay.

She made her bed, pulling up the simple patchwork quilt her mother had sewn for her, using scraps of fabric she'd collected from people at work. Hannah had debated putting it in mothballs, but her mother had never been one to not use what she owned—and she'd sewn things to be used. They'd been living in the hollow out on the river then. Mary Shay had never liked town. She'd learned the names of the different birds in the area and had enjoyed putting up feeders during the winter. She'd aspired to so little and yet had suffered so much. She'd fallen for the wrong man. She'd been bitten by the wrong tick.

Hannah shot out of her bedroom. Better to think about how to get her absentee landlord to spring for needed maintenance on his Vermont house.

Anything, she thought, to keep her mind off cold-blooded killers.

She headed up the short hall to the small kitchen. Its window—one of the ones that needed replacing—looked down on Elm Street and the jut of the one-story ell that had been added to the house eighty years ago and was now part of the Three Sisters Café.

Neither of her brothers was up yet. She hadn't heard Devin pacing in the night or tossing and turning in his bedroom next to hers. She hoped that was a good sign. He'd graduated high school in June but hadn't decided on a course for his life. He'd moved out over the summer, living up at Black Falls Lodge while he worked for A.J.

and Lauren Cameron, but he'd returned home just before Thanksgiving, after nearly becoming a victim of the hired killers who'd left Drew Cameron to die in the cold in April.

Although not specifically targeted by the killers as Devin had been, Toby wasn't unaffected by the bloodshed in November, but he was optimistic and driven by nature. He'd already made plans for the future. In two days, Sean Cameron would fly the younger of her two brothers, his mountain bike and all his mountain-biking paraphernalia to Southern California for a minimum of three months as an exchange student. Toby would be living with the family of a mountain-biker friend, another avid downhill racer. Hannah had met them all last summer. As much as she would miss him, she had no worries for her brother's safety or care. Toby was still a minor and had needed her permission to go to school in California, but how could she have denied him this chance?

She noticed a mountain-biking magazine he'd left open on the table. She'd done her best by both her brothers, never pretending she was anything but their older sister. She knew their relationship was different—given the gap in their ages, it would have been even if both their parents had lived.

Hannah peeked at the thermometer in the window above the table.

Seventeen degrees.

She smiled to herself. It wasn't mountain-biking weather, but it wasn't bad for a late-December dawn in northern New England. She wouldn't mind a break from the long Vermont winter herself, but she had friends who were such serious winter-sports enthusiasts, they cheered every inch of new snow.

Letting both her brothers sleep, Hannah tiptoed out of the small apartment and took the curving stairs down to the center-hall entrance of the old house. It had such character—such potential—but its owner seemed only interested in the basic maintenance necessary to keep the place from falling down, presumably until he decided the time was right to kick everyone out—her and her brothers, the small first-floor gallery and the café—and gut it, renovate it and sell it for a fortune.

Hannah unlocked a solid-wood door that

was original to the house and entered the café's dining room. It had its own entrance onto Main Street, as well as one off the center hall. She'd heard Dominique Belair and Beth Harper, her two partners, arrive earlier. They'd decided on the name Three Sisters Café, considering themselves sisters in spirit if not by blood. Each of them knew what had to be done to get scones, muffins, homemade yogurt, fresh-cut fruit and other goodies ready for the café's 7:00 a.m. opening.

Her heartbeat quickening at the same time her pace slowed, Hannah took in the gray early-morning light, the gleaming hardwood floor and the dozen-plus wood tables and chairs. On the interior wall, the countertops and glass case were empty, spotless. Before long, the bright winter sun would stream in through the tall windows and customers would start arriving.

But mentally, Hannah was back in April—eight months ago—as small, black-haired Melanie Kendall sat across from Thomas Asher in the café and pretended to be an interior decorator from Washington, D.C., taking a break from her busy schedule. She and Kyle Rigby, her partner in killing, had already made sure Drew Cameron had died of hypothermia on Cameron Mountain.

Hannah stopped breathing. *Don't* . . .

She couldn't stop the images.

After years of searching, Drew had discovered the site of the Camerons' original house in Vermont in what was now a wilderness on the north side of the mountain. He hadn't told anyone while he secretly built a small cabin on the remains of the old foundation. What supplies and equipment he couldn't get up the mountain on his own, he'd enlisted a local high school senior—Hannah's brother Devin—to carry for him, never admitting why or showing off his work-in-progress.

He'd meant the cabin as a surprise for his four adult children.

Melanie had flirted with Thomas Asher while the children of her and Rigby's victim had called in search teams and headed up the mountain themselves to look for their father. She had known Drew was dead—that the cold had done its work before anyone had realized he was missing.

Hannah eased behind the glass counter. For the past five weeks, every morning had been the same, and she knew what the next rush of images would be. She stared across the counter toward the windows overlooking the river, the landscape taking shape under the lightening sky. She'd been the one who'd hired Nora Asher, Thomas Asher's eighteen-year-old daughter, to work at the café when Nora had moved to Black Falls after dropping out of Dartmouth College in September. Nora had wanted to experience life in small-town Vermont. By then, her father and Melanie Kendall were engaged. Already suspicious of Melanie, Nora had enlisted Devin's help to conduct their own background check on her future stepmother.

In November, Nora's stepfather, Alexander Bruni, a prominent ambassador, was killed in a hit-and-run in Washington, D.C. Nora panicked at the news of his likely murder and took off up Cameron Mountain.

Devin went after her, as a friend, telling no one.

Clever, calculating Melanie manipulated her fiancé into hiring Kyle Rigby to search for his missing daughter.

Hannah could see Kyle on that bleak

November morning, his broad shoulders, his aura of competence and reassurance as he'd walked into the café. Posing as a mountain rescuer, he'd asked her to tell him what she could about where Devin and Nora might be.

He had fooled everyone. He hadn't wanted to help. He'd wanted to make sure Nora and Devin didn't get off Cameron Mountain alive and had tried to paint Devin as a troubled teenager whose obsessions and recklessness had led to tragedy.

Kyle Rigby and Melanie Kendall were killers who were themselves now dead.

With a gasp for air, Hannah broke the cycle of images. Investigators believed Kyle and Melanie had been part of a sophisticated network that paired clients who wanted someone dead and were willing to pay with professional killers who'd do the job—a network that didn't tolerate screw-ups. Elijah Cameron had shot and killed Kyle Rigby in Kyle's do-or-die mission on Cameron Mountain. Hours later, Melanie Kendall was killed at Black Falls Lodge when a bomb went off in her car, presumably triggered, or arranged to be triggered, by her employer, for whom failure was not an option.

So many unanswered questions, Hannah thought as she burst through the swinging door into the kitchen. Dominique and Beth were on backless stools at the counter-height worktable. Beth, a copper-haired, high-energy paramedic a year older than Hannah, was willing to do anything to keep the café running but focused her efforts on maintenance and comfort food. Small, dark-haired Dominique was, at thirty-four, the eldest of the three "sisters" and decidedly not a local. Something of a mystery in town, she was an expert cook and the creative vision behind the café's success.

Without a word, Hannah reached for a dark green canvas apron. Dominique and Beth each wore one, too. They'd agreed on evergreen as the café's signature color. The kitchen was toasty warm. It was one of Hannah's favorite rooms in the house. They'd kept the design simple, with an emphasis on efficiency, openness and food safety.

"Is Toby packed?" Beth asked, lifting a thick round of dough onto a baking sheet.

"He started packing his bike paraphernalia Christmas night. The rest doesn't matter." Welcoming the distraction from her post-trauma visions, Hannah filled a mug—also evergreen—with coffee. "He wants to get in shape for a big race in California in late January."

Beth looked up from the worktable. "You should go out there for the race. While you're at it, you can make Sean take you shopping on Rodeo Drive."

Hannah laughed as she leaned back against the counter with her coffee. "What on earth would I buy on Rodeo Drive?"

"Five-hundred-dollar shoes," Beth said without hesitation.

"To tramp through snowbanks when I got home? I don't think so. Toby's caught up in the excitement of getting to go mountain-biking during the winter. I don't blame him. At least his host family in California wasn't scared off by what happened here in November."

Beth's deep turquoise eyes darkened. She'd been on the search-and-rescue team that had gone up Cameron Mountain in November. She'd strapped Devin to a stretcher herself. He'd been injured after

Kyle Rigby had taken Devin's own walking stick from him and beat him with it—but not before Devin was able to warn Nora, giving her a chance to run and almost certainly saving her life.

"Sean will look after Toby," Beth said, shoving the tray of plump buttermilk scones into the oven. "He's every bit the hard-ass mountain man as Elijah is. Or A.J., for that matter." She shut the oven and grinned. "Hell, or Rose."

After two sips, Hannah set her mug on the counter. She'd come to rely on Beth's restless energy and good humor to help her through the past five weeks. "The Camerons are all mission-oriented types. Not knowing who ordered their father killed and why is tough on all of them."

"It won't last." Dominique didn't look up from her bowl of cut fresh fruit as she spoke. "They'll get their answers."

Beth nodded thoughtfully. "Yes, they will." She pulled open the freezer and turned to Dominique. "Wild blueberry muffins for a cold post-Christmas morning?"

Dominique, never one for surprises, frowned. "I hadn't planned on making blueberry muffins."

"All the more reason to get out the blueberries," Beth said, grinning as she reached into the freezer for a container of wild blueberries she and Hannah had picked back in August.

Dispelling the last of her early-morning visions, Hannah returned to the dining room, just in time to greet Scott Thorne, Beth's boyfriend, a state trooper and a member of the task force investigating the violence in Black Falls. He was a man with a limited sense of humor, but then again he'd been working night and day since he'd joined Beth hiking up Cameron Mountain in mid-November and had discovered Elijah Cameron standing over Kyle Rigby's body.

Scott ordered coffee, which he took to the largest of the café's tables.

Zack Harper, Beth's younger brother and a local firefighter, arrived next and ordered coffee, a cranberry-nut muffin and a scone. "Did Jo get you out running this morning already?" Hannah asked cheerfully. With their Secret Service agent sister back in town, both Zack and Beth liked to complain that Jo was killing them with exercise.

Zack shook his head. "Grit Taylor did. Guy's got one leg, and he's up at oh-dark-thirty to do three miles along the lake."

Hannah had met Ryan "Grit" Taylor, a Navy SEAL, several times at the cafe. He and Elijah Cameron had both been wounded in combat in Afghanistan in April, around the same time Elijah's father had died of the cold in Vermont. Shot in the femoral artery, Elijah had managed to tie a tourniquet on his thigh and save his own life. He'd eventually made a full recovery. Grit's progress was slower. He had helped find an eyewitness to Alex Bruni's murder in Washington, D.C., and had joined Elijah in Black Falls after Kyle Rigby and Melanie Kendall were dead. He'd been back and forth to Washington since mid-November, with no apparent official role in the investigation.

Zack took his coffee, muffin and scone from Hannah and headed over to Scott's table. As a firefighter, Zack was primarily interested in the particulars of how Melanie Kendall's car had blown up. Who'd placed the crude pipe bomb in her car? Who'd set it off? Were there other bombs tucked away in Black Falls for future use?

Zack and Scott were followed by Jo Harper and Elijah Cameron. Jo, two years older than Beth and a Secret Service agent, happened to be in her hometown in November when Kyle Rigby and Melanie Kendall had targeted the two teenagers. She and Elijah had stopped them, and Jo had been assigned to the joint federal, state and local task force investigating the tangle of crimes.

Jo might be stuck in Black Falls, Hannah thought, but she was stuck there with Elijah. Their rekindled romance amid the violence in November was the talk of the town.

Of all the Cameron brothers, Hannah had the easiest relationship with Elijah. “What’s good today?” he asked.

“Beth and Dominique did all the cooking,” Hannah said, “which means everything’s good.”

He laughed. “Then I’ll have one of each.”

Jo rolled her eyes, but she was obviously amused. “He’s trying to learn charm from Sean. Speaking of whom—” She nodded to the main entrance. “Here he is right now.”

Hannah felt the draft from the open door

as Sean walked into the café and approached the glass case. Unable to stop herself, she noted the shape of his shoulders and hips and the cut of his dark hair. He had on his mountain man jacket, not his long black cashmere coat, and, like his older brother, was bareheaded.

Hannah cleared her throat and saw that Elijah had noticed her sudden awkwardness, but he made no comment. If Jo noticed, she didn't show it. Hannah handed them two mugs of coffee and two plates with muffins and scones, and they retreated to the table with Zack and Scott. Investigators had made the café a regular stop, but this morning's gathering was more one of family and friends than anything official, never mind that it included a local firefighter, a state cop and a federal agent.

And an experienced Special Forces soldier. According to Beth Harper, the shots Elijah had fired to stop Kyle Rigby from killing him, Devin, Nora and Jo on Cameron Mountain five weeks ago had been dead-on.

Hannah hadn't been up to the spot yet

where her brother had nearly died. She knew she'd go. It was just a question of when.

Sunlight was spreading into the café, sparkling on the snow-covered river, but it would be dark again by four o'clock. She was aware of how much daylight had leaked out of the shortened winter days.

Sean eyed the offerings in the glass case. He had flown to Black Falls in November the moment he'd learned about Melanie Kendall and Kyle Rigby and their trail of violence and bloodshed. He'd stayed through Thanksgiving, then returned a few weeks later to spend Christmas with his family. He'd be heading back to California in two days.

Taking Toby to his host family.

"I have a list of repairs for you," Hannah blurted.

"What kind of repairs?" Sean asked without looking up at her.

"The place needs work—not fun work, either. Stripping wallpaper, scraping paint, caulking windows. Several windows need to be replaced. There are wiring issues in the upstairs hall."

He glanced at her now with a smile. "Wiring issues?"

She met his gaze. His eyes so reminded her of his father. "I can get Zack Harper to go up and have a look, if you'd like. He doesn't like a fire hazard."

"There's no fire hazard."

"I didn't say there was. I said Zack—"

"Anything else?"

She pivoted, her back to him, and filled a mug from the urn on the counter behind her. Sean was an experienced firefighter himself. He'd left Vermont after college and headed west to realize his dream of becoming a smoke jumper, one of the elite firefighters who parachuted into remote wildfires. For the past decade, he'd tackled one raging fire after another. He and another smoke jumper, a Californian Hannah had never met named Nick Martini, had pooled their resources and invested in a run-down Los Angeles building in a great location. They renovated it, leveraged it, bought more buildings, and now were worth a fortune, although they both still fought wildfires.

Hannah turned to him with his coffee. "There's water in the cellar."

"There's been water in that cellar for two hundred years."

"Not quite two hundred. The house was only built in 1835."

A muscle in Sean's jaw worked. She didn't know if he was amused or irritated—or both. "All right," he said. "I'll have a look."

"I looked. I'm not an expert, but I can recognize water on a cellar floor when I see it."

His very blue eyes leveled on her. "Sleep at all last night, Hannah?"

She ignored his question as well as the flutter in the pit of her stomach and let her voice soften. "I have the list upstairs. I can fetch it when things quiet down."

"Ah. Please do."

He took his coffee and sat across from Elijah, facing Hannah behind the glass case. She could feel the focus as well as the frustration of the men and one woman at the table. In the first frenetic days of the investigation, everyone had hoped answers would come quickly. They hadn't. They still didn't know who had hired Kyle and Melanie to kill Drew Cameron and make his death look like an accident and why. How had they known he'd be on the mountain? How had they known *where* he'd be on the mountain?

What had *he* known about them and their network of killers?

How was Drew's murder connected to the hit-and-run murder of Ambassador Bruni seven months later?

How many murders was this network of paid assassins responsible for?

How many killers were still out there, and who were their next targets?

As far as Hannah could see, the law enforcement agencies working on the investigation were as determined and unyielding now as they had been five weeks ago. They'd put together time lines and maps, figured out the movements of perpetrators, victims and possible victims—not just in Black Falls and Washington but throughout the U.S. and even internationally.

Hannah also understood that everyone in town was hoping for a break in the investigation that would take it in a new direction—preferably away from Black Falls.

She busied herself going back and forth to the kitchen for fresh, warm scones and muffins—Beth had indeed talked Dominique into making wild blueberry muffins—and arranging them on the shelves of the glass case.

She noticed Sean stiffen visibly at the table, his attention directed toward the café's main entrance.

Uneasy, Hannah followed his gaze.

She saw what was wrong.

Bowie O'Rourke, out of jail and back in Black Falls, had entered the café for the first time since his arrest two weeks before Drew Cameron was murdered.

Three

Hannah placed the blueberry muffins inside the glass case and tried to focus on their smell, the smell of coffee, the sounds of the radiators clanking against the winter cold.

"Hey, Hannah," Bowie said as he walked over to her.

She stood up. "Bowie. It's been a long time."

"I heard you were looking for me."

She glanced at the table of law enforcement officers, Camerons and one firefighter and saw they all were eyeing the man in front of her. She could hardly blame them. After getting out of jail, Bowie worked in Burlington through the summer and fall. In late November, he'd taken a job repairing a stone culvert in a cemetery down the road from Black Falls Lodge, and just before Christmas, he'd returned to his place on the river.

Hannah hadn't actually seen or spoken to him since his return to Black Falls. She'd only heard rumors about him. She'd stopped at the cemetery late yesterday looking for him, but he hadn't been there. The elderly couple who lived across the road from the cemetery must have mentioned her to Bowie, and now here he was.

His timing couldn't have been worse.

"I'd have called," she said, "but you don't have a phone."

"Correct. No phone—no landline, no cell phone."

"No e-mail, either."

He shrugged his big shoulders. He was wearing his habitual down vest and orange sweatshirt. "I get by without any of them. What can I do for you?"

"Water's getting in the cellar here." She avoided even glancing in Sean's direction. "I was wondering if you could check it out."

Bowie's brown eyes were without expression. "What does your landlord have to say?"

"He lives in California. I look after the place in exchange for a break in rent."

"I worked on the cellar here with your father when I was a kid. Whatever needs to be done, it'll either be in the part we didn't work on or it won't be much. I'm on my way to a job now. I'll come by later."

Hannah nodded. "Thanks, Bowie. Can I get you anything?"

He grinned at her suddenly. "You're kidding, right?"

"No. What's the difference between a blueberry muffin I make in my kitchen and one we make here?"

"One's free and the other isn't."

She laughed and grabbed a muffin she'd accidentally broken in half. He wouldn't accept anything that smacked of charity. "Here, take this one. I didn't make it, though. Beth and Dominique did."

"Even better." He pointed to the coffee urn behind her. "I'll take a coffee to go. I'll pay for it. *Regular* coffee. Don't give me coffee with raspberry flavoring or something in it."

She filled a large to-go cup and handed it to him. He left money on the counter and walked over to the small coffee station. He added two sugars to his cup and put on a lid. As he reached for a napkin for his muffin, he addressed the gathering at the large table. “I heard about Drew. I know it’s a tough loss. He always tried to give everyone a fair shake.”

Elijah tilted back in his chair. “Appreciate the thought.”

If a wisecrack entered Bowie’s head, he had the self-control—or the survival instinct—to keep it to himself. “See you around. I have to get to work.”

“Bowie,” Jo said, rising, “I hear you’ve moved back to town in the past few days. Why now?”

“I never left. My place here’s my legal address.”

Jo bristled visibly, but Bowie just turned and walked out the front door of the café, the door thudding softly behind him.

Hannah didn’t wait for Jo or the men at the table to pounce. She ducked through the swinging door to the kitchen, untying her apron and hanging it on a hook. She ignored Beth’s and Dominique’s looks of concern, not stopping until she was through the hall door and in the mudroom.

Seeing Bowie. His past. Her past.

It was time, and she knew it. She was haunted by questions. Bowie. Drew Cameron. The old cellar hole on Cameron Mountain.

She had to know.

She reached for Devin's empty daypack on the floor in a corner. He'd had it with him on the mountain in November. He'd tried to do everything right and still he'd almost been killed.

Hannah yanked open a closet door and pulled out energy bars, a water bottle, a flashlight, waterproof matches, trash bags that could be used as an emergency shelter—she grabbed everything she could think of to take on a winter hike and shoved it into the pack.

"What're you doing?"

Hannah was so startled, she dropped the pack on the floor. But it was Devin, not Jo Harper or a Cameron. *Not Sean.* She picked up the pack. "I'm getting ready for a hike."

Her brother frowned at her. Always thin, he'd lost weight in the weeks since his ordeal on Cameron Mountain, but he was up and showered and dressed, not lying in bed staring at the ceiling. His eyes, as pale a blue as hers, showed the strain of the past weeks as he took in her pack, her obviously agitated state. "Where are you going?"

She shut the closet door. "Cameron Mountain."

Devin didn't respond.

She lifted her winter jacket from a hook by the back door. It wasn't suited for a prolonged hike in late December, but she'd compensate with proper layers that would protect her from the elements. Drew Cameron hadn't succumbed to hypothermia because he wasn't prepared for the conditions on the mountain, even in the worse-than-expected April snowstorm. He'd succumbed because Melanie Kendall and Kyle Rigby had killed him. They'd made sure he slipped into hypothermia. As his body temperature continued to drop, he would have become increasingly disoriented and confused, stumbling around, until he finally lay down in the freshly fallen spring snow and didn't get up again.

Hannah shrugged on her jacket as her brother frowned at her. "You're going to Drew's cabin." His tone was without emotion, but his face had lost color. "Aren't you?"

"If I can find it. I think I can."

Devin's breathing was shallow. "I haven't been back up there."

Hannah touched his rail-thin upper arm. "When you're ready, we'll all go. You, Toby, me."

"Who's going with you?"

She grabbed a pair of ski poles and snowshoes she'd picked up at a yard sale. "No one."

"What, are you crazy? You can't go alone."

"The Camerons would have my head for hiking alone, I know—especially Elijah. I'll be fine. I'll take the falls trail. It's longer than the trail up the back of the mountain, but it's easier, and I'll be able to use my cell phone more of the way. Trust me, I won't be lingering up there."

"Hannah," Devin said, an edge of worry creeping into his voice, "what if whoever hired those two to kill Nora and me follows you up there?"

"The police have already searched Drew's cabin and the surrounding area. It was a crime scene, Dev. Whatever bad guys are still on the loose aren't going to care if I go up and take a look."

"I can go with you," her brother said simply.

"Are you supposed to work this morning?"

"Just for a few hours. I can call A.J.—"

She shook her head. "Go on to work, Dev. Don't worry about me. I need to get moving or I'll run out of daylight before I can get back here." She opened the back door, barely noticed the rush of cold air. "The Robinsons invited me to dinner tonight. I'll be back in plenty of time to get ready."

Everett Robinson was a Vermont district court judge and her friend and mentor, and Hannah suspected he'd push her at dinner to describe her plans for studying for the bar. Thanksgiving and Christmas were behind them. New Year's was almost over. He'd want her to get serious.

Devin still looked uneasy but didn't try to stop her. She headed out back and followed the icy stone walk through a white-painted wooden gate to the driveway.

Elijah Cameron's truck was parked very close to her beat-up car, but before she could get annoyed at his nerve for not parking in the street, she realized Sean must have borrowed the truck from his older brother.

And since Sean owned the place, he could park wherever he wanted.

She managed to maneuver her way out of the driveway without scratching either vehicle and headed up Main Street past the green toward the back road up to Cameron Mountain.

After the bar fight in March, Bowie had slipped out the back before the police arrived at O'Rourke's. Drew Cameron had gone out to the hollow the next morning to find him.

Hannah was already there.

Drew had tried to talk her into going back to town. She hadn't listened. Instead she'd led him through the woods out to an old cellar hole down by the river. It was where Bowie had always gone to escape his drunken father. As she and Drew picked their way through the mud and wet snow, he had moved steadily, no sign the uneven terrain or conditions bothered him in his late seventies.

"In the old days," he'd said, "you could have a scuffle in a bar, and if no one was seriously hurt, all was forgotten. Lessons were learned. People figured out who they could mess with and who they couldn't. Nowadays . . ." He'd shrugged, not finishing his thought. "Bowie's been in trouble before. He knows what he has to do."

They'd found him standing in the mud at the edge of the cellar hole. The outer foundation wall and the caved-in chimney were all that remained of the tiny, original nineteenth-century house. His back to them, Bowie stared through the trees down at the river, the water high with runoff from the melting snow in the mountains and huge chunks of ice up on the banks as spring slowly came to Vermont.

"Wes Harper has a warrant for your arrest," Drew said. "He's on his way."

"Sean and Elijah and A.J. weren't involved. The three of them can finish any fight anyone starts."

Drew nodded thoughtfully. "They can.

So can you. That's not the point, though, is it?"

"I suppose not."

"They gave statements. Hannah here did, too."

Bowie continued to stare at the river. "I'll go." He'd turned to Drew. "Give me a ten-minute head start. I don't want Hannah to see." Then he'd turned to her. "You understand, don't you?"

"Sure, Bowie. I'm sorry—"

"Don't be sorry."

"If I hadn't been there, none of this would have happened."

"You don't know that," he'd said, and started up the mix of snow and mud toward the road.

Drew put a hand on Hannah's shoulder. "You're not going to cry, are you?"

She'd managed a smile. "Not in front of a Cameron."

"Sean's going back to California in the morning. The police have his statement."

"Do you want me to pack him some scones?"

She immediately regretted her bite of sarcasm. Drew dropped his hand back to his side and didn't smile. When he'd first heard about Three Sisters Café, he hadn't understood the day-to-day appeal of things like hand-ground coffee, scones and "comfort food" that could be made at home. Nonetheless, he'd been the café's first customer. He'd ordered a buttermilk scone and wished the three "sisters" well, leaving a ten-dollar tip and going on his way, never to return.

His eyes—the same riveting blue as the eyes of all four of his children—had stayed on Hannah that cold March morning as if he could see right through her to all her fears and secrets. She'd noticed the lines in his face, the shape of his jaw that she'd noticed more in A.J. than any of his other children.

"You'll make a good prosecutor," he'd said. "You're a gentle soul who believes in getting to the truth, but that's not why. You don't let your emotions dictate your actions."

"Don't I?"

"You could have let Bowie run."

"No, I couldn't have. That's what you've never understood about me. I'm not here to preserve my options for the future. I showed you here because Bowie's a friend."

Instead of being offended or irritated, Drew had seemed satisfied. "He won't necessarily see it that way when he's sitting behind bars."

"I can't help that."

The old man had studied her a moment in that incisive, uncompromising way he'd had. "You were missing your mother. That's why you went to O'Rourke's."

"It's a good place."

"Your mother always wanted you to make something of yourself, but she made something of herself, too. Never forget that."

"I never will. Thank you. Your sons respect you as well as love you. You never forget that, okay?"

He winked at her. "Okay, kid."

Hannah had gazed up through the woods, no sign of life yet on the bare tree limbs dark against the gray sky. Except for the softening ground, the flowing river, spring had seemed impossibly far away. She'd first come out here as a little girl with her father and had pictured the house that had stood on the old cellar hole and wondered who'd lived here, what had brought them to this quiet, beautiful spot on the river and what had become of them.

It was the last time she'd encountered Drew Cameron. By mid-April, captivated by an old cellar hole up on the mountain, he was dead.

Four

Sean Cameron abandoned his cranberry-nut muffin, which he didn't much like, anyway, and got to his feet. The sight of Hannah's banged-up red sedan that she'd been driving for years heading down Main Street seconds behind Bowie O'Rourke's rusted van didn't sit well with him.

He could see it didn't sit well with Jo Harper, either. She sat back, her gaze cool as she raised her eyes to Sean. They'd graduated in the same high school class, but she'd been a lunatic about his brother Elijah for as long as anyone could remember. They'd run off for a time when she was eighteen and Elijah was nineteen, but they hadn't gone far—just to the lake below Black Falls Lodge. Both their fathers had hunted for them, but it was Elijah's who'd discovered them. By the end of the summer, he had left Black Falls for army boot camp and a career in the Special Forces and Jo for college and a career in the U.S. Secret Service.

She'd never wanted to stay in town. He'd never wanted to leave. Now they were back together again, one of the few positives that had come out of the events of mid-November.

It was a different kind of love, Sean thought, the love between two people who'd grown up together, who'd been in snowball fights and seen each other at awkward ages, who knew each other's families. He didn't have such relationships. He'd never sought them. There wasn't, and never had been, anyone in Black Falls for him.

At least that's what he kept telling himself, but he hadn't been thinking so straight on the subject since hauling Hannah Shay out of the brawl at O'Rourke's in late March. He still could feel her slim little body as he'd lifted her off her feet. Her passion had caught him by surprise. The elbow in his gut, the flash of her eyes, the willingness to jump into the middle of a bar fight, outnumbered and outmuscled.

There'd been no question among him and his two brothers that he'd be the one to take care of her.

Just as there wouldn't be now.

"Never come between Hannah and one of her missions," Jo said, nodding toward the street, "and she's on a mission."

Elijah, who had a soft spot for Hannah, didn't look nearly as concerned. "Maybe she's gone to the store for bananas."

Jo kept her gaze on Sean. "Are you going after her?"

"I'll find out what she's up to."

"Be warned, Sean," Jo said, breaking off a piece of scone. She had on the simple diamond engagement ring Elijah had bought for her fifteen years ago, only giving it to her last month when he'd finally proposed. She obviously wasn't thinking about love and romance at the moment. "Don't let Hannah's unassuming manner put you off your guard. In her own quiet way, she can slice any of you Cameron boys to ribbons."

Of that, Sean had no doubt. He could see Hannah turning to him in high school Latin class and giving him one of her cool, superior looks. Thirteen years old, and she knew she was smarter than anyone else in the room. He didn't remember what he'd done to earn her disdain. Probably said something asinine.

He reminded himself that Jo was a federal agent and Scott Thorne, sitting across from her, was a state trooper. He chose his words carefully. "Do we know if Bowie was ever in town at the same time as Melanie Kendall or Kyle Rigby?"

Jo didn't respond. Neither did anyone else at the table. They didn't have to. Sean knew what was on their minds. The bomb that had killed Melanie Kendall had exploded while Jo and Elijah had tried to talk her out of her car. It hadn't been on a timer, and it had gone off *after* Kyle Rigby was already dead. It was a simple device constructed of a cell phone, copper wire, black powder and gunpowder, set off by the electric charge caused when a call came into the cell phone, completing the circuit and igniting the explosives.

Who'd made the call?

Who'd bought the materials and assembled the bomb and placed it in the car?

Who'd wanted Melanie Kendall dead?

Whoever had dialed the number of the cell phone and triggered the bomb had known that Melanie Kendall was in that car. How?

Was it someone local, or was there a local accomplice? Sean looked at his brother. "Maybe you should go after Hannah."

Elijah shook his head. "Not me. I didn't haul her butt out of the bar that night. You did. I'd have let her bloody those bastards. Even if Wes Harper had arrested her, there isn't a jury in Vermont that would have convicted her."

"She was about to get beat up and trampled."

His brother shrugged. "Just would have made her madder."

Sean had participated in enough negotiations to know when he'd lost. "I'll let you know what I find out."

Jo's eyes fastened on Elijah, then Sean, in that kick-ass Secret Service manner of hers. "You two are on a short leash."

Sean grinned at Elijah. “She hasn’t changed since she was twelve, has she?”

“Four,” Elijah said.

She didn’t so much as crack a smile. “You two can do your Cameron brothers thing,” she said, “but I’m still a member of the task force working this investigation.”

“So your life’s not on hold up here in the sticks?”

Sean had kept his tone light, but Jo didn’t answer for a half beat. “My life is not on hold.”

He saw he’d hit a raw nerve and regretted opening his mouth.

Elijah saved him. “I can follow you and cover you when Hannah checks out of the grocery with her bananas. She’ll never know I’m there.”

Given his brother’s fifteen years’ experience as a soldier, Sean had no reason to doubt him. “Hannah’s scary but not that scary.”

Jo still didn’t smile.

Sean headed out of the café into the center hall and found Devin Shay untangling ski poles in the mudroom. He was agitated, spots of color high on his thin cheeks. "I need a ride up to the lodge," Devin said. "Hannah's crazy."

"What's going on, Devin?"

"She's hiking to your dad's cabin. Alone. I can't— I'm going with her."

"Hang on. Hannah can take care of herself, and I can go up to the lodge and check on her. Are you working there today?"

"No."

"Have you given A.J. notice?" Sean asked him.

Devin shoved the ski poles against the wall. Two clattered to the floor. "I don't even know why we have so many stupid ski poles. Hannah already took two with her. She's snowshoeing."

"Devin—"

"Not yet. No. I will."

"Get a ride up to the lodge and do it today. Be responsible and up-front. Unless you've changed your mind—"

"I haven't."

Sean went still a moment, eyeing the teenager. "You haven't told Hannah yet, either, have you?"

Devin looked away and shook his head. "Have you said anything to A.J.?"

"It's not my place to tell him or your sister. Devin, you're almost nineteen. You can make your own decisions about your life. Including Hannah in the process is a good idea. It's the right thing to do. But ultimately what you do is up to you."

Toby Shay bounded down the stairs. He was a few inches shorter than Devin, his hair cropped so close, his head almost looked shaved. His obsession with mountain biking kept him in top-notch condition. He was a champion rider, but, according to what his older brother had told Sean, he'd promised his sister he wouldn't let mountain biking take over his life and fully intended to go to college.

"Hey, what's going on?"

Devin repeated the information about their sister.

Sean put up a hand before Toby could grab poles and snowshoes and head up the mountain, too. Hannah had delicate features and a small frame, which, Sean knew, people often mistook as an indication she was a fragile person. Her brothers, for example. His brothers, too. Sean didn't. He'd learned a long time ago that she had a spine of iron.

"I'll see to your sister," he said. "Devin, you need to tell her—"

"I will." He looked guilty but less agitated. "Tonight. I promise."

"Damn right tonight. I'm not keeping secrets from her. Enough procrastinating. It's time to be straight with her and give her the news."

The brothers squirmed under Sean's scrutiny, but he didn't care. Hannah had gone along with Toby's desire to head to Southern California to go to school and indulge his passion for mountain biking, but she didn't know that Devin was on his way west, too. He'd presented his plan to Sean and asked him for a job, and Sean had agreed to give him one. He'd had his doubts that Devin was ready to make such a big decision after what he'd experienced in November, but he'd proved otherwise. Devin had joined Sean and his brothers and sister on a Christmas Eve search for twelve-year-old twin sisters lost snowshoeing on Cameron Mountain. Physically recovered from the beating he'd received at Rigby's hands, Devin had shown a mental resilience and confidence that Sean had found reassuring. But the search hadn't taken them anywhere near the north side of the mountain, and it hadn't put Devin in the position of worrying and disappointing the sister who'd sacrificed so much to raise her two much-younger brothers.

Sean remembered what it was like to have a burning desire to be on his own and see other places. He'd always been restless, driven and ambitious—and his family hadn't always approved of his choices.

"Hannah could nail my hide to the wall as a coconspirator," Sean said.

Devin raked a hand over the top of his head. "I'd be going to California even if you weren't helping me get there."

"But I know your plans and haven't told her. That's the point. See where I'm going with this?" Sean didn't wait for an answer. "Talk or I talk. What route is Hannah taking?"

"She's going up past the falls," Devin said.

Sean hesitated, then asked, "Is she meeting someone?"

Toby's eyebrows went up. "You mean like a boyfriend? Hannah? No way."

"She's going alone as far as I know," Devin said. "That's why I—"

"Forget it." Sean was relieved her brothers hadn't immediately thought of Bowie but decided not to bring him up. If Devin and Toby weren't aware Bowie had been to the café, they didn't need to know now. "Stick to your plans for the day. I'll go after your sister."

They didn't argue with him, and Sean left through the back door. He climbed into the pickup truck he'd borrowed from Elijah, who wouldn't hear of his brother spending money on a car rental. Being a soldier and an expert in wilderness survival skills, Elijah had a ready pack loaded with enough supplies to keep anyone alive on a frozen hilltop for days.

On his way out of town, Sean dialed Elijah's cell phone. "Jo there?"

"She is. You want to talk to her?"

"No. Hannah's hiking up to the cabin by herself."

"She's taking a big risk."

"That's her style. She just tells herself and the rest of us she's careful."

His brother would have his misgivings. He wasn't one for solo operations. Given his own years fighting wildland fires out west, Sean wasn't, either, but he wanted answers bad enough to take a few risks.

And he didn't want to see Hannah get hurt.

"All right," Elijah said. "You go argue with her in the cold. A.J. and I will meet you in front of the fire at the lodge before dark."

"Well before dark. I'm not hiking up there the long way."

Sean disconnected. He passed O'Rourke's, not yet open for the day, a red-bowed wreath hanging crookedly on its front door. The temperature had risen to the low twenties, but if the temperature was above zero, Liam O'Rourke got outside. He loved Vermont winters. Sean didn't know if Hannah did or not, but he wasn't concerned about her freezing on her solo hike up to his father's cabin. She knew every shortcut on the mountain, and she knew how to handle herself in winter conditions. She was smart, reserved and utterly fearless.

Plus, he planned to catch up with her before she had a chance to go too far wrong.

Five

Hannah paused at the edge of a cluster of spruce trees on the flat of a quiet knoll on the remote north side of Cameron Mountain. All that disturbed the blanket of snow was a twisting rabbit trail that disappeared under a low-hanging evergreen branch. There were no other tracks or prints. It had been at least a week since any investigators had made the trek up this way.

She stepped among the evergreens, her snowshoes and ski poles sinking into the fresh powder. The snow sparkled in the midday sun. There was no wind. The air was cold and dry, the trees creating still shadows under the cloudless, clear late-December sky. Exertion and her layers had kept her warm on her hike. She'd kept hydrated with sips of water, and although not hungry, she'd forced herself to eat a couple of energy bars.

Devin had found Drew's body at the top of the shorter, steeper trail up the north side of the mountain, two hundred yards back through the woods. By then, much of the wet spring snow had melted and there were no tracks left to follow, at least none that anyone had noticed. As a result, no one had known about the cabin until five weeks ago, when Nora Asher, with Devin right behind her, had discovered it.

On sleepless nights, Devin would describe the cabin's location in detail. He'd drawn maps and noted landmarks—the trail, the tree-covered but distinctive knoll, the cluster of spruce trees.

This was the right place.

A clump of snow dropped into a drift as Hannah brushed past a gnarled spruce.

A chickadee fluttered out from among

the evergreen branches and flew up into a tall, bare oak tree.

She couldn't remember when she'd been to a place so quiet, so isolated.

Why had she come alone?

"You don't let emotions dictate your actions," Drew had told her.

Well, she just had.

"I wouldn't feel nearly as crazy if I'd brought a dog," she said half aloud. Rose Cameron, Drew's only daughter, trained search-and-rescue dogs and handled one of her own. She could have recommended a dog who'd have appreciated a good run in the snow.

But Hannah couldn't make herself smile. She continued past the spruce into a small clearing, which Devin had also described. After years of searching, Drew Cameron had finally come upon what he'd believed to be the site of the original Cameron dwelling in Black Falls. He'd cut down trees in the immediate area and, in apparent secret, had built a post-and-beam cabin on the old foundation.

Hannah spotted a tiny, batten-wood cabin on the far edge of the knoll and almost sank to her knees with emotion. This was it—this was Drew's cabin.

This was the place where Devin and the three people with him had almost died.

Where his would-be killer *had* died.

Her snowshoes almost floating in the drifts, she hardly made a sound as she crossed the clearing. She had no time to waste. She leaned her poles against the exterior of the cabin and squatted down, using both hands to scoop snow away from any exposed section of the foundation.

About ten inches of the foundation extended aboveground. She wasn't a stonemason herself, but she could see it was rubble-stone construction, which made sense. Two hundred years ago, breakage would have been more practical—easier to find, dig up and haul—than whole stones.

Drew had placed a thick sill beam on the foundation, creating even more of a protective barrier between the ground and the cabin itself.

Hannah dug as much snow as possible out of the rock and saw that both the remains of the original foundation and any rebuilding Drew had done were dry construction. That meant he hadn't had to figure out how to get mortar up here or decide between using an old-style lime-and-sand mortar or a modern cement. A strict historic renovation would have called for original materials where possible.

Hannah had crawled around in enough old cellar holes to have an idea of the work involved in rebuilding a foundation that had been left to the elements for generations. She remembered the fallen stones, caved-in dirt, trees and brush often growing right in the middle of what had once been someone's home.

She stood up on her snowshoes. Drew hadn't rebuilt the original chimney, opting instead for a woodstove that he hadn't lived to hook up. He could have used stones from the chimney in repairing and extending the foundation wall. Still, he'd have needed equipment to do the job—trowels, stone hammers, drills, pry bars, fulcrums, rollers—and he'd have needed know-how. He was handy, but he wasn't a stonemason.

If he hadn't had help with the work itself, he'd at least had advice.

"Maybe," Hannah said aloud.

She could be wrong. Drew had been a Cameron, after all. Who was to say he couldn't have managed on his own, without help *or* advice?

She'd learned to keep her mouth shut until she was sure she had her facts straight.

Especially when the facts involved her past.

Leaving her poles outside, she pushed open the solid wood door, wincing at the loud creak of the hinges, as if it might wake someone, or alert someone to her presence. She stepped inside, pulled the door shut and tugged off her snowshoes. She didn't want to stop moving for too long. Once she got cold, she'd have a hard time warming back up.

The cabin was just one room with windows, a front door and back door and the woodstove, which hadn't been hooked up yet.

She went still, certain she'd heard a sound outside.

Not a chickadee or the wind.

A deer? A moose?

She tiptoed to the front window next to the door. Kyle Rigby, hidden among the spruce trees with an assault rifle, had shot out the glass. After the police had released the cabin as a crime scene, Jo and Elijah had nailed thick, translucent plastic over the opening and cleaned up the shards.

Hannah tried to peer through the plastic but couldn't see anything except blurry white snow and the vague outline of trees.

Again she heard a *whooshing* sound.

Someone on snowshoes or skis?

She held her breath and listened but heard nothing now.

Had whoever was out there paused to eye her tracks in the snow—her ski poles leaned up against the outside of the cabin?

Not waiting any longer, Hannah grabbed her backpack and snowshoes and bolted across the plywood floor for the back door. It wouldn't be locked. There was nothing in the cabin to steal except the woodstove, and who would bother hauling it down the mountain in winter conditions?

"Hannah. It's me—Sean Cameron."

Before Hannah had a chance to adjust to the idea of who it was out there, she heard the creak of the front door and spun around just as it opened.

Sean lifted his sunglasses onto the brim

of his wool cap and frowned at her from just outside his father's cabin. "Hannah, what are you doing?"

"Getting ready to bolt. Sean. Damn." She took in a sharp breath. "Scare me to death, why don't you?"

"I'm sorry I startled you." He nodded to the snowshoes in her arms. "Were you going to beat me over the head with one of those?"

"I was just trying to get out of here." She hoped she sounded calm, sure of herself. "I figured I'd need snowshoes once I outran you—or whoever it was." She smiled. "Of course, I was hoping it'd be someone I could outrun."

"Or a friend," he said.

"Yes. Or a friend."

Sean stayed just outside in the snow. He didn't look particularly winded or tired from his trek up the mountain. But he wouldn't. Hannah had never seen him in action as a smoke jumper, a job that required him to maintain a high level of fitness.

She followed his gaze to the plastic-covered window. "I finally had to come up here and see for myself," she said.

"Why now?"

"Initially law enforcement wouldn't let anyone near this part of the mountain. Then we had the holidays, and I was so busy. This morning I knew it was time."

"What made you know?"

Sean wasn't letting her off the hook, but she had no intention of lying to him, or of giving him a full explanation. She'd been thinking about Drew's old cellar hole for days, and seeing Bowie walk into the café with Elijah and Sean and the law there—their reaction to him—had forced her into action. Bowie was a stonemason. They shared a difficult past. He'd worked with her father and knew as much as anyone in the area about historic stonework.

"I wanted to get things settled in my own head," she said simply.

"Did you succeed?"

"I don't know yet." She walked past the woodstove, where Devin and Nora had taken cover when shots started flying. "Devin's recovered physically. Psychologically—he seems to be doing all right. I think he is, anyway."

"A.J. and Lauren do, too."

Hannah started to say more, to tell Sean she was concerned about the effects of the trauma of the past months on her brother and his lack of direction, but she caught herself. “He’s strong. He’ll get through it.”

“He’s had a hell of a time. You, too.”

She let the snowshoes slide down her legs and stood them upright, leaning them against her thighs as she took in shallow breaths and looked around the small cabin. She pictured Elijah and Jo—armed, having headed up the mountain prepared for trouble—and the two teenagers huddled in the dark, a storm raging through the long night. They all had known a killer was out there in the cold. Had he run? Would he be back?

Still suffering from his encounter with Kyle Rigby before nightfall, Devin had been semiconscious, barely aware of the storm.

Then came morning . . . a foot of fresh snow . . . and the first shots that shattered the window.

“When the shooting started, there was nothing Devin could do. Being so helpless was hard for him. . . .” Hannah pointed at the rough-wood beams high on the back wall, her hand shaking. She wondered if Sean noticed. “You can see where bullets struck the wood. One lucky shot, and anyone in here could have been hit."

"Jo and Elijah had positioned themselves and Devin and Nora as best as possible." Sean spoke with little detectable emotion. "Rigby had to have known what he was in for when he started shooting. He could have gone on his way. Instead, he waited out the storm and assaulted a cabin with an armed soldier and federal agent inside."

"Jo pinned Rigby down from the front window while Elijah sneaked out the back door to go after him." Balancing the snowshoes leaning against her thighs, Hannah looked back at the woodstove. "Jo told Devin and Nora to stay low. He said she was cool and focused under fire. Rigby had a chance to give up, but he kept shooting."

"Devin did fine, too," Sean said. "Eighteen years old, scared, targeted by contract killers—he still managed to save Nora Asher's life. He warned her Rigby was after her."

"He and Nora survived thanks to Jo and Elijah," Hannah said, picking up her snowshoes. She tucked them under one arm and walked past Sean in the doorway, brushing against his arm, remembering—for no reason she could fathom—the feel of it around her back in March when he'd hauled her out of O'Rourke's.

She stepped into the snow in her hiking boots, hyper-aware of Sean watching her as she dropped her snowshoes side by side in front of her.

"Hannah," he said, "what's going on?"

She didn't give him a direct answer. "Devin had his suspicions, but he didn't know about this place. The police didn't find it, either, when they investigated his death. It seems so easy to find now, but if you don't know where to look . . ." With the heel of her boot, she dragged one snowshoe closer to her. "Everything seems more obvious in hindsight."

Sean steadied his gaze on the sunlit snow and still shadows. "Rigby didn't have to come back here after the storm," he said, "but he knew he'd be marked for death himself if he failed."

Hannah looked at the evergreens where Kyle Rigby had concealed himself and taken cover in preparation for his assault on the cabin. "He knew what he was doing.

He wasn't crazy or suicidal." She spoke in a steady voice, consciously keeping her emotions contained. This had always been her way, she thought, and wasn't a skill she'd learned in law school. "He gauged his chances and did what he had to do."

"He assessed the terrain and picked his spot."

She took in a shallow breath, hearing, in her mind, the gunfire that frozen morning, picturing Elijah's and Jo's focus and intensity as they'd confronted the hidden shooter. "Rigby knew that failure wasn't an option. His own people would kill him if he didn't succeed up here. It didn't matter to him that he was taking on a Green Beret and a federal agent."

"It was kill or be killed."

And he'd been killed, Hannah thought. A few hours later, his partner, Melanie Kendall, was blown up in her car at the lodge, presumably by the people who'd hired her and Rigby.

Sean pulled the cabin door shut. "Why are you here alone?" he asked quietly. "Any of us would have come with you."

"Devin would have, too." She eased her boot into the binding of her snowshoe. "I guess I just needed to come on my own. What about you? Are you alone?" She looked back at him with a quick smile. "Your brothers aren't hiding in the trees, are they?"

He didn't return her smile. He lowered his sunglasses, making his eyes impossible to read. "I'm alone."

Hannah pulled off a glove and squatted down to adjust the strap on the back of her boot. "So you must not be afraid I'm the mastermind of this network of killers."

Sean leaned into one of his ski poles. "Long hike?"

She realized she'd gone too far in trying to compensate for her self-consciousness around him—for not telling him the whole story about why she'd come up here. "Longer than I wanted it to be." She stood up, feeling downright warm. "Did you follow me?"

"I parked on the old logging road and came up the back trail." His tone was even, pragmatic. "You can ride back with me."

She quickly put on her other snowshoe. Hike down the mountain with Sean? Sit next to him for the ten-mile drive back around the mountain to the lodge? She'd hiked up here for a reason, and he knew it, and he wanted to pry it out of her. Even under normal circumstances, she'd be reluctant to go with him, just because he was Sean Cameron.

These weren't normal circumstances.

She tried to keep him from seeing her turmoil of emotions. "I don't mind hiking the way I came," she said, adjusting the strap on her second boot.

"It'll be dusk by the time you get back." Sean spoke calmly, without pleading. "One wrong turn, and you'll be spending the night on the mountain. Elijah would have your head for hiking up here by yourself."

"I'm prepared for the conditions."

"Of course you are. You're always prepared for anything."

She gave him a sharp glance, but she didn't see the slightest hint of impatience in him.

Just pure, uncompromising Cameron determination.

"You choose the route," he said. "I'm going with you."

Hannah reached for the ski poles leaning against the cabin. Now that she'd been still for a while, the cold was seeping into her. Even so, she felt the blood rush hot to her face. "I'm not going to get rid of you, am I?"

There was just the glimmer of a smile. "No."

"Why, because I'm alone—or because you don't trust me?"

"Something's on your mind, Hannah. You ran out of the café this morning right after Bowie left and headed straight up here."

"I didn't run."

"Does he blame you for his arrest?"

"I don't know. I haven't asked him. This morning was the first time I've talked to him since his arrest. You were there. You all heard what we said to each other. We talked about the leak in the cellar."

"You went looking for him. The leak's not a crisis. You wanted an excuse to talk to him."

"I've known Bowie since I was a tot. I don't need an excuse to talk to him, and the only way to get hold of him is to go looking for him."

Sean sighed. "All right. I give up. I'd rather argue with you someplace warm."

"Sounds like a plan." She'd meant it as

a light comment but saw his mouth twitch with sudden humor and immediately realized what she'd said. She decided she'd only make matters worse by trying to explain. "Supposedly the Cameron who first built up here was a bit of a hermit. Makes sense, considering how isolated it is."

"It wasn't as isolated then. The land was cleared for farming, and there were houses scattered along the river and up onto the mountain slopes."

"It was never crowded, that's for sure. You Camerons always have liked things a little rugged. You might live in Beverly Hills and not be used to Vermont winters anymore, but you fight wildfires." Hannah started across the clearing. "I've never been west of the Mississippi." Thinking of Toby's imminent departure, she glanced back at Sean. "Would I like Southern California?"

"To visit, at least. Everyone likes Southern California to visit."

"I hope Toby likes it," she said in a half whisper, but knew she couldn't let that line of thinking take hold.

She paused, looking out at the snow and the mix of evergreens and hardwood trees, really feeling the cold now. She knew Sean wasn't going to leave her to head back alone. Never mind his questions about her motives for coming up here, his father had died on this part of the mountain.

She turned to him, her ski pole striking a rock or ice under the snow. "Since I'm on Cameron land, I suppose I should do as you suggest and go back with you."

Sean tilted back his head but said nothing, and she followed her tracks back through the cluster of spruce trees. A rabbit scampered in front of her, then disappeared under drooping, snow-covered branches as Sean came up next to her.

Hannah glanced up at him. "Being here can't be easy for you," she said quietly.

"It isn't."

"You and your brothers and sister have enough on your minds without beating yourselves up because your father didn't come to you for help."

"He wanted the cabin to be a surprise," Sean said. "We get that."

Hannah angled a look up at him. "I don't mean just with the cabin. He went to Washington two weeks before his death to talk to Alex Bruni. I hear investigators speculate at the café, and I've talked to enough of them myself. They believe whatever your father discussed with Ambassador Bruni ultimately got them targeted by these killers. Whatever it was, neither of them realized it was incendiary at the time, or they'd have gone to the police."

"It was enough for my father to drive to D.C."

"But it wasn't enough for Bruni not to blow him off. Nora doesn't know what they talked about, but she says her stepfather wasn't very nice to your father. It wasn't until she started asking questions about Melanie Kendall that he took another look at what Drew had told him that day back in April." Hannah stared down at the twisting trail the rabbit had left behind before scurrying out of sight. "Then he was killed."

Sean was very still next to her. "You'll make a good prosecutor."

"Your father wasn't protecting you," she said. "He would have protected you, but he wasn't. You know what kind of man he was. He went to Alex Bruni because he thought that's where he could get the answers he was looking for. He saw Jo in D.C., too, and didn't say a word to her about what was on his mind."

A sudden wind blew down from the summit and cut through her thin jacket and layers. Sean didn't seem to notice. "Bowie was in jail in April," he said.

She pretended she hadn't heard him and pushed off through the snow, following his tracks when they diverged from hers. She came to the steep trail down to the old logging road. Fine snow blew off a six-foot rock outcropping next to her. The wind was steady now, harsh, numbing her face. She lifted her jacket collar to better cover her chin and mouth.

Sean pulled off his gray wool scarf and handed it to her. "Take it," he said. "I don't need it. We can finish this discussion later."

Hannah didn't argue. The scarf was soft and still warm from him. She draped it around her neck, pulled it up over her mouth and nose, wishing suddenly that she hadn't come up here at all. She thought of Bowie standing out at the old cellar hole on the river when she and Drew had traipsed through the snow and mud to find him. Had Bowie already been up to see the old cellar hole Drew had found? Had the two men already talked about the work involved in rebuilding an old foundation?

Hannah plunged down the steep trail, knowing Sean would be right behind her if she tripped—or if she decided to tell him her real reasons for finally hiking up to see his father's cabin.

Six

Sean had his hood off and his jacket unzipped even before the heat in Elijah's truck kicked in. Hannah had already unwound his scarf from her neck, letting it dangle down her front. She sat stiffly next to him, her eyes pinned straight ahead as if she were trying to pretend she really wasn't driving the ten miles back to the lodge with him. She'd moved fast on the mountain trail, sleeker, more lithe and agile, than he was comfortable noticing.

Just keep driving, he told himself as he navigated the rutted, icy, one-lane logging road at the bottom of the trail. Ordinarily it would be closed to vehicles by December, but after the violence five weeks ago, law enforcement saw that it was kept plowed. It led to a back road, almost as narrow, that wound through the hills and the isolated hollow where Hannah Shay and Bowie O'Rourke had grown up.

Sean remembered his father talking about the Shays. "They've always lived hand-to-mouth," he'd said on one of his rare visits to Southern California. "It's what they know. Hannah and her brothers could be different, but they won't be if they don't want to be. I guess it's easy for me to say. I've never had to leave behind what I've always known."

As he drove down close to the river, Sean glanced at Hannah, her cheeks rosy, her eyes a pale gray-blue against the winter landscape. He'd always recognized that she was attractive. There'd never been any doubt about that. She was just impossible. She had a wall up around her as impenetrable as a force field, and never let anyone in.

"I can imagine your father's excitement when he found that old Cameron cellar hole," she said.

Sean could, too. "I always thought searching for it gave him an excuse to be up on the mountain, but he was serious about finding it. He took A.J., Rose and me up a few times, but most of the time, it was Elijah. They butted heads all their lives, but they understood each other."

"I think in his own way, your father understood all four of you, even if he didn't always approve of your choices."

"Maybe so."

Sean felt the familiar rush of grief mixed with guilt, anger and regret when he thought about his father and how he'd died, but he allowed it to wash over him and didn't, this time, drown in it. He wanted to get his hands on whoever had hired the two killers to leave an old man to die alone in the cold. He wanted it as much as he'd wanted anything in his life, and he wasn't a man easily deterred once he'd put his mind to getting something.

Hannah stared out her window without speaking for a couple miles.

"How's law school?" Sean asked when her silence finally got to him.

She shrugged. "I've finished."

"Studying for the bar?"

"Yes."

"Any job prospects?"

She continued to sit rigid in her seat without glancing at him. "Not yet. I'm looking into a clerkship. With Toby in California for a few months . . ." She paused. "I'll have time on my hands."

What would she do when she found out Devin was heading to California, too? Sean tried not to think about how alone she'd be. She had her friends, the café, her budding law career, and she'd just be irritated if she thought he was feeling a little sorry for her.

"You can manage the café and a clerkship?" he asked.

"I managed law school and the café."

The late December sun was very low in the sky. An arc of bright, harsh afternoon light hit the windshield. Then it was gone, disappearing behind the hills as he took a tight turn down close to the river, just a few small pools of clear, fast-moving water not yet frozen in the winter cold.

Sean assumed Hannah's short answers were a clue she didn't want to talk, but he didn't care. He wanted to know more about her reasons for going up the mountain so suddenly on her own. "The café seems to be doing well," he said.

She smoothed a finger over the soft fabric of his scarf. "It is, thanks."

"Holiday season was busy?"

"Yes."

"A.J. says reporters and investigators made up for the drop-off in tourists at the lodge after the violence. I imagine it was the same at the café."

She nodded again. "It was."

"Hannah . . ." Sean turned onto Cameron Mountain Road, which would take them up from the river to the long, picturesque ridge where Black Falls Lodge was located and where he and his brothers and sister and the Harpers had all grown up. "You know, I wouldn't have to ask so many questions if you'd work with me here."

"Maybe I'm tired after my long hike and don't want to talk."

"You could just say so."

She turned to him finally and smiled. "I'm tired after my long hike and don't want to talk."

He grinned at her. "Could have told me eight miles ago."

She seemed to relax slightly. “I guess I could have.”

Not that she hadn’t made it obvious. He’d just ignored her signals.

He passed his sister’s little house and continued down to Harper Four Corners, the oldest settled section of Black Falls, where Cameron Mountain Road and Ridge Road intersected. On the corner to his right was a former early-nineteenth-century tavern, rumored to be haunted. To his left was an abandoned post-and-beam barn. On the corners directly across the road were a cemetery and a small, white-steepled church.

Sean turned right, onto Ridge Road, heading past snow-covered fields and stately, bare sugar maples that grew along stone walls constructed by long-ago farmers who’d cleared the rocky, inhospitable land.

He resisted the temptation to push the private, guarded woman next to him about her reasons for hiking up to the cabin—what they had to do with Bowie O’Rourke, why she wouldn’t just say what was on her mind. She’d never been one to knuckle under to pressure. It just had a way of getting her back up.

They came to Black Falls Lodge, a string of rustic buildings at the top of a sloping, snow-covered meadow dotted with evergreens. The views of the endless mountains, blue and white in the December afternoon, were the subject of countless postcards and tourist photographs.

On his most tortured nights since April, Sean would lie awake in his bed in Beverly Hills and picture standing with his father on the lodge's stone terrace. Drew Cameron had lived in Black Falls his entire life, marrying there, pulling together parcels of land on the mountain named for his ancestors, opening the original lodge with his wife as a young couple. He'd never expected her to die first. He'd had enemies—people he'd irritated over the years—but Sean couldn't think of anyone who'd hated his father enough to have him killed.

"Sean?"

He glanced at Hannah and realized she'd seen his pain. He quickly masked it and turned into the lodge parking lot, the truck's tires crunching on the packed ice and snow as he pulled in next to her car.

A.J. and Elijah walked out the side door to the main lodge. They weren't wearing coats, just heavy sweaters. Jo would be on the premises, and Lauren, A.J.'s wife. Lauren worked at the lodge, but it wouldn't have mattered. A.J. had kept his family close since two hired assassins had turned up and been killed, one of them within sight of the lodge.

Hannah unfastened her seat belt. "Not going to complain about the cold in front of your brothers, are you?"

Sean looked over at her and laughed. "Not a chance."

She touched the door handle. "Thanks for the ride. Stay warm. You'll be back in Beverly Hills soon."

Her tone was cool, reserved, and he knew he wouldn't get anywhere with her, not with his brothers watching, not with her on high alert. He smiled instead. "I can't persuade you to stay for hot chocolate?"

"Hot chocolate and the third-degree. No, thanks. You all know where to find me if you have any specific questions. I have to check on Toby and his packing. He'll remember all his mountain-biking gear and forget his driver's license."

"Toby's old enough to see to his own packing."

"So he is." She pushed open the door, letting in the frigid air. Her gaze settled on a spot out on the plowed, sanded parking lot. "I wasn't here when Melanie Kendall's car blew up. It was after the search-and-rescue team brought Nora and Devin down off the mountain. I was with Devin at the hospital."

"She had a bad end coming, but no one wanted to see her murdered."

"Jo and Elijah witnessed the explosion. He got Nora out of Melanie's car before it blew up. I hear from her every now and then—she's in Washington with her mother. Her father, too. It's tough, but she's talking about going back to school."

The blast that killed Melanie Kendall, Sean knew, could have killed his brother, or Jo Harper, or anyone else who'd been at the lodge that day. "I should have been here," he said. "I was drinking damn *mojitos* by the pool—"

"No one knew we had two killers in our midst. Guilt will eat you alive, Sean," Hannah said, her voice deathly quiet. "Believe me, I know. Don't let it."

Sean suddenly was aware of the afternoon shadows and the lavender shade of the sky as dusk slowly settled over the mountains. His life in California almost seemed to belong to another man, not to him.

"I'm glad I didn't witness Melanie or Kyle's deaths, or see their bodies." Hannah seemed to draw herself in against the cold as the heat seeped out of the truck. "If I'm going to be a prosecutor, I have to learn to steel myself to what I'll have to see."

"This was different. You met them. They tried to frame Devin for stalking Nora Asher and stealing from her, the café, the lodge."

"Melanie was attractive and personable. I never would have pegged her as a killer."

"That's what she and Rigby counted on."

"Her own people killed her. Right here." Hannah shook her head as if she were telling herself she had to stop now, before she could spin out of control. "Rigby was already dead. Jo figured out that Melanie was Rigby's partner, but whoever triggered the bomb in her car didn't necessarily know that. It wasn't why she was killed. Nora and Devin were still alive. Melanie had screwed up, and she had to die."

Sean stayed where he was behind the wheel. He saw the tremor in Hannah's lower jaw. Next, her teeth started to chatter. Her eyes were wide, focused, he knew, not on the present but on the images of what had happened five weeks ago.

He reached over to her and touched her elbow. "Hannah. Breathe."

His words, his touch, seemed to penetrate whatever was coming at her, and she exhaled and turned to him. "Sorry. Every day's better, but I still . . ."

"I know," he said softly.

"The police have cleared everyone who was at the lodge when Melanie's car exploded. The killer could have had a spotter, but why make two calls when one would do? This is a practical, calculating killer."

"It's also one who will take tremendous chances if necessary."

"A man? A woman? A team?"

Sean shook his head. “I couldn’t tell you. I couldn’t even guess.”

Hannah looked out toward the mountains in the distance. “Even up here, it’s easy to go unnoticed. Who’d remember a car parked on the side of the road, or a cross-country skier out enjoying the first snow of the season? Make a discreet call and . . . mission accomplished. Melanie Kendall is dead.”

Sean saw his opening and took it. “What if whoever’s behind this network had an accomplice here in Black Falls? An unwitting accomplice, perhaps. Someone who was used or manipulated into helping to set off the bomb.”

Hannah shifted her gaze from the view, her pale blue eyes reflecting a hint of the lavender in the sky. “Do you have anyone in mind?” she asked, her self-control back in place.

“I don’t.” His eyes narrowed on her. “What about you?”

“It’s your theory,” she said, “not mine.”

“You’re letting the police run the investigation, aren’t you, Hannah? You’re not a prosecutor yet.”

Her look was unreadable now. “I’m familiar with who does what in a criminal investigation."

She pushed open the door and climbed down out of the truck. Sean nodded back toward his brothers. "A.J. and Elijah will want to know you're all right after going up to Pop's cabin. They know being up there can be emotional. Why don't you come into the lodge with me and we all have a drink?"

"I really can't," she said, grabbing her pack, snowshoes and ski poles.

Sean leaned across the seat, ready to charge after her. "Hannah, what did you figure out up there?"

"That I should have done a better job of protecting my brother."

"You have a law degree. You're smart. You see everything. It'd be natural to have questions—"

"Yes. Devin almost getting killed definitely sparked questions."

Her arms loaded, she shut the door with her knee and made it to her car without dropping a snowshoe or poking an eye with a ski pole. She managed to get the passenger door open and dump in her pack and snowshoes, then went around to the driver's side and climbed in.

Sean could have gone after her, but he got out of the truck and headed across the parking lot, trying to ignore just how tense and aggravated he was. He'd sit across a negotiating table with the worst of the sharks he'd encountered in Beverly Hills before taking on Hannah Shay.

No one, he thought, had ever gotten to him the way she did.

He could feel the approach of dusk in the cold, still air. Nightfall would come early. He had never noticed the relentless winter dark as a kid, only later, when he'd come home for the holidays. He'd had no intention of returning to Vermont to live, but he'd always thought he could.

Now he wasn't sure. His father's death . . . Hannah . . . her brothers . . .

His brothers.

Sean waited until Hannah's old car was rattling down the road before he joined A.J. and Elijah on the walk.

"Let's go inside," he said to his brothers. "We need to talk."

Seven

Hannah smiled as Lester and Gloria McBane both came to answer her knock on the side door of the old Four Corners tavern. They were in their eighties, white-haired and noticeably frailer in recent months. Reverend McBane had performed the funeral service for Hannah's father but had already retired when her mother died. He and his wife, a former librarian, had attended her funeral and supported Hannah's decision to become her brothers' legal guardian. The run-down tavern had been their home for the past twenty years. They liked to say the place was as comfortable and familiar as a worn-out pair of slippers. Hannah had heard rumors that Sean Cameron had his eye on it, but she couldn't fathom what he needed with another property in Black Falls.

She held a small box that she, Dominique and Beth had packed last night. Hannah had set it in her car before bed, figuring she'd make her way up here at some point during the day. She hadn't imagined it would be after hiking up Cameron Mountain. She handed the box to Gloria McBane. "We thought you might like a few goodies for a cold winter night. Beth says she got the coffee cake recipe from you."

"You all are much better cooks than I ever was," the older woman said. "I hardly cook anymore these days. Won't you come in and have some with us?"

Suddenly aching with the cold, Hannah glanced down the road for a Cameron on her tail. None so far. She turned back to the McBanes. "I should get back to town. I've been hiking."

Lester McBane pointed a thin finger at her. "I can see that. Your face is chapped from the wind and the cold. Were you hiking with Sean Cameron?" The old man smiled. "You look surprised. Gloria and I saw you two in Elijah's truck a little while ago."

"Ah." Hannah laughed. "No secrets in a small town." But she felt herself blush and added quickly, "Not that Sean and I . . . We just ran into each other up at his father's cabin and he gave me a ride back to the lodge."

"It's terrible, what happened out there before Thanksgiving," Mrs. McBane said, setting the box of goodies on a counter behind her. She was a small woman, her fine white hair neatly curled. "We only get out twice a week in the cold weather. We haven't seen any of the Camerons since before Christmas. How are they? And how are *you,* Hannah?"

"Everyone seems to be coping. My brothers and the café keep me busy, and I've just started to study for the bar. Devin had a rough time with those killers, but the Camerons lost their father."

Reverend McBane nodded thoughtfully. "It'll take time."

"It would help if the police could figure out who triggered the bomb in Melanie

Kendall's car." Hannah didn't mince words. The McBanes had been through plenty in their lives and were well aware of what had happened down the road at Black Falls Lodge. "If you were the one watching and waiting for her to get in the car, where would you be? Would you be out in the open and subtly dial your cell phone? Or would you hide? Those are the kinds of questions everyone's asking."

"We've been thinking about that," Mrs. McBane said. "Lester and I have come up with dozens of options ourselves."

He immediately warmed to the topic. "Cell-phone service is spotty up here," he said. "I suppose the killer could have found a landline to use. We didn't see anyone out here. We were in watching television when the bomb went off."

Mrs. McBane buttoned her sweater, baggy on her thin frame. "I remember the storm the night before. We drank brandy in front of the fire and went to bed early." She shuddered. "I'm just glad those two killers were the only ones who ended up dead. How's your brother?"

"He's still working at the lodge," Hannah said. "He had a room above the shop there, but he's moved back with Toby and me for now."

"A.J.'s been good to him," Mrs. McBane said.

It was just an innocent comment by a kind woman, but Hannah automatically felt herself go on the defensive and realized how on edge she was. She pushed back any irritation. "Yes, he and Lauren have both been great. Devin works hard." She smiled again at the older couple. "I shouldn't keep you standing here in the cold. It's perfect weather for tea and a few goodies."

"You're all good to think of us," Reverend McBane said.

He and his wife had done the same for other people for dozens of years. Now it was their turn to need a helping hand, which they accepted graciously, without any hint of the stubborn pride or defensiveness Hannah had to fight when people offered to help her and her brothers.

She wished them good-night and headed back down the well-sanded walk to the driveway, glancing down the road again. She only saw leafless sugar maples silhouetted against the slowly darkening sky. There was no question in her mind that Sean, A.J. and Elijah had gathered in front of the lodge's big stone fireplace to discuss what she was up to and how they could get it out of her.

She'd never been good at lying or pretending. She'd always found she did best when she looked at life straight on.

But this was different.

Sean knew she was holding back. But she wasn't, really. She didn't know anything the police didn't. She'd answered all their questions fully. They and the Camerons and their friends had all crawled through Drew's cabin after Kyle Rigby's assault and subsequent death. Any one of them could have wondered how and if Drew had managed to reconstruct the old foundation on his own.

Just as any one of them could have wondered if Bowie O'Rourke had helped Drew with his secret project on Cameron Mountain.

If, by whatever means, for whatever reason, Kyle Rigby and Melanie Kendall had found the cabin because of Bowie.

As she came to her car, Hannah heard the muffled barking of a dog across the road. She peered out at the cemetery, slabs of gray headstones standing out against the white of the snow. The air was frigid and still. There were no lights or cars at the church on the corner opposite the cemetery. Four Corners Burying Ground, it was called. Its oldest grave—that of a Harper—was dated 1796.

The barking continued. The dog sounded agitated. Hannah walked out to the end of the dirt driveway, wondering if deer or wild turkeys were crossing the cemetery and driving the poor dog nuts. She noticed a van parked just down Cameron Mountain Road next to the stone wall that bordered the cemetery.

Bowie's van. It had to be his black lab, Poe, creating the racket.

She shoved her hands into her pockets and told herself she should go back to the village and see to her brothers, the café, her studying. Instead, she crossed Ridge Road and walked along the edge of the cemetery to the corner.

She noticed snowshoe tracks and boot prints in the snow, most leading to the oldest of the headstones, simple rectangular slabs leaning crookedly in different directions. The McBanes had told her they didn't worry about living in a haunted house with so many ghosts right across the road. People came from all over the country to research their family roots and locate the graves of ancestors. Many of the graves had metal markers identifying a veteran of the Civil War, the Spanish-American War, the two World Wars, Vietnam. There was even a handful commemorating those who'd fought in the American Revolution.

Drew Cameron was buried in the Cameron family plot on the far southeast corner of the cemetery. Hannah and her brothers had attended his funeral but not the graveside service. She doubted any of her ancestors were buried at Four Corners. Her parents were buried at a little church graveyard past the hollow where she'd grown up.

She zipped up her jacket and hunched her shoulders against the cold as she came to the corner. Bowie's van was parked a little ways down Cameron Mountain Road, at the end of a narrow lane cut between the cemetery and a steep, wooded hill.

Hannah crossed her arms on her chest, really cold now.

Poe continued his barking and growling.

She looked out across the old headstones just as a breeze kicked up, blowing fine snow into the air.

Creepy, she thought, and kept walking toward the parked van.

Eight

Poe, who had to be at least six or seven years old, jumped up in a side window, yapping madly as Hannah eased between the van and the snowbank on the side of Cameron Mountain Road. “Hey, Poe,” she said, trying to soothe the agitated dog. “What are you all excited about? Did you see a rabbit?”

He calmed slightly as she reached the lane. Exertion and adrenaline had warmed her up, if only slightly. She glanced around for Bowie. He’d never leave Poe in the van in the cold for too long, but she didn’t see him. Could he have scooted across the street into the church?

"Easy, Poe. I'll find Bowie, okay?" The lab's barking was more intermittent now, and she raised her voice as she called for his master. "Bowie, where are you? Poe's going crazy here."

She listened for any response, any indication of what had gotten the dog so excited. She could see that Bowie had done a careful, thorough job on the old stone culvert that ran along the edge of the lane and provided drainage for the cemetery. He must have stopped by to clean up or check on a potential problem. Whatever his other faults, Bowie was an expert mason who did quality work.

Poe settled down, and Hannah called Bowie again. She could feel the effects of her long hike and the day's tension in her legs now. She debated going back to the van and letting Bowie's dog out to come help her find him. She wasn't sure she believed in ghosts, but she definitely didn't like being alone in an isolated, cold cemetery at dusk.

"Hannah."

It was as if someone had just whispered her name into the wind.

She stopped abruptly, her boots crunching on the packed snow.

"Bowie?" She heard a slight catch in her voice. "Is that you? Are you hurt?"

A stiff breeze blew across the cemetery, cracking naked tree limbs together and whooshing through the branches of the hemlocks and white pines on the hillside.

"Hannah . . . Hannah . . . Hannah."

The voice—rhythmic and unnerving—came from near the stone-and-concrete crypt built into the hillside farther down the lane. Hannah felt her throat tighten and her hands stiffen inside her jacket pockets. She went as still as she could, listening, but she heard only the wind in the trees.

Where was Bowie?

Who was whispering her name?

She noticed several long-handled tools leaned up against the end of the crypt close to her and decided she'd arm herself with a shovel, then head back to the McBanes' and get help if Bowie didn't surface.

She crept a few steps closer to the crypt. She didn't know if there were any bodies inside. The McBanes could be pragmatic about cemeteries, but she wondered if she'd be as spooked if she'd heard someone whispering her name at the old church across the street. It had to be Bowie. Who else could it be?

She reached for a shovel that was leaned against the crypt. On the other side of its thick wood door was a four-foot pallet of granite blocks. Next to it was a taller pile of what looked like debris Bowie had collected in repairing the culvert. Rock, dirt and broken bits of concrete had dislodged from the pile and fallen, bringing along most of the black tarp that had been draped crookedly over both the debris and the pallet of blocks.

The tarp flapped in the steadying wind.

Hannah took a tentative step forward to investigate, but there was no sign of Bowie—or a deer, moose, wild turkeys or anything else that might have disturbed the pile of debris.

Various scenarios ran through her head. Bowie could be under the fallen debris. He could have hit his head and be disoriented, wandering in the woods or among the headstones.

He could be hiding from her. He could be deliberately trying to scare her.

No.

The tarp blew into her, and she batted it with the shovel, her heel slipping on a glistening patch of ice. As she regained her balance, more of the tarp came at her. She tried to get clear of it, but snow, ice, dirt and chunks of rock were crashing onto her.

She leaped backward against the crypt's door as something sharp—a bit of broken granite or ice—cut her left cheek, and a baseball-size rock struck her left wrist. She ignored the sudden pain, batting aside the tarp with her shovel, kicking past stones, dirt and chunks of ice.

Still holding on to her shovel, she burst out from the rubble and ran into the middle of the lane. She was freezing now, her face and wrist stinging where she'd been hit, but she saw footprints in the snow on the edge of the woods and charged over to a trail that led straight downhill through the white pines.

Had Bowie just knocked her over and run off?

"Hannah!"

This time it was a shout—a distinctly

male voice coming from behind her in the cemetery. She pivoted, shovel raised.

Sean leaped over the stone wall to the crypt, and in another two bounds was onto the lane, grabbing her around the middle before she could launch herself off down the trail.

"Someone just . . ." She was aching, gasping for air.

Sean tightened his hold on her. "Just what?"

"I don't know. I have to find Bowie. I can't tell if these prints are new." Most were boot prints, not ski or snowshoe tracks. "It'd be easy to lose someone in all these evergreens. I don't even know if he's out here." She realized Poe was barking madly again. "Did you see him? Bowie?"

"No." Sean eased back from her, holding her by her upper arms as he assessed her. "You're hurt."

"Not badly." She pointed the shovel at the mess in front of the crypt. "That pile came down on me. I didn't see anyone, but I heard someone calling my name. It was barely a whisper."

Sean peered more closely at her. "Are you sure you're okay?"

She nodded, realized with a jolt that she didn't want him to release her and forced herself to stand back from him. Her breathing was calmer. "It's creepy out here," she said, giving an exaggerated shudder. "Damn. I do *not* like cemeteries."

"Hold on—"

Before Sean could stop her, she picked her way over fallen blocks and grabbed an edge of the tarp, still flapping in the wind, and heaped it into a pile in the snow in front of the crypt.

She caught a glimpse of torn orange fabric on the other side of the main pile of debris.

Then it was gone, snatched away.

"Bowie, is that you?" She scrambled over dislodged, frozen dirt and rock to get a better look. "What's going on?"

She heard a moan and started to move faster, but Sean leaped up behind her, got one arm around her middle again and lifted her off her feet. Before she could catch her breath, he set her back down on the ground, staying on the pile of rock, ice and dirt between her and whoever was on the other side of the crypt.

"Relax, Cameron." Bowie stood up and

grunted in obvious pain. Blood dripped from gashes on his left hand and the left side of his face. He was ashen, his orange sweatshirt covered in dirt, his down vest unzipped, his breathing hard and fast. "I just got my butt kicked by a wall of granite. I'm in no condition to kick anyone else's butt."

Sean's expression was tight. "What the hell happened to you?"

Bowie staggered out to the lane, blood dripping from his hand into the snow, dirt and rock dust in his hair. He ignored Sean and looked at Hannah. "I heard Poe barking like crazy, but I didn't know you were here."

"I can call an ambulance," she said.

"Nah." He shook his gashed hand, a gob of blood dropping onto an icy patch on the lane. "It's nothing."

Sean eyed Bowie warily, making no apparent effort to hide his suspicion. "Were you in a fight?" he asked.

Bowie shrugged. "A fight with granite." He touched the cuff of his sweatshirt to his cut, swelling face as he nodded to Hannah. "You okay? Your cheek's bleeding."

"Just a little. I'm fine. I got out of the way in time."

"Most of this mess fell on me," Bowie said. "It knocked the wind out of me."

Hannah winced at the blood dripping from his hand and face. "You should get yourself checked out. You might need stitches, and if you have a concussion—"

"I've got a med kit in my van. If I went to the emergency room for every nick and scratch I get in this work, I'd never finish a job." He grimaced at the tarp, rock and dirt. "I stopped by to pick up some tools I left out here and heard a noise."

"What kind of noise?" Sean asked.

Bowie glanced back at him, slightly less hostile. "Probably the tarp. I'd secured it with rocks, but it was blowing around in the wind. I figured a critter crawled under it looking for a warm place to sleep. I climbed onto the edge of the pallet to secure the tarp and must have knocked this stuff over on myself. Stupid." Clearly in pain, he turned back to Hannah. "I didn't mean to scare you."

"I thought I heard someone calling my name . . . it was weird." She saw Sean's eyes darken, but he said nothing as she continued. "Honestly, Bowie, you should see a doctor. Don't take chances."

"I've been hit in the head before. This time—hey, at least it was an accident."

She didn't smile at his stab at humor. "Are you sure?"

"Why wouldn't I be?" He gave her a crooked grin. "Prosecutor Hannah."

Sean didn't smile, his expression serious as he toed a pile of small rocks. "Where were you when you heard the noise?"

Bowie picked up the shovel from the frozen ground and leaned it against the front of the crypt. "I was at the end of the lane by my van. Thought at first it might be a deer or a moose. Poe started barking. I couldn't hear anything after that. I came down here, and next thing, I was fighting off granite."

"Bowie . . ." Hannah hesitated. "Could it have been an attack?"

His gaze settled on her, practical. "I don't see how. It was probably just a big old raccoon making trouble." He grinned, blood trickling into the corner of his mouth. "Or maybe a ghost."

"Funny, Bowie." Hannah cradled her injured wrist, felt it swelling. She shivered, very cold now. "Look, with everything that's been going on lately, it'd be a good idea for us to tell our story to the police and let them check out what happened."

"You do what you want. I'm getting a couple Band-Aids."

Next to her, Sean inhaled sharply and reached into his parka for his cell phone. He hit a couple of buttons. "Hey, Elijah. I'm at the crypt at Four Corners cemetery. Hannah and Bowie got banged up. You and Jo need to get over here." He disconnected and turned to Hannah. "What did you mean you heard someone calling your name?"

"Just what I said. It was a whisper—I don't know. Maybe it was the wind and my imagination is so fired up I just turned it into my name." She made an effort to smile. "Or there *is* a ghost out here."

Sean returned his cell phone to his coat pocket. "Whatever you heard, it wasn't a damn ghost."

"Bowie," Hannah said, "did you hear someone call my name, or was it you?"

He clenched his cut finger with his uninjured hand, stemming some of the bleeding. "I didn't hear anyone, and no, it wasn't me. That I'd remember."

"You could have hurt your head more than you realize—"

"No. I didn't call your name, Hannah."

She frowned. "Maybe no one did."

Sean settled in alongside her, more out of suspicion, she thought, than any protective impulse. "Why did you run out to the trail after you were hurt?" he asked.

It was Bowie who answered. "Because she thought I'd knocked over the debris on her and was getting away, and she took off after me. Hannah has a temper, in case you haven't noticed. She controls it most of the time. Most people don't realize what a hothead she can be."

Hannah took no offense. She *had* been mad. "Come on, Bowie. I can at least get your first-aid kit out for you."

He started down the lane toward his van. Except for the dark green of the pines and hemlocks, there was no hint of color in the landscape of gray sky, bare trees, granite headstones and endless snow.

As she headed back down the lane, Sean stayed close to her. "Why did you come here alone?" he asked.

"I wasn't about to ask Reverend McBane to escort me."

Sean inhaled sharply. "All right." His tone was even. "Why did you come at all?"

None of the fight eased out of her. "I heard Poe barking."

"You could have called the lodge."

"To get you or one of your brothers to check out a barking dog with me?"

"You knew it was Bowie's dog."

"Exactly."

Sean narrowed his gaze on her injured cheek. Hannah remembered that as a smoke jumper he was trained in emergency medical care. "You should get some ice on that bruise," he said. "On your wrist, too."

"My main problem right now is that I'm freezing."

"Ah. Just what you need, the cold weather stiffening your spine even more."

She smiled suddenly, in spite of herself. "I'm being combative. Sorry. You raced across a bone-cold cemetery to my rescue. Thank you. If it'd been a particularly mean raccoon or ghost—"

"Whatever it was, Hannah, we're all going to want to know what really happened out here."

"Because it involves Bowie. If it didn't, you wouldn't care."

She picked up her pace and went ahead of him, but she realized he just had to lengthen a couple of strides and he'd catch up with her. But he didn't, and as she approached the van, her head was throbbing. She felt a little unsteady on her feet and made herself take a couple of deep breaths as she stood behind Bowie at the passenger door.

Without looking at her, he said, "What's on your mind, Hannah?"

She rubbed her fingertips over her bruised wrist. "I guess we were lucky we didn't break any bones."

"Go back to your car before you get frostbite." He glanced at her, the swelling on the side of his face reaching his eye now. "You look as if you've spent some time out in the wind today."

"I hiked up to Drew's cabin this afternoon."

Sean stopped at the end of the lane, and Hannah was aware of him eyeing Bowie for his reaction.

Bowie merely shrugged and stood up with a small black bag. "Cold day for a hike." His black lab was up and barking again. Bowie tapped the window. "Poe. Settle down. You know Hannah. She's a friend."

She noticed he didn't mention Sean.

Bowie set the bag on the passenger seat. "How'd you do up on the mountain?"

"It wasn't easy seeing Drew's cabin. Devin gave me good directions, but no wonder it took Drew forty years to find that old cellar hole. It's in the middle of nowhere. There's no trail—nothing but woods and more woods."

"Yep." Bowie unzipped the bag and pulled out a large bandage, tearing it open with his teeth. "Drew must have had an idea it was on that part of the mountain, or he just stumbled upon it one day."

Sean was silent, as still and stiff as a man could be, Hannah thought, and not crack into pieces. She watched as Bowie tossed the packaging into the van and secured the bandage to his cut face. It looked as if the worst of the bleeding had stopped. She assumed if anything looked seriously awry with Bowie or the bandaging, Sean would step forward.

"One more scar to go with all the others." Bowie splayed the thick, callused fingers of his injured hand, still bleeding freely. "Mind grabbing a bandage for this thing?"

"Of course not." Hannah stepped past him and rummaged in the med kit for the supplies. Bowie had always been stubborn, and he had a high tolerance for physical pain. For good reason, she thought. "Are you sure you don't want Sean to do this? He's—"

"I'm sure."

"Hold out your hand, then." She ripped open the bandage as she frowned at the gash on his hand. "Are you going straight home?"

"I have a stop to make."

"Where?"

"The Whittakers. I'm starting work on their guesthouse tomorrow. It's a good winter job."

Hannah had no doubt it was. Lowell and Vivian Whittaker were wealthy New Yorkers who'd bought a "gentleman's farm" in Black Falls a little over a year ago. It was just a few miles from Bowie's place on the river. They had befriended Alexander Bruni, a longtime regular in Black Falls, and his wife, Carolyn, Nora Asher's mother—which eventually had led Melanie Kendall and Kyle Rigby to the Whittakers' Vermont estate in November as guests.

"What kind of work are they having done?" Sean asked.

"Carpentry and some masonry work on the exterior and the chimney." Bowie winced as Hannah tightened the bandage on his cut hand. "It's not a tourniquet, you know."

"You want it tight enough to help stop the bleeding, especially if you're not getting stitches."

"Doesn't need stitches."

"Dr. Bowie . . ." She stood back, examining her handiwork. Blood was already oozing through the gauze. "If you won't get medical attention, at least stop at your place first and clean these wounds and put on fresh bandages."

He grinned at her. "Sure thing."

Hannah didn't say anything more. Bowie wasn't accustomed to having anyone worry about him any more than she was.

"I work in stone," he said, zipping the black bag shut. Poe was back out of sight again and quiet. "I'm used to getting cut. You should get moving before you freeze.

I'll come by later and take a look at your cellar leak."

"If you feel up to it. Are you sure you can drive?"

"I can drive."

"Jo will want to talk to you," Sean said.

"Anytime." Bowie peeled the bandage off his face with his uninjured hand and balled it up. "I like talking to the law. Agent Harper knows how to find me. If she wants to arrest me for being stupid and knocking over a pile of rock on myself, she can have at it."

Hannah ached, the cold exacerbating the sharp sting of her scrapes and bruises. "No one's accusing you of anything."

Bowie shut the van's passenger door. "I'm glad you weren't hurt any worse. I'm sorry you were scared. Next time you hear Poe barking, let him bark."

"It's cold out here. If I hadn't investigated, maybe you wouldn't have survived."

"Me? This sweatshirt's warm as sin." He grinned at her and winked. "And I know sin."

He headed around the front of the van to the driver's side. Hannah stood back even farther, almost bumping into Sean, as

Bowie got in behind the wheel, started the engine and made a U-turn back to the corner, then headed across Ridge Road and up Cameron Mountain Road. It was getting dark fast, the stark trees creating long shadows on the snow, the mountains a deep blue-gray against the darkening sky.

"I'm not afraid of Bowie," Hannah said without looking at Sean next to her.

"Why not?" His tone wasn't demanding or hostile, but it wasn't gentle, either.

"He's had his run-ins with people around here, and he's made mistakes and paid for them, but I grew up with him. I didn't grow up with Camerons and Harpers." She crossed her arms, wincing at the pain in her wrist as she added softly, "I don't expect you to understand. We may be from the same small Vermont town, but we're from two different worlds."

"Los Angeles and Black Falls are two different worlds. Black Falls and Black Falls are the same."

"To you." She dropped her arms to her sides. "You're just stalling until Jo and Elijah can get here. Jo may be a federal agent, but she doesn't have jurisdiction over falling rock, snow and ice."

Sean didn't respond at once. "We can go across the street and wait where it's warm."

Hannah looked back toward the wooded hillside, feeling shaken and off balance. The cold, the wind, the exertion and adrenaline were all taking their toll. So was being around Sean Cameron, but she didn't want to think about that now. "It could have been kids. They could have parked down the hill and come up the trail through the woods. They ran into Bowie and then me and decided to hide and have some fun. It's a cemetery. I can see a couple of kids playing ghost, thinking they're funny. Why not?"

"They'd know your name?"

"Sure. Toby's still in high school, and Devin just graduated in June." She felt a sudden twinge of pain in her side where she'd slipped getting out of the way of the falling rock. "It makes more sense than a lot of the alternatives."

"What about Bowie? Is it possible he knocked that rock over on you?"

"Why would he?"

"Just because you're not afraid of him doesn't mean you don't have reason to be."

Hannah's teeth were chattering now. "I can't stand this cold any longer." She shuddered against the brutal windchill. "I'm going to my car."

She was already marching up Cameron Mountain Road to the corner. She heard Sean take in a sharp breath. He fell in next to her, not shivering at all. She reminded herself that he hadn't been outside as long as she had—and her shivering wasn't just from the cold. She was tired, hurting and unnerved by what had happened at the crypt.

And reassured, she thought, to have Sean with her, even if he didn't entirely trust her.

"Thank you," she said as she crossed the road to the old tavern.

"For what?"

"For charging through the cemetery after me."

"I heard the rock falling, and I heard you scream—"

"I was startled."

"And you were scared," he said.

Lights were on in the tavern's front windows. Hannah pictured the McBanes pulling back the curtains and checking out the goings-on by the cemetery. Had they called the local police? Would Jo?

When they reached the driveway, she looked at Sean in the dim light and noticed that the shadows of the fading afternoon highlighted the stubborn set to his jaw and the black lashes of his Cameron blue eyes.

She gestured down Ridge Road. "You can't see the lodge from here. It's too far."

He settled back on his heels. "You mean this isn't a good place for someone to have waited and watched for Melanie Kendall to get in her car."

"It's what you're thinking, isn't it? That Bowie—"

"I'm not thinking anything. I'm trying to figure out what the hell just happened."

"So am I," she said, past the point of being reasonable. "You can tell Jo and Elijah I'll be at the café."

With his index finger, Sean touched her cheek just under the swelling. "If Beth's not there, call her. Let her check you out. Promise me."

She nodded, softening. "All right. I promise. You're being a little unfair, you know."

He let his finger drift to the corner of her

mouth. "Who's to say what would have happened if I hadn't come along?"

Hannah opened her car door. "I might have caught the little bastards who knocked over that rock on Bowie and me."

Sean stood back and watched her as she got into her car and shut the door. As she turned on the ignition, she acknowledged that she was reacting to being so close to him for the past few hours. First in the cabin, then on the trail down on the mountain, in Elijah's truck. Had she *ever* been in a vehicle with him?

Nope, she thought. She'd remember.

Then, in the cemetery. She still could hear the intensity with which he'd called her name, grabbed her—kept her safe.

And just now. Touching her that way.

Her fingers aching, her face and wrist screaming in pain, she turned up the heat but knew she'd probably be back at the café before the car was warm.

Would Jo and Elijah believe stone blocks and debris had toppled over on Bowie by accident?

Did *she* believe it?

If law enforcement was looking for someone in Black Falls who'd make an ideal local recruit for a network of professional killers, Hannah knew that Bowie O'Rourke would be at the top of their list.

As she turned down Cameron Mountain Road, she glanced to her right and saw the oldest headstones, flat rectangles silhouetted against the snow and the gray.

Whoever or whatever had whispered her name in the shadows, she and Bowie hadn't been alone in the cemetery.

Nine

Sean reached into the truck's glove compartment for a flashlight. Behind him, Lester McBane shuffled down the walk in a worn parka and unlaced boots. He wasn't wearing a hat, but his fine white hair wasn't much protection against the dropping temperatures. "Everything all right out here?" he asked.

"Everything's fine, Reverend. Some rock and debris Bowie O'Rourke left behind after he worked on the culvert came down on him and Hannah. They got a little cut and bruised. Nothing serious." Sean flicked the flashlight on and off to check the battery; it was fine. Of course. It was Elijah's flashlight. He kept his tone casual as he continued. "You see much of Bowie out here?"

"Some. I think he's finished up work on the culvert. He'd start early and seemed to work hard."

"By himself?"

"He'd hire help when he needed it. I'd walk over and talk to him when it wasn't too cold. He's very knowledgeable about stonework." The old minister shuddered in the dropping temperature but made no move to head back inside. "There are those of us who do things in the moment that we later regret. We have a conscience. We suffer the consequences of our mistakes, but we learn from them."

"That's what you think Bowie is—a guy who made a mistake he regrets?"

"What do you think he is?"

"He's a bad-tempered ex-con with a grudge against half the town. I've seen him in enough fights to know I don't want to get into it with him, but it doesn't matter what I think." He thought of Hannah and started to say more. "Never mind. You should go back in where it's warm."

McBane studied Sean a moment. "You're worried about Hannah. She has a blind spot when it comes to Bowie. Everyone knows that, but she's always been levelheaded."

"She hiked up to my father's cabin alone today. How levelheaded is that?"

"She could have known you'd go after her." The old man paused, then added, "She could have hoped you would."

"Don't count on it," Sean muttered.

McBane barely reacted to a gust of wind that seemed to blow straight across from the cemetery. "Your father and I would sometimes walk among the old graves together. It's a peaceful spot."

Sean almost smiled. "There are a lot of peaceful spots around here where people aren't buried."

"You live, you make mistakes, you see your friends die. You don't worry so much about taking an afternoon walk in a cemetery." The old man grinned suddenly. "Or being in the ground yourself."

"Did my father say anything that in retrospect suggests why he was targeted by those two killers?"

"No. He was introspective. Thoughtful.

He knew he had fewer days ahead of him than behind him. He said he was looking forward to being a burden to his children."

Sean smiled. "That sounds like him."

"He was proud of all of you, Sean. Rightly so."

"Did you talk to him about Bowie?"

McBane shook his head. "No, I didn't. I don't think we had one of our walks after Bowie's arrest."

"What about Hannah?"

"Ah. She's another story. Drew was like the rest of us in that he wanted to see her happy. There isn't anyone in Black Falls who doesn't wish Hannah well, but she doesn't know it."

"She thinks she's on her own and we're all out to judge her." Sean noticed car headlights far down Ridge Road. That would be Jo and Elijah. "You should go back inside, Reverend. Lock your doors just in case."

"Just in case what, Sean?"

"That it wasn't a ghost or the wind that knocked over that rock onto Bowie and Hannah."

"Hannah's good to us. So are you."

Sean smiled in spite of his uneasiness.

"Well, don't tell anyone and ruin my reputation."

McBane shuffled back up the sanded walk. Sean was aware that, by his own design, very few people knew he had bought the former tavern a year ago and made the McBanes life tenants. They paid for utilities and basic upkeep and were entitled to live there rent-free the rest of their days. He'd run and biked past the tavern as a kid and pictured it fixed up, with vegetable gardens and fruit trees and a clothesline, with a tire swing tied to the sugar maple near its old stone wall. Wanderlust hadn't gripped him yet, and he'd yet to even hear about the people who parachuted into wildland fires out west—or to experience January in Southern California versus January in Vermont.

When he'd heard the McBanes were struggling to stay in their home—after decades in parsonages—he'd knocked on their door and made them an offer.

He'd told them he liked the idea of owning a haunted house.

He headed back across the road and took the shortcut through the cemetery, as he had when he'd heard the falling rock and Hannah's yell of pain and surprise. He hadn't seen anyone else, human or animal—just the tarp blowing in the wind, and then Hannah leaping for the wooded hill. Would she have been as sure of herself if it'd been anyone but Bowie's van, Bowie's dog barking?

Sean didn't turn on the flashlight until he came to the crypt. Jo would have his head if he interfered with a crime scene. He circled the beam of light at the rock and debris, the tarp, the splatters of blood. Bowie's blood. Hannah hadn't bled as much.

The thick wood door to the crypt was shut, its only "lock" a stick shoved into the latch where a padlock should have been. Sean removed the stick and managed a smile at what passed for security. The door creaked as he opened it, shining the flashlight into the dark, windowless space. It was surprisingly high—at least eight feet, presumably to provide space for stacking coffins.

With a grimace, Sean stepped inside. There was no electricity. He shone the beam of light into the corners of the crypt, just to make sure a raccoon or other animal hadn't somehow taken up residence there. Heavy metal scaffolding provided spots for coffins, but despite the cold weather, no bodies were yet being held over the winter for spring interment. A wooden shelf kept coffins from having to rest on the concrete floor. The walls were laid stone that had been pointed and in some places sealed with cement. The ceiling was framed in, plastic-backed plywood added as a protective measure against moisture.

It was one dark, dank and creepy place, but there was nothing there.

Sean returned to the lane. Maybe Bowie had a point. He was a stonemason. Stonemasons got hurt.

Jo and Elijah arrived, greeting Sean briefly, and he filled them in on what had happened. When he finished, Jo squatted down in front of the fallen rock and debris. Blood had splattered on chunks of ice.

"Is Hannah with Bowie now?" Jo asked without looking up.

"They left separately." Sean glanced at his brother. "I'm not jumping to any conclusions. Bowie hit his head. He could have called Hannah's name and not realized it. This all could be nothing."

"You know Jo," Elijah said. "She loves to check out nothing."

Sean lowered his flashlight beam to the end of the trail that led down through the woods, impenetrable now in the dark. "Bowie's still on probation. It's easier for him if it was just the wind that knocked over the pile and had Hannah thinking she heard someone whispering her name. Maybe it's easier for us if it wasn't."

"What's that supposed to mean?" Jo asked sharply.

"The investigation's stalled," Sean said. "We're all getting restless and impatient."

"I'm not." She waited, as if she expected Elijah to argue with her, then said, "I just want to know what happened here."

Sean sighed. "I know. Something's not right with Hannah."

Jo stood up next to Elijah, both looking at Sean as if *he'd* been hit on the head with a rock. "Sean," Elijah said, "you want to tell us—"

"No. I don't." He nodded to the stone, dirt and ice, the tarp still now that the wind had died down. "Bowie needs to get some equipment up here and clear out this mess before someone else gets hurt."

Sean recognized Rose's Jeep out on Cameron Mountain Road. She stopped in front of the church and ran across the road with her golden retriever, Ranger. When they got to the crypt, Elijah quickly explained the situation. She listened, pacing but not interrupting. "Ranger and I can take a look in the woods, if you like," she said. "We can see what we can turn up."

"It's best you stay up here," Jo said.

Rose nodded. Her hair, the same medium color as Elijah's, was tangled, and she was pale and pensive. She'd gone to the Midwest in November after devastating tornadoes and hadn't been in Black Falls when Kyle Rigby and Melanie Kendall had turned their sights on two teenagers. A.J. had been the one to call her and give her the news that their father's death hadn't been an accident after all.

A.J. had called Sean in California, too.

Rose rubbed the top of Ranger's head. He sat at her side, patient. Rose didn't look at her brothers or Jo as she spoke. "Hannah's used to handling things on her own and being judged—"

"No one's judging her, Rose," Jo interjected.

Rose didn't back down. "Being up at the cabin, seeing for herself where Devin and Nora and you and Elijah were almost killed, had to be emotional for her."

Elijah opened the heavy door to the dark crypt and looked inside. "Rigby knew what he went up the mountain to do. Things worked out the only way they could. Him dead. Jo and those two kids alive."

"And you, too, Elijah," Rose said.

He glanced back from the threshold of the crypt and grinned at his sister. "Well, yeah. Goes without saying."

That was Elijah, Sean thought. His soldier brother was a survivor, something their father had believed and in which he'd found comfort—until the final weeks of his life. He'd called Sean in early April. "I just don't have a good feeling," his father had said. "I think Elijah's in Afghanistan, but who knows? Sean . . . I'd trade my life for Elijah's. For yours or A.J.'s or Rose's. I swear I would."

Sean had tried to reassure him. "We know that, Pop. Don't worry."

"Elijah's seen combat. He can't talk about most of it, but he's never been seriously wounded. What if his luck's run out?"

"Not Elijah. He's the luckiest man alive."

"He'd be here in Black Falls if I hadn't kicked him out—"

"Or in a prison cell, or the ground. Elijah wasn't on a good path, Pop."

"Jo would have straightened him out if I hadn't interfered. If I'd just let nature—fate—take its course."

Drew Cameron hadn't been an introspective man, but his fear for his soldier son's safety had been real and deep—and, as it turned out, warranted. Elijah had survived the firefight and his life-threatening injury. By October, he was back in Black Falls, the hometown he'd never wanted to leave. A month later, he'd confronted the killing partners hired to murder his father on Cameron Mountain.

Sean had never thought much about staying or leaving Vermont. He'd thought in terms of objectives. What did he want? What did he have to do to get it? He was thinking in those terms now. His main objective was to figure out what Hannah was up to before he left for California with her brothers.

"If Hannah is withholding information," Jo said, "she needs to start talking. Now."

Elijah walked across the lane to the edge of the woods. “If this network of hired killers is planning more murders and Hannah can help—”

“She’d want to,” Rose said, not letting him finish.

“Not me,” Ryan “Grit” Taylor said in his light Southern accent as he ambled up the lane. He had a small apple in one hand. He bit into it. “I’d keep my mouth shut and bake cookies. Stay the hell out of this mess.”

Sean had noticed the Navy SEAL arrive in a car he’d borrowed from A.J. at the lodge. Dark, wiry and ultrafit, Grit had lost his lower right leg in the same firefight that had nearly taken Elijah’s life in Afghanistan in April. A member of Grit’s team, another SEAL named Michael Ferrerra, had been killed. While in rehab in Washington, Grit had helped Elijah look into Alex Bruni’s hit-and-run death. He’d flown back and forth between Washington and Vermont in the past five weeks, but basically he’d been camped out in one of Jo’s run-down cabins on the frozen lake below the lodge.

Jo frowned at him. “Why?”

“Fear. No good options. Make a wrong

move and end up a target of unknown killers. Make a wrong move and end up irritating a Cameron or Harper." Grit pointed his apple in the general direction of Jo and the Camerons. "You people are scary."

"You don't know Hannah Shay," Jo said.

"I've been to Three Sisters Café. Hannah wears a green apron and bakes cupcakes, and she's studying to be a lawyer. Small. Prettier than she thinks she is."

"And hard as nails," Sean said. "She's not afraid of us."

"I am," Grit said. "I've had quite the immersion into you hard-bitten Yankees since November. You don't let up. Really scary."

Elijah rolled his eyes. "Eat your apple, Grit."

Myrtle Smith picked her way along the lane. She must have come with Grit. Her Washington home had caught fire a few hours after Kyle Rigby's death on Cameron Mountain. It was an electrical fire that was contained to her home office, but no one believed it had been an accident. Myrtle had been looking into the sudden death of a Russian diplomat in London—a former lover, from what Sean could gather—

and had her suspicions about a network of killers. All her notes had been destroyed in the fire.

Grit Taylor had saved her life.

In his limited experience with Myrtle, Sean had learned she didn't like the cold, never mind that she couldn't seem to stay away from Vermont. She was fiftyish, tiny and black-haired, with perfectly manicured red nails and lavender eyes. She'd arrived in Black Falls with Grit in November, returned to Washington in early December, then came back before Christmas.

"They say you burn more calories in cold weather," she said, eyes on the terrain as she carefully navigated icy patches. "I hope so, because I'm frozen."

Rose's mouth twitched, and Sean was relieved to see his sister display at least some hint of amusement.

Myrtle continued down the lane. "It's too damn dark for me to be hanging out in a cemetery, but Grit and I saw all these cars and had to stop. Old reporter's habit. Otherwise you wouldn't catch me here except in broad daylight."

Elijah turned to Jo, his mind clearly not on Myrtle's complaints. "Can you give

Sean and me a minute? Take Myrtle and Grit and check the crypt. Whatever." Then he shifted to Rose. "You can go, too."

Rose gave him a cool look. "As you wish." She smiled at Grit and the other two women. "My brothers want to confer on their own. I vote for going back to the lodge for hot chocolate with real whipped cream over checking out a crypt, but it's up to you."

"I had warm apple pie at lunch," Myrtle said, her Southern accent more pronounced than Grit's. "If I indulge in whipped cream, I'll have to go cross-country skiing or something at the crack of dawn and burn it off. It's supposed to drop below zero tonight."

"Best weather for investigating a crypt," Grit said.

"A first time for everything," she said without enthusiasm.

Rose's golden retriever flopped in front of the entrance as Grit and then the three women entered the crypt. Sean didn't notice any indication of stiffness or a limp in Grit's gait. He'd had a long, difficult recovery, but he was almost back to his pre-injury fitness level, a remarkable achievement given what that had been as a SEAL.

Once Rose and the non-Camerons were inside, Elijah narrowed his eyes on Sean. "What the hell's going on? Bowie turns up at the café. Hannah hikes up to see Pop's cabin. Now this." Elijah lifted the shovel and stirred the heap of debris, jagged chunks of rock, bits of mica catching the beam of the flashlight. "As far as I know, Bowie hasn't been in trouble since he got out of jail. He's only been back in his house for a few days, and already there's a drama involving him."

"Where did he stay while he worked on the culvert?" Sean asked.

"He roomed with a cousin in Ludlow." Elijah blew out a breath at the charcoal-colored sky. "The guy's good-looking, rugged and familiar, and he knows how to knock heads together. He and Hannah share a past that we can't understand." He turned to Sean, the cold having no apparent effect on him. "No wonder she's defensive about him."

Sean hardly noticed the cold, either.

"She's on the defensive. It's not easy to get through to her when she's got her shield up."

Elijah managed a half smile. "Threaten to send in Jo."

Rose stepped out of the crypt, not giving any indication she'd overheard her brothers. "I'm not stepping foot into another crypt until I'm embalmed."

Elijah grinned at her. "And you think you're tough."

"You'd sleep in a crypt, wouldn't you?"

He shrugged. "I have."

Ranger got up onto all fours and yawned. Rose scratched his head. "We should go home, huh, boy? Get away from these macho brothers of mine." Still bent down over her dog, she looked up at Elijah. "I've had a lot of requests for information on dogs since that business went down in November. I tell people if they want protection, a puppy isn't it."

Sean couldn't read his sister—her tone, her attitude, her feelings—but now, with the biting cold and the situation at the crypt, wasn't the time to push her about whatever was going on with her.

Jo had her cell phone out as she joined

them. "The local police and Scott Thorne are on the way. They'll take a look around here. They'll want to talk to you, too, Sean."

"No problem."

"And Hannah," she added.

It was an unnecessary comment, which told him Jo had wanted to see his reaction.

"Devin was framed as well as nearly killed a few weeks ago," she went on. "Hannah could think people were too willing to believe he was guilty."

"Meaning you, Jo?" Sean asked quietly.

"Keeping an open mind isn't the same thing. Hannah has to be angry, Sean. Anyone would be. We're all angry."

"She's used to holding her emotions in check."

Jo slipped her cell phone into her jacket pocket. "Bolting up a mountain by herself in twenty-degree weather isn't holding her emotions in check. Neither is looking for Bowie O'Rourke in a cemetery."

"I get your point," Sean said, careful to keep his tone even.

"I just want to be sure you're seeing this situation clearly."

"It's not your problem, is it, Jo?"

"Don't make it mine." She softened, rubbing her gloved hands together. "Damn, it's cold. Sean, you know what I'm getting at. You were at O'Rourke's in March when Bowie got into trouble. Now you were at . . . whatever this was here. If he has his eye on Hannah and sees you as a threat—well, I guess it doesn't matter, does it? You'll be back in Beverly Hills soon."

"You should come out, Jo. Get some sunlight. It'll cheer you up."

She rolled her eyes. "As if one Cameron man isn't enough to deal with, Elijah comes with two brothers." She looked at the pallet holding the granite blocks. "Did your dad have much to do with Bowie before his arrest in March?"

"I don't know." Sean wasn't fooled by Jo's show of interest in the pallet. Jo's focus was entirely on interrogating him. "I wasn't around much then, either."

"Pop was a trustee for the cemetery and the Four Corners church," Elijah said, standing close behind her. "He recommended Bowie for a job at the church last winter."

"That doesn't mean anything by itself," Jo said. "Bowie's a natural for any mason work. If I had any that needed doing at the lake, I'd call him, but right now I just think I need a sledgehammer." She glanced up at the two brothers and grinned. "For those old cabins. Not for you boys."

A town police cruiser pulled in behind Myrtle Smith's rented car.

"They're going to be thinking what I am," Jo said. "Bowie's a question mark. We don't have anything that points to him, but this—it won't help ease any suspicion."

"He was in police custody when Pop was killed," Rose said.

Jo nodded. "That doesn't mean he wasn't involved. I'm not suggesting he was, but it's not a good idea for Hannah to be around him right now. Bowie's too much of a loose cannon."

Elijah settled back on his heels. "You're not used to having a personal stake in an investigation. You can't control what we all do. And you can't protect us."

She pulled her jacket hood up over her head. "You're right. I can't."

Grit and Myrtle stepped out of the crypt, shutting the creaky door behind them and replacing the stick in the latch. "I'm going for that hot chocolate and whipped cream,"

Myrtle said, giving an exaggerated shudder. "I believe in ghosts, you know."

Grit sighed. "Of course you do."

A town police officer headed down the lane. Sean recognized him from high school. His life in California suddenly seemed distant, surreal, as if he'd never get back there—as if he'd never left Black Falls and it was his home and always would be.

Jo eased in next to him, away from the others, her gaze narrowed on the dark woods. "Some days I feel like a stranger here," she said with some sympathy, then angled her turquoise eyes at him. "What do you think, Sean? Did Hannah really hear someone whispering her name?"

He considered her question a moment. "Yes."

"Was it Bowie or her imagination?"

"If I'd gotten here ten minutes sooner," he said, "I'd know."

A cruiser arrived at the end of the lane. Scott Thorne got out and joined the town officer. Sean put up his own jacket hood, aware of Jo falling in next to Elijah by the crypt, automatically, casually. However she felt about being in Black Falls, she was no stranger to his brother.

Sean thought of Hannah, then decided maybe it wasn't a good idea to think of her, and he walked out the lane to meet the two officers.

Ten

Vivian Whittaker felt a draft and looked up from the book she was reading at the kitchen table, a pot of hot English Breakfast tea at her side. "Lowell, please," she said sharply. "Close that door. I'm freezing."

Her husband set a bag of groceries on the granite counter. "It's already closed, dear. It took a moment for the cold to reach you."

She tightened her sweater around her. It was a cast-off, store-brand black cashmere cardigan she kept here at their Vermont country house. She was chilly and had thrown on the sweater to warm her up, but she'd take it off before leaving for dinner later with Judge Robinson and his wife. Vivian was already dressed in a cream silk top and black wool slacks. She was pleased with the invitation. She had been trying to cultivate friendships with the locals, although this was the first time since November she was truly looking forward to anything in Black Falls.

She always seemed to be cold these days, but she loved their rambling farmhouse with its beautiful, established landscaping and stunning, updated interior of polished wood, stark white walls and modern art. It was located among rolling fields and woods on a branch of the Black River, with several small outbuildings and a classic Vermont stone guesthouse. Large windows in the kitchen overlooked the backyard and the river, frozen and dark now, with no ambient light or stars or even a sliver of moon to illuminate it. After the horror in Black Falls—the horror *here,* Vivian thought, on this property—they'd spent Thanksgiving in New York, but had returned for Christmas. Their children, both young singles, had joined them, but she'd insisted they not bring any friends. Family only this year.

Alex Bruni. Melanie Kendall, Kyle Rigby. Vivian shivered. Three recent guests, now dead. Two of them paid killers who had sat at this very table. Kyle Rigby and Melanie Kendall had just teamed up to run Alex down in Washington. He'd been rushing to a breakfast meeting with Thomas to discuss Nora's concerns about her father's fiancée. After killing Alex, they'd set their sights on Nora.

Vivian gave an inward shudder but tried not to let her anxiety get the better of her. She didn't know Thomas as well as she had Alex, but the two had been friends since college. That Alex had basically stolen Thomas's wife from him had to have been a terrible blow, but Thomas wasn't one for displays of strong emotion. He'd admirably accepted his fate with a stiff upper lip, only to succumb to the charms of a clever, sociopathic killer. He'd gone so far as to ask Melanie Kendall to marry him. Of course she'd accepted his proposal.

Then she'd tried to kill her own fiancé's daughter after Nora had become suspicious of her future stepmother. Melanie's shocking lack of empathy and narcissism had her believing right up until the end that she and Thomas would still go forward with their wedding once Nora was dead.

Nora was back in Washington now with both Thomas and her mother, Alex's widow, all of them attempting to put their lives together. Vivian sympathized with their situation, but she didn't want to maintain contact with them. She was sick of all of it, but Christmas had been quiet and pleasant, with a spark of hope for better in the future. The police had finished asking questions of her and her husband. They hadn't had to deal with anyone in law enforcement in more than two weeks.

She warmed her hands on her mug of tea. "Where have you been?"

"Supply run." Lowell lifted cans of soup and diced tomatoes out of the bag and set them on the counter. "The grocery store here has such a limited selection of items. I always forget."

Vivian looked out the window but saw only her reflection. Her hair, which was fine and straight, seemed thin. She was only forty-seven but had started to notice more gray showing through her natural dark blond. She had no intention of dyeing it. Its light color helped, not that she cared. She'd never been one for such vanities.

"I don't know how people live up here all winter." She turned back to her tea and book with a scowl. "It's so dark. It's depressing."

Lowell folded the empty paper bag. He was lanky and fair-haired, a year older than she was, but he still had no sign of gray in *his* hair. "I find the dark, cold nights up here cozy and comforting," he said. "They make me want to curl up by the fire with a good book."

"Yes, I suppose there's that advantage."

He opened a lower cupboard and placed the paper bag on a stack of other bags he'd saved. She'd have tossed them all on the fire. He loved to play the frugal country farmer, but he'd been a reasonably successful investment banker for fifteen years. Vivian had finally talked him into leaving the working world two years ago, after their younger daughter had graduated college. They could easily live off her trust fund. He had his own money, but it was for his little projects.

He pulled out a chair across the round table from her and sat down heavily, as if he'd been chopping wood all day instead of running to the grocery. Vivian abruptly pushed back her chair but didn't get up. Having Lowell at the table immediately irritated her. She'd been enjoying her time alone, and now he was crowding her. She flipped the book shut. It was one her book club in New York had assigned, but she couldn't concentrate on it now.

She tried to suppress her irritation as Lowell spoke. "Bowie O'Rourke is supposed to stop by. He's obviously running a little late. I imagine he'll be here any minute. I'm going over the work on the guesthouse with him. It won't take long. He already has a good idea of what needs to be done. This is just a last-minute check before he starts tomorrow. I wasn't sure at first about having the guesthouse redone, but I see your point now. Fresh paint will help erase some of the bad memories. We'll all be happier here."

"You do know that Bowie is an ex-convict, don't you, Lowell?"

"He was in a scuffle at his cousin's bar with several drunken ski bums who, from what I've heard, had it coming."

"He went to *jail.* He's on probation."

"He didn't really fight the charges against him. If it'd been a Cameron who'd drawn blood, I wonder if there'd even have been an arrest."

Vivian noticed her tea was cold and decided she didn't want it any longer. "Hannah Shay was the one the ski bums were insulting when Bowie lost control and started throwing punches. Are you sure hiring him isn't just a means for you to get closer to her?"

Lowell looked uncomfortable. "You know I have no romantic interest in anyone in Black Falls—or anywhere else, for that matter."

"Who do you prefer, Hannah or Rose Cameron?" Vivian thought a moment, ignoring her husband's obvious discomfort. "Hannah, I believe. She's the safer choice, for certain. Her brothers are just teenagers. Rose's brothers are all in their thirties and very competent—true New England mountain men."

Lowell leaned back in his chair and

glanced at his own reflection in the window.

"Are you still pestering Rose about dogs?" Vivian asked him.

"We've talked, yes."

"A dog won't protect us. You just want one because you'd feel more like a country squire with a golden retriever at your side."

Her husband's interest in getting a dog and Rose Cameron's work with search-and-rescue dogs had preceded the violence in Black Falls, anyway, and had nothing to do with protection. Vivian no longer believed she was without enemies. *Everyone* had enemies. She wanted to install an alarm system and a panic room, but Lowell argued that it would destroy the sense of refuge he felt being in Vermont. She was adamant about not having guns in the house.

She rose and took her teapot and mug to the counter. "I spoke to Ginny Robinson earlier. She wants me to get involved in the local historical society. I think that'd be fun, don't you? Even if they are just looking for a donation."

"I'm sure—"

"They say all the right things. I figure it's a way to be let into the community, assuming we don't give up and sell this place." She set the dishes in the porcelain sink; she was still cold. "The Robinsons have invited Sean Cameron to dinner, too."

"Is that right?" Lowell didn't meet her eye.

"I wonder if Hannah will be there. I understand that Ginny and Everett have been very good to her over the years. She's had a considerable amount of help from people in town, but from the way she behaves, you'd think she did everything on her own. Sean seems to look after her." Vivian walked back across the hardwood floor to the table and picked up her book, standing over her husband. "Do you suppose he's attracted to her?"

"I wouldn't know."

"She's definitely attracted to *him.* I can see it when he's at the café. She's so fetchingly self-conscious, don't you think?" Vivian didn't bother to hide her sarcasm.

Lowell stared at the table. "I haven't noticed."

"Oh, of course you have, Lowell. Sean's handsome and rich. He's a self-made multimillionaire. He's also skilled in mountain rescue, and he fights wildfires out west. He's an elite smoke jumper."

Lowell traced a circle on the table in front of him. "Yes, dear, I know."

"He has to stay incredibly fit even to work on a voluntary basis."

"No doubt."

"Hannah's pretty, even if she doesn't know how to dress, and she has grit and intelligence, but she's also vulnerable. Every man's fantasy." Vivian watched Lowell for a reaction. "Men want to take care of her."

"Is that what you think? I hadn't noticed."

Vivian wanted to scream. Just once she'd like to see her husband display some real backbone, but he never would. He'd never stand up to her or anyone else. If Kyle Rigby had decided to cut their throats in the middle of the night, would Lowell have protected her?

What a ridiculous thought. Her husband would have expected *her* to protect *him.*

She didn't know whether to laugh or cry at the sudden image of Lowell cowering at her side in bed. She knew she was being unfair and irrational. He was a good man and a good husband. He was sophisticated, civilized and decent. She'd never have been happy with someone like Bowie O'Rourke or A.J. or Elijah Cameron.

But Sean Cameron?

Vivian shook off the thought. She accepted that she was drawn to him because of the vulnerability she'd been feeling since November. It was understandable, even inevitable. She wasn't as happy about being in Vermont as she had been before Alex Bruni's death. She had to admit she'd enjoyed the prestige of being friends with an intelligent, respected ambassador more than she'd liked Alex himself. He could be abrasive and arrogant. He hadn't been one to suffer fools gladly. Nonetheless, he hadn't deserved to be deliberately run over and killed.

When his stepdaughter had dropped out of college and wanted to move to Black Falls, Alex had hinted that he'd appreciate any help Vivian and Lowell could offer. They'd invited Nora to stay at an apartment in their guesthouse. Lowell would have let her stay with no strings attached, but Vivian had insisted the teenager do odd jobs around the property and run errands, if not pay rent. It would be good for her character. Nothing in this life was free, was it?

Vivian couldn't stand the terror that suddenly gripped her. Tea, a book—distractions hadn't worked to calm her. "I want the police to find their bomb-maker and be done with this," she said under her breath.

"I know, Vivian," Lowell said. "We all do."

"The Camerons won't rest until they have the answers to every last question they have about who hired these killers, who else they killed, who else might be out there—additional killers, potential victims. Jo Harper, either. She's as driven as the Camerons are."

"Given what they've all been through, one can see why."

Vivian didn't know why, but his comment annoyed her. "We need to see these people as they are, Lowell, and not romanticize them and their lives here in Vermont. You agree with me, don't you?"

"Of course, dear."

His response increased her annoyance.

She glared at him. “Lowell, I’m serious. I don’t want us to get caught in the middle again.”

“Nor do I,” he said, rising from the table. “I’ll check my e-mail and then head to the guesthouse to meet Bowie.”

She didn’t respond, and Lowell left her alone in the kitchen. She rinsed the dishes in the sink. When she turned off the faucet, she stared out the window into the darkness. She couldn’t move. It was as if she were paralyzed, trapped by the memory of meeting Drew for the first time more than a year ago. She’d run into him in front of the library in the village. He’d been so sure of himself—so rooted and content in this small, picturesque northern New England town. Black Falls wasn’t an escape for him. It was home.

It’s become a nightmare for me, she thought.

How she wished she could pick up their estate and put it down somewhere else. Black Falls wasn’t one of the more prestigious towns in Vermont for second-home owners. One had to truly want a life in rural northern New England to live there.

Vivian headed down the hall to the study. She had overseen its decorating, but it was Lowell's space. Lined with dark wood shelves, the room had deep mountain colors that were a deliberate contrast to the brightness of the rest of the house. She remained in the doorway. Her husband was at his massive, solid oak desk, his back to her. She knew he was wishing and hoping this network of killers the police were after would just go away. That was what he'd always done when faced with any difficulty. Wished and hoped and left the hard decisions to her.

"Don't bother building a fire now," she said, startled at how loud her voice seemed in the quiet house.

Lowell pivoted to her in his oak chair. He didn't seem startled. "Yes, I suppose there's no reason to start a fire now, since we're leaving for dinner soon."

Why *suppose?* Why not just say *there's no point*? She wanted to scream at him. Why couldn't he be decisive and strong?

She checked her temper. "You're not going to the Robinsons dressed like that, are you?"

He gave her a blank look. “What?”

She pointed at his barn jacket and wide-wale corduroy pants. “You’re wearing your wannabe mountain man clothes, Lowell. People will think you’re trying to pretend you’re a Cameron.”

“Oh. I’ll change if there’s time after I talk to Bowie. I’d hoped to stock the wood box before I got ready for dinner.”

“There’s no time for the wood box. These aren’t fancy people, but at least put on a sweater and a sport coat. You don’t want Sean showing you up.” She waited a half beat, but Lowell didn’t respond. Of course he wouldn’t. She felt a ripple of irritation. He was so damn *annoying* these days. “There doesn’t seem to be anything the Camerons can’t do, does there? Of course, you have your virtues, too.”

Lowell turned to his computer, an old desktop from their home in New York. Vivian felt dismissed, but she didn’t leave. She watched as he flipped on his computer, its sudden hum the only sound in the quiet house.

“Lowell,” she said finally.

He looked back at her. “Yes, Vivian?”

She sighed. “Nothing. Never mind. I’ll

see you after you meet with Bowie. Let me know if either of you has any questions."

He didn't even seem to notice when she withdrew from the doorway. They planned to celebrate New Year's in Vermont and stay through the following week. She hoped overseeing the work on the guesthouse would prove to be a welcome distraction and the fresh start she needed.

Dinner tonight would be pleasant. She liked the Robinsons, and she looked forward to spending an evening with Sean Cameron. Whatever his faults might be, the man definitely wasn't hard to look at, and he was strong, fit, competent and utterly masculine, as well as a self-made multimillionaire.

Perhaps her husband would learn a thing or two from him.

Eleven

Hannah had forgotten she still had Sean's scarf and draped it over her coat and hung both on a hook in the mudroom. She kicked off her boots, changed into her sneakers and headed to the café kitchen. Her brothers weren't home. She'd left messages on their cell phones letting them know that she'd had a slight accident at Four Corners and the police might be stopping by but that they shouldn't worry.

And why should they worry? If it hadn't been Bowie O'Rourke in the cemetery, would Sean have bothered to call Jo and

Elijah? Would *she* have reacted the way she had?

When she entered the kitchen, Dominique and Beth were there, still working. They'd laid out a dozen chocolate and vanilla cupcakes on the worktable and had piles of assorted decorations and little bowls of icings in different colors.

Beth eased off her high stool. "Yikes, what happened to you?"

"I fell up at Four Corners cemetery. It's a long story. I just need some ice." Hannah opened the freezer and grabbed a handful of ice cubes, tucking them in a flour-cloth towel, which she put to her swollen cheek. "You'd think ice is the last thing I'd want after being outside most of the day."

"Hiking up Cameron Mountain," Beth said. "We heard. Is that how you hurt yourself? Here, let me take a look."

"I didn't get hurt on the mountain."

"Sean followed you up there," Dominique said.

Hannah could see that her friends had been kept in the loop, at least up until the incident at the crypt. "Yes, he did," she said, feeling the cold from the ice penetrate the towel. "A.J. and Elijah were at the lodge when we got back, but I didn't get a chance to talk to them."

"Chance?" Beth snorted skeptically. "You mean you got out of there before they could pin you down about what you were up to, hiking up to their dad's cabin by yourself."

Hannah smiled. "Yes, that's what I mean. I stopped at Four Corners to give the McBanes the goodies, and I had a bit of an accident at the cemetery. Bowie was there checking on the culvert. He had some rock and debris piled up. . . ." She noticed that her hands shook. "That's how I got hurt."

Beth's eyes narrowed. "You're leaving a lot out." She sighed. "Might want to put some ice on your wrist, too."

"It doesn't hurt that much."

"Not now, maybe. Later it will. Clean it, too." Beth sighed. "And pour yourself a stiff drink. The Camerons on your case. A fall in a cemetery at dusk. Damn. Pour two drinks, one for me."

Hannah set the ice pack on the counter and turned to the sink to wash her hands. Her wrist was puffy and turning multiple shades of blue, but she doubted it would bother her for more than a day or two. Beth stood next to her. "Indulge me. You're so damn stoic, Hannah, you could have a broken wrist and just not notice your pain."

"Or not want to trouble anyone," Dominique added quietly behind them.

"Have a look, then." Hannah leaned back against the sink and let Beth examine her wrist. "Thank you."

"Sean took a look, too? He's an EMT."

"You're assuming he was at the cemetery."

"Was he?"

It would be a mistake, Hannah knew, to think that Beth's good nature meant she wasn't as sharp, skeptical and relentless as her federal agent sister. "Yes." Before either Beth or Dominique could respond, Hannah continued. "So, what's the verdict on my wrist?"

Beth grinned at her. "Bruised. Ice is the best thing."

Hannah washed her hands and retrieved her ice pack, putting it on her wrist, figuring she could alternate with her bruised cheek. "What's with all the cupcakes?"

"Myrtle Smith suggested we have New

Year's cupcakes," Dominique said. "We're experimenting with designs. She doesn't know what to do with herself. She's one of the few reporters left in town but she has a personal stake in the investigation. I suppose we all do."

"I should tell you," Hannah said, "Jo might be stopping by. In fact, she probably will be stopping by."

Beth tapped a fingertip onto a little pile of edible silver stars, three of them sticking; she carefully placed them atop a vanilla cupcake with bright blue icing. "With my sister on the way, does that mean that whatever happened to you could be considered a criminal act?"

Hannah transferred her ice pack to her cheek. "It means what Dominique just said. Everyone's restless."

Beth tapped more stars. "And Jo would know something happened at the cemetery because . . ."

"Sean called Elijah." Hannah sank onto one of the stools at the worktable. "Cell phone."

Dominique dumped out chunks of black licorice. "I don't care for licorice," she said, then sighed at Hannah. "Will you just tell us what happened?"

"I'm sorry. I don't want anyone to worry, because it was nothing."

"If it was nothing," Beth said, "you wouldn't be sitting here with an ice pack on your face and my sister would be out at the lake with Elijah."

"Fair point," Hannah said, relenting. She told her friends the basics of how she'd ended up with a bruised, scraped cheek and wrist.

Dominique shuddered. "You heard someone whispering your name in a *cemetery?* I'd have passed out on the spot."

"I could have been mistaken."

"Whatever the case," Beth said, "Jo probably grabbed Scott and maybe a local guy and went to talk to Bowie first. That gives us a few minutes before she swoops in here in federal agent mode." Beth added more stars to her blue-iced cupcake, then sat back and assessed her handiwork. "What do you think?"

"Pretty," Hannah said.

"People might not think the stars are edible," Beth said.

Dominique added a hunk of the black licorice. "There. That looks real. It'll cue people everything on the cupcake is edible. Hannah?"

She appreciated their obvious but sincere attempt at normalcy. "I like the sparkle, but not everyone likes licorice . . . including you."

Dominique sighed. "All right. Next."

"Do you think my crazy sister will actually marry Elijah?" Beth was teasing, but there was a note of concern in her voice, too. "He can be called back for some secret mission at any time, and she can't stay up here forever. What would she do? She'll have to go back to D.C. or get a new assignment, or quit the Secret Service altogether. There's no guarantee this'll work now any more than it did when they were teenagers."

"Jo's still wearing the ring he gave her," Dominique reminded her friend.

The same ring he'd bought at nineteen for her. "A sentimental Cameron," Hannah said, trying to keep her tone light. "Hard to believe one exists."

"Deep down, all the Camerons are sentimental." Beth pointed to the middle row of cupcakes. “Buttercream frosting with gold sprinkles—delicious but not special enough.” She lifted a cupcake with white frosting and a bright red number one, for the first day of the new year. “This one. Oh, my. It’s perfect.” She peeled off the paper wrapper. “Absolutely perfect.”

“Hannah?” Dominique asked.

She nodded. “A series of simple, elegant and delicious cupcakes will go over well.”

“All right, then.” Obviously satisfied, Dominique jumped off her high stool. “I’ll do more designs along these lines. Three should do it.”

Beth took another bite of the cupcake. “All the cops and such hanging out here will love some happy cupcakes. We’ll cheer them up yet.”

Dominique untied her apron. “Hannah, why don’t you take some of these sample cupcakes for Devin and Toby? An occasional treat, especially this time of year, is good for the soul.”

Hannah picked up one of the cupcakes, peeled off the wrapper and bit into the rich, sweet cake and icing. She smiled at her friends, despite her fatigue and dread at having to face Jo Harper. "Who needs ice when there are cupcakes?" She reached for two chocolate ones decorated with white buttercream frosting and sprinkles. "I'll take these. You can both head on out. I'll be fine on my own with Jo and whoever else turns up."

"Scott's working tonight," Beth said, peeling off her canvas apron. "I promised I'd help Jo clean out one of the cabins. She's tackling them one by one. I think the work helps her process the investigation—and her life. How about you two?"

Hannah set the two cupcakes on a plate. "The Robinsons invited me to dinner, and if Bowie's up to it, he's stopping by to take a look at the water in the cellar—"

"Whoa, whoa." Beth put up a hand. "Bowie? Hannah, what are you doing?"

"He's a stonemason, Beth. He knows cellar leaks. If you're worried, which I'm not, Devin and Toby will both be here."

"All right, I'll stay out of it. I just hope what happened up at the cemetery was an accident." Beth grabbed her jacket off a hook by the door. "Have fun at dinner. You and the judge can go off on one of your tangents about Thomas Jefferson and John Adams. It'll take your mind off things. Dom, you want to join Jo and me at the lake?"

"Not tonight, but thanks," she said.

It was Dominique's standard response when she was invited anywhere in the evening. She rarely went out after work, saying she preferred to stick close to the little house she was renovating in the village and the café provided most of the social contact she needed. She and Beth left together. Hannah wrapped the rest of the cupcakes, got fresh ice and a fresh towel and locked the café for the night. She went out into the center hall and stared out the side windows at the Christmas lights twinkling on the trees across the street on the common. Dominique was a stickler about keeping decorations fresh. The wreaths, lights and baubles they'd put up in the café would be down by New Year's Day.

As if on cue, Jo Harper's car angled into a parking spot in front of the building and she and Elijah got out. Hannah wondered if they could see her standing there in the hall or if she could run upstairs and lock herself in her apartment and refuse to talk to them.

Best to get this done, she thought, setting the plate of cupcakes on the curving stairs to the second floor. She held her ice pack in one hand and opened the front door. “Elijah, Jo,” she said as the pair mounted the stone steps. “I’ve been expecting you. Beth and Dominique have gone home. We can talk in the café.”

Even as a senior in high school, when Hannah was a freshman, Jo Harper, the eldest of the town police chief’s three children, had been direct and uncompromising. Her one weakness had been the man across the café table from her now—badboy Elijah. Their days holed up together in a cabin on the lake were probably her only departure from the straight-and-narrow.

Fate in the form of the sixteen-year-old son of the vice president of the United States had brought her to Black Falls in November. While assigned to protect Marissa Neal, the eldest of Preston and Holly Neal’s five children, Jo had become the victim of one of Charlie Neal’s infamous pranks. Charlie was the youngest and the only boy. He’d hosted an airsoft battle at the vice president’s residence. Jo believed one of the guns was in fact real and jumped into the teenage fray, intercepting what turned out to be a barrage of airsoft pellets.

The incident, captured on video by one of the boys, ended up on YouTube. The subsequent media sensation and Jo's disgruntled boss had landed her back in her hometown until things settled down.

Hannah had heard rumors that Charlie, who had a genius IQ, had played a role in discovering the existence of the network of killers-for-hire. It wasn't anything Jo was willing to discuss.

Regardless, Jo had always had a knack for rubbing Hannah the wrong way.

Elijah had walked over to a riverside window while Jo stepped behind the glass case and poured herself a mug of coffee as if she owned the place. She brought her mug to a small table overlooking Elm Street and pulled out a chair. Her jacket was open, a black scarf hanging from her neck.

She nodded to Hannah. "Have a seat."

Hannah tried not to bristle and sat opposite Jo, her back to the street window. She reminded herself that Jo was in a difficult position and she and Elijah had saved Devin's life. Devin had said she'd been good to him on the mountain, careful with him, putting herself at risk to make sure he and Nora Asher were as safe as possible when the bullets had started flying. Jo had stood up to the pressure of a life-threatening situation and hadn't taken care of just herself.

"Can I get you anything else?" Hannah asked. "Soup, a sandwich—cupcakes?"

"Not for me. Help yourself if you want anything."

Hannah understood that Jo was indicating this wasn't a casual conversation among friends. "I just had a cupcake, thanks. I assume you've already talked to Sean and Bowie."

Jo nodded. "Sean's still up at the cemetery. Scott Thorne and I went out to Bowie's place and talked to him."

"How are his injuries?"

"He says fine. He was on his way to see about some work he's doing for the Whittakers. How're your injuries?"

"Nothing ice and a hot bath later tonight won't cure."

Elijah turned from the window and walked

over to their table, his deep, clear blue eyes fastening on Hannah for a half beat, but he said nothing and sat next to Jo.

Stifling a surge of self-consciousness, Hannah kept her attention on the federal agent across from her. “It makes sense you’d want to check out what happened in the cemetery. Even if you weren’t in the middle of a major investigation, that was weird.”

Jo drank some of her coffee, holding the evergreen mug in both hands. “Tell us what happened.”

Hannah gave her account as thoroughly and objectively as she could, leaving out as much emotion and speculating as she could manage. Neither Jo nor Elijah interrupted.

When Hannah finished, Jo set her mug on the table and looked out the window at the dark, quiet street. “We’ve been tracking Melanie Kendall’s and Kyle Rigby’s movements. We know for sure they were in Black Falls in April and again in November. Melanie met Thomas Asher here in the café in April.” Jo sat back in her chair. “Did you see Kyle then?”

Hannah shook her head. “No, but he

stopped by in November before he went up Cameron Mountain to look for Nora. You know that, Jo. He interviewed all of us. Dominique, Beth, me. He said he was a mountain rescuer."

"He wanted us to believe Devin was a troubled teenager," Jo said. "Money turned up missing at the lodge, at Nora's apartment and here at the café."

"That's what we assume," Hannah said, hesitant. "It's not clear . . ."

"What's not clear, Hannah?"

She saw it now. She'd stepped right into Jo's trap. She had little choice but to press ahead. "We don't know it was actually Rigby who stole the money. The cash stolen from the café was in a blue willow jar in the kitchen. If he'd come in here before his search for Nora and any of us had seen him, we'd almost certainly have remembered him. If we'd seen him anywhere near the kitchen, we *definitely* would have remembered him."

Jo drank some of her coffee. She was steady, as focused as Hannah had ever seen her. "Are you suggesting he and Melanie had an accomplice here in town?"

"I'm not suggesting anything," Hannah said.

"No one at the lodge remembers seeing him or Melanie near the shop where the money was stolen," Jo went on. "Nora's apartment at the Whittaker place is more isolated, but it still would have been risky for him to duck in and out of there with cash from her kitchen."

"I'm not a law enforcement officer, Jo. Or a prosecutor. I don't have to build a case."

"That's right. You're a witness."

"I have no intention of meddling in your investigation. I just know how easy it is for any of us to jump to conclusions. It's been a long five weeks and we're all frustrated and maybe scared—"

"Scared of what?"

Another trap, Hannah thought. She didn't hesitate before answering. "We're all afraid there are more killers out there. More murders in the works. That scares you, doesn't it, Jo?"

"It doesn't matter what scares me."

"What about the prospect of this network having a connection to Black Falls? Does that scare you?"

Jo's rich, deep turquoise eyes stayed on Hannah. "Did you help Drew with his cabin, Hannah?"

"No," Hannah said, recognizing the question as a deliberate non sequitur.

"You know I'm a federal agent. Telling the truth—"

"I am telling the truth, and I know the law. I didn't help Drew with his cabin. My brother didn't help him, either. He carried supplies up the trail and left them where Drew asked him to leave them."

"And you had no idea what was going on?"

"Not until late October." Hannah glanced at Elijah, who hadn't said a word; his expression was neutral, making it impossible even to guess what he was thinking. She turned back to Jo. "Devin had a hard time after finding Drew's body. He thought he could have done more to save him. We all know he couldn't have."

Jo pushed back her chair slightly, stretching out her legs. She rubbed the engagement ring on her finger. Hannah saw Elijah notice, too.

"Do you know who helped Drew with the cabin?" Jo asked.

"I don't know that anyone did," Hannah said.

"Did you know he'd found that old cellar hole?"

"No."

"Why did you go up there today?"

"I wanted to see for myself where my brother nearly died."

"You went on impulse. Alone."

Hannah shrugged. "So I did."

Elijah settled back in his chair, his gaze on Hannah. "Bowie had just been in the café."

"So had you, Jo, Sean, Zack Harper, Scott Thorne and who knows who else."

"We're not ex-cons who grew up with you," Jo said. "We don't blame you for a bar fight that got us thrown in jail and put on probation and disrupted our lives. We don't blame you for leading Drew Cameron to us so that the chief of police could arrest us."

"You're assuming Bowie blames me, and he doesn't."

Jo touched the rim of her mug with one finger. "Now who's assuming, Hannah?"

Her wrist throbbing now, Hannah resisted the urge to jump up and run out of there, get away from Jo Harper and her suspicions and attitude. “Bowie wasn’t an ex-con when we were kids. He was a boy with dreams and a hard row to hoe.” Her voice was under control, even as her heart raced. “Be grateful you didn’t have his childhood.”

Jo started to say something else, but Elijah spoke first. “How’d you do up at the cabin?”

“I was only there for a short time. It was cold and I’d been hiking for several hours. I didn’t want to stop moving. That’d only make me colder.”

“Sean was there,” Elijah said.

Hannah forced herself not to react. “He saved me from a long hike back to my car.”

“What about Bowie?” Jo asked. “Has he ever been up to the cabin?”

“I don’t know. I haven’t asked him. Until this morning, I hadn’t seen him since his arrest. If you want to know if he’s been up to the cabin,” she added coolly, “you can ask him yourself.”

“I did. He says he hasn’t been up there.”

Hannah wondered if she’d stepped into another of Jo’s traps. As much as she’d learned in law school, she didn’t have Jo

Harper's experience as a federal agent. Best, she knew, to shut up now. "Are you sure you don't want something to eat?" she asked. "What about a scone? Jo, I know how much you love Dominique's scones."

Jo surprised Hannah with a smile. "I keep trying to get Elijah to try them."

Hannah sighed. "It's no secret you all are looking for a Black Falls connection to these killers. I understand that, and I understand that Bowie's convenient—"

"It's not about convenience," Jo said, rising. "We didn't find anything up at the cemetery that definitively suggests you and Bowie were attacked. Sean says you ran straight to the hillside after you got back on your feet. Why?"

Hannah shut her eyes briefly, remembering those first seconds after the rock fell, before Sean arrived. She looked at Jo. "I can't say for sure. I don't know if I saw or heard something and was so hyped up on adrenaline I can't remember—or if I just operated on instinct."

"You didn't go down the hill," Jo said. "Why not?"

Hannah kept her gaze steady. "Sean had arrived by then."

"Ah." Jo nodded with understanding. "I see. He stopped you."

Elijah surprised her with a grin. "Sean didn't tell us that part, either." He stood up. "Next time you want to take off onto the mountain by yourself, call me."

"Take care of that wrist and cheek," Jo said, rising next to Elijah. "I'm glad you weren't hurt any worse. Bowie, too."

"On that," Hannah said with a small smile, "we agree."

"I suspect we agree on more than you want to admit," Jo said quietly.

She headed for the door to the center hall, but Elijah remained behind, his Cameron blue eyes leveled on Hannah with an intensity that made her glad she'd never had to encounter him on a battlefield. "Let's be clear," he said. "No one's lumping you and Bowie together just because you grew up on the same part of the river, or because you were at O'Rourke's in March when the fists started flying. You're not responsible for what he does."

"You've never had to prove yourself. You don't know—"

"I do know, Hannah." He gave her a

quick smile. "Try boot camp and then tell me I've never had to prove myself."

"I didn't mean it that way."

"We'd all do well not to let our pride keep us from recognizing our friends," Elijah said. "Stay in touch. Let us know if there's anything we can do for you."

She nodded, feeling tears forming in her eyes. He had the grace to pretend not to notice and left without saying anything more.

Twelve

Although she felt steadier on her feet now that she'd finished talking to Jo and Elijah and had devoured another cupcake, Hannah descended the cellar stairs slowly. They were straight, steep and utilitarian, not as graceful as those in the center hall. They needed painting—on the to-do list she had made up for her absentee landlord.

She pulled a string hanging from a light-bulb socket, revealing spiderwebs, dust-covered pipes, stored furnishings and junk cast in dim, yellowish light. The cellar's cement floor was reasonably new, but the old stone foundation was original. She remembered her father working on it one summer when she was a child.

A summer he hadn't been in prison.

She edged to the back wall, on the river side of the house. There was no standing water right now, probably because it was coming from outside and the ground was frozen.

That couldn't be good.

She started to push a dusty, heavy, flat-topped trunk away from the wall. She had no idea what was inside. Treasure, maybe? She smiled to herself at the thought, but jumped, startled, when she heard footsteps behind her on the stairs.

"Hannah," Sean called to her. "Are you down here?"

"Just me and the spiders."

He appeared under the seventy-five-watt bulb. He'd changed out of his mountain parka into his long, black cashmere coat. "I ran into Jo and Elijah on the street," he said.

"Ah." Hannah scraped the trunk another few inches across the cement. "We just had a nice chat up in the café."

"They're meeting A.J. at the lodge and filling him in. I'm heading up there next."

She regretted her sarcasm. "Poor Jo's caught between a rock and a hard place, and Elijah—"

"Jo?" Sean's eyebrows went up in surprise. "Are you kidding? She's mad as hell, and she has a job to do. Kyle Rigby tried to kill her. She saw Melanie Kendall get blown up. Jo wants answers, and she doesn't care if she has to irritate friends and family to get them."

"She's also in a holding pattern with her life," Hannah said with some sympathy. "She could go back to Washington and decide everything that went on up here was too much of a whirlwind and just forget it all."

"You mean her and Elijah?" Sean said.

Hannah stood up from the old trunk. "They got back together in a few high-adrenaline days. Once things settle down, who knows?"

"They do. They're for real. They always have been. It just took them fifteen years to realize it." Sean ducked under a low pipe and came closer to her. He reached out to brush a strand of hair out of her eyes. "What about you, Hannah? Are you okay?"

"I am. Yes. Thanks for asking." She fought back a wave of self-consciousness at his touch and pushed the trunk with a toe, but it didn't move. She could hear her name in the wind, the flapping of the tarp, the initial scraping sounds of the rock and dirt falling onto her. "If you came here to argue about what happened at the cemetery, you can go up to the lodge now and leave me to my spiders."

"I didn't come here to argue."

The dim light created shadows on Sean's face that made him look less the charming Cameron. Hannah ran her fingertips over a mustard-painted hinge on the trunk. Her wrist and cheek ached, and she was suddenly hot, choking on the stirred-up dust in the air. "There's probably radon down here. All this stone. Perfect breeding ground for radon."

Sean smiled. "Adding radon testing to my to-do list?"

She didn't answer as more footsteps sounded on the stairs. She remembered Bowie had promised to stop by and started to call out to warn him Sean was on the premises, but Devin ducked into the dim light.

He was halfway through one of the cupcakes. “I figured this was meant for me.”

Hannah collected herself, but she was aware of Sean’s eyes on her. Their clear blue had turned to a dark, smoky color in the cellar light. Whatever was going on between them, she would do well to remember that he was as relentless and mission-oriented as any Cameron ever born. He believed she was holding back on him, his brothers, Jo. He hadn’t given up the fight.

“Toby’s back, too,” Devin said. “Your message—we were worried about you.”

“Everything’s fine,” she said, trying not to sound breathless, self-conscious. “Toby has to finish a trigonometry take-home test before he heads to California.”

Devin peeled off more of the cupcake wrapper. “I hated trig.”

“You hated math, period. Did you work at the lodge at all today?”

“Nope. Tomorrow.” He stopped, glancing at Sean, then back at his sister. “I’ll talk to you later.”

“Dev, you can say what you have to say in front of Sean.”

Her brother finished off the cupcake, his

eyes on the old trunk now, as if he just needed to have something to focus on that wasn't Hannah or Sean. "Even if what happened up at Four Corners wasn't his fault, Bowie's trouble," Devin said. "He always has been. I remember Mom saying trouble will find him if he doesn't find it for himself."

"She liked Bowie."

"Yeah, he's a great guy when he's not punching someone's face in."

Hannah felt Sean's stillness next to her. "The police didn't find anything up at the crypt," she said, "and Bowie was hurt worse than I was."

Devin balled up the cupcake wrapper in one hand. "Maybe you don't know him as well as you think you do. You go tearing up Cameron Mountain, and then this." He looked at her again. "You should see your face."

"It'll heal in no time." She gave him a light smile. "All's well that ends well."

Sean squatted down behind the trunk and examined the leak damage in front of shelves of dusty canning jars. "I gather you haven't told your sister what we talked about this morning," he said.

Devin rubbed the back of his neck as

the hulking furnace came on in full force. It had been churning away against Vermont winters for at least two decades. "Think this thing'll make it through the winter?"

Hannah sighed, recognizing her brother's behavior as his way of avoiding telling her something he didn't think she wanted to hear. "Beth, Dominique and I have a pool going. I say it dies before Valentine's Day. Dom's giving it until the first day of spring. Beth's the optimist—she thinks it'll last through this winter *and* next."

Sean grunted. "That furnace will last another five years."

Hannah looked at him with amusement. "Well, if it dies when it's four degrees out, I'm calling you in Beverly Hills. I don't care if I have to get you out of bed."

He smiled. "You do that."

His voice was husky, sexy, which she told herself she only noticed because of her fatigue, pain and adrenaline.

Devin, mercifully, was oblivious. "Wish I knew something about furnaces," he said.

"Ha. Don't we all."

Hannah abandoned the trunk and suddenly wished she hadn't come down here at all—hadn't hiked up the mountain or checked on Poe and Bowie at the cemetery. If she'd just stayed at the café and baked cupcakes and studied for her bar exam, she wouldn't have Sean Cameron on her case right now.

She stepped back, right into cobwebs hanging from the ductwork. "What did you and Sean talk about this morning, Dev?"

Sean rose and Devin averted his eyes. "Nothing," he mumbled. "It can wait. We can talk after you're done down here."

"Dev," Hannah said, "just tell me what's on your mind. If it's something you think I don't want to hear, that's my problem, not yours."

Sean dipped behind the trunk, examining more water spots on the cement floor and the stone foundation. Without looking at either Shay, he said, "Devin, you need to tell your sister your plans."

Devin swiped at the remains of her cobweb. "You ever think about leaving Vermont?"

Hannah went still. "You mean move?"

"Yeah. Start over somewhere else."

"How would I—" She stopped herself. "No, I haven't thought about moving. Why?"

"I've been thinking . . ." He gave her a

weak smile. "Let's at least talk up where there are no spiders."

Finally Sean rose again, with a sharp look at her brother. Hannah gulped in a breath. A collage of images came at her. The California desktop background on the computer she shared with her brothers. The searches she'd found for smoke jumpers and Beverly Hills. The talk about needing to figure out what came next for him now that he'd graduated high school.

The nightmares, the pacing, the certainty that he had to do *something*.

"Toby's leaving for California with Sean the day after tomorrow." Hannah tried to keep her emotions under control. "Is that what you're up to? Going out there with your brother?"

Devin grimaced and looked down at the floor. "Sean offered me a job."

"Sean Cameron?" She spoke as if he weren't right there. "What kind of job?"

"Basic step-and-fetch-it until I figure out what comes next."

Hannah felt as if the dust were settling on her, encasing her, as if she were another cast-off in the old, musty cellar. "How long do you plan to stay in California?"

"I don't know. It's open-ended."

"So—what? A month to start? Five months?"

"I've committed to three months to start. Same as Toby."

"Where will you live?"

"I said he could stay at my place until he gets on his feet," Sean said.

"Not a bad deal, right, Hannah?" Devin seemed desperate for her approval. "Sean also said I could fly out with him and Toby."

"The day after tomorrow," Hannah repeated dully.

"That's right. I'm eighteen," he added, with a hint of defiance. "Almost nineteen."

"Of course. You don't need my permission." She raked both hands through her hair, not even sure what she felt. "You can do whatever you want now. Toby turns eighteen soon, too. Then he can do whatever he wants, too. Stay in California and mountain bike his life away."

Devin looked crushed. "I can stay here. I don't have to go."

"No—no, Dev." She shook her head, pulling herself together. "If this is something you want to do and you can make it happen, I'm not going to stand in your way just to keep you here." She was aware of Sean's presence. The coconspirator. But she wasn't going to let Devin get sucked into whatever was going on between the two of them. "I'll be upstairs in a few minutes. We can talk more then."

His face brightened with obvious relief. "Yeah. Great. I'll go up and figure out supper."

Hannah waited stiffly for him to get back up the cellar stairs. Her side throbbed now in addition to her cheek and wrist. She forced back the pain and turned to Sean. "How long have you known?"

"Two days."

Sean came around to her, his coat open to a dark, soft-looking sweater. He'd changed since she'd left him at Four Corners. She was still in her hiking clothes, still had rock dust and dirt on her, the cuff of her shirt wet from her ice pack.

"Hannah—"

"When did he start talking to you about California?"

"During the search for the twelve-year-olds on Christmas Eve. He'd been thinking about it for some time. He convinced me he's serious."

"He's romanticizing your life, smoke jumping, California."

"Then he'll find that out for himself."

She heard more footsteps, heavier than either Devin's or Sean's. It had to be Bowie. She called up to him. "Come on down, Bowie. You can handle the stairs, right? You're not going to pass out from loss of blood, are you?"

"Ha. Funny, Hannah."

He thumped down the stairs and, dodging the string hanging from the lightbulb, headed over to the back wall. His face was badly swollen and bruised. He'd changed into a heavy gray sweatshirt and put a fresh bandage on his hand, no blood yet seeping through.

He glanced at Sean, then turned to Hannah. "I can come back."

"No, it's fine," she said quickly. "The leak's right over there. Please, have a look now. Sean owns the building. It's not a problem that he's here."

Bowie's expression was unreadable, controlled. Sean said nothing, just watched, impassive, as Bowie dipped behind the trunk and had a look at the water damage.

Hannah leaned over the trunk. "Do you need more light?"

"Nope." He stood up. "It's not an active leak right now because of the outside temperatures, but water's obviously getting in. My guess, the wall here's rotted. I'll have to get a closer look."

"Can you fix it?" she asked.

"Yes, I can. I'll have to figure out exactly where and how the water's getting in, but I think I can just repoint the stone, do some resealing. A little mortar and hydraulic cement should do the trick."

Sean was cool. "I'll want an estimate—"

"I estimate I can fix it."

Hannah checked her irritation with both of them and focused on the task at hand. "It has to be done. When do you think you could get to it?"

"A week or two. It'll keep until then. If it doesn't, call me."

She nodded. "Fair enough."

"Take care of yourself," he said, and left, the old stairs creaking and groaning as he headed up.

Hannah didn't move, didn't look at Sean. She listened for the center-hall door to open and shut and then crossed her arms on her chest, careful with her injured wrist. She felt tight, emotional, on the verge of spinning out of control. "I need to check on Toby," she said half to herself.

"Hannah," Sean said. "What's going on?"

She shot him a look. "Other than my brothers taking off for California? Other than hiking up to see where one of them was nearly murdered? Where a man we all loved . . ." She pushed back the rush of emotion. "I'm sorry. You have enough on your mind. You lost your father to those people. I'll be fine."

He stepped closer to her. "That's your refrain, isn't it? You'll always be fine." He moved another few strands of her hair from off her face and smiled at her. "There's something sexy about a woman with cobwebs in her hair and dust on her nose."

"Are you the big charmer in Beverly Hills?"

"I'm an amateur out there." With his fingertip, he touched her cheek, just under where the rock had struck her. "You don't want dust getting into an open cut."

"It hardly counts as a cut. It's mostly just a bruise."

His fingertip drifted down to her mouth,

brushed her lower lip. "No one wants to see you hurt and alone." His smile had vanished. "I don't."

"My brothers shouldn't have to worry about me. Neither should you."

"Is it okay for anyone to worry about you?"

"Sean . . ." Hannah cleared her throat, feeling more than a little hot now. "It's been a long day. I'm not sure I trust myself with you."

His eyes sparked. "Does that mean you want me to kiss you or you don't want me to kiss you?" Before she could respond, he stood up straight and winked at her. "I won't make you answer."

She pushed the trunk with one foot, feeling ragged, wishing she had gone upstairs to her apartment and not answered the door for Jo and Elijah after all, just locked herself in her bedroom and studied for her bar exam.

She *did* want Sean to kiss her. She wanted to kiss him. She'd wanted it since she was fourteen years old, and it had been crazy then and was crazy now. They'd both know it come morning. This was adrenaline and circumstances at work.

She'd been impulsive enough for one day.

"I need to see Devin and Toby. I'm having dinner with the Robinsons tonight. I probably should cancel." With her uninjured hand, she caught Sean's fingers into hers and gave him a quick smile. "*Long* day."

She ran for the stairs. Sean didn't stop her, and, despite her hike up and down Cameron Mountain and the incident at Four Corners, she didn't break her stride on the two flights of stairs to her apartment.

By the time she reached her apartment, all the hounds of hell might as well have been after her. Her head was pounding and she was breathing hard, her heart racing, her stomach churning.

Having Bowie there—the competition and open animosity between him and Sean—must have prompted Sean to touch her that way. Talk to her that way. *Look* at her that way.

She caught her breath and raked her uninjured hand through her hair, coming up with, indeed, cobwebs. What kind of fool was she? Of *course* cobwebs in the hair weren't sexy. Sean had simply thought of something to say and said it.

She entered the living room. It had a working fireplace and windows that looked out on the village green with its white Christmas lights shining in the black night. Ever since Devin had found Drew Cameron's body on Cameron Mountain, and in particular since his own encounter with Kyle Rigby and Melanie Kendall, Devin had seemed unfocused and rootless, as if he were caught between his past and his future.

No wonder he'd jumped at the chance to move to Southern California.

Hannah found Toby hunched over a mountain-biking magazine at the kitchen table. "I thought you were working on your take-home test," she said.

"It's all done." He looked up at her. "Dev told you?"

"Yes," she said, more sharply than she meant to. "He told me he's heading to California, too."

Toby leaned back in his chair. "I only sort of knew. I kept it to myself in case it didn't work out."

"That I understand." She hesitated. "Are you sure about going to California yourself? You have so much to do before you graduate."

"I'm finishing my last college application tonight. If I don't do this now, when?"

Her throat felt constricted. For the past seven years, she'd been responsible for her two brothers. She'd been their sole legal guardian. She'd worked and sacrificed for them and laughed with them and cried with them. They were a family.

She'd bought Toby his first mountain bike.

"I don't have to go," he said in a small voice.

"No—no, Toby. It's okay. You're right. If not now, when? It's a great opportunity." She found herself blinking back tears. "You and Dev need to get on with your own lives."

"Hannah, we don't want to you to feel bad—"

"I'm studying for the bar. I've got the café. Friends." She smiled through her sudden anxiety. She'd never been apart from one or both of her brothers for more than a few nights. "I'll be fine."

"What about Bowie?"

"Bowie? He's a stonemason I grew up with. That's all, Toby."

Toby got up from the table. "You could come out to California. I have that big race at the end of January."

"I'd love to see you race. If I can make it happen—I will, okay?"

"You've put your own life on hold long enough for us," Toby said.

"That's not how I've looked at things."

"I know, but maybe it's time you did." He gave her a crooked grin. "You'll be turning gray before you know it."

Hannah looked down at the books and papers on the table. Hers, Toby's. Devin had gotten halfway through one college application before he quit, saying he'd decided to postpone college for at least a year. Was he going to California because Toby was? Or because it was what he himself wanted to do?

Or because handsome, rich, rugged Sean Cameron had offered him a job?

Devin came into the dining room, looking sheepish. Hannah felt a stab of guilt. He should be excited about his trip. She didn't want to be a wet blanket and have either of her brothers put their dreams on hold because of her.

Wind rattled the old window by the table. She could feel a cold draft and forced a smile. “I don’t blame you for wanting to check out sunny California.”

She headed for her bedroom. In warm weather, with the windows open, she could hear the river. Now she could only hear the clanking of the ancient heating system. She had no desire to go out into the cold night and be sociable, but Devin’s news helped motivate her not to back out of dinner with the Robinsons. She needed to prove to her brothers—and to herself—that she had a life.

And that she was still safe in Black Falls.

Thirteen

"Bowie hasn't been in since the fight," Liam O'Rourke said from behind his rough-wood bar. "I expect his probation officer wouldn't want him here."

"Do you?" Sean asked. He hadn't gone to the lodge after Hannah had run upstairs. Instead he'd walked down to O'Rourke's.

Liam shrugged, his shoulders as powerful as his cousin's. "I stopped wanting or not wanting anything concerning Bowie a long time ago. I stay neutral. He does what he does. Always has."

"Do you like having him back in town?"

"Neutral. No opinion."

Sean stood up from the stool. He'd had only two sips of his beer. His head was already screwed up enough with his reaction to Hannah in her cellar. It wasn't thinking about kissing her that he regretted. It was *not* kissing her—a line of thinking, he knew, that was the path to frustration.

"What about Bowie and Hannah?"

"I've never understood their relationship." Liam reached for Sean's glass. "She saw my uncle in action. Bowie's father. He's a great guy to the rest of the world, but he was rough on Bowie. A bad drunk. When your father's against you, maybe you feel like the whole world's against you."

"Does Bowie blame Hannah for his arrest—for being here that night, then for showing my father where to find him?"

"Anything's possible. I don't claim to know how Bowie thinks. All I know is it's a good thing you grabbed her that night. Those guys weren't going to stop. Who knows how far they'd have gone with it. With her."

"Bowie should just have walked out of here."

"The insults were tough to listen to."

Sean noticed his friend hesitate. "What is it?"

"Nothing. I don't know." Liam scratched the side of his mouth, awkward now. "I haven't seen those stupid bastards in here since March. Derek Cutshaw. That guy's a prick. I don't know if he was just talking about Hannah."

"Who else?"

Liam dumped Sean's beer into the small sink in front of him, below the bar. "Doesn't matter." He looked up. "Was that trip out here in March the last time you saw your father?"

Sean nodded.

"I'm sorry, Sean. I'm really sorry."

He left the bar, buttoning his coat as he walked down Main Street to the building he owned and rented out to Hannah Shay and her brothers. The gallery on the west end of the first floor was struggling. Three Sisters Café was thriving. His father had been surprised by the café's immediate success. He'd never expected there were enough people in Black Falls who'd keep such a place in business.

He dialed Elijah. "Police done at the crypt?"

"All set. They didn't find anything that disputes either Hannah's or Bowie's story."

"Elijah, was it an attack?"

"It wasn't a raccoon or a ghost," his brother said.

"Kids? Could Bowie have walked into the middle of a drug payoff? Could he have been in the middle of one and Hannah—"

"No evidence of either."

"Does Jo believe Hannah told her the truth?"

"The truth," Elijah said, "just not the whole truth."

"Meaning she stuck to the facts and didn't tell Jo what she's thinking."

"Hannah never tells anyone what she's thinking. Keep that in mind, brother."

"I'll do what I can," Sean said, and disconnected.

He stood on the shoveled, sanded sidewalk and watched Hannah pull open the heavy front door and trot down the stone steps. She had on a simple black wool dress coat, her skirt even longer, her flat-heeled boots suited to a walk on a cold Vermont winter evening. She wasn't wearing gloves or a hat, her fair hair not pulled back, shining in the glow of the Christmas lights.

She handed him his scarf. “I forgot to return this,” she said nonchalantly, as if seeing him on Main Street was an everyday occurrence and nothing had just happened between them.

“Go ahead and wear it.” He wrapped the scarf around her neck. Her bruised cheek wasn’t badly discolored, and the swelling appeared to be no worse. “I’ll walk over to the Robinsons’ with you.”

“You’re coming to dinner?”

He smiled at her slightly stricken look. “I am.”

She didn’t seem tired or self-conscious as they walked up the street. They turned onto a side street and crossed a covered bridge, rebuilt after the original had come apart in a flood fifty years ago. The Robinsons’ Greek Revival house was another twenty yards past the river. Its white wooden fence was draped with holiday greenery. Multicolored lights sparkled on a spruce tree in the front yard.

“Is Judge Robinson helping you prepare for the bar exam?” Sean asked.

“He’s bugging me to get a study partner

and cut back on work at the café. He'd like me to quit and devote myself to studying full-time."

"He'd put you through your paces in a courtroom, wouldn't he?"

"Without a split-second's hesitation."

"Are you looking forward to becoming a full-fledged lawyer?"

"Most days. Some days I dread it."

"Is today a dread day?"

"In more than one way," she said half to herself, then angled a smile at him. "I mean my brothers and their California adventure in addition to figuring out my career. I don't mean you, Sean."

"Hannah, I don't want to add to your stress—"

"It's okay," she said.

He almost told her he didn't believe the insults about her sex life that Derek Cutshaw and his friends had shouted at O'Rourke's back in March, but he figured that would just remind her of them, as well as be an admission that he'd been thinking about that night himself.

He followed her up the steps to the Robinsons' front door. Statues of Dickens-style carolers—fully dressed in Victorian garb—

stood next to the glass front door. Ginny Robinson was known in town for her elaborate Christmas decorations.

Hannah rang the doorbell, positioned below a simple pinecone wreath. “I’ll have more time and space to study with Devin and Toby off in California,” she said. “I could be admitted to the bar before Toby gets back.”

“Then on to becoming a prosecutor?”

“That’s the plan. We’ll see what happens.”

Everett Robinson opened the door. He was in his early sixties, a stocky man with a gray beard and thinning gray hair in perpetual need of a trim. His wife, a homemaker, was generous and patient with her husband’s sometimes black moods after twenty years on the bench and forty years practicing law.

“Help, help,” he said cheerfully, leading his guests into the comfortable house. “Ginny tried new, heart-healthy hors d’oeuvres, and I don’t want to be the first to take a bite.” The judge stood back and frowned at Hannah. “Good heavens. What happened to you?”

She smiled. "I learned the hard way never to get into a fight with a rock."

He didn't press for more details. Given his position, he would easily be able to find out about the incident at the cemetery. Hannah started to pull off her coat, but Sean helped her, careful of her bruised wrist. He then shrugged off his own coat and hung both on a coat tree surrounded by the Robinsons' winter gear.

The judge led his guests down a hallway decked out in Christmas decorations and into a comfortable living room with a fire in a brick fireplace and more Victorian carolers on the mantel. Lowell and Vivian Whittaker had already arrived and were seated opposite each other by the fire. Ginny Robinson, who barely skimmed five feet, joined them with a silver tray of marinated mushrooms, sardines, toasted pita points and a few other things Sean wasn't sure he wanted to identify.

"Looks wonderful," Hannah said with a sideways smile at the judge.

He grinned at Sean. "See what a good prosecutor she'll make? Fearless."

Ginny glanced at Sean, her eyes wide

with surprise as she turned to Hannah and mouthed something that he suspected amounted to *"Is he your date?"*

Hannah smiled and shook her head.

Everett settled into a worn leather chair. Sean helped himself to a mushroom and a glass of wine and sat on the couch. Hannah stayed on her feet. He sensed her restlessness and wondered if she might bolt at any moment. The judge lifted a glass of wine from a nearby side table. He had a friendly, open face, but the way he narrowed his eyes on his protégée was a reminder of the keen mind behind them and the many tough decisions he'd had to make in his long career.

Vivian Whittaker nibbled on a sardine on a pita triangle. "Hannah, your face—did you have an accident at the café?"

Lowell leaned forward with his wine. "I met with Bowie O'Rourke a little while ago. He's doing some work for us. He told me about the incident in the cemetery. He feels terrible. Vivian, I didn't think to tell you."

"What incident?" she asked sharply.

Her husband relayed Bowie's rendition

of what had happened. The judge sat back, listening intently, Sean thought, but saying nothing.

When Lowell finished, his wife was visibly pale. "I don't know if I want Bowie on the premises now."

"Let's just see how it goes tomorrow," Lowell said quietly.

Everett sipped his wine. "What work are you having done?"

"We're repainting the guesthouse and having some minor repairs done," Vivian said. "Both apartments. The one where Nora stayed and the one where . . ." She held her hors d'oeuvre in midair. "Where that killer stayed. Kyle Rigby. Melanie Kendall stayed with Thomas Asher in one of our guestrooms. I'll tackle it next. I don't know if fresh paint will help, but it can't hurt. But if Bowie . . ."

"He's considered one of the best stonemasons in the area," Lowell said.

Sean noticed that Everett Robinson's incisive gaze was on Hannah. "Bowie's had his struggles," the judge said, "and he knows he has to stay out of trouble. He's still on probation."

"We heard about the bar fight in March," Vivian said, turning to Hannah. "You were involved, weren't you?"

"I was there," Hannah said simply.

Vivian shifted her attention to Sean. "You and your brothers were there, as well, weren't you?"

Sean nodded and started to change the subject, but Lowell interrupted him, addressing Hannah. "We heard that some drunk young men insulted you. Of course, that's no excuse for Bowie bloodying the perpetrator, but one can understand. You and Bowie go way back. I walk out to where you grew up almost every day when we're up here. It's so peaceful."

"It's beautiful," Vivian said, "but I can't imagine being a child there. Were you bored?"

"Never," Hannah said, without any hint of defensiveness.

Ginny announced dinner, breaking the tension, and they all drifted into the dining room. Sean liked the Robinsons and had nothing against the Whittakers, but he wished he hadn't come to dinner but instead had whisked Hannah up to the ridge and watched the stars come out with her.

He didn't know if it was the aftereffects of being alone with her on the mountain, or charging after her when she was in danger at the crypt, or finding her among the cobwebs in the cellar, but he was having a hard time maintaining any objectivity with her.

But who was he kidding? It'd started back in March, this unsettling attraction to Hannah. Seeing her sipping wine by herself at O'Rourke's. Watching her self-control and reserve as she'd tried to ignore Derek Cutshaw and his friends, then her anger and passion as she'd jumped into action.

Sean could still feel the fight in her when he'd carried her out of O'Rourke's—and how alone she'd looked as she'd headed home in the freezing rain. He'd never understood Hannah, and he hadn't that night, either.

That was before his father's death. Before Elijah's life-threatening wound in Afghanistan. Before Melanie Kendall and Kyle Rigby had gone after Devin Shay and themselves been killed.

Sean had convinced himself there was no one in Black Falls for him and he no longer belonged there, but on every visit to Vermont since March, he'd found himself at Three Sisters Café. In California, he'd told himself he was too busy to date when he knew he wasn't. It was Hannah and his inexplicable desire to be with her.

And now here he was, caught between his mission to get the truth out of her and his urge to reach for her hand under the table.

What did he know about Hannah and her life, her dreams?

Vivian Whittaker sat next to him at the dining table. "I understand you're a smoke jumper," she said abruptly, with a coy smile. "It sounds fascinating. Tell us about it."

Sean was accustomed to interest in that part of his life and offered his usual answer. "It's hard work that I enjoy. I used to do it full-time. Now I volunteer when needed."

She reached for her wineglass. "Smoke jumpers parachute into the middle of raging wildfires, don't they?"

"We try to get to a fire when it's small and put it out before it's had a chance to spread. We work mostly in remote areas and choose our jump spots carefully."

"Is it dangerous?"

"We mitigate the dangers as much as possible through training and planning."

"You obviously have to stay in top shape," she said, eyeing him over the rim of her wineglass.

Sean smiled through his discomfort. "The point of any training is for us to be able to do the job we're called to do."

"I read that you have to be able to climb a tree to retrieve your parachute and gear. Is that true?"

He managed a smile. "It wouldn't do to leave the stuff up there, would it?"

Vivian took a big gulp of wine and set her glass back down. "It's hard to picture you in full firefighter gear, out in some western canyon with a fire raging around you. I suppose jumping out of an airplane to fight a fire sounds romantic to those of us who've never done it." She gave a mock shudder. "Have you ever been in danger?"

"I'd rather not—"

"Ah. Just what I expected. You're not going to tell us the details, are you?" She glanced across the table at her husband as she continued. "True heroes never want to discuss their exploits. You should brag, Sean. You've earned the right."

Sean thought about a fire a year ago and a mistake that had led to the near-death of his business partner and a fellow smoke jumper, Nick Martini. It had been Nick's mistake. He'd be the first to say so—and the first to say he was glad he'd been the one hurt and no one else.

Hannah's eyes were on him, as if she knew he was reliving a bad moment. Sitting there in the Robinsons' festive dining room on a cold Vermont winter night, he could feel the fire exploding around them, propelled by high winds and fed by dry underbrush. They'd been building a fireline, back-breaking, necessary work that they'd done scores of times. He and Nick were able to deploy their emergency shelters at the last second and managed to survive.

He was relieved when Lowell Whittaker changed the subject. "Everyone I've run into at Three Sisters Café has told me you're famous for your Christmas decorations," he said to Ginny Robinson. "I can see why."

Ginny was obviously pleased with the compliment. "Everett and I love decorating for Christmas. Putting away the decorations—now, that's another story."

As she and Everett served the simple meal of baked cod and assorted side dishes, Sean could see that Hannah was preoccupied, and likely tired and aching, too. She barely participated as the dinner conversation shifted to other topics—the weather, winter sports, the status of various inns in and around town and the end of the holidays.

After dinner, Lowell Whittaker got Hannah's coat for her as they prepared to leave. "I hope your bruises heal quickly," he said. "You must be exhausted after all you've done today. Shall I walk you home?"

She smiled, taking her coat. "Thanks, but I don't have to go that far."

"It's very cold."

"I'm used to the cold."

The judge stood back in the front hall. He obviously knew something was up, but didn't press Hannah as she quickly excused herself and thanked him and his wife for dinner. "I'll see you at the café tomorrow," Ginny said cheerfully. "I'm going cross-country skiing first thing in the morning with two friends. We believe in exercise first. Then scones."

"I'll be watching for you," Hannah mumbled as she headed out the front door and down the steps.

Sean said goodbye to the Robinsons and the Whittakers and slipped outside, catching up with Hannah by the covered bridge. "Let's go for a walk."

"It's dark and probably below zero by now."

He smiled. "That's why you have a coat and my scarf."

They crossed the bridge and headed down to Main Street. There was little traffic in the village, few people out on the cold late-December night. Even O'Rourke's looked quiet. A high-end restaurant in a Victorian building around the corner had a few diners—it tended to attract tourists and people from surrounding towns more than Black Falls residents.

Sean felt the bite of the dry, frigid air. "I'm sorry you had to find out about Devin and Toby's California plans the way you did," he said.

"I don't want them to feel as if they have to stay here and not follow their dreams because of me." She raised her collar against the cold. “It was decent of you to offer Devin a job.”

“He just needs a paycheck while he sorts out what’s next for him.”

“Military recruiters have been calling. I think he’s tempted. He’s always looked up to A.J., Elijah and you.” Hannah hunched her shoulders against the cold as they started across the street to the common. “Elijah’s friend Grit is a Navy SEAL. It doesn’t matter that they were both shot to pieces. Devin sees what he could do.”

Sean had just arrived in Black Falls to search for his missing father when the notification came about Elijah’s brush with death. Rose had flown to Germany to visit him in the military hospital at Landstuhl airbase.

“It’s been a tough year for your family,” Hannah said as she stepped onto a walk that cut through the snow-covered common. “Would Jo tell you if there were any new leads in the investigation?”

“Elijah would get it out of Jo, and he’d tell A.J., Rose and me.”

“That’s what I figured.” She paused at a snowman someone had built by the bandstand. "This is dead-of-winter cold. You remember what it's like?"

"I remember."

She frowned at the three-foot-tall snowman. "He has a pirate look about him, doesn't he?"

"I don't know, I think he looks kind of roguish."

She grinned at him. "What would I know about rogues?" But her mind obviously wasn't on snowmen. "Devin and Toby are excited about going out to California. Thank you for taking them. Toby's biked all over New England and upstate New York. There are some great trails out here, but he's been itching to get out west."

"It's new territory for him."

"He and Devin have never lived in a city. Neither have I, for that matter."

Sean bent down and scooped up a fistful of snow into his gloved hand, but it didn't hold together. The lights on the trees seemed to sparkle in Hannah's eyes. "Lousy snow for a snowball fight. My siblings and I used to have some no-holds-barred snowball fights when we were kids. Jo, too."

"Must have been something."

"You were a little younger and—"

"And I grew up in the hollow. Sean, why did you ask me out here? You might as well get to the point before we freeze."

He dusted the snow off his gloves. A year ago, her tone would have irritated him, or he wouldn't have even noticed. Now he was intrigued by the contrasts that were Hannah Shay—her directness and her reserve, her pride and her vulnerability. He remembered watching her in Latin class and thinking he'd never figure her out. But he had a mission, and in the glow of the Christmas lights, he could see the shadows of her bruised cheek.

"Okay. I'll get to the point. I want to know the rest—whatever you're holding back about why you went up the mountain today. Jo, Elijah and A.J. want to know, too." Sean waited a half beat, then added, "We're not sure about your judgment where Bowie O'Rourke is concerned."

She'd gone slightly pale. "Well." She gave a small, fake laugh. "I asked."

"You saw Judge Robinson tonight," Sean said. "He clearly doesn't like what's going on."

She adjusted the snowman's stone eye. "And what's going on, Sean?"

"You're getting sucked into Bowie's world."

"Well, I guess that's true, since his world is rock and I just had a pile of rock fall on top of me." She stood back from the snowman. "I think he looks more like a lawyer now, don't you?"

"Hannah—"

"Did Jo and your brothers put you up to prying the truth out of me? Do they think I'll be more likely to talk to you than to one of them? Is that what *you* think?" She shook her head. "Don't answer. I understand that you think I'm not leveling with you, but maybe it's not a question of leveling. Maybe I'm just keeping things to myself that should be kept to myself."

Sean suppressed his frustration with her. "You're exhausted, and you're in pain. We can talk tomorrow."

"No, we can talk now," she said. "You all don't need everyone with a harebrained theory distracting investigators from real clues to these killers. Do you think I'd protect Bowie if I had even the slightest suspicion he was involved with them?"

"I think you'd resist being suspicious of him in the first place. You're not objective where Bowie's concerned."

"And you are?"

Sean could see her reserve, her self-control, drop into place. She shoved her hands into her coat pockets, obviously forgetting momentarily about her injured wrist. She bit down on her lower lip in pain but didn't moan or make any sound. Then she bolted back across the common.

He caught up with her across the street in front of the café entrance.

She held up a hand before he could speak. "I know," she said stiffly. "I pushed you into saying that."

"No one's trying to make things harder for you."

She peeled his scarf off her neck and handed it to him. "Good night, Sean."

"If you decide you want to talk, you know where to find me."

She pretended not to hear him and headed down to the main entrance, running up the steps to the center-hall door. She glanced back at him. "You're not hiring Devin out of charity or some sense of guilt, are you?"

He stood at the bottom of the steps. “If you know anything about me, Hannah, you know I do almost nothing out of guilt, and you’re not a charity case.”

“Fair enough.” She seemed to make an effort to smile. “You’re not used to cold-weather hiking. You might want to soak in a hot tub tonight.”

“You do the same.”

“I would,” she said cheerfully, “except my cheap landlord won’t install a tub in our bathroom.”

He grinned at her. “Then come up to the lodge. You can use the tub in my room.”

A picture came into his head of Hannah settling into a scented bath in his warm, comfortable room at Black Falls Lodge.

“I’ll keep you posted on cellar repairs,” she said crisply.

He wondered if she was fighting similar images of him, her and a hot bath but forced himself to return to the issue at hand. “We all understand you want to believe Bowie has his act together. With your brothers away—”

“I’ll be alone.” Her tone wasn’t combative. “Yes, Sean, I know.”

"Hannah," he said, "is there more of a history between you and Bowie than my brothers and I are aware of?"

She gave him a cool smile. "How would that be possible? Nothing goes on in Black Falls that you Camerons don't know about," she said, and ducked inside.

Sean waited for the door to shut behind her before he walked back up the street to Elijah's truck and the dark drive back up the mountain. He'd figure out how much he'd tell Jo and his brothers about his evening in town.

It wouldn't be everything, that was for damn sure.

Hannah lay awake, the shades pulled, her brothers' voices and the television in the next room part of the background noise that was life in their small apartment. Devin had tried to explain more about his plans to her—the mix of impulsiveness and long-held dreams that had gone into them—but Hannah was so tired and distracted, trying not to feel rejected, that she took in only half the details, finally promising to sit down with him tomorrow and get everything sorted out.

"It's just a seven-hour flight to Los Angeles, Hannah."

A day to get there. A continent between them. The time, the money—the distance. The world her brothers had grown up in versus the one they wanted to embrace.

She stared at the old plaster ceiling. Her parents had dreamed of being a normal family. She wasn't sure anymore who knew her father had been to prison, serving sentences for brawls, theft, disorderly conduct and simple assault. She wasn't even sure at this point how much Devin and Toby knew. They'd probably learned more about their father from town gossip than from her.

He'd failed them and himself. And he'd known it.

As she went over the events of the day in her mind, Hannah concluded Sean's little hit on her in the cellar had been largely tactical, perhaps subconsciously so. He'd been trying to win her trust, worm his way into her psyche. Even if his reaction to her hadn't been calculated or deliberate, it was, she decided, intended to get her to let down her guard.

"**Hannah . . . Hannah . . . Hannah . . .**"

She tried to block out the voice and

rolled over onto her side, her wrist throbbing as she replayed the day in her head. Hiking up Cameron Mountain. Checking the old stone foundation of Drew's cabin. Realizing Sean was out there. Seeing the Cameron brothers out by the lodge.

Hearing Poe barking, and the voice at the crypt.

"Hannah."

Had Bowie been playing games with her—protecting himself, trying to scare her off, distract her? He could compartmentalize—he'd learned to as a boy, as a way to cope with his father's drunken rages.

Had he managed to compartmentalize having let himself be used by Melanie Kendall and Kyle Rigby? Had he fallen in with them to indulge his resentments against the Camerons?

Hannah couldn't stop the flood of questions and possibilities. Bowie could have spotted her crossing the road to the cemetery to check on Poe. Had he dislodged the debris pile in order to cover up the retreat of someone he'd met there?

Even if he wouldn't have hurt her, it didn't mean he wasn't involved in the network responsible for the murders of Drew Cameron, Alex Bruni and possibly others.

It didn't mean he wasn't a danger to himself and others.

She turned over again. She didn't believe Bowie was capable of being involved with killers. And that was what Sean had been trying to tell her was the problem.

She heard snoring down the hall and sighed, satisfied that at least her brothers were sleeping tonight.

Fourteen

December 29—Black Falls, Vermont

Ryan "Grit" Taylor was cold under the blankets on the lumpy twin bed in one of the dozen small, falling-down cabins Jo Harper owned on the frozen Vermont lake below Black Falls Lodge. He'd stoked up the woodstove before going to sleep, but the fire had died down by dawn. There was no insulation in the cabin and it was the dead of winter. The last forecast he saw had the temperature dropping into single digits overnight, and he had no doubt it had. An offense to his Southern soul. He could have stayed at the lodge, but he hadn't wanted to. Too many people.

Not being a coward, having faced bullets, blood and death, he figured he might as well get up. He donned his prosthesis, following a procedure that wasn't quite routine but wasn't new, either. He sat up on the side of the bed and put a prosthetic sock over the stump, made sure there were no wrinkles or folds, and grabbed the PTB—patella tendon bearing—socket that stood upright on the floor. Quickly but carefully, he inserted the stump into the socket and secured it with an elastic cuff.

"Done," he said, part of his ritual.

Life sucked, but whatever.

He added kindling to the hot coals in the woodstove and shut the door, hoping he wouldn't have to baby the fire to get it going. He looked out the picture window and saw Myrtle Smith coming up the path, which he'd cleared of snow himself, using a shovel that had to be a hundred years old. Jo had found it in another cabin. He'd discovered she was a waste-not-want-not type.

Myrtle wasn't, but if she ever needed any shoveling to be done, she'd get someone else to do it.

Grit opened the door. “Myrtle, what are you doing?”

“Trying not to fall,” she said without looking up from the narrow path. “If you were dead in there, no one would find me until fishing season.”

Myrtle, too, had a Southern soul. She hated cold weather. She hated snow and ice.

“Hurry up,” Grit said. “I don’t want to let the heat out.”

“What heat? You’re in a cabin in the boonies.”

“I’ve got the woodstove going.”

“Ah. I’m reassured,” she said, picking her way across an icy patch directly in front of the cabin door. “It’s Vermont. My car thermometer reads four degrees below zero. A woodstove isn’t going to get me to forget that.”

Grit had met Myrtle in mid-November at the spot in front of the Washington, D.C., hotel where Ambassador Alex Bruni was killed in a hit-and-run masterminded and executed by the two killers who’d then headed to Vermont to kill more people. In the weeks he’d known her, Grit had concluded that Myrtle was a drama queen who wasn't happy unless she was bitching.

"I'm not hurrying," she said. "I almost went ass-over-teakettle on the ice by the lake. I spend half my time up here trying not to fall and break something, I swear."

Grit grinned at her. "Think of it, though. I could rescue you. Throw you over my shoulder and carry you to safety. Oh, wait. I already did that when I pulled you out of your burning house."

Myrtle rolled her violet eyes as she walked past him into the cabin. She'd never been inside, and from her frown, Grit guessed she didn't appreciate what she saw. She glanced at him. "Do your own cleaning, do you?"

He shut the cabin door. "You always been a pain in the butt, Myrtle?"

"It's gotten worse since my Russian friend had his toothpaste poisoned by unnamed assassins and my house was set on fire."

"Just your office burned," Grit said. "Your house is intact."

Andrei Petrov, a controversial Russian diplomat, had died in London over the summer under mysterious circumstances. Myrtle hadn't been satisfied that he'd just keeled over while brushing his teeth and had launched her own personal investigation. She'd begun to suspect a network of professional killers was responsible for Petrov's death and started looking into other similar deaths, which had led her to venture out to the site of the hit-and-run that had killed Bruni. Police now could place Melanie Kendall and Kyle Rigby in London at the time of Petrov's death.

Myrtle had good reason for being a little dramatic.

She stood by the woodstove and put her gloved hands out toward the fire. "This investigation is dead in the water. We're not getting anywhere. Some rocks fall up in a cemetery and a tarp blows in the wind, and everyone gets all excited."

"The stonemason's on probation."

"For a *bar fight,* Petty Officer Taylor. In my day, bar fights between stonemasons and mountain men were par for the course. Nobody called the damn police."

"In your day, duels to the death were legal, too."

She ignored him. "Whoever hired Kyle

Rigby and Melanie Kendall has gone to ground. Their network's probably disbanded. Law enforcement's being tight with information, but we'd know if they had a freaking clue."

Grit shrugged and said nothing.

Myrtle opened up the woodstove. "I grew up in a little town in southern Georgia. We had a woodstove. My grandma would put on a pot of white beans. . . ." She drifted off and got more kindling out of the bucket next to the stove and set it on the anemic fire, blew on the coals and stood back as if she knew what she was doing. She shook bits of wood and sawdust from her glove. "Goatskin. Cost me a fortune. Those mountain men, Elijah and A.J., told me to get some windproof blah-blah-blah gloves. Ugly as sin."

A.J. had outfitted Grit with just such a pair of gloves. They were fine. "Why are you here, Myrtle?"

She watched flames slowly spread through the kindling. She didn't look as cold. Grit figured it was the psychological effect of seeing the fire. It wasn't any warmer in the cabin. "You never told anyone that Charlie Neal was switching places with his lookalike cousin," she said without looking at Grit.

He didn't say anything. Instead he pulled on a fleece-lined sweatshirt. If he'd had his way, Myrtle wouldn't have known about Charlie Neal and his cousin, Conor, either. Feeling guilty over causing Jo Harper to be sent into exile in Vermont, Charlie had done his own investigating after Alex Bruni's death. He'd conducted his research mostly on the Internet, but he'd also switched places with Conor and headed out into the city on his own, without benefit of Secret Service protection. He'd come to believe, as Myrtle had, that paid assassins were at work and had produced a list of potential victims. Not everyone on his list had checked out—but authorities were paying attention to it. They just didn't know it came from the vice president's son.

"The Secret Service think they have Charlie buttoned up," Myrtle said. "But you know he's still on this thing. He's got an IQ of one-eighty and he gets bored easily, and he wants to matter. He'll find a way to meddle."

"He can take anything he learns straight to the Secret Service."

"What if he doesn't trust the Secret Service?"

Grit pulled the covers up on his bed.

Myrtle kept her sights on him. She wasn't one to quit. "I'm not saying they don't deserve to be trusted. It's just that Charlie idolizes you and Elijah. The hero SEAL and the hero Special Forces soldier."

"I'm not a hero," Grit said.

"Eye of the beholder."

"What do you want me to do?"

She lifted a small birch log and set it on the burning kindling. "You sweep this place for listening devices? Jo Harper's still Secret Service. She knows how to bug an old cabin. She'll throw both our butts in jail if she—"

"Cabin's not bugged."

"So you *did* sweep for bugs. Damn, Grit. All right. I have a phone number." She handed him a piece of paper. "Call it."

"We're playing with fire, Myrtle."

She picked one last wood chip off a glove. "At least it's warm."

Being a bold type, Grit dialed the number Myrtle gave him from a big icy boulder on the steep trail up to the lodge. He had a view of the lake and Elijah's house. That meant Jo Harper could look out the kitchen window and see her cabin guest up there with a cell phone and wonder who the hell he was calling in the cold.

Grit didn't know for sure, but he had a feeling who it was.

Special Agent Harper would go berserk if he was right and she found out.

Someone picked up on the other end. "Is this Petty Officer Taylor?"

Grit recognized the boyish voice of the sixteen-year-old son of the vice president of the United States. If Jo had her Secret Service listening devices in Elijah's house, or if Elijah had his Special Forces listening devices in his house, and one or both could hear Charlie Neal on the other end of the connection, Grit knew he'd be hauled off his icy rock.

"It is," Grit said. "Do you have a Secret Service detail with you, Charlie?"

"Sort of. My cousin and I are in the control room in our school auditorium."

"Aren't you on break for the holidays?"

"Yes, sir, but we're dismantling the lighting we did for the freshman Christmas play. It's a private school. We can have a Christmas play."

"Don't call me 'sir.' I work for a living. You're both there? You and Conor?"

"That's right."

Then the two teenagers hadn't done one of their prince-and-the-pauper switches.

"Listen," Charlie said, "I've been thinking."

"Scary when you start thinking with that one-eighty IQ."

Charlie brushed him off. "We need to expand our view of this group of killers and not just focus on Melanie Kendall and Kyle Rigby."

"*We?* You aren't on this investigation, and neither am I. I'm filling time between PT appointments. You're in high school. You're under Secret Service protection."

"We know that Rigby was the senior partner," Charlie said as if Grit hadn't spoken. "Kendall was newer. I think Rigby knew or was in contact with at least one other killer."

The kid was relentless.

Grit realized he should hang up, march down to Jo Harper and rat out Charlie Neal, but instead he played devil's advocate. "What if they were the only killers? Rigby and the woman. What if there's no network? They found their own clients and pretended there was a middleman."

"Why would they do that?"

"To keep their clients comfortable in their anonymity."

"Ah. To mislead people." Charlie was thoughtful. "Nah. Doesn't work. Then who blew up Kendall's car?"

"Some friend of Rigby's. A one-time deal. 'I get killed, you blow her ass up.' Like that."

"Still doesn't work," Charlie said, as if, of course, he knew better.

"You wanted me to call you so you could theorize? You can do that with your cousin and your Secret Service detail."

"You sound as if you're in pain, Petty Officer Taylor. How's the leg?"

"Which one?"

"The one that got blown off. What's left of it. That one."

Grit gave the kid credit for not backing down. "I don't like the cold, and I don't like the son of the vice president of the United States talking to me about killers. Think about something else."

"I am. My mind can work on different tracks all at once. I get bored easily."

"Don't we all."

"And I didn't just set up this call to theorize."

Anyone else, and Grit would have thought—okay, the kid feels bad. Hurt at being dismissed. Not with Charlie Neal. "Why *did* you set up this call, Charlie?"

"Sean Cameron and his business partner, Nick Martini, met each other when they were full-time smoke jumpers."

Grit waited. The cold didn't bother him that much. The lake and the surrounding hills were white and shades of gray and evergreen under a clear blue winter sky. It was a nice view. He could stay out here awhile.

"The sister—Rose Cameron—trains and handles search-and-rescue dogs," Charlie said. "She's a search management expert. Very experienced. She's been at the scene of a number of devastating western wildfires."

Grit was unimpressed. "The Camerons are active types. I've been chopping and hauling wood and running and fixing things since I got to Vermont. Jo's the same. She had me up on the roof of her cabin the other day looking for how bats get in."

"Bats can squeeze into—"

"Don't start with me, and forget what you're thinking."

"Firefighters are sometimes themselves firebugs. A volunteer firefighter started horrible fires in Australia that killed hundreds. It's unfortunate, but it happens." Charlie paused. "Sean Cameron and Nick Martini both are volunteers now."

"So?"

"So who blew up Melanie Kendall's car? Who blew up Myrtle Smith's house?"

"A Cameron didn't."

"But maybe someone the Camerons know did."

"It's a thought. Keep it to yourself."

"I'm not telling anyone but you."

Great. Lucky him. "When's school start?"

"Couple more weeks. Public school starts up right after New Year's. Talk to me, Petty Officer. I haven't actually met Elijah, but we've spoken on the phone. He's a disciplined soldier—"

"Sergeant Cameron. Mr. Cameron. Either one's okay. Not Elijah."

"He said I could call him by his first name."

"I didn't say you could, and you're talking to me."

"He's a hero. What about Sean and Rose? A.J.?"

"Go back to un-lighting Santa Claus, Charlie."

"It's a crèche. Again, private school. You should keep your eyes open."

"Always, my friend. Always."

"Sean Cameron, Rose Cameron, Nick Martini, firebugs. I'm telling you. There's something there."

Grit disconnected and debated walking down to Elijah's house and telling Jo that the vice president's son was back at it, sticking his nose into a criminal investigation. At least Charlie was just speculating and not showing up at a murder scene as he had in November. Everyone in Black Falls was speculating. No harm in that.

Sean Cameron seemed to fit in just fine with his mountain man brothers. The only difference was that he fought fires out west and had a tan and a lot more money. Grit was a warrior sailor whose family made honey in the Florida Panhandle. His idea of having money was a hundred-dollar bill in his pocket.

Grit sighed. What to do on a cold winter day in Vermont?

He could call Admiral Jenkins back. The admiral, whom Grit had heard of but did not know, had left messages six times in the past week. Grit was to get in touch with him. It was an unofficial summons and undoubtedly had to do with the admiral having an idea about a wounded Navy SEAL's future.

It didn't do not to return an admiral's call, but Grit figured he could always blame bad service up here in the boonies.

He decided he'd have breakfast with Jo and Elijah and maybe work Sean and Rose and firebugs into the conversation.

He headed down the trail through the snow. Ever since helping to pinpoint the identity of the killers who'd targeted Drew Cameron and Alexander Bruni and dealing with the mischievous, genius son of the vice president of the United States,

Grit had been thinking less and less about his leg. Dealing with it was becoming more routine, more automatic.

He didn't know if he liked that. He didn't know if he was ready to leave behind the man he'd been and the life he'd led.

Fifteen

"I dreamed about . . . you know."

Devin rubbed a hand over his head, awkward and, in his own way, self-conscious, uncomfortable about sharing his emotions—his vulnerabilities. Hannah sat with him at a small table by the café's front door. It was early, the café cold as the heat kicked in for the day. Since surviving his ordeal on Cameron Mountain, Devin had insisted he was okay, but he had recurring nightmares, reliving the shots Rigby had fired into the cabin and then the shots Elijah had fired. Finally, the silence, and the knowledge that one of the two men was dead.

He stared out the café window at Main Street. “I think California will help. The change of scenery will do me good.”

“I hope so,” Hannah said. The swelling on her cheek had died down overnight. Her wrist had turned shades of purple and blue. “If you get homesick—if you need to talk to someone—just do it, okay? Don’t wait. You’re as tough and resilient as anyone, but you went through hell last month.”

“Yeah. We all could have died up on the mountain in about ten different ways. Beaten to death. Frozen. Shot.” He turned from the window and sipped hot cocoa from an evergreen mug. “Rigby wasn’t a maniac, you know.”

“I know, Dev. He was a cold-blooded killer.”

Her brother raised his eyes, still haunted from his nightmare. “What was he like when you talked to him?”

“Convincing.” They’d gone over this ground before. “I didn’t question that he was a mountain rescuer. No one did. It makes me sick to think I gave him any information that helped him find you.”

"He already knew about the cabin from when he and Melanie Kendall killed Drew. They must have followed Drew up there one day or something. I didn't know about it until Nora found it in November. She pretty much stumbled onto it." Devin licked chocolate foam off his lips. "I keep hearing the shots that killed Rigby." He paused, staring into his mug. "Elijah saved my life. He and Jo. I was useless."

"So was I, Dev. We all did what we could, but maybe events unfolded the way they were meant to." Hannah smiled, hoping to help shake Devin out of the aftereffects of his nightmare. "Look at Jo and Elijah now."

Devin gave a small smile back at her. "Planning a wedding."

"Nora was so excited when she found Drew's cabin. I'd told her I'd brought supplies up there, and she was determined to figure out what he'd been up to."

"She'd never have made it back there in the storm if you hadn't warned her about Rigby."

"He nearly beat me to death."

"But you got away from him and found Jo and Elijah—"

"I was lucky," Devin said.

"You made your own luck. You were able to show Jo where the cabin was and take shelter there. Elijah knew he had to find Nora before she succumbed to hypothermia. He got her to the cabin." Hannah sat back in her chair. She'd had coffee, but she wasn't hungry. She hadn't slept that well herself. "You held your own with experienced pros."

Toby bounded into the café from the center-hall door and grabbed a corn muffin off a tray on the glass case. "Hey, Dev, Hannah," he said. "Tomorrow's the big day. All set for our adventure, Dev?"

"Yeah, I guess," Devin said.

"We better not annoy Sean. Don't want him to pitch us out of his airplane." Toby grinned, obviously not worried about any such thing. "I wonder if he has any parachutes on board. Probably, given his other life as a smoke jumper."

Toby bit into his muffin, crumbs falling into his lap. He hadn't grabbed a plate or a napkin, no butter, no jam. He ate all the time—he'd probably had scrambled eggs before heading down to the café.

"What're you up to this morning?" Hannah asked him.

"I'm hitting the weight room at school. It's open."

"I can drop you off—"

"Nah. I'll walk. It'll be above zero by the time I get out of here. Dev, you want to go with me?"

Devin shook his head. "I'm working up at the lodge today. My last day."

Even if he hadn't been working, Hannah knew he wouldn't weight-lift with his younger brother. Toby was a competitive athlete, and while Devin was fit, he was more likely to hike than to spend time in a gym. Neither brother was the student she'd been, but Devin's grades had really suffered after Drew Cameron's death in April. He almost hadn't graduated. Then came a summer of aimlessness and trouble. His friendship with Nora Asher after her move to Black Falls had offered a glimmer of hope. They'd both had to sort out their options.

Lowell and Vivian Whittaker entered the café with Everett and Ginny Robinson. Hannah got to her feet. "Duty calls," she said to her brothers with a wink.

They grabbed muffins and headed out through the café kitchen. Hannah dipped behind the glass case, the two couples having made up their minds about what they wanted. From what she gathered, they'd run into each other on Main Street and come into the café together.

As Hannah took their orders and gathered muffins and scones, Everett quizzed her about her plans for studying. "Are you keeping your law books handy?"

"I'm still getting organized," she said.

The Whittakers decided to have their muffins and coffee to go. "Lowell and I want to be at the guesthouse when Bowie O'Rourke starts work there today," Vivian Whittaker said. "I think that's always for the best. I really do hope repainting will help. I can't get rid of the memories of those two killers on our property."

"At least nothing actually happened there," Lowell said.

"That does make a difference," his wife said. "I wish the same were true for the Camerons' lodge. Alex Bruni stayed there many times and loved it there, but I can't imagine how it will recover. I wouldn't want to stay in a place where someone blew up in a car."

Judge Robinson looked a little shocked at Vivian's bluntness. "I'm sure it will be easier once the police find the person who triggered the bomb."

"Assuming they can." Vivian picked up two coffees from the counter where Hannah had set them. "It's been weeks. I'm not convinced we'll ever know who it was. Of course, we all want to find the rest of these people before they can hurt anyone else."

Lowell quickly paid, and he and Vivian left, the Robinsons heading to a table. Hannah wanted to avoid Everett's scrutiny and went into the kitchen while there was a lull in customers.

Dominique looked up from the worktable, where she was filling muffin tins with thick batter. "I had to step outside for a minute, and I saw the Camerons arriving in force. Any idea what they're doing here?"

"I haven't seen them yet."

Dominique frowned. "Do you want me—"

"No, I'll go."

Hannah returned to the dining room

just as the Cameron men entered the café. A.J., usually busy with the lodge or his two young children, was a rare presence. He and his brothers left on their coats as they approached her behind the glass case. Their sister, Rose, wasn't with them.

All three men looked focused and edgy, understandable, Hannah reminded herself, given the circumstances. Then again, when hadn't a Cameron looked focused and edgy?

"Dominique just pulled cinnamon scones out of the oven," she said. "Interested?"

"Just coffee," A.J. said.

"Where's Jo? Usually she's with you—"

"She's taking a look at the crypt in daylight," Elijah said.

"I guess that makes sense," Hannah said.

A.J.'s gaze was hard on her. "I guess it does."

He took his coffee to a table by the window. She noticed that Sean was back to normal, whatever had bubbled up between them last night well below the surface again now. She got coffee and muffins for them, and they joined A.J. at his table by the river.

Dominique came through the swinging door with a bowl of homemade yogurt that she placed in the glass case. She sighed at Hannah and nodded toward the Cameron table. "You want to go butt heads with them, don't you?"

"I think it's the other way around."

"Go ahead. I'll keep an eye out here."

"If you need me," Hannah said, "just let me know and I'll come right back."

Leaving on her evergreen apron, Hannah headed across the dining room to the Cameron men. Sean was seated next to A.J., their backs to the river, the morning sun glinting on the ice formations and drifts of undisturbed snow.

Elijah was at the end of the table, his long legs stretched out. With one foot, he slid out a chair. "Have a seat," he said.

As she sat down, Hannah tried to look casual rather than irritated, self-conscious or guilty, when, in fact, she felt a little of each. "Is Rose joining you?"

"She's snowshoeing with Ranger," A.J. said. "We've finally started cleaning out our folks' place. It's not easy on any of us, but it's especially hard on her."

"She and your mom were close. It hasn't been long since you lost her, either. It's good you all have one another."

No one spoke for a moment. "So, Hannah," A.J. said, "how are you after your hike up to the cabin and your incident at Four Corners yesterday?"

"Sore."

A.J. bristled at her response, but he kept his temper in check. "It's still hard to figure out what went on in the cemetery—if Bowie just knocked the wrong rock and the whole thing came tumbling down, if it was the wind or what. Your face looks good." He nodded to her wrist. "That's not pretty. Any other scrapes and bruises?"

"Nothing I'm worried about."

Hannah realized her breathing was light, rapid. She figured they'd decided that Sean had failed on his own and now the three of them would try to get answers out of her. But she had no answers, and she wasn't accustomed to such scrutiny.

"Why go alone up to the cabin?" A.J. asked. "Any of us would have gone with you."

"So Sean told me yesterday. I appreciate that. I know I was on Cameron land, but—"

"That's not the point. Hiking alone in winter conditions isn't safe. Why did you do it?"

"I knew I could count on you Camerons to come rescue me," Hannah said with a deliberately fake smile.

A.J. didn't so much as crack a smile back at her. Sean and Elijah drank their coffee, letting their older brother do the interrogating. They'd probably figured it out in advance. Of the three brothers, A.J. had the least patience with her and had never treated her with kid gloves. But she'd never been intimidated by him, either.

"What were you looking for?" he asked.

"Peace of mind."

Technically it was true. She didn't care if she was being obstinate. She didn't want to drag them on a wild-goose chase—and she didn't want to subject Bowie to unfair scrutiny.

A.J. gave a small hiss of irritation. Sean didn't move. Elijah leaned forward and placed a hand on Hannah's arm, probably aware his older brother was about to throttle her. “We’re not ganging up on you, Hannah. We want to help.”

“Help with what? The leak in the cellar? The lunch menu?”

A.J. shot to his feet. “I knew this would be a waste of time.”

If Jo Harper had a knack for rubbing her the wrong way, Hannah thought, she, on the other hand, had a knack for rubbing A.J. Cameron the wrong way. He was as hard-bitten as his father had been, and as devoted to Black Falls.

His expression softened slightly as he glared down at her. “We’re on the same side. Keep that in mind.”

As he stalked out of the café, Hannah wanted to jump up and run, but where to? The kitchen? Upstairs to her apartment? She supposed she could lock herself in the cellar with the water leak and the spiders. The Camerons and the Harpers were two of the most prominent and beloved families in Black Falls, and she didn’t like being confronted—targeted—by them.

Elijah tried again. “Hannah, this isn’t an inquisition. We know the past month’s been tough on you. You almost lost Devin. We're here to help."

But how could they? She'd been truthful with Sean last night. She didn't want to distract them with some useless tidbits when they had enough on *their* minds. After five weeks, all of them—herself included—were ripe to latch onto the slightest lead, no matter how unsubstantiated or ridiculous or wrong-headed.

"I just want to see my brothers off to California." Rising abruptly, she forced herself to stay steady, contained, and turned to Sean. "They're excited about their trip. They'll be ready tomorrow whenever you are."

Before Sean could respond, she pivoted and headed back across the café and behind the glass case. Dominique mumbled that she'd be back in the kitchen and ducked through the swinging door.

Beth Harper passed A.J. in the main entrance, taking in the scene as she approached Hannah. "Uh-oh. A Cameron gathering."

Hannah managed a smile in spite of her tension. "They had a few questions for me, which I've answered. Would you mind staying out here while I—"

"Go ahead. Do what you have to do." Beth's eyes narrowed. "Hannah, you're not going to cry, are you?"

"Not because of them," she said, and fled into the kitchen.

Dominique was in the storage room. Hannah ripped paper towels off a roll, dampened them with cold water and applied them to her cheeks as she fought back tears. Did they *all* have to come to the café?

If they thought she was holding back something that would help them find out who'd ordered Drew Cameron's death, yes.

She couldn't very well blame them.

She heard the swinging door open and shut and assumed it was Dominique or Beth, but the footsteps on the old wood floor had a distinctly male sound to them. Resisting the impulse to turn around, Hannah tossed the paper towels in the trash and got out of there, grabbing her car keys and her jacket and charging out the back door.

Sean followed her out to her car. "I'll go with you."

"You don't even know where I'm headed."

"To see Bowie."

"Then you can just drive fast and beat me there."

She climbed into her car and started the engine. Drew had told her she wasn't one to let her emotions dictate her actions, but she had the night at O'Rourke's when some idiots started flinging insults—and now she was again, letting the Cameron brothers get to her. They were just trying to find out answers to their father's murder.

"So am I," she whispered to herself, and backed out of the driveway, leaving Sean standing in the frigid air as she drove past him and out toward the hollow where she and Bowie O'Rourke had spent their childhoods.

Sixteen

Hannah checked Bowie's place on the river first, but his van wasn't in the short driveway. He lived in a wreck of a house that he claimed to be renovating. Wood was stacked neatly under a homemade lean-to, smoke curling out of a stovepipe chimney. This wasn't the romanticized Vermont of postcards, nostalgia or tourists. There were a few houses strung along the river on what was now a back road, a stone wall running along one side of what used to be a more traveled road.

Keep going, and she'd end up back at the logging road at the base of the north side of Cameron Mountain where Sean had parked yesterday. Could Kyle Rigby and Melanie Kendall simply have had Drew Cameron under surveillance and followed him up the mountain? The April snowstorm would have covered their tracks. No one was sure of Drew's exact route, but he hadn't parked at the old logging road at the bottom of the short, steep trail down from the north side of the mountain. As near as anyone could figure, he'd taken one of the main trails that started out by the lodge.

The police didn't believe the two killers had followed him. They believed they'd waited for him in his cabin.

Which meant they'd known about it in advance.

The wind stirred up snow as Hannah got out of her car. The river was frozen, the silence almost eerie. The landscape seemed so desolate. Or maybe it was her mood.

She didn't linger and headed back down the road to the open stretch of the river that was light-years from the narrow, isolated hollow where she had spent the first twenty years of her life. The house where she'd grown up had been condemned and torn down. Her mother used to joke about setting fire to it, but she'd loved its quiet, pretty location. She'd commuted from home to Castleton State College, until she finally saved enough money to rent a room at the Robinsons' house. She'd just graduated from college when her mother died, leaving Devin and Toby underage orphans. Foster care had loomed if Hannah hadn't gone to Judge Robinson and begged him to help her figure out how to become their legal guardian.

She came to the Whittaker estate, which had always been owned by out-of-staters. Bowie's van was parked in the turnaround by the stone guesthouse. It had been divided into two side-by-side apartments. Hannah followed an icy walk to the front porch and called to him. He didn't answer, but she went inside anyway, finding him in the apartment where Nora Asher had lived briefly. All her belongings had been removed, and Bowie had already moved furniture out of his way and covered it up with paint cloths.

His face had blossomed into purple splotches. The bandage on his hand seemed to be free of blood. "Hey." He barely looked up from a small tub of Spackle set out on newspaper. "What can I do for you, Hannah?"

"Just wanted to check on you. How's your head?"

"A handful of ibuprofen does wonders." He stood up with a dab of thick white paste on the end of a small putty knife. "Crazy to paint this place if you ask me. Doesn't it look fine to you? Just a few nail holes to patch. There's some minor work to do on the chimney, too."

"Hard to believe Melanie Kendall and Kyle Rigby had the gall to stay here right under everyone's noses. Did you run into them at all in November or back in April?"

"I told the Cameron boys and Jo Harper *and* Scott Thorne yesterday that I saw Kendall with Thomas Asher at the Four Corners church when they were up here in October. They were taking pictures. I only saw her that one time."

"What were you doing in town?"

"Looking at a potential job."

"The culvert?"

He glanced over at her. "Does it matter? I don't recall ever running into Rigby. Jo showed me a picture of him, but I'd seen his picture in the newspaper and on television. I'd remember him if I'd seen him."

Hannah watched Bowie work for a moment. "I imagine your probation officer wants you to stay as far away from this business as possible. That mishap yesterday . . ."

He slapped the Spackle onto the living room wall. "Bad timing."

"Bowie, when I was up on the mountain yesterday, I got a good look at part of the foundation to Drew's cabin. The original foundation would be almost two hundred years old. You can imagine the damage done over the years. He must have rebuilt it entirely."

"I imagine so," Bowie said.

"Even if he could have done the actual work on his own, I don't know that he had the expertise in stonework to manage without help of some kind. What do you think?"

"You asking me from a technical point of view?"

She let his suspicion slide past her. "I'd appreciate your expert opinion, yes."

"I could do the job on my own. Drew could if he knew what he was doing and had the right equipment and materials."

"*Did* he know what he was doing?"

Bowie worked the paste into the nail hole with his thumb and smoothed it out with the side of his uninjured hand. "I wouldn't know."

"Your guess?"

"I'm not guessing, Hannah."

"Cutting down trees, trimming them, constructing the cabin itself—I can see Drew handling that part on his own. But the stonework . . ."

Bowie didn't look back at her as he spoke. "If he had help with any of it, not just the stonework, that means someone else knew about the cabin. Is that what you're getting at, Hannah?"

She watched him dip his putty knife back into the Spackle tub. "Bowie . . ."

He stood up with fresh paste on the end of his knife and gave her a cool look. "I didn't help Drew. If I had, I'd have said something by now."

"Did you help him find that old cellar hole?"

"No. What about you? Your dad's hobby was looking for old cellar holes. I went with him a few times. So did you. Did you two ever run into the old Cameron cellar hole?"

"My father had an idea it was on the north side of the mountain. We looked for it a few times. Drew had been looking for it on and off for years. That wasn't a secret." She stepped back as he slapped the Spackle onto the wall. "Did you point him in the right direction?"

"We talked about possibilities from time to time," Bowie said, obviously reluctant to talk. "I gave him pointers on what to look for—trees, shrubs, groundcover, abandoned wells, the lay of the land. That's it. I might be able to find it on my own now, but only because of what I've heard since November."

"There's no love lost between you and the Camerons."

"I may have a short fuse, but I don't hold grudges. Drew mellowed some. He'd come by and talk when I was doing a job at the Four Corners church the winter before he died."

"About what?"

"Stonework, mostly."

By then, Drew had already had Devin haul supplies up the back side of the mountain for his secret project building his small post-and-beam cabin on the site where Camerons had first settled in Black Falls.

"Did you know Drew was missing in April?" Hannah asked. "You were in jail—"

"I know where I was," he said, not harshly. "I didn't know until after Devin had already found him. It wouldn't have mattered. I didn't know about the cabin. If I had and I'd realized he was missing and had probably gone up there, I'd have said something. I sure as hell wouldn't have left your brother to find him."

"Bowie," Hannah said, "you know what I'm getting at."

"Yeah. I'm going to end up on the cops' radar. I guess I'm already there."

"On Cameron radar, too. Especially after yesterday."

"I don't need you looking after me."

She picked up a pebble-size piece of dried Spackle. "What about Alex Bruni, Nora Asher's stepfather? He was the ambassador who was killed in the hit-and-run in Washington."

"Yeah. I know. I saw him in town a few times. I knew who he was, but we never spoke."

"How did you know who he was?"

"People talk."

"What people?"

"People who stop at O'Rourke's for a beer after a hard day's work." He sighed at her. "Who put you on this investigation?"

"I'm not on the investigation," Hannah said, keeping her tone neutral.

He shook his head at her. "You're a hound on a trail, Hannah. Drew never took me up the mountain with him, but I knew he was up to something. I didn't ask a lot of questions. He obviously didn't want to talk." Bowie turned and smoothed the Spackle with the flat of his knife. "Something I can respect."

She ignored his gibe. "If you had information that would help the investigation, you'd tell the police, wouldn't you? You wouldn't wait to be specifically asked—"

"I already told you as much." He continued with his work without looking at her. "Ever wonder if Sean or A.J. or Elijah killed Melanie Kendall? Elijah managed to get Nora Asher out of the car in time. How? What if he knew A.J. would trigger the bomb? What if he knew his friend Grit would—if he'd called Grit before heading out to the parking lot?'

"You don't believe that."

"What if a Cameron's your killer mastermind? Ever think of that?"

"No."

Bowie finally stood back from the wall and turned to her. "Anything else, Hannah?"

"Are you mad at me for being at O'Rourke's that night?"

"Nope. You had a right to be there."

"The insults—"

"Those guys are dolts. They deserved what they got, but I was stupid to give it to them. Derek Cutshaw, especially, is an idiot."

"What he said . . ." Hannah hesitated. "The prejudices about how I grew up I'm used to. The rest. The really personal stuff. You kept them from going into detail." She licked her lips, awkward now, but also determined to learn the truth. "Bowie, were those comments about me?"

He steadied his dark eyes on her. "Does it matter? It's over. I've got a job to do here." He turned back to the wall and rubbed his callused fingers over the drying Spackle. “Did Sean send you out here? Or was it a joint decision between him and his brothers?”

“No one sent me.”

“Good. I don’t need the Camerons and the Harpers on my case. Jo’s a pit bull these days.” He glanced back at her. “You don’t need them on your case, either, Hannah. Let the police investigate what they want to investigate. Do you know something they don’t?”

“About stonework, maybe.”

“Your dad taught you a few things,” Bowie said.

“Yes, he did.”

When he wasn’t in prison. It wasn’t until she was a teenager and he’d already been dead for several years that she’d finally understood that his troubled history explained the big age difference between her and her brothers.

“He didn’t kill himself,” she whispered. “I know you’ve wondered—”

“Doesn’t matter anymore.”

“His death was hard on you, too. He wasn’t perfect. We know that, but he never laid a hand on either of us. He believed in both of us." She fought back unexpected tears. "Bowie, he always hoped you'd stay out of jail. He didn't want you following in his footsteps in that way."

His eyes were half-closed again, the bruises and swelling on his face making him look even more like a man a woman alone would be smart to avoid. "I never would have hurt you or let anyone else hurt you that night at Liam's."

"I know that, Bowie."

"The Camerons don't."

She didn't argue with him.

"They think you have a blind spot where I'm concerned," he said, then looked at her. "Maybe you do."

She shrugged. "All right. Maybe I do."

"Can you become a prosecutor with a father who was in prison?"

"I am who I am. My past, my family, my friends—I can't change any of it."

"Would you if you could?"

"And what, grow up on a dairy farm?" Despite her tension, she managed a smile. "Cows give me the creeps."

He didn't return her smile. "You deserved

better than what you got. Your dad wanted to do the right thing. When you stand in judgment of someone, remember that."

"I will, but I won't be standing in judgment of anyone. That's for the jury."

"You'll be the prosecutor. You'll decide whether to take a case to trial or drop the charges."

"The prosecutor is a truth-seeker."

He laughed. "Yeah, right. You know better. Prosecutors are just like any other lawyer. They want to win their case." His laughter faded. "What truth are you seeking now, Hannah?"

"The same as everyone else in town."

Through the front window, she saw Sean coming up the walk, the morning sunlight outlining the uncompromising angles of his face. He mounted the steps to the porch, moving deliberately, in no apparent hurry. Hannah wondered if Bowie saw him, too.

Of *course* Sean hadn't resisted coming after her. The man was on a mission, and she was it.

She stifled a surge of warmth and turned back to Bowie. "I want to know who's behind these killings," she said.

“It’s not your job to find out.”

“If you ever want to talk to me, you know where to find me.”

Sean stepped into the entry and stood in the doorway to the apartment Nora Asher had occupied for such a short time. Bowie looked at him without expression as he addressed Hannah. “Go bake cookies and study to be a lawyer.”

She shot out the door, passing Sean without a word. He could have grabbed her and stopped her, or said something, but he just let her go. She didn’t slow her pace until she hit the icy walk. She paused, letting her eyes adjust to the bright sun on the snow.

Vivian Whittaker was on cross-country skis, making her way down from the dark gray farmhouse visible on top of a long, open slope above the river. “Brr.” She gave an exaggerated shiver as she came to the edge of the guesthouse walk. She wore expensive cross-country ski clothes. Only her red cheeks looked cold. “I can’t believe how cold it is. I should have checked the thermometer. I was fooled by the sun. It makes everything sparkle and look so warm and inviting.”

"It can be deceptive," Hannah said, a gust of wind penetrating her thin jacket.

"Are you here to see Bowie?"

"I just stopped to say hello."

"I see. I have to admit . . ." Vivian looked toward the guesthouse. "He makes me a little nervous. I think he does Lowell, too."

Hannah said nothing. What was there to say? Maybe the Whittakers were smart to be nervous and she was the one who was making no sense.

"I understand you two go way back." Vivian shuffled closer to the walk, the tips of her long skis edging out of the snow. "I don't mean to be intrusive, but you know what I'm asking. Bowie will be working here for at least the next two weeks. We're having company for New Year's. He has a criminal record."

"Honestly, Mrs. Whittaker—"

"Vivian."

"Vivian. Honestly, I don't know what you're asking."

She lifted her ski poles out of the snow and seemed to struggle to hold back a caustic response. "I'm asking, Hannah," she said coolly, "if you and Bowie O'Rourke are romantically involved and if that's going to be a problem for Lowell and me. That's all. I'm sorry to be blunt, but with all that's gone on here this year, I feel the need to speak my mind."

"No problem."

She settled back on her skis. "But you're not going to answer me, are you?"

"No, I'm not."

Sean came out of the guesthouse and walked down the porch steps, but Vivian ignored him, her gaze leveled on Hannah. "I understand your parents are both gone and you're alone in the world. Bowie must be a force of strength and continuity in your life."

Hannah tried to keep any defensiveness out of her tone. "I'm not alone in the world. I have two brothers. We have assorted relatives, just none in a position to have been their guardian." She glanced back at Sean, who seemed unconcerned about the ice on the walk. She turned to Vivian Whittaker. Why was she explaining herself to this woman? "I have to go."

"The Robinsons have enormous respect for you and your accomplishments. I trust their judgment." Vivian gestured toward her sprawling farmhouse on the hill.

"Do you have time for coffee or tea? We've a fire going. Lowell's filled the wood box to the brim. He loves his country chores."

"Thank you, but I can't stay."

"Another time, perhaps." Vivian smiled at Sean as he came closer. "I imagine you can't wait to be back in California, given this cold weather."

Hannah didn't wait for his response. She lost her footing on a slippery section of the walk but didn't fall. She was used to ice. Cold. Long winters. This was her world, she thought as she headed to her car. Sean was from Black Falls, but it wasn't his world any longer.

She half expected him to have blocked her in with Elijah's truck, but he hadn't. She yanked open her frozen car door. How much did Sean know about her father? How much did all the Camerons know and not say? Drew undoubtedly had been aware of Tobias Shay's multiple arrests.

"I've done a lot of stupid things," her father had told Hannah when she was eleven. "I'm not proud."

"Then why don't you be good?"

"I don't know. I just don't know."

He hadn't been an alcoholic, a drug addict or a sociopath. He'd been a man who'd made some very bad decisions and had never quite been able to keep his life together.

"I wouldn't trade your father for a Prince Charming," her mother had said.

Then again, maybe that hadn't been a good decision on her mother's part. Hannah had loved them both, just as she loved her brothers, who were now about to go off to California. She shivered, the cold wind downright painful.

Why did it feel as if Sean Cameron were stealing her brothers from her?

She knew it was ridiculous. Devin and Toby were doing what they wanted to do. Sean was just helping them.

He was suddenly behind her. "Your hands must be cold," he said.

"Frozen. I should have worn gloves."

"You were in a hurry."

"I wasn't thinking."

"I shouldn't have let you come out here alone."

"And how would you have stopped me?"

He smiled, the cold having no apparent effect on him. "Would you like me to count the ways?" Before she could respond, he touched a thumb to her injured cheek. "Looks better today."

"It feels better. My wrist, too. I see you're not wearing gloves, either."

"Serves us both right if we get frostbite. Bowie's injuries look bad, but he's just cut, scraped and bruised. And oblivious." Sean eyed her a moment. "He wouldn't tell me what you two talked about."

"Stonework," Hannah said. "He's a stonemason. I'm the daughter of a stonemason. We often talk about stonework."

Sean's eyes narrowed as he stood back from her. Finally he said, "Go on. I won't keep you out here in the cold. I'll see you in town."

"Sean—"

"It's okay. Go."

She climbed into her car. She could see Vivian Whittaker shuffling gracefully on her skis down to the little duck pond, covered now in snow, below the guesthouse. Hannah didn't blame the woman for being suspicious. Who wasn't, after the events of the past year?

As she backed out onto the road, she noticed Sean didn't get into the truck and figured he'd go back and try again with

Bowie. Would Bowie tell him about her questions about Drew and stonework and old cellar holes? Would he invite more Cameron scrutiny?

"I never should have come out here," Hannah said to herself.

Her car had lost most of its heat. By the time she got it warm again, she'd be back at the café, with the same questions she'd started out with and no answers.

Seventeen

Vivian paused in the soft snow on the bank of the pond. The ducks that had been there all summer and through the fall had vanished. She supposed it was because of the ice and cold, but maybe on some level they'd been aware of the violence in Black Falls and hadn't wanted to be there any longer. It was how *she* felt, but she'd made a conscious decision not to give in to her fear and revulsion and be driven from her dream home in Vermont.

At least this morning. By this afternoon, she could easily change her mind and call a real estate agent.

She hated her conflicting emotions. All these strong emotions, period. She preferred a more sedate, predictable life.

A groomed trail would have been helpful, but she'd enjoyed breaking through the fresh snow. She'd dressed appropriately for the conditions, but the cold was worse than she'd anticipated, freezing her face, chapping her lips. She refused to give in to her discomfort.

She skied over to Lowell, who stood next to a weeping willow in front of an old stone wall. He'd tramped down the road in his boots and then through the snow to the pond.

"Hannah was here," she said. "Did you see her?"

"Not to speak to, no."

"I'm sure that's a huge disappointment."

"Vivian, please. Hannah's an intriguing, lovely woman, but she's not—"

"You've had an eye for her ever since we started to come up here. She's not as pretty as Dominique, though, is she? And Beth with her copper hair and those deep turquoise eyes of hers. Hannah seems rather mousy in comparison."

He reached down and dug snow out of

the top edge of his boot. He had on a leather jacket that was perpetually either too warm or not warm enough for the conditions, never quite right. Typical.

"Are you going to speak?" she asked sharply.

"Hannah is hardworking and intelligent. She's proved herself to everyone in Black Falls. We should applaud her success."

Vivian scoffed at him. "What success? She and two friends own a small Vermont café, and she's been in law school forever. She's finally finished, but she hasn't taken the bar exam yet. She's not working as an attorney."

"Judge Robinson thinks very highly of her." Lowell rose, teetering slightly. He'd have been better off on skis or snowshoes than in boots. "Vivian, I don't have my eye on Hannah or anyone else in Black Falls—or anywhere else for that matter. You do believe me, don't you?"

Vivian felt a little aghast, and annoyed, at his crushed look. "Of course. I didn't mean . . ." She suddenly realized she didn't know what she'd meant. "Sean was with her just now. I think there's something between the two of them. I really do."

"I'd trust your instincts." He raised a gloved hand and pointed at the guesthouse. "Have you talked to Bowie yet this morning?"

"No, I haven't. I think he's a complication for Hannah and Sean. It'll be interesting to see what happens when Sean returns to California. I just don't want us to get caught in the middle."

"I stopped in to see Bowie just now," Lowell said. "I only stayed a minute. His injuries don't seem to bother him or to be impeding his work."

"It's a hazardous occupation, being a stonemason." Vivian repositioned her ski poles in the snow. "I wish he didn't live just up the road. It's unnerving. We're here alone at night. He could just—" She stopped herself, then said, "Anything could happen. I hadn't realized he'd moved back. Did you know?"

"I noticed smoke coming out of his chimney when I took a walk out past his place before Christmas. I assumed he'd moved back but didn't think anything of it."

"I wish you'd told me. If he's got a temper, we don't want to provoke him."

She looked back toward the guesthouse and felt a dryness in her throat, a sense of dread she'd never felt before, even when Kyle Rigby and Melanie Kendall were guests there. But she hadn't known they were killers. Bowie O'Rourke? What was he?

"Everything will be all right, Vivian," Lowell said quietly.

Even his reassurances irritated her. She glared at him. "Just don't start in on me again about getting a dog. I don't want to hear it."

She skied back over to the guesthouse, staying in the snow to the side of the walk as Bowie came out onto the porch. He looked terrible. In addition to his bruises and cuts, his heavily bandaged hand, she noticed his stubble of beard, his torn orange sweatshirt, his muscular build. Although he'd spent only sixty days in jail, he had the air of a hardened ex-convict about him.

"Mrs. Whittaker," he said, his tone polite if not friendly.

"Is everything all right here?" she asked. "I know my husband stopped by, but do you have any questions I can answer?"

"All set."

He barely looked at her, and his distant manner made her wonder if he'd overheard her and Lowell. Well, what of it? She and her husband had been together for decades. They had a way of talking to each other that other people could either understand or not. She didn't care if Bowie O'Rourke disapproved.

Bowie went back inside without further comment, and Vivian headed back to the tracks she'd made skiing down the slope from the farmhouse. Even with a trail, the going was much more difficult going back. She had to fight the wind as well as ski uphill, and seeing Hannah, Sean and Bowie had left her drained and uneasy.

She found Lowell coming out of the small woodshed behind the house. He'd carefully stacked cordwood inside and outside the shed all fall. "You'll fill the wood box, won't you?" Vivian asked him. "I want to keep a fire going all day. Just looking at flames makes me feel warmer. Doesn't it you?"

"Yes, of course."

"You're not even paying attention. Don't just humor me."

He tightened the latch on the shed door.

"Are you sure you can tolerate being here? If you can't, we can leave."

"I can. I refuse . . ." She looked down the slope toward the guesthouse. "The more I think about Bowie, the less I like having him here. Do you suppose he could be involved with the murders?"

"I don't want to believe anyone from here is involved."

"No one does, Lowell, but we have to face reality. Whoever the mastermind of these killers is must be intelligent and calculating. Bowie seems too simple."

"I suppose he could be involved without being the mastermind."

She shuddered but felt a wave of irritation at her husband. "You say that without conviction. You like Bowie, don't you? You think my concerns are ridiculous."

"I didn't say that."

No passion. No emotion whatsoever. She stepped onto the back walk, suddenly feeling trapped in her skis. She couldn't wait to be out of them. "Even if I'm wrong about Hannah and Sean, there's still something going on between her and Bowie," Vivian said, then sighed. "Well, these small-town connections are impossible for an outsider to follow. Joining the local historical society won't change anything. These people will never let us in."

"Would you want to be let in?" Lowell asked.

"I might. You never know. The Camerons and Harpers are interesting families." She breathed in the cold air and took a moment to appreciate the beauty of their spot on the river, the play of light and shadows on the ice and snow, the starkness and stillness of the landscape. "I don't want these killings to ruin this place for us."

Lowell pretended not to hear her and headed to his neat woodpile in front of the shed. Vivian skied over to the back door of the farmhouse to tackle getting her skis off. "I'm going up to shower," she called to him. "Please build a fire before I come back down, won't you?"

He waved to her. "Of course."

She left her skis by the back door and peeled off her winter clothing just inside. She took the stairs up to the master suite, welcoming its neutral colors and clean lines. She hadn't wanted any fussy, clunky country furnishings. She immediately felt more centered. She looked out the window and saw a deer prancing through the leafless brush down by the frozen river. She'd left the bedroom door open and could hear Lowell clanking fireplace tools. The smell of woody smoke soothed her and irritated her at the same time. A *little* smoke was fine, even homey, but he always created too much smoke when he started a fire.

She placed her forehead against the smooth, painted wood trim. Had she ever asked for much in life? A good husband and children. Friends. Holidays. Buying this place had been her idea, but it fit Lowell's fantasies of playing the Vermont country gentleman.

What damn fools they'd been.

As she raised her head, a movement far to her left caught her eye, and she noticed a solitary male figure down by the duck pond. She couldn't see him clearly from this distance, but it had to be Bowie. She stood a moment and watched him.

She heard a sound behind her and turned. Lowell was standing in the bedroom doorway. "Please don't worry, Vivian," he said. "All will be well."

"I just don't want any more disruptions to our lives. These people will never stop searching, digging. The Camerons, the Harpers." She tried to stem a sudden sense of panic—and anger, she thought. Everything about the past five weeks infuriated her. "They'll have their answers, no matter who's hurt in the process. I don't know if I could be so relentless. I think if I had the choice I'd just pretend nothing happened."

Lowell didn't respond for a moment. "Would you have me killed if you could?" he asked quietly.

Vivian gasped. "What a terrible thing to say! Of course not."

He shrugged, standing still in the doorway. "You didn't ask me if I'd have you killed."

"You have a bizarre sense of humor," she said irritably. "Let's not talk about killing."

He looked past her toward the window. "These killers aren't about passion, Vivian. They're just doing a job."

"On behalf of people who *are* about passion."

"Yes," he said, "I suppose you're right."

His shoulders slumped and he turned back into the hall. In another moment,

Vivian heard his footsteps as he headed back downstairs.

She wanted to throw a shoe at him. Why couldn't he ever show some spine?

She peered out the window again, but saw only the wind blowing the fine snow into sunlit drifts.

Lowell sat in his favorite chair in front of the fire, roaring now, not so smoky—more to Vivian's liking. He could hear the shower running upstairs and appreciated having the fire to himself. The big, comfortable room. His wife had decorated it, of course, but he'd approved her choices, the blend of modern and traditional. Neither of them had wanted moose heads on the wall or log-cabin quilts on the beds.

He slowly opened his fingers, giving a low moan at the pain that coursed through his hand. Fortunately, whatever bruising there was was faint, not obviously discoloring the skin.

He shut his eyes, forcing himself to remain calm. He'd always been cerebral and quiet, not one to let emotions intrude on his work. Lately, however, he felt as if his life were spinning out of control and he were hanging on by his fingernails, just trying to survive.

Vivian would just tell him what a fool and a failure he was.

In a few minutes, when he heard her on the stairs, he got to his feet and slipped out to the back hall. He took his coat and walking stick and eased outside, not making a sound. He didn't want her to follow him. He didn't want company right now.

He walked down their long driveway back out to the road that wound along the river. The cold made him feel alive, energized. He continued down to the turnaround, but Bowie's van wasn't there. He must have gone for supplies, or to take a lunch break.

Lowell paused, out of breath.

Vivian's concerns about Bowie weren't an overreaction. *He* was concerned. Bowie O'Rourke was the perfect choice for opportunistic killers looking for an ally in Black Falls—for someone to deal with a potential liability.

Melanie Kendall had become a liability. That was why she was dead now. If Elijah Cameron hadn't killed Kyle Rigby and Kyle had failed in his mission to get rid of Nora Asher and Devin Shay, he, too, would have been a liability, marked for death. Both he and Melanie were professionals who'd understood the score.

The less you know about some things, the better.

Lowell forced himself not to think about matters over which he had no control.

Hannah.

Thinking about her calmed him. She was so brave, so beautiful. Seeing her with Sean Cameron didn't sit well with him. Last night, again just now. Was she in love with Sean? With Bowie?

Were both men in love with her?

Lowell hardly felt the cold anymore. Vivian was right. Sean was everything her husband wasn't.

He continued down the narrow road. It curved close to the river along an old stone wall. Would he have survived here two hundred years ago, with such harsh conditions?

Yes.

He was a survivor.

He pictured Hannah's soft mouth, her

pale eyes and the gentlest spray of freckles on her cheeks. He'd been fascinated with her ever since he'd first walked into Three Sisters Café shortly after it had opened, when its future was still uncertain. He and Vivian had come to Black Falls shortly after the bar fight at O'Rourke's. He'd heard different accounts about Hannah's role. He'd run into Drew Cameron not long after he and Chief Harper had gone to the river hollow to find Bowie.

"Bowie screwed up," Drew had said. "No question. But I have a feeling he's not telling all he knows about why he did what he did."

"Do you think he was protecting someone?"

The older man had shrugged without comment.

Lowell had persisted. "Was he protecting Hannah?"

Again Drew hadn't answered.

Lowell stared out at the ice formations on a bend in the river. What had Hannah seen yesterday at the crypt? What did she suspect?

What did she *know?*

She wasn't as meek as Lowell had thought. He'd expected her to run after she'd heard her name eerily whispered in the isolated cemetery. Instead she'd grabbed a shovel and kept coming, determined to find Bowie. She was strong—in her own way as tough as any Cameron or Harper, if softer, more vulnerable.

Lowell reminded himself that he'd succeeded. Bowie's arrival at the cemetery had caught him by surprise, but he'd managed to hide in time, then thought quickly, acted decisively, and knocked the rocks and debris on him and dealt with Hannah. He'd escaped down the wooded hillside without her or Bowie or Sean Cameron spotting him.

He hadn't intended to take such an enormous risk. It'd just worked out that way. He'd seized the first clear—or what he'd thought was clear—opportunity to retrieve the copper wire he'd stored in the crypt. Now it was safely tucked in his woodshed.

By itself, the wire wasn't incriminating. With black powder, gunpowder, a pile of cell phones—then it would be a problem.

He'd never meant to be an operator, but

he'd done what he'd had to do. He'd proved to himself a thousand times in the past year that he could step up to the plate and get the job done himself when necessary.

He was strong, too. Yes, he was a survivor.

Eighteen

Sean came to a crooked stop at a meter down from Three Sisters Café and didn't bother to straighten out the truck. He didn't feed the meter, either. He was too impatient, and he had no intention of staying in the spot for long. He'd pay the damn parking ticket if he got one.

He launched himself up the sidewalk. The café lunch crowd had geared up, people ordering sandwiches on twelve-grain bread, wraps, quiches, the homemade soup of the day and servings of shepherd's pie, chili and chicken pot pie.

He didn't care. He went in through the

main door and headed down the center hall, under the sweeping stairs to the kitchen.

Dominique Belair came at him, her fists clenched, her brown eyes wide with emotion. “I can’t believe you let her go out there alone.”

“I didn’t let her go alone.”

“She went to see Bowie O’Rourke, didn’t she?”

Reluctant to give an answer, Sean saw that Dominique didn’t need one.

“She did,” Dominique said with a sigh of resignation. “She sees a childhood friend where the rest of us see a man with a temper he can’t always control.”

“Where is Hannah now?”

Her friend clamped her mouth shut without responding. Dominique was the most private of the three “sisters” and, not being a Black Falls native, was an outsider to the good and the bad that came with growing up in a tight-knit small town.

Finally she pointed to the kitchen door that led to the mudroom. “Back there.”

Sean left her alone in the kitchen and headed back out into the hall. He saw Hannah’s jacket hung neatly on a peg in the mudroom and heard the scraping of a chair or stool across the floor in the adjoining pantry. He had no idea what it'd been back in 1835. A place to hang meat, for all he knew.

Hannah had her back to him as she stood on tiptoes on a wood chair and grabbed a can of tomato puree from a high shelf. "I know you're here, Sean," she said without looking around at him.

Holding the can in both arms, she stepped down from the chair. The bruising on her wrist stood out in the storage room light. Sean saw that she had tears in her eyes, but her protective shield was up, too, and he wondered if the emotions she was fighting were more than she could handle. He suddenly wasn't sure he could handle them, either. Best, he thought, to keep an objective distance and focus on what he was there to do.

"Jo called me on my way back here," he said. "She took a good look up at the crypt. She's impressed you and Bowie weren't hurt worse yesterday."

"Did she find anything new?"

"No."

"Frustrated?"

"We'd all be smart not to provoke her right now."

"If you mean by going to see Bowie on my own, I'm not under arrest. Neither is he." Hannah set the tomatoes on a shelf behind her. "You're not afraid of Jo, are you, Sean?"

He grinned. "Jo? I can see her cutting the rope on the tire swing on Elijah when we were kids. She was so mad at him, she climbed up the tree and had at it while he was in the swing."

"And you watched her and let her get away with it."

"She did it before A.J. and I knew what she was up to."

Hannah laughed, tightening the tie on her evergreen apron. "I remember that tire swing. I'd see it when we drove past her house. I was never . . ." She reached for another can on a lower shelf. "Dominique uses locally grown and canned tomatoes when she can. Beth doesn't care."

"I wish I had memories of you in a tire swing, squealing with laughter, hair flying." Sean felt a pang of regret that caught him by surprise. “We grew up just down the road from the Harpers. It was natural for us to get together as kids.”

“Yes, and there’s a bond now among you all that was formed during your childhood.”

“Just as there is between you and Bowie.”

“All this drama, Sean,” she said, turning back to him with the second can of tomatoes. “No wonder you’re a millionaire. Who can win against you?”

He winked at her. “Now you’re with the program.”

“You’re afraid Bowie will hurt me, and I’m not.”

He nodded to her injured cheek and wrist. “Maybe he did hurt you.”

“I don’t believe that,” she said quietly. “I’m not so sure you do, either. If you thought he was dangerous, why did you come barreling across the cemetery? You saw his van. How’d you know Bowie wouldn’t attack you?”

“I didn’t know. I was only thinking about getting to you.”

Color rose in her cheeks, and she quickly picked up her other can. “Something you might want to keep in mind when you all start in on me about being impulsive and reckless. I guess we're both lucky things worked out the way they did."

"You don't think I could have taken on Bowie?" Sean asked, amused.

"That's not what I said. If he and I both were attacked, then someone else was out there."

"All the more reason for me to have been there with you."

Hannah held her tomato cans close to her chest. She was slim, smart and one who prided herself on not needing anything from anyone. Maybe it was the tension of knowing she was holding back on him that had him noticing everything about her—had him wanting to keep her safe. He'd never met anyone more capable or self-reliant, but she looked so small standing there with her can of tomato puree. Even back in high school, she'd had a way of tying him in knots.

He'd never liked being tied up in knots. He liked having things straightforward, and he liked being in control as much as she did.

"You went out there this morning because

you think Bowie knows something," Sean said, forcing any gruffness out of his voice. "But you're not sure, and you don't want to focus attention on him if you're wrong—"

"I already got all you Camerons focused on him."

"He got us focused on him himself."

"How, by returning home?"

"You're not naive," Sean said. "You know that Bowie's . . ."

"What? From the wrong side of town? Yes, Sean, that I do know, because I am, too."

He fought a surge of exasperation at the same time he wanted to take her into his arms and carry her upstairs to her apartment. Toby and Devin could be there, and Dominique was down in the café kitchen with her knives and doubts about him and his motives.

Was Hannah ever alone—and how long had it been since she'd had a man in her life?

Sean watched her, acknowledging a disturbing thought. Had she gone to O'Rourke's in March in part because she'd hoped Bowie would turn up? Now that he was back in town, was she tempted to strike up a relationship with him?

Just as well he was heading back to California in the morning. As clear-eyed as he was in business and on a fire call, he'd never been clear-eyed where Hannah Shay was concerned.

"All I'm asking," he said, noticing a few strands of her hair slipping from her ponytail into her face, "is for you to trust me. We're not on opposite sides."

She looked down at her bruised wrist. "I do trust you, Sean." Any anger and defensiveness seemed to have drained out of her. "I appreciate what you're doing for Devin. You've worked hard and done well. Good for you."

"Feel even less guilty about sending me the bill for the repairs to the cellar?"

Her eyes finally sparked with humor. "I never did feel guilty."

"I should have known." He laughed and tucked the stray hairs behind her ear, the bruising on her face a reminder of what was at stake if she were wrong about Bowie O'Rourke. "I'm going up to the lodge if you decide to—"

"Come clean?"

He smiled, dropping his hand back to his side. "That's one way of putting it."

"I have work to do here. I also promised Devin and Toby we'd do something special for dinner on their last night here."

She seemed determined not to dampen her brothers' excitement, but Sean saw how much she'd miss them. He wished he could think of something to say to make her feel better but just left her to her work and returned to the café dining room.

The lunch crowd had dissipated, but Rose was there, in front of a riverside window, staring down at the snow and ice. She didn't look up as he stood next to her. "You're a bastard, Sean, you know that?"

"That seems to be the general consensus today."

She turned and glared at him. "Hannah's been half in love with you since ninth grade, and you and A.J. and Elijah are all playing on that because you think she's got some insight or information about these killers."

"Rose, what the hell's the matter with you?"

She didn't seem to hear him. "You're going to break her damn heart, Sean."

He frowned at his sister and said nothing.

"You, Elijah and A.J. are taking your frustrations with the slow pace of the investigation out on Hannah. She's an easy target." Rose shifted her gaze back to the river. "You're all bastards. All three of you."

"Anything else?"

"You're leaving tomorrow and taking her brothers with you. Hannah will be here alone."

"She won't be alone. She has you, Dominique and Beth and half the cops in town are here on a daily basis. Come on, Rose. Get a grip. Hannah's never been alone."

"I mean alone here. In this building. At night. She's never lived by herself. Even when she rented a room at Judge Robinson's, he and Ginny were around."

"You live by yourself."

"That's different." She inhaled, glancing up at him with a directness that immediately struck him as feigned, as if she were desperate to have him think she had nothing to hide. "I'm used to it."

"Rose, what's going on with you?"

"Other than Pop getting murdered and

people blown up and shot and more killings likely in the works?"

Sean felt a jolt of fear for his sister. "Rose . . . what's wrong?"

She looked back out the window, softening ever so slightly. "What's your big hurry to get back to California?"

"I only came out here for Christmas. I stay in touch with the investigation. If I need to be back here, I'll get on a plane. I have responsibilities there." He tried to smile and ease the tension between them. "And it's cold here."

"But Hannah—"

"She's tougher than most people think."

His sister angled her eyes at him, still combative and tense. "So that means you can lead her on for your own purposes and then dump her?"

Sean settled back on his heels. "Who are we talking about here, Rose?"

"I've said my piece. You know where I'm coming from."

She bolted across the café, nearly knocking over Myrtle Smith, who had on a down vest, a heavy wool sweater and pants and boots with thick soles. No gloves. She waved her fingers, the nails painted a deep red, as she joined him at the window. "I just had a manicure here in town. Not bad. It's all that saves me from turning into a mountain woman. I swore I wouldn't cave and invest in a parka, but I hit the lodge shop today. I noticed your brother sells the pricey stuff there and wears Carhartt himself."

Sean had come to appreciate Myrtle's crusty charm, as well as her keen, uncompromising instincts as a reporter. "The lodge offers a range of prices."

"Very diplomatic of you. You own this building, right?" She didn't wait for him to answer. "Here's what I think. Get rid of the gallery across the hall. It's struggling, and the owners just need a nudge to move to a cheaper place. Then expand the café and add a dinner service on that side of the house. There's a working fireplace over there. It could be nice. Intimate."

"I don't run either business—"

"But you have influence." She gave a small moan. "Listen to me. I'm desperate. I'm bored out of my mind."

"You could go home to Washington."

"I could," she said without looking at him.

He was silent a moment. “It’s still hard, isn’t it?” he asked.

She turned to him with a smile that didn’t reach her eyes. “Ever wish you’d taken a different path in life? Never mind. You’re too young.”

“Grit tells me you’re not a romantic and I shouldn’t be fooled.”

“He’s suffering. The leg’s bad, but the friend he lost in Afghanistan still weighs on his mind. Moose Ferrerra. He was a SEAL, too. His wife had a baby boy after he died and named him for Grit and Elijah. Did you know that?”

“No, I didn’t.”

“I’ve seen a lot of tragedy in my work, but that one . . .” She sighed again and turned back to the window. “Grit’s just a kid. I should quit complaining.”

“You had a friend who was killed by this network.”

“Andrei. He was intense, interesting. One of my flings. It wouldn’t have lasted, but he didn’t deserve to have his toothpaste poisoned. Someone paid someone to make it happen.” She glanced up at Sean, her lavender eyes shimmering with barely suppressed anger. “I want them all.

Who paid to have him killed, who arranged for someone to kill him, who did the killing."

"The police know Rigby and Kendall were in London when Petrov was killed."

"What if they met another killer there? I want everything. Every detail." She resumed staring out the tall window. "What about you? Anyone else besides your father who could be a part of this thing?"

"Do you have someone in mind?"

Her eyes were a dark lavender as she glanced sideways at him. "Think about giving the gallery the boot. You'd be doing them a favor."

Nineteen

A fire roared in the big stone fireplace just down from the front desk of Black Falls Lodge. Sean stood with Elijah facing the flames. On a normal winter day, the comfortable couches and chairs behind them would attract guests settling in with a book or wanting an afternoon nap. Sean was staying in one of the cottages and had insisted on paying full price. He couldn't bring himself to sleep at his childhood home, and he wasn't about to intrude on Elijah and Jo at the lake or sleep in one of Jo's cabins. Rose didn't give any indication she'd wanted company.

"Do you and Jo always stay at your house," he asked Elijah, "or do you ever stay in the cabin where you ran off to, for old times' sake?"

"It's cold in the cabin. Jo likes her creature comforts."

"I thought you were a creature comfort."

Elijah rolled his eyes. "Miss having you around here all the time, brother."

Sean managed a laugh. Their father had surprised his offspring by leaving the dozen run-down cabins and thirty-five acres on the lake to Jo. He'd bought them from old Pete Harper, her grandfather's brother, who hadn't touched the property in decades and had since died. Everyone in Black Falls—including the Cameron siblings—had expected the land to go to the lodge. A.J. had even drawn up preliminary plans for what to do with the lakefront property. Elijah's house, which he'd built himself when he was home on leave over the past three years, had no lake frontage. He had to go on Jo's land. Which he did, and would have even if he weren't sleeping with her.

"You two really engaged?" Sean asked.

"I asked her to marry me, and she said

yes." Elijah didn't look up from the flames. He'd been pensive since Sean had found him there. After a long silence, he continued, "It was close up on the mountain. Rigby could have killed us all."

"You and Jo didn't let that happen."

"I almost lost her."

Sean nodded. Elijah wasn't a brooder, but he was thoughtful. Down the hall, A.J.'s four-year-old son and two-year-old daughter squealed and laughed in the main dining room, both parents with them.

"What's on your mind, Elijah?" Sean asked.

"Maybe by killing Rigby I lost the chance to stop more murders."

"We can't second-guess ourselves," Jo said, walking down the hall from the dining room in a sweater, jeans and boots. "We did what we had to do to get off the mountain alive." She narrowed her turquoise eyes on Sean. "Get anything more out of Hannah?"

"No, but I'm doing this because of her, not for any other reason."

"Understood."

Grit Taylor walked in through the lodge's main door and headed over to the fire. He put his hands out toward the flames. "Hannah Shay's here. Her car's stuck on ice on that mess you all call a parking lot. She'll spin her way out of it and be in a fine mood by the time she gets in here."

Elijah regarded his friend with a mix of amusement and respect. "Any theories about what's going on, Grit?"

Grit's gaze settled on Sean and then shifted back to Elijah. "Plenty. Doesn't mean any of them is worth spit." He opened and closed his fingers, the fire glowing in his dark eyes as he glanced again at Sean. "Are you still planning to head back to California tomorrow?"

"Yes."

"Got a New Year's party to attend?"

"Yes, but that's not why I'm going back."

"Fire season's already peaked, hasn't it?"

"It normally peaks in October," Sean said, "but fires can flare up anytime if the conditions are favorable."

Grit adjusted his stance, as if his leg hurt. "You still get out there, jump out of a plane to fight fires?"

"When needed." Sean eased back away from the massive fireplace. A giant stuffed moose—a fake one—stood in the corner.

"You did SEAL training in Southern California. You must know about wildfires in remote areas."

"Yep. Some. Your partner—he's a smoke jumper, too?"

"That's right. Doing research, Grit?"

"Me? Nah. Just yakking while I warm up and wait for Hannah. There's nothing the cops don't know about any of us by now. Hell, if we put a tack on our teacher's seat in fourth grade, Jo and Company know about it."

Jo had gone very still but didn't speak. Sean figured Grit's questions had sparked her interest, too. Maybe things had gotten to the point that none of them could make idle talk without drawing suspicion, but Grit wasn't even being subtle.

Elijah eased in next to the man he'd fought with—had almost died with. "Has our friend in Washington been in touch again?"

"Some people don't like to leave well enough alone," Grit said cryptically. He nodded at the main door as it opened. "What do you know, here comes one who does just that."

"Hannah's fearless," Jo said. "It's what scares me about her."

"That I understand." Grit pulled his hands from the fire and shoved them into the pockets of his jacket. "I'll go make myself scarce. Let me know if you three can't handle our would-be prosecutor and need my help."

He headed down the hall toward the sounds of the young, squealing Camerons. Hannah entered the lodge, her coat unzipped, her head bare, her long, fine hair pulled back. Sean noticed that some of the anger had gone out of her, but his reaction to her unnerved him. This time, all he wanted to do was sweep her away to his cottage through the snowy meadow, light a fire in the fireplace there and keep her safe.

Well. That wasn't all.

He wanted to make love to her. He avoided glancing at his brother or Jo lest it showed in his eyes just what he was thinking.

"I'm not staying," Hannah said as she approached the fire, acknowledging him, Jo and Elijah with a stiff smile. "Nice to see you all. I'll just get straight to the point. I came to tell you that I got to thinking about the foundation at your father's cabin and decided to check it out. My father was a stonemason. A good one. I thought . . ."

When she stopped, Elijah stepped closer to her. "Go on."

Her bruised cheek stood out against the glow of the fire. "I've been wondering how Drew found that old cellar hole and if he could have handled rebuilding the foundation on his own. I went up to see if being there would help me figure out the answers. It didn't. That's it. That's all I know."

No one said anything. Sean realized they were fixed on Hannah. No wonder she was defensive and felt isolated, as if they were ganging up on her.

He couldn't let that deter him, and finally he said, "What about Bowie?"

"What about him, Sean?"

"He walked into the café yesterday, and you bolted up the mountain in twenty-degree weather by yourself."

"One thing doesn't necessarily have to do with the other."

"In this case—"

"I used to go out hunting cellar holes with my father as a kid. Bowie did, too. After my father died, I'd go out in the woods by myself. I'd find an old cellar hole and see a rosebush still growing by a stone wall, and I'd imagine myself back in time." She paused. "I remember seeing your dad and Elijah hiking up on the mountain."

"I don't remember that," Elijah said.

"You never knew I was there. I was hiding by a stone wall. Your father had you go on ahead, and he came back to me and saw me home."

"How old were you?"

"Thirteen. That means you were seventeen."

"Did you ever find the cellar hole where Drew built his cabin?" Jo interjected.

Hannah shook her head. "No, I didn't. I don't know if anyone else did."

"Bowie or your father, you mean."

Her turquoise eyes were cool and controlled, but Hannah reacted by straightening her spine, as if she knew Jo suspected her, knew she was still keeping secrets.

Jo grabbed a black iron poker and stirred the coals in the fire as she spoke. "You hike up to the cabin and not thirty minutes after you're back down the mountain, you hear someone calling your name, and you're knocked over in the cemetery."

"Correct."

Jo set the poker back on its rack. "You're protective of your brothers. Anyone in your position would be."

"My position?"

"Devin's just been through an ordeal. He was suspected of stalking another teenager and stealing—"

"But he didn't stalk Nora, and he didn't steal. He was framed."

"He had a rough time after he found Drew's body on Cameron Mountain. He was in some trouble—"

"I'm not making excuses for him."

Sean exchanged a look with Elijah, but neither of them spoke, letting the federal agent and the budding lawyer go.

"Devin found Drew when no one else could," Jo said, "but he should have told one of us."

"I know." Hannah's voice was just above a whisper. "I'd give anything if I'd gone up the mountain instead of him. If I'd at least been with him."

Jo didn't relent. "Then you of all people know that you should tell us what's on your mind now, Hannah. What you know, what you theorize, what you suspect. What you're afraid of."

Hannah tightened her hands into fists. Sean noticed her wince in pain and figured she must have momentarily forgotten about her injured wrist. She didn't so much as glance at either him or Elijah. "What else, Agent Harper?" she asked.

"How well do your brothers know Bowie?"

"They hardly know him at all," Hannah said, guarded, her emotions contained.

"You want Bowie to be innocent."

"Of course. Don't you?"

"That's not the point."

Elijah eased in next to Jo and winked at Hannah. "You don't like being wrong, Hannah," he said. "Never have. But we all are wrong sometimes."

She shifted to Sean. "What time do you need Toby and Devin to be ready?"

Sean decided just to answer her. "I'll pick them up at seven."

"They'll be waiting for you on the front steps." She turned back to Jo. "I have nothing to hide. I was curious about the cabin's stonework and checked it out. Maybe we'll never know how Drew found that cellar hole, or how he managed to build the cabin on his own."

"Or how those two killers found out about it," Jo said quietly. "Do you have a theory of your own, Hannah?"

"I imagine everyone in Black Falls has a theory."

Jo gritted her teeth visibly. "That's not an answer."

"I told you what I know," Hannah said. "Now, if you'll excuse me . . ."

No one stopped her as she walked back to the entrance. Once the door shut firmly behind her, Elijah fastened his gaze on Sean. "Go," he said to his younger brother. "Talk to her."

Jo looked more exasperated. "Try to get past that stubborn pride of hers and make her understand we're on the same side."

"Maybe we're not," Sean said. "Just now, Jo. What do you know?"

Her eyes were distant. "Ask Hannah about her father," she said, and turned, shutting out even Elijah as she gazed at the fire.

Twenty

Sean parked in the driveway of the house he owned in Black Falls, not on the street this time. When he got out of Elijah's truck, the wind was even worse than up on the ridge, howling down from the summit of Cameron Mountain as if their father himself were steering it, trying to tell his third-born something—something he'd been trying to get through to him for a long time, but Sean kept missing it.

Too many ghosts in Black Falls, he thought, heading in through the mudroom.

The cellar door was open. He heard a

scraping sound and went down the dusty stairs.

Hannah was moving an old oak desk near the trunk and shelves of canning jars. "Hello, Sean," she said, pointing vaguely at the floor. "I'm clearing space so Bowie can start work on the leak."

"When does he start?"

"I'm not sure yet," she said. "After you all head out to California. I first noticed the leak this fall. I'd open up the bulkhead periodically to get some air in here and let things dry out. There wasn't much damage."

"Why didn't you have Bowie look at it then?"

She stood up from the desk, her front smeared with thick dust. "He wasn't living in town at the time. He hadn't started work on the culvert up at the cemetery yet. By then . . ." Her shrug was anything but casual. "It was right after Thanksgiving. I had enough to think about."

"If he'd noticed the bulkhead open and stopped by out of curiosity, would you have noticed?"

"I noticed yesterday, didn't I?" She drew a fingertip across the layer of dust on top of the desk. "I know what you're getting at, Sean. I've had the same thought. It's hard to believe Kyle Rigby or Melanie Kendall would risk stealing money from the café to set Devin up. Why not find an easier way? Whoever was paying them didn't want his and Nora's deaths seen as murders by a stranger. Two teenagers overwhelmed by their own problems get lost on Cameron Mountain . . ." She trailed off and gave the desk a shove with her slim hips.

"We can talk about this later," Sean said. "Would you like some help with that desk?"

"No, I think there's enough room for Bowie to get back here. He can move whatever else he needs out of the way himself. I'm just looking for distractions." She glanced around the dank cellar. "Tourists who stop at the café love that it's in an old house. They're drawn to the sense of history here. Is that why you bought it?"

"I didn't think much about it."

"Then it was just a good investment opportunity?"

He smiled. "It's not that good an investment. From what you've told me about your to-do list—"

"Oh, my to-do list doesn't even scratch the surface of what this place needs."

Sean settled his gaze on her and noted she was paler than usual, but she looked away, ducking behind the desk, squeezing between it and the old trunk as she stepped back under the dim lightbulb. She was closer to him now. He could see dust on her jeans and shoes, even a few cobwebs.

She seemed unaware of his scrutiny. "Bowie's place on the river is of no historic consequence, but it's an old part of town," she said. "He's fixing it up. I'm surprised he wanted to go back there. He didn't have it easy as a kid. Everyone loved his father, but they didn't know what he was like in private—especially with his son."

"It's hard to love people who aren't good for you. Who hurt you."

Hannah brushed off the front of her shirt. "Bowie's escape was to hunt for old cellar holes. It got him interested in historic stonework."

Sean glanced at the old cellar with its stone foundation. The exterior of the house was brick, and there was a hundred-year-old stone wall out back. The former tavern up at Four Corners had an old stone foundation and stone walls, too. He was familiar with "historic" stonework.

Tobias Shay, Sean remembered, had laid the stone terrace at the lodge.

He rubbed a rough, whole stone on the foundation, then turned back to Hannah, knowing he had to ask. "What was your father's relationship with Bowie?"

Her pale, pretty eyes were suddenly distant. "Did Jo tell you to ask me about him?"

Sean nodded. "She did, yes."

Hannah remained very still. "He and Bowie got along well. He died when I was fourteen and Bowie was eighteen. He ran his car into a tree on an icy road."

"I remember."

Her expression was impossible to read, deliberately so, he thought. "Do you remember anything else about him?" she asked.

"I was seventeen—"

"No," she said, answering for him, without a trace of bitterness. "There's no reason you should. Most people don't remember my father, and those who do don't talk about him. *I* don't talk about him. Devin and Toby have no memories of him at all." With one hand, she batted the long string on the lightbulb and watched it swing into the dusty air. “I figure Jo looked him up or talked to her father about him.”

“Why Chief Harper?” Sean asked.

Hannah didn’t hesitate. “My father served time in prison when I was small. It’s not a secret—it’s just not something anyone ever talks about. People didn’t even talk about it when he was alive.”

Sean recalled vague references to Hannah’s father, a gifted stonemason, having a troubled past. “Jo’s thorough,” he said. “It’s her job.”

“I understand that. I figured when I was up at the lodge that she either knew about my father and hadn’t thought about him until Bowie turned up, or she asked her father. Chief Harper arrested my father at least twice.”

“What did he do?”

Her cheeks were pink now, her emotions high if in check. “Broke the law.”

“Hannah—”

“I try to focus on the good times I had with my father. He convinced my mother he’d gotten his act together when I was ten. She took him back, and they had Devin and Toby.”

"Did he get into trouble again after that?"

"Not that I know of."

"When Nora Asher talked to Jo and Elijah after their ordeal on the mountain, she mentioned that Devin had told her that his father had abandoned his family."

"He must have heard that around town. I guess it's true in a way, isn't it? He never abandoned Devin and Toby, but he did my mother and me by doing stupid things and ending up behind bars."

Sean considered her words, tried to be objective about them—about her. It wasn't easy. "It's also possible Rigby played up your father's past and put it out there to help raise suspicions against Devin."

"Maybe. I don't know. I always studied hard and knew that getting a good education was my path to a different life than what my parents had. My father encouraged me. He was beset by demons I'll never understand, but he didn't want me to make the same mistakes he had."

"You're worried about your brothers," Sean said, seeing it now. "You don't want them in trouble."

She grabbed a rag that hung on a nail and returned to the desk, dusting its scarred surface. “I hope going to California is the right choice for them.”

“They’ll figure that out for themselves.”

“They don’t have the same upbringing you’d had when you left Black Falls.”

“Not the same,” Sean said, “but Devin and Toby know they have you behind them. Trust them. Trust yourself.”

“I wish it were that simple.” She carefully wiped off the top of the desk. “I don’t know why I’m bothering. It’ll be dusty again in a day down here.”

“Hannah, you’re an emotional mess.”

“Just get my brothers safely to California.”

“You could go with them.”

She shook her head. “I can’t. Not now. The next few days will be busy at the café, and then I have to get organized and start studying for the bar. Plus, Bowie will be working on the leak.” She made an attempt at a smile. “I keep hoping to find hidden treasure down here, but so far, there’s just a lot of junk and spiderwebs.”

“Would you tell anyone if you found treasure?”

This time, her eyes gleamed as she smiled. “I could buy a house next to yours in Beverly Hills and let you wonder how I got the money, except that'd never work. There are no secrets in Black Falls. The truth would find its way to you in California."

"There are loads of secrets in Black Falls. They're just not that easy to keep."

She softened, even laughed a little. "Come on. I assume you're having dinner at the lodge or out at Elijah's, but I can at least give you one of our New Year's cup-cakes." As she started past him for the stairs, she stopped next to him abruptly. "Your plane—do you fly it yourself?"

"Not yet. I'm still learning."

"Is there nothing you can't do, Sean Cameron?"

Her tone was light, but he saw the dis-coloration on her cheek and the pain in her eyes, even as she smiled. "Figure you out," he said, brushing his fingertip along the edge of her jaw. "I think I've been try-ing to figure you out since Latin class."

"You hated Latin."

"Yeah, I did."

He tucked a finger under her chin, and when she didn't run for the stairs, he low-ered his mouth to hers. "Hannah," he whis-pered, kissing her gently. She didn't back away from his kiss or, at first, quite return it. Then she put her hand on his hip and kissed him back—but only for a half second, just long enough, he thought, to let him know that she wanted more.

She stood up straight and swiped at a cobweb above her with a shudder. "I've gotten used to dealing with spiders," she said, "but that doesn't mean I like them."

Sean kept his gaze on her. "You can't pretend this isn't happening."

She grinned at him. "Yes, I can. I have a favor to ask you. And I didn't let you kiss me because of it."

"You wanted that kiss," he said.

"Well, yes. Yes, I did, because it's been just that crazy around here." She seemed suddenly self-conscious. "I can't deny or begrudge my brothers this chance in their lives, or blame them for wanting to get out of here, especially after what's happened. Even without what happened—what can I offer them?"

"You're their sister."

"I don't have a house in Beverly Hills with a pool," she said lightly.

"They'll miss you." Sean brushed the

back of his hand over her cheek and onto her hair and was glad when she didn't bolt for the stairs. "They're teenagers. They're not necessarily good at expressing that sort of thing."

"It's not as if I haven't known this day was coming. I *want* Toby and Devin both to figure out their lives."

"You have your own life to figure out." He thought of his sister's accusation about breaking Hannah's heart and wished he hadn't come down here—even as he acknowledged that he wanted to kiss her again.

"When your brothers are in California and you're here alone . . ." Sean hesitated, struggling to find the right words. "There's still a killer out there. Don't try to be a prosecutor before it's time. You need to back off."

"You can tell Jo that my father was a positive influence on Bowie. Not a negative one. Or she can ask me, and I'll tell her myself."

"You can trust me, Hannah. I hope you know that."

"Do you trust me?"

"It's not just a question of trust."

"I should go," she said.

"Hannah—"

But she finally ran for the stairs, taking them two at a time, fast.

Sean moved the damn desk, just to get rid of some of his pent-up energy, then turned out the light and headed upstairs.

Rose was waiting for him in the hall, frowning, eyebrows raised in suspicion as she spotted Sean. Ranger lay obediently at her feet. The golden retriever wagged his tale when he saw Sean, but his sister didn't seem to take it as a vote of approval. "I'm decorating cupcakes with Beth, Dominique and Hannah," Rose said. "They threatened to kidnap me if I didn't get out of the house."

Sean could hear Beth and Dominique laughing in the kitchen.

Girls' night.

"Then," Rose added, her tone hardening, "I'm going up to the lodge and out to the lake and throttling Jo and my three big brothers. Get off Hannah's case, all of you. She's Bowie O'Rourke's friend, maybe the only friend he has left in the world. That should be commended instead of turned into a source of suspicion."

Sean scrutinized his sister. "Rose? What the hell are you talking about?"

"I'm throttling you first. In the meantime—" She smiled, although her eyes were still fiery. "Dominique's buttercream frosting awaits."

She headed for the kitchen. Ranger stayed put in the hall. Sean stepped over him and went into the mudroom. He wasn't going near Rose and her friends and the cupcake decorating.

Devin was coming in from the back with a duffel bag he'd borrowed from Elijah. He looked nervous as well as excited.

Sean didn't blame him.

It wasn't easy to think about leaving Hannah behind in Black Falls.

Hannah dipped a finger into the buttercream frosting heaped atop her chocolate cupcake. She knew that Dominique, Beth and Rose weren't there decorating cupcakes because of the café.

They were there because her brothers were leaving in the morning.

Rose sat on a high stool at the worktable, a tiny jar of sparkling silver stars in hand. "I love the smell of baking cakes," she said happily, then turned to Hannah, her Cameron blue eyes serious. "Sean can be a heel, you know."

Beth set a cookie tray in the stainless-steel sink. "Pardon me for saying so, but it's true. He owns property in town, but that doesn't mean he ever plans to come back here to live."

Hannah licked the frosting off her finger, aware of her friends' scrutiny. "No worries, my friends. There's nothing between Sean and me."

"Ha," Beth said.

"Okay, maybe a momentary thing because we were in a dark cellar and covered in cobwebs."

Dominique raised her dark eyebrows. "Cobwebs?"

"He *is* cute," Beth said.

"All the Cameron men are dreamy," Dominique added, as only she could.

Rose groaned. "Cute? Dreamy? Try tripping over their size-twelve shoes at the bottom of the stairs."

"Try coming between them and something they want," Beth added.

"Or hurting one of their own," Hannah said.

Rose averted her eyes. She looked agonized, but Hannah said nothing, although she was more and more certain her friend was fighting off the aftereffects of a failed love affair on the road. There'd been hints, but Hannah knew Rose well enough to be cautious about confronting her. Rose was very private and naturally solitary, and she was still angry and grief-stricken over her father's death.

Whatever romantic disaster Rose had experienced, Hannah doubted the Cameron men had a clue. As much as they might argue, A.J., Elijah and Sean wouldn't be happy with any man who had broken their baby sister's heart, and Rose would know to keep them away from whoever it was.

"When you're ready, we can talk," Hannah whispered. "I know it's torture for you to confide in anyone."

"Thanks," Rose said under her breath.

Beth and Dominique either didn't hear the exchange or pretended not to.

For the next hour, they turned their attention to cupcakes and laughter, as if there were nothing more pressing on their minds than frosting, sprinkles and little silver stars. Hannah welcomed the show of support and friendship. It would make saying goodbye to her brothers in the morning easier knowing she had these women behind her.

And saying goodbye to Sean, she thought. She'd let herself go too far with him when she knew he'd be back in Beverly Hills in twenty-four hours, by his pool, making deals, attacking fires.

Rose left, and Beth and Dominique helped Hannah pick out the boys' favorite café offerings for a winter smorgasbord and put together goody bags for their trip, then helped carry everything upstairs. Devin and Toby both had their stuff heaped in the living room, their excitement about their upcoming adventure obvious as they greeted the three "sisters."

"Watch it," Beth said good-naturedly, "Hannah can turn your bedroom into a sewing room while you're gone. What if all that winter warmth and sunshine gets to you?"

They just grinned at her. After she and Dominique left, Devin turned serious. "Toby and I have to ask you something before we leave," he said.

Hannah sank onto the couch. “All right. What’s on your mind?”

Devin remained on his feet, rubbing the back of his neck. Toby rubbed his thumb on a scratch on a bike helmet in his lap. Whatever they needed to talk to her about, it was making them uncomfortable.

Finally Devin plopped down on a chair opposite her. “Hannah, were you and Bowie O’Rourke ever—are you now—you know . . .” He squirmed. “Romantically involved?”

Of all the things that had run through her head, that was one of the least intrusive and upsetting. They could, for instance, Hannah thought, have asked her about Sean Cameron. She shook her head. “No. No romance. Never in the past and not now. I haven’t seen that much of Bowie in recent years, but he’s more like an older brother to me than anything else.”

“The Camerons don’t trust him,” Toby blurted, looking up from his helmet.

“The Camerons are hard on everyone,” she said, then added diplomatically, “but they’re hardest on themselves.”

Devin was watching her. It would be a mistake, she knew, to think his slumped posture meant he was disinterested—or satisfied with her answers. Her brother noticed everything. "A.J., Elijah and Sean were all three at O'Rourke's when Bowie—"

"Yes," Hannah said, "they were."

Devin's pale blue eyes stayed on her. "We've heard stories about what happened."

Meaning stories about what Derek Cutshaw and his friends had said. She'd never discussed the specifics of that night with Devin and Toby and had no intention of doing so now. "People love to tell stories," she said, rising. "I'll get dinner on the table while you two finish up in here."

Both Toby and Devin got to their feet. "Hannah," Toby said, "Devin and I have talked, and we'll postpone California if—"

"*No*. No cold feet. I'll get out there to see you. I have some money saved. I'll take a break from studying." She smiled at them. "Even if Judge Robinson is watching me like a hawk and won't want me to."

"I'm glad he doesn't live far from here," Devin said.

"Don't worry about me. After yesterday, I'll be on Cameron radar for a while." She suddenly noticed everything in the room that belonged to her brothers and would remind her of them when they were gone. "If you hate California, I'll get you back here."

As she headed for the kitchen and unloaded shepherd's pie, chili, salads and cupcakes, she knew they wouldn't hate it. Sean had never come back to Black Falls to live once he got out west. Why should her brothers?

Devin and Toby were up at six and on the sidewalk in front of the house before seven. It wasn't yet light out. They'd set all their stuff in the hall before they'd gone to bed. Devin just had the duffel bag he'd borrowed from Elijah. Toby had all his biking paraphernalia—helmets, gloves, goggles, repair kits—as well as his racing bike, a full-suspension model he'd saved for.

"It's a good thing Sean's taking you with him," Hannah said, grinning at the pile of equipment. "It would have cost a fortune to ship all this out to California with you."

"I probably would have sold some of it and just bought new out there." Toby shivered in the frosty air. "I am definitely not going to miss zero-degree weather."

Their excitement was palpable as Sean and Elijah pulled up to the curb promptly at seven, as promised. They were in the lodge van, Elijah behind the wheel to drive them to the airport where Sean's plane awaited them. Hannah helped her brothers load up their stuff and didn't embarrass them by hugging them goodbye.

Sean stood next to her as Devin and Toby climbed into the back of the van. He had his coat unbuttoned, as if he knew he didn't have to be out in the cold again for a while. He started to speak, but Hannah jumped in before he could get a word out. "Have a safe flight," she said quickly, then forced a smile. "Devin and Toby promised to call me when you land."

His blue eyes narrowed in the gray early-morning light. "It'll happen."

Meaning he'd make sure her brothers didn't get carried away with their excitement about their adventure and forget.

"You have my numbers," he said. "Call anytime."

She wasn't sure what he meant but didn't ask. "I will. Thanks."

He hesitated, then got into the front passenger seat next to Elijah. Devin and Toby were laughing now, and they both turned and blew her silly kisses, as they had when they were little boys and barely realized how much older she was.

Hannah laughed and blew kisses back to them.

Then the wind blew, and she groaned at the cold and fought back tears as she ran inside to the warm café kitchen, Beth, Dominique and their work of the morning.

Twenty-One

Four days later—January 2—Black Falls, Vermont

Grit woke up on the second day of the new year to the same dark and cold he'd woken up to on the first day of the new year and the last day of the old year. A.J. and Lauren Cameron had set off fireworks up at Black Falls Lodge, as they did every New Year's Eve. Elijah had dragged Grit up there. It was minus two outside, but he'd liked looking at the stars in the black Vermont sky.

The fireworks were fine. A couple of guests from the lodge, all bundled up in their Patagonia coats, had heard that he was a SEAL and Elijah a Special Forces soldier and had asked them if the fireworks bothered them. Elijah had politely said he liked fireworks. He hadn't been home for them in years.

Grit had been tempted to take the head off a nearby snowman and shove it down their pants.

He was in that kind of mood.

"Ah, Moose," he said aloud, "where the hell are you when I need you?"

Moose didn't answer, and Grit decided it was okay. Michael "Moose" Ferrerra was at peace.

Grit climbed out of bed, performed his morning routine, which now included cursing the cold, the dark, the killers who were dead, the killers who remained elusive and—most of all—woodstoves.

He'd really come to hate woodstoves.

He was tempted to call Admiral Jenkins back—the admiral's last message included a threat to send MPs after him—but Myrtle had called two minutes before Grit was fully awake with instructions for his morning.

Per those instructions, he left a note on his bed for Jo and Elijah that he was on an errand. Myrtle hadn't considered a car.

He borrowed Jo's without her permission—he figured she wouldn't mind—and drove up to Black Falls Lodge. Myrtle was waiting on the front walk in her new parka.

"Drive me to the village," she said. "Don't talk. Why'd you borrow a Secret Service agent's car? What if it's bugged?"

Grit grinned at her. "You and the drama. Being up here's getting to you, too, isn't it? One of these days we'll have to go back to Washington and sort out our lives."

"Let's just hope we don't go back in handcuffs."

Again per her instructions, he drove her into the village. The sun was up. It was a bright, sparkling, bone-chilling morning in the Green Mountain State. Grit parked next to a snowbank. Myrtle complained she couldn't get out and launched into a tirade about ice, snow, plows and town budgets, and he pulled up a few yards to where someone had shoveled a cutout in the snowbank to the sidewalk.

"You want to tell me what's going on?" Grit asked her.

"In my next life, I'm managing a spa. I

swear." She kept her gaze forward. "We'll talk on the sidewalk. I'm serious about this car."

She got out, and Grit backed up and parked. He walked on the street up to the cutout and met her on the sidewalk. His leg hurt this morning. He ignored the pain as Myrtle finally looked at him with her lavender eyes and said, "Charlie Neal's cousin Conor called my room at Black Falls Lodge thirty minutes ago. He's in Rutland."

The cousin. Grit looked across Main Street at the frozen tundra of the pretty town green. "How'd he get to Rutland, Myrtle?"

"He took the train. He got in last night."

"Where is he now?"

"He's at a roadside motel on Route 4 just outside Rutland."

"He's sixteen," Grit said. "Don't they check ID?"

"He's very smart. All the Neals are smart."

Grit glanced at Myrtle, who was trembling, from nerves or the cold, he didn't know. She definitely didn't look happy.

"He says he has a message for you from Charlie."

"Myrtle."

"He's not under Secret Service protection. Conor Neal. The cousin."

Grit knew better. It wasn't Conor Neal in Rutland. It was Charlie. He was up to his prince-and-the-pauper tricks again, which Myrtle, being a smart Washington reporter, was pretending she didn't know about. "Doesn't mean they're not watching him," Grit said.

"No, it doesn't. The motel's not busy."

"What did he do, hitch a ride from the train station?"

"I didn't ask."

Up the street, a woman bundled from head to toe was walking a couple of little white dogs. Grit wondered if she had a normal life and decided probably not. What was normal, anyway?

"Let's go inside for muffins," Myrtle said. "You can leave me there and go to Rutland. I'll keep an eye on everyone for you."

The café was warm and filled with people, including various law enforcement officers. The state trooper that Jo's sister, Beth, was dating was adding half-and-half to a mug of coffee.

Jo was already there with Elijah. Also at their table was Jo's boss, Mark Francona, up from Washington on a frigid New England morning.

That couldn't be good.

Grit had met Francona in Washington in November and, being an experienced Navy SEAL, suspected the senior Secret Service agent's presence had something to do with Myrtle's errand.

"Myrtle," he said under his breath.

She grimaced. "I see. We walked right into the lion's mouth. I thought we'd have more time before anyone got here."

"So the note on my bed and borrowing a Secret Service agent's car—"

"Shut up, Grit," Myrtle said.

She went ahead of him to the glass case and put in her order with a frowning Beth Harper.

Elijah, who wasn't law enforcement, got up from the table with Jo and Francona and ambled over to Grit in such a controlled manner it could only signal the proverbial shit was hitting the fan. "Francona turned up ten minutes ago," Elijah said. "He flew in from D.C. first thing this morning. He wants to talk to you."

"Maybe I should have stopped at the gas station for coffee."

Beth Harper was attractive, and Grit had seen her and her sister running on the lake in skintight leggings, but he kept looking at the women in Black Falls as sisters. Jo, of course. She was Elijah's woman. But Beth, Rose Cameron, Dominique Belair, Hannah Shay. He'd had the same reaction to each one. They were untouchables.

Grit didn't like that. It wasn't like him.

Myrtle took a mug and muffin to a table next to the one with the feds.

Ignoring Elijah for the moment, Grit smiled at Beth and pointed at muffins heaped on a plate inside the glass case. "What kind are those?" he asked.

"Pumpkin," she said.

"You're serious? Pumpkin muffins? Do they taste like pumpkin pie?"

"Similar spices. They're dense. We make them with whole-grain flour."

"What kind are the ones next to them?"

"Cranberry-walnut."

"No Krispy Kreme around the corner, is there?"

Beth smiled. "No, Petty Officer Taylor, there is not."

"I'll go with the pumpkin."

"Would you like butter or ricotta cheese with it?"

He stared at her. "Ricotta? You serious? Ricotta goes in lasagna and ravioli. Why would I want it on my muffin?"

"Because it's a low-fat alternative to butter, and it's loaded with calcium."

Grit looked at Elijah, still standing in front of the glass case with him. "This is a strange little town."

Being an experienced special operations soldier, Elijah wasn't buying the distraction. "Jo and Francona want to talk to you."

"They armed?"

"Always."

"Why don't they want to talk to Myrtle? Look at her. She's sitting there by herself with her fluffy coffee and muffin."

"Latte," Beth said.

"I see she went for the pumpkin muffin, too. Scary."

Elijah had that same look Grit had seen in April right before their helicopter went down in an isolated Afghan mountain pass. That hadn't been a good night. Elijah's eyes got dark. "Grit . . ."

He looked at Beth. "I'll have a small

coffee, too." While she filled his order, he dug out a few bills and left them on the counter, operating under the assumption he would have to make a fast getaway with two Secret Service agents a few yards from him and Myrtle's errand to complete. "I'm going for a pleasant morning drive in Vermont."

"Grit," Elijah said, "we need to talk."

"Tell Jo and her boss they can meet me at my cabin later. They can search it if they want. Just have them put a log in the stove."

Elijah backed off, and Grit gave Beth a friendly smile as she handed him his muffin and coffee to go. Since he took his coffee black, all he had to do next was walk out of there and be on his way to Rutland and the roadside motel where, as far as he knew, Conor Neal was waiting to deliver his message from his cousin Charlie, the vice president's son. It was called plausible deniability.

Francona and Jo intercepted him before he got the café door open.

Jo said, "Let's try not to let in the cold air. Why don't you come sit with us?"

"Can't."

"Why not?" Francona asked. He was in his early forties, a straight-backed type with a peculiar sense of humor.

"I'm taking a drive." Grit didn't mention it was in Jo's car. "I want to see some Vermont winter vistas."

Elijah winced behind his fiancée and Francona and mouthed, "Vistas?"

Jo's eyes narrowed in a way that probably fired up Elijah but didn't do much for Grit. She said, "You'd tell us if you were contacted by a Secret Service protectee, wouldn't you, Grit?"

"You bet."

"Because," Francona said, "we're all on the same page here. We all want the same thing. Right?"

"If by the same thing you mean spring," Grit said, "yes, sir. We are definitely on the same page."

Grit opened the door. His left shoe felt tight and achy. That hadn't happened in a while. He had a left shoe but not a left foot. He figured the phantom pain had something to do with the two unsmiling Secret Service agents with him. Jo, a native Vermonter, didn't look cold. Francona, who probably wasn't a native of anywhere, didn't look cold, either. He just looked as if he wanted to shoot someone.

Not much of a sense of humor this morning.

They didn't stop Grit as he walked out of the café onto Main Street. The sun glinting off the snow hurt his eyes. He put on his sunglasses and got behind the wheel of Jo's car. He had a bite of his muffin, which didn't taste like pumpkin pie at all, and a sip of his coffee, and stared past the quaint town common. He called Myrtle on his cell phone.

She picked up on the first ring. "The Secret Service is about to gang up on me," she said. "I'll do what I can, but I'm not good with cops unless it's a First Amendment issue."

Meaning she'd cave if it meant saving her ass. "I'll break you out of jail."

"What a champ," she said, and disconnected.

Grit found the motel with no trouble. It was on the road to the massive Killington ski area, and when he pulled into the parking lot, he was pretty sure no one had followed him. He didn't know if Myrtle had broken, though, and was on high alert in case state cops and feds were about to pour out of the mountains and nail him.

He spotted a fair-haired teenager who resembled Prince Harry at sixteen making waffles at the free breakfast bar. It wasn't Conor Neal. It was Charles Preston Neal, son of the vice president of the United States.

Big surprise.

Charlie appeared to be alone.

Grit hated being unarmed with a high-value target right in front of him. What if bad guys had followed Charlie last night and were already in the breakfast room?

Charlie motioned for Grit to join him at the waffle iron.

"Thanks for coming," the kid said.

Grit smelled waffles and coffee. "I thought I told you not to pull this stunt again. You and your cousin switching places. It's not smart." He frowned. "Secret Service is onto you."

"No, they're not. They just think they are. What are they going to do if they find me? Arrest me?"

"I would," Grit said.

Charlie shivered as steam rolled out of

the waffle iron. "It's cold in here. The heating system is inadequate for the conditions. Do you want waffles?"

"No. It's cold in Black Falls, too. It's cold everywhere up here."

Charlie's light blue eyes fastened on Grit. "It's not cold in Southern California."

Grit said nothing.

"I'll make a deal," Charlie said. "You let me tell you about California, and I'll go back under Secret Service protection."

"Or what? I don't let you tell me about California and I put you back under Secret Service protection myself?"

"My way, and no one knows I was ever up here. Your way—"

"It's not going to be your way. Whatever we do, it's my way. Understood?"

"Yes, Petty Officer Taylor, I understand."

A tactical decision. There was nothing meek or humble about Charlie Neal.

"Nobody's trying to kill me, Petty Officer."

"I'll bet a lot of people are thinking about it." Like Deputy Special Agent in Charge Mark Francona and Special Agent Jo Harper. Probably Myrtle Smith by now. "Call your parents."

"Why? They think I'm with my cousin.

You'll just get some poor Secret Service agent fired."

"Maybe some poor Secret Service agent deserves to be fired."

Charlie lifted the lid on the waffle iron and grinned at the browned waffle inside. "Perfect. Come on. Who can resist fresh waffles?"

Grit's cell phone rang. He saw Elijah's number on the screen and knew he had to answer. "You have a bead on me?"

"On Jo's car."

"Were you going to shoot out the tires and leave me here in the cold if I didn't answer?"

"Not me. Jo."

"You didn't follow me. You're good, but I'd have spotted you. Francona have a homing device on Jo's car?"

"It wasn't Francona."

Myrtle. She'd said she'd cave. "Where do we meet?"

"Jo says to sit tight. She likes waffles."

Grit shut his phone. "Talk fast," he said. "They're coming for you."

Charlie didn't look perturbed. He pried his waffle loose, put it on a plate and headed to his table. Grit followed him and sat down across from Charlie. He smeared butter on his waffle. "You can't have too much butter on a waffle." He glanced up at Grit. "Sean Cameron's back in Beverly Hills."

Charlie was such a know-it-all that Grit wasn't sure if it was a question. "He headed back out there a few days ago."

"With Devin and Toby Shay. Hannah stayed behind in Black Falls."

Charlie spoke as if they were all personal friends, but that was the way he was. Grit dipped a finger into a pool of syrup on Charlie's plate and licked it. "It's not tupelo honey, but it's not bad. Yeah. Sean and the Shay brothers are in California. Hannah's here. So?"

"Think they'll see stars? I don't mean stars in the sky." Charlie ate another forkful of dripping pancakes. "I mean celebrities."

"I need to warn you. You haven't seen Jo Harper since you shot her in the butt with airsoft pellets. She and the Camerons have had a rough time since then."

"I know. My cousin Charlie helped figure out a network of killers was behind Drew Cameron's death in April."

Grit decided it was just as well Charlie

kept up the charade that he was his cousin Conor and not the son of the vice president of the United States. He could claim he thought he was talking to Conor Neal. Not that anyone would believe him. But he could. "My point is, Jo's still a Secret Service agent. Badge, gun, no sense of humor when it comes to your prince-and-the-pauper antics."

"*Any* of my antics," Charlie said. "Not that I'm always the one responsible. Conor does his share of damage."

"What, Charlie, giving up on pretending to be your cousin?"

He shrugged. "I tried. Agent Harper had no sense of humor even when she was assigned to my sister Marissa. Marissa's never any trouble. She's the history teacher who was almost burned to death a few months ago—"

"An accident. Don't reach for problems."

"You met Marissa, remember?"

"I do."

Marissa was the eldest of Charlie's four sisters. Grit had run into her in November when he'd dropped her little brother—her only brother—at his private school in northern Virginia, where she taught history.

Myrtle had been with him. Neither woman had wanted details on just what all Charlie had been up to out on his own on the streets of Washington. He had, in fact, provided information that had led police to a critical eyewitness to the hit-and-run that had killed Ambassador Alexander Bruni.

Grit hadn't had a brotherly reaction to Marissa Neal. He'd forgotten about that. It had to be a good sign.

He stayed focused on Charlie and prompted him. "Southern California."

"Marissa is suspicious. I tried to get her to take me to Beverly Hills with her to see the stars. She has an ex-boyfriend in Los Angeles. He's an actor. He dumped her when our dad was elected vice president. He didn't want the scrutiny, which I can understand, can't you?"

"No."

"You really can't?"

"I'm not judging. I just don't understand why you'd dump someone because you didn't want scrutiny."

"That's because you've been through SEAL training."

"It's because I grew up in a swamp," Grit said. "What do you want?"

If Charlie was worried about Secret Service agents descending on him, he didn't show it. He slid a CD case across the table to Grit. "I wanted to give you this information. I told you when we spoke a few days ago. I've been doing research."

"You could have e-mailed it to me."

"I don't have your e-mail address."

"You could have asked for it. You could have set one up for me. You're a genius. You could have figured out something besides sneaking on a train and checking yourself into a cheap motel."

"It's not that cheap. I paid cash. Conor and I—"

"Enough."

The kid could be a real pain. Grit drank some ice water. Charlie wasn't chastened at all. It wasn't how he was wired. "If you'll recall," the vice president's son said, "in November I put an arson investigator named Jasper Vanderhorn on the list of potential victims of our assassins' network." He soaked up syrup with a piece of his waffle. "Don't say it's not 'our' network. I'm not being literal."

"Police are investigating any suspicious

deaths that even remotely could be connected to these killers."

"Vanderhorn died in a fire in Southern California this past June. The fire was supposed to be out, but it wasn't. It flared up and he was caught in the flames and burned to death. Rose Cameron happened to be in Southern California doing a training session."

"Did she participate in a search for Vanderhorn?"

"Not that I know of, but she was on the scene."

"Did she and Vanderhorn know each other?"

Spots of color appeared high in Charlie's smooth cheeks. "I don't know. It's possible. He's on my list because his death fit the parameters of my search. Then I found out about Rose, and I learned Sean Cameron and his business partner are smoke jumpers."

"Were Sean and his partner at this fire?" Grit asked.

"I think so. So far Vanderhorn is our only California victim." Charlie pushed his plate to the center of the table. "Check what I gave you on the CD. It's nothing the police need to see. I mean, it's not official evidence."

"If it is, I'm turning it over to the authorities."

"I'd expect nothing less."

"If Jo catches me, she'll peel it off me. She's tough. She carries a badge. I only have one leg."

"You rescued Myrtle Smith from her burning house. You only had the one leg then. You're a hero, even if—"

"Myrtle's the one who gave you up to the Secret Service."

"She's a frustrated mother, don't you think?"

"I think she'd rub your face in syrup if she heard you say that. Would you say she was a frustrated father if she were a man?"

"She's not a man."

"True."

Charlie was thoughtful. "Grit—Petty Officer Taylor, I mean. We have a firebug."

Grit didn't say a word. His cell phone rang. The screen indicated it was a private number. He picked up, and a soft female voice said, "Are you with my brother?"

Marissa Neal. Grit pictured her on the

manicured campus of the school where she taught and which her no-account brother and cousin Conor attended.

No point lying. “Someone who looks just like him is sharing his waffle with me.”

A sigh of relief. “Thank God.” She sighed again. “I want him back here safe and sound, and I don’t want him to become the butt of media jokes. Do you understand, Petty Officer Taylor?”

“Yes, ma’am, I do.”

“Then make it happen.”

“Aye-aye.”

“If it doesn’t, I will hold you both responsible.”

Charlie was mouthing the words “my sister?” Grit nodded, and Charlie said, “She’s threatening to choke you and me to death, isn’t she?” He leaned over the table. “Love to you, too, sis.”

“Don’t encourage him, Petty Officer Taylor,” Marissa Neal said.

“Or you’ll choke me to death?”

“That’d make your day, wouldn’t it?”

He shrugged. “Probably.”

She gasped and disconnected. Grit pocketed his phone.

“She won’t rat me out,” Charlie said,

confident. "Here they come now." He motioned toward the window overlooking the parking lot. "Listen. The fire at Myrtle's house was a professional job. It was made to look like an accidental electrical fire. That took skill. It wasn't an accident. It wasn't Kyle Rigby or Melanie Kendall, either."

"Mice chewing the wires?"

"Our firebug."

Grit narrowed his eyes on the boy across from him. He didn't care if Charlie Neal had a genius IQ, he was still a kid. "There is no 'our,'" Grit said.

Charlie ignored him. "I did some more research. Have you run into a stonemason named Bowie O'Rourke in Black Falls?"

Leaning back in his chair, his shoe no longer feeling tight, his left foot not aching, Grit didn't respond.

"Ah," Charlie said. "You have. O'Rourke pled guilty to simple assault and was sentenced to time served in county jail—sixty days—and a couple years' probation. The assault occurred in Black Falls, at a bar owned by his cousin who, by the way, is the one who called the police."

"I know about the bar fight."

"It was a couple weeks before Drew Cameron was killed."

"So was April Fool's Day. What do you have on me?"

Charlie waved a hand. "It's not easy to find out about you. Too many top-secret missions. I wouldn't have that kind of access."

Which meant he knew everything.

The kid didn't miss a beat. "Sean and Elijah—Sergeant Cameron—were both in Black Falls for the bar fight. Not long after, Drew Cameron visited Ambassador Bruni and Jo in Washington."

"Agent Harper," Grit corrected.

"Right, right. Agent Harper. Do you think she missed anything when Drew—Mr. Cameron—visited her?"

"I think she worries about it."

"That's not the same," Charlie said thoughtfully. "Hannah Shay's father was an ex-con. Did you know that?"

"Nope. Makes no difference to me."

"It might to her." He licked the last of his syrup off his fork. "I'm missing something. It's like I have a two, a four and an eighty-three, and I'm supposed to come up with the formula for a rocket to land on Venus."

"You don't have to do anything but be a kid. Go play basketball or flirt with girls."

"Girls still scare me."

Grit smiled. At rock bottom, Charlie Neal was just a sixteen-year-old boy. "Girls will always scare you."

Myrtle, Jo and Elijah walked into the little free-breakfast room together. If Jo could have taken Charlie Neal and his waffles out of the motel at gunpoint, she probably would have, but she just addressed him through clenched teeth. "Give Elijah the key to your room. He'll check you out and get your stuff."

"It's good to see you, Special Agent Harper," Charlie said cheerfully. "I gather you've recovered—"

"On your feet. Let's go."

Charlie remained in his seat and gave Grit a plaintive look. "No wonder my cousin Charlie complains about her. He says she has no sense of humor." He shifted back to Jo. "Charlie's a pain, isn't he?"

Jo's eyes darkened but she didn't speak.

"He felt bad about the airsoft prank. You know. Shooting you in the butt. Those pellets sting, don't they?"

Grit leaned over the table. Charlie wasn't

hoping Jo didn't recognize him. He was deliberately playing games with her. "I did tell you she's armed, didn't I? And her gun is loaded with real bullets? You're smart. Figure out when you're beat."

"People used to think my cousin and I were identical twins."

"You're not," Elijah said.

Jo turned her Secret Service face to Grit. "What are you doing here, Petty Officer?"

Definitely not in a happy mood. Grit said, "I told Mr. Neal here that I'd listen to what he had to say."

"And?"

"I listened. He's a kid. He has a lot on his mind."

Charlie started to protest, but seeing how he had a 180 IQ, he finally figured out that Jo was looking for an excuse to shoot him. "I'm finished with my waffle," he said instead, not exactly meek but not argumentative, either. He handed Elijah a key card. "Room 17."

Before Elijah could leave, Mark Francona entered the motel. Charlie didn't wither at all. Francona breathed in through his nostrils before he spoke. "Special

Agent Harper and Mr. Neal here can come with me." He pointed at Myrtle, then Grit, then Elijah. "You three can find your own way home."

"Mr. Neal wants me to go back to Washington with him," Grit said. It wasn't in him to leave the kid to the feds for such a long trip, even if he deserved it.

Francona looked at him. "Yeah? I want to read a book by a fire. Neither is going to happen." He turned back to Charlie. "Let's go."

Charlie got to his feet and put his hand out to Grit. "Thank you," he said, shaking hands as if he were about to have his last cigarette and go before the firing squad.

Jo fell in with her boss and the vice president's son and headed out.

"Francona's mad," Myrtle said after they left.

Elijah shrugged. "He's always mad. His sense of humor just covers it up most of the time."

Myrtle sputtered. "What sense of humor?"

"Come on," Grit said, rising. "Let's go back to Black Falls and pack. You and me on a road trip, Mom."

"Call me Mom again and I'll run us off a cliff. I'm driving."

Elijah was quiet. Grit understood why. Jo was gone. He said, "She'll be back."

"Maybe we went too fast," Elijah said, half to himself.

"Myrtle and I will look her up in D.C. and figure out what's going on. Jo needs to be back in her old life. She needs to be sure that who she is and what she wants will be the same when she's back in D.C."

"What did Charlie want?"

"To help find these killers. It's past time, Elijah."

Elijah didn't budge. He'd had his own dealings with Charlie Neal. Charlie had called him about paid assassins in November, after Ambassador Bruni's murder. "Charlie didn't make the effort to come up here without specific intel," Elijah said. "You know what he's like."

"Your brother Sean and his partner are smoke jumpers. They fight some bad wildfires."

Elijah's eyes narrowed, and he showed no emotion whatsoever.

Which told Grit that he had his friend's

full attention. "We have a lot of dots. Not all of them will connect."

"Did Charlie mention Bowie O'Rourke as well as my brother?"

"Jo leave you out here in the cold? Need a ride? We can talk on the drive back to Black Falls."

Twenty-Two

January 2—Beverly Hills, California

Devin Shay fished debris out of the pool with a long-handled net while Sean stood on the patio of his Beverly Hills house and buttoned his jacket. Another black-tie event tonight. He hoped it'd be a distraction. It was all wrong that he was in California. Yesterday he and Devin had dropped Toby off at his host family's house outside Malibu. The place was spectacular, but all Toby had wanted to do was get out on the trails with his bike.

All Sean wanted to do, then and now, was to get back to their sister.

Her brothers clearly missed her. They

didn't want to show that they did, but it was obvious. Whether or not any of the Shays—including Hannah—would admit it, she was a second mother to them. Given the gap in their ages, the bond between them would have been different, anyway, but Devin and Toby had lost their mother as young boys and Hannah had stepped up to keep them together as a family.

Sean had been so preoccupied with what she was up to with his father's cabin and Bowie O'Rourke, with the force of the sudden, surprising, no-win attraction he had to her, that he hadn't fully considered the emotional turmoil this separation would cause for her and her brothers.

Meanwhile, he was in close touch with A.J. and Elijah. Jo hadn't let up on finding out exactly what had happened in the cemetery, but she was on her way back to Washington. Elijah was being circumspect and was obviously miserable.

Devin reached out to the middle of the sparkling pool with his net. "I'm worried Hannah's going to end up a spinster hanging judge," he said abruptly.

Nick Martini, stretched out on a lounge chair by the pool, nearly spit out his beer, but after three days with Devin as a houseguest, Sean had come to expect such blurts from the eighteen-year-old. He'd start work tomorrow at the Cameron & Martini high-rise offices on Wilshire Boulevard, which, Sean thought, should prove interesting. Nick had turned up fifteen minutes ago in shorts and a T-shirt. He was the son of a navy submarine captain and a former submariner himself, with prematurely gray hair that suited him in a boardroom, a ballroom or the middle of a wildfire. They'd met ten years ago as young smoke jumpers and formed a partnership that had profited them both and suited their personalities.

"Careful, kid," Nick said. "Spinster? Those are fighting words."

"I know. I don't care. Facts are facts."

"Her marital status shouldn't matter. Being a hanging judge, though . . ." Nick gave a cheerful shudder. "That matters. Wouldn't want to step out of line with her."

Devin nodded eagerly in agreement. "You're not kidding. She likes telling Toby and me about Royall Tyler, this Vermont judge who sentenced a pirate to execution. Cyrus Dean. Ten thousand people showed up for his hanging."

"I don't sympathize with pirates," Nick said.

"Not my point," Devin said, his attention apparently focused on a tiny leaf a few yards out into the blue water of the pool. "Hannah looks mild-mannered. Kind of mousy, even. Like Donna Reed in *It's a Wonderful Life.* You see that movie? Hannah makes Toby and me watch it with her every year at Christmas. She makes butter cookies." Devin paused a moment, staring at the water. "They're good. Her butter cookies."

"That's the movie with Jimmy Stewart and the town who takes him for granted after he sticks around and helps them, and then he ends up thinking he was happy?" Nick drank more of his beer. "I hate that movie."

"Donna Reed didn't end up a spinster because of him."

"She'd have been better off."

Sean grinned. "What about their kids?"

"Now you're getting too complicated." Nick nodded to the pool and said to Devin,

"Take a swim. It'll get your mind off hanging. You'd have to chip ice to swim in Vermont."

Devin rallied with a smile. "That's true."

Nick sighed. "Quit worrying about your sister. She's smart. She'll be fine."

Devin slowly dragged his net back across the water toward him. "Sean, you talk to Hannah lately?"

"Not since we left Black Falls. Why?"

"I worry about her being there alone, without both Toby and me."

"She's a grown woman, Devin. She can take care of herself. Worry about getting on with your own life."

"It's not that." He lifted the net out of the water and shook out the contents onto the tile next to him. "If she doesn't start doing something fun once in a while, I don't know. I'm serious. She's going to end up being a hanging judge or one of those prosecutors that goes for the jugular every time."

Nick shrugged, philosophical. "Maybe that's what she wants."

Devin glanced at Sean. The teenager's eyes were flat, but it wasn't hard to see his pain. "Since we left Vermont, Bowie's been coming by at night to work on the cellar. I called a little while ago and Beth picked up, and she told me. Hannah and Bowie aren't seeing each other. I don't mean that. Just—there's just something about him."

"Is Beth concerned?" Sean asked, his collar suddenly feeling tight.

"Yes and no." Devin turned back to his work, his contained emotions reminiscent of his older sister. "Hannah won't talk about the fight at O'Rourke's. I heard these ski bums insulted her, and you got her out of there before she could get hurt."

"Or hurt someone," Sean said.

"That, too." Her younger brother scooped up debris with his net. "Maybe I shouldn't have come out here now. I could have waited."

"For what?" Nick asked.

"Hannah's got too much on her mind right now," Devin said. "That accident in the cemetery threw her."

"Being in a cemetery at all would throw me," Nick said.

"So did going up to see the cabin where I was almost killed. Elijah, Jo and Nora, too." Devin's voice was steady, low, as he eased the net back into the water. "All of us."

Nick was silent now. He had voiced his suspicions about the death of Sean's father early on, refusing to believe that a seventy-seven-year-old man who'd been hiking on Cameron Mountain his entire life had become lost and disoriented in a snowstorm, ultimately dying of hypothermia. Nick had been blunt: either Drew Cameron had decided to check out in a spot he loved or foul play was involved.

"Now Hannah's talking about flying out here to California sooner rather than later." Devin angled a look back at the two men. "My sister spending that kind of money? *Not* normal. She's not herself, Sean. You know how tight she is with a buck. You should hear Beth and Dominique going on about how the café wouldn't be as successful as it is without Hannah's money sense."

"Maybe her money sense is why she can afford to fly out here," Sean said.

"If she comes out here and goes shopping on Rodeo Drive," Devin said, "then I'm going to start thinking she and Bowie O'Rourke are robbing banks together."

Nick propped up one knee, making himself at home on his lounge chair. He had a condo in Beverly Hills, but he'd spent a lot of time on submarines. He was content anywhere. "Sounds as if you're nervous because you left your sister alone in Vermont with this guy Bowie." He glanced up at Sean. "Is Hannah pretty, or does she look like Devin here?"

Devin managed a grin, Nick's humor penetrating his worry. "Sean? What do you think? Is Hannah pretty?"

"She seems more vulnerable than she is," Sean said, figuring that he needed to say something; if he took the Fifth, he was doomed altogether. Devin and Nick would know for sure he was falling for her and fighting it.

"She's got no clothes sense," Devin said. "Dominique could go into Hannah's closet and come out looking great, and Hannah—you know what I mean, Sean. She ends up looking frumpy."

Now Sean did take the Fifth. "I'm not going there, Devin."

Nick drank some of his beer. "You and your brother shouldn't have to worry about your sister. She wouldn't want that."

"She worries about us. She's never had a life. Toby says so, too. She sacrificed herself for us. She'd argue with us if she heard us saying that, but Sean knows I'm right."

Sean let his gaze drift to the red bougainvillea spilling over the wall behind his pool and the bright Southern California late-afternoon sunshine. He understood why Devin was going on about his sister. It wasn't just idle worry, and he was very far from home. Yet this *was* his home, a buff-colored, multilevel stucco house in Beverly Hills with a pool, expensive landscaping and a three-car garage. He didn't know why he owned three cars, but he did.

Well. Three vehicles. One was an old pickup truck he used as a smoke jumper and took up into the mountains to camp, hike, bike.

Devin had been asking him and Nick questions—mature, serious questions—about smoke jumping since his arrival in Southern California. The long route to becoming a smoke jumper didn't seem to dampen his interest.

Sean pictured going off with Hannah into the California mountains and shook off his own worries about her. A kiss among the cobwebs and a million questions unanswered aside, his life—his work—was out here in California.

He looked at Devin. "Sure you don't want to borrow a suit and head over to the Beverly Hilton with me?"

"Thanks, but I'll stay here. Anything you need me to do?"

Sean shook his head. "Finish up with the pool and relax."

"Would you mind if I used your weight room?" Devin asked tentatively.

"Help yourself."

"Thanks."

"I have to go," Sean said. "Nick, you coming?"

"Nope. Going involves a suit. I'll send a check."

Sean headed through the gate and down a stone walk to the garage. He climbed into his car and sank against the cool leather seats. It'd only been a few days since he'd left Hannah in Vermont, but at least it was a new year. No one on the task force investigating the murders-for-hire had slacked off for the holidays and they wouldn't now, but they needed a break—a new lead. It would be easy for everyone—including Hannah—to let Bowie and old stonework and whatever had gone on at the cemetery become distractions.

Sean remembered his father railing about Hannah after her mother had died. “That girl has no business trying to raise those two boys. A foster home would be better. She’s just a kid herself. Hell, though. No one’s ever been able to tell Hannah—or any Shay—what to do.”

In March, he’d admitted he’d been wrong. It was just after Bowie’s arrest, before Sean had returned to California. “Hannah would do anything for her brothers, and they’d do anything for her,” his father had told him. “Devin and Toby wouldn’t have been better off in a foster home. I’d just like to see her smile more. Cut loose a little, you know? She’s a good soul. You should have her and her friends out to Beverly Hills for a visit.”

Sean smiled at the memory. His father had hated Southern California. The weather’s nice, he’d say, but that was it. Sean had never taken his father’s comments as a condemnation of his choice to move west. Drew Cameron had just always been a man to state his opinions. Agree, disagree, argue, don’t argue—he didn’t care.

Sean started his car. He envisioned Hannah in an evening gown next to him, smiling as they headed out together for a night on the town. Her pale blue eyes would be gleaming with excitement, and all her troubles would be behind her.

No question, he thought. The woman definitely had him tied up in knots.

When he reached the hotel lobby, Sean dug out his cell phone and dialed A.J. Enough, already. He had to stay focused on his real mission, and it wasn't having Hannah on his arm for a fancy Beverly Hills event. "You and Elijah keeping an eye on Bowie?" he asked his older brother.

"As best we can," A.J. said. "Elijah's in a bad mood with Jo in Washington. He's not talking, or can't talk, about what she's up to."

"Bowie's been stopping at the café at night to work on the cellar."

A.J. was silent a moment. "I know. I haven't said anything to Hannah. It wouldn't do any good. Elijah and I hiked up to the cabin and took a look at the foundation ourselves. We have a fair idea of Pop's capabilities, but who the hell knows if he had help, didn't have help, needed any. No wonder Hannah didn't want to say anything."

"It does sound nuts," Sean said, "but if Bowie advised him on rebuilding an old dry-wall foundation, then he could have put the pieces together and figured out what Pop was up to. Bowie would have had more of an idea than most people about where the old cellar hole could be."

"He could have hiked up the mountain one day and found it."

"Then told the wrong person. He ends up in jail, and Pop's killed—"

"And here we are." A.J. sighed heavily.

"I'm not out to get Bowie," Sean said, "but I'm not assuming he's just misunderstood, either."

"Same here. I'm keeping an open mind." He paused, then added, "Hannah's not."

Sean gripped his phone, watching well-dressed men and women pass him in the hotel lobby. What was he doing here? "I shouldn't have come back here, A.J. I should be there."

A.J. grunted. "Yeah, well, you're not. I should warn you—Elijah will be calling."

Two minutes later, he did. "Tell me about an arson investigator named Jasper Vanderhorn. And tell me about Nick Martini. We've never met."

Sean stepped out of the path of two actors he recognized and their entourage. "Elijah, what's this about?"

"Hell if I know."

"I didn't know Vanderhorn. He was killed in June."

"Rose was out there then."

"Yes, she was," Sean said, feeling a strange coolness run down his spine.

"Jo and Grit are onto something," his brother said curtly. "I can't explain. I'm asking you to understand that."

"Fair enough. Nick's a friend. I'd trust him with my life."

"With our sister? Scratch that. I'm speculating. I don't know anything."

Sean skipped his event and got back into his car. He shut his eyes, seeing in his mind every detail of the canyons, not that far from Beverly Hills, where Jasper Vanderhorn had died. A hot spot had flared up in the high winds and dry conditions and blazed out of control, jumping a fireline and trapping Vanderhorn, an experienced firefighter himself as well as an arson investigator.

Nick and Sean had tried to get to him and failed.

Rose had been there, close enough to be in danger herself but helpless to save Vanderhorn.

The land was still charred, but Sean had noticed signs of life when he'd last gone out there. Green shoots poked up out of the ground. The air didn't smell as foul as it had.

When he got back to his house, he headed straight to his bedroom and dragged out a suitcase. He packed his warmest clothes. His head was spinning with questions, but if he knew one thing, it was that January in Vermont would be cold.

And Hannah would be there.

He zipped his suitcase shut and looked out the tall bedroom windows. Devin was sitting on the edge of the pool with his feet in the water. Nick was still stretched out on a lounge with a glass of ice water.

Sean dialed Elijah's cell-phone number, but it was Jo who answered. "I ended up with Elijah's phone," she said. "I'm in D.C."

"Fight?"

"No. Damn, Sean. *No.*"

He heard the anguish in her voice and felt a pang of guilt. "Sorry."

"You've talked to him," Jo said.

"Yes." No fool, Jo was. "I gather we're all on a need-to-know basis with whatever you're up to. How *are* you and Elijah, Jo?"

"Arguing about the fate of the cabins. He's all for getting a bulldozer out there. He's not sentimental."

"He saved that engagement ring he bought you. Still wearing it?"

"Forever, Sean."

"You're both a couple of romantics under a tough shell and wearing guns."

Jo waited a moment before she spoke. "Do you want to tell me about Hannah? She's why you called, isn't she?"

"I shouldn't have left her."

"She's not alone. You just think she is because you're a rock-headed Cameron who doesn't— Never mind. Your relationship with Hannah's none of my business. The unanswered questions are getting to everyone. It's just the way it is. We all have to deal with it."

"Who are we talking about here, Jo?"

"How was New Year's in Beverly Hills?"

Sean sighed. Jo wasn't going to give him anything. "Chilly. I had to wear a sweater."

She cursed him cheerfully as she disconnected.

He clicked off his phone and headed out to the pool. The water rippled in a breeze. Nick had put on a sweatshirt.

Devin had rolled his jeans up to his knees and stuck his feet in the water. He had on a T-shirt and didn't look cold. "How was the fund-raiser?" he asked. "You weren't gone long. Did you even go?"

"I didn't stay," Sean said as he walked over to Nick's lounge chair. "My sister?"

Nick glanced up, meeting his friend's eye. "She's good with dogs."

Sean gritted his teeth. "Nick—"

"I'm heading home." Nick rolled onto his feet. "Let me know if you need me in Vermont."

"My sister and Jasper Vanderhorn?"

"You're going to Vermont. Ask her."

As a smoke jumper, Nick was fit, agile, committed, reliable—and daring without being reckless. He brought that same intensity and commitment to their business partnership. Sean trusted him without question.

Just not with his sister.

“I never should have left Vermont,” he said half to himself.

“Hannah?” Devin was slightly pale.

Sean turned to the teenager. He wondered if he was pale himself.

Devin’s eyes narrowed. “You’re going back to Vermont, aren’t you?”

“Late red-eye.”

Devin leaned back onto his elbows and squinted up at Sean. “Hannah’s onto something, isn’t she?”

Sean felt a tightness in his throat. “I hope not.”

Twenty-Three

January 3—Black Falls, Vermont

Hannah shut her law book and put away her study notes on the small table in her apartment kitchen. Now she could see why Everett Robinson had been encouraging her to get a study partner and sign up for a review course. The dedication and focus she needed to pass the bar exam couldn't be on and off. It had to be sustained.

She noticed a mountain-biking magazine Toby had left behind and a pair of old sneakers Devin had decided not to take with him at the last minute. She couldn't pretend that her brothers were at work or on a hike or mountain biking for a few hours, or even at a friend's house for a few days. They were in California—on the other side of the continent.

For now, she planned to leave everything of theirs in place and continue with her own life as normal. She'd work in the café, study for the bar and figure out options for her own future. She'd been locked into her routines for so long, and now they were changing, regardless of Devin and Toby's departure.

Regardless, she thought of Sean Cameron and the attraction that had flared up between them. It had been a momentary thing, understandable given the high emotions of the past weeks, and best forgotten.

She ran downstairs, suddenly excited for her brothers even as she pushed back her own loneliness. Toby would be ensconced with his upper-middle-class host family and hitting the bike trails. Devin would be swimming in Sean Cameron's heated pool and figuring out his new job.

She paused in the hall, peering out the narrow side window into the gray, drizzly January afternoon. There'd been nothing in terms of a lunch crowd at the café, and

Dominique had shooed both her and Beth out early. The drizzle was expected to turn to snow showers later in the day, with colder temperatures back tomorrow. She and Beth and a few of their other friends planned to take the initiative and spend a day cross-country skiing. Just get away from everything.

"Can't do *that* in Beverly Hills," Hannah said under her breath with a quick smile.

She headed out through the mudroom and jumped in her car, driving up to Rose's house on Cameron Mountain Road. It was nestled into a hillside, small and without any immediate neighbors, which Rose seemed to like.

Hannah was surprised when she passed Lowell Whittaker at the bottom of the plowed, sanded driveway. Rose's golden retriever was bounding toward him. Hannah parked next to a BMW—presumably Lowell's. Rose was standing in front of her open garage as she watched Ranger scoop up a stick in his mouth, pivot and race up the hill to her.

As she got out of her car, Hannah noticed fog swirling in the evergreens on the edge of the yard and rising up from the melting snow. There was a lull in the precipitation, but water dropped off pine needles and small puddles had formed in dips in the driveway.

"I'd rather have a clear, cold winter day than this wet weather," she said as she approached Rose. "The dampness gets into my bones."

Rose kept her eyes on her dog. She was dressed for the weather in a waterproof jacket, the hood pulled up over her tawny hair. "I feel closed-in on days like today, but it won't last. All this water will freeze tonight and we'll be in the cold again tomorrow."

Hannah stood next to her friend and nodded toward Lowell Whittaker. "What's he doing here?"

"He's interested in getting a dog," Rose said without inflection.

"Does he want to get into search-and-rescue?"

"I doubt it. He's talking about adopting a failed or injured search dog. I think he's more curious than anything else, or just looking for a distraction." She put out a hand as Ranger sat in front of her, and he dropped his stick into her palm. "How're you doing with your two brothers in California?"

"Different. I didn't realize how little sleep I've gotten since November. I'd wake up several times a night and check on Devin, just listen in case he was pacing."

"He went through hell. You all did. I wish . . ." Rose paused, throwing the stick back down the driveway. Ranger immediately charged after it, legs pumping, golden fur gleaming. "I'm sorry I wasn't here."

"You were on a job. You didn't know what was happening."

"That's my point." She went on quickly, "How do Devin and Toby like California?"

Hannah hesitated, but decided to take Rose's lead in changing the subject. "They love it." She watched Ranger return with his stick, clumps of wet snow clinging to his tail and undercoat. "They both say Sean's place is nice."

Her friend laughed unexpectedly. "I've been there. It's incredible, is what it is. Are you afraid Devin will get spoiled? Sean won't let him. He'll make him work. He didn't get rich robbing banks."

Hannah smiled but said nothing. Her father had served time for robbery.

Rose petted Ranger, praising him for a job well done, then squinted down through the gloom at Lowell, still at the bottom of the driveway. "He's heading home soon. He's cold. How's he going to take care of a dog if he can't handle a little weather?" Her tone was only half-teasing. "I won't say anything to him, of course."

"Of course not. You're the nice Cameron."

Rose's eyes narrowed.

"Sorry," Hannah said quickly.

"It's okay. I understand where you're coming from. We can be a hardheaded lot. Lowell says his wife is freaked out about what happened here. I don't know that having a dog would make her feel more secure, though."

"Maybe a bomb-sniffing dog would," Hannah said, and realized she wasn't joking. Ranger was an air-scenting dog, trained to find people in an area versus tracking a specific person, but Rose was an expert in every kind of search dog.

Lowell picked his way through puddles and patches where the rain had washed away the sand, exposing ice. "Ranger is a well-behaved dog, Rose," he said, clapping his thick gloves together as if his hands were cold in spite of them. "He's also handsome. I don't know if I can ever talk Vivian into a dog, but I'd love to have one—just as a pet. The work you do requires an enormous commitment."

"It does," she said, "but owning any dog takes a certain commitment."

He sighed. "Yes, I understand your point." He turned to Hannah and smiled. "What a welcome surprise to see you here. You and Rose don't look the least bit cold. Now, why is that, I wonder?"

"Warm clothes," Rose muttered.

He had the grace to laugh. "You're native Vermonters. A little cold weather doesn't bother you."

A cold breeze penetrated the fog and intermittent drizzle. "If you go up to the lodge," Rose said, "A.J. and Elijah will outfit you with winter gear that'd hold you through any dog outings in the Vermont winter."

"They won't want anyone in Black Falls to freeze to death," Lowell said.

Rose narrowed her blue eyes on him. "That's correct."

"Oh, dear. I'm so sorry. I wasn't thinking. Your father—"

"He didn't die of hypothermia because he wasn't dressed properly for the conditions or was in over his head in that storm." Rose's voice was steady, without any obvious emotion. "He died because he was murdered."

"Yes. Yes, that's true. Awful." Lowell glanced at Ranger as the golden retriever bolted back up the driveway with his stick. "What a remarkable dog. I should go, though. A nice hot fire awaits me at home."

"How long will you be staying in Black Falls?" Hannah asked.

"As long as Vivian wants to. At least a few more days. We're overseeing the work on the guesthouse. It's going well. Bowie O'Rourke keeps to himself and seems to be doing an excellent job. How's work coming on your cellar?"

"He's almost done."

The wind and drizzle picked up. Lowell said goodbye, patted Ranger and headed for his car. After he was down the driveway and back on the road, Hannah picked up the stick again and threw it for Ranger, who looked eager for more fetching. He ran after it with just as much energy as the last time. Hannah watched him, aware of the drizzle dampening her hair, collecting on her jacket.

"You were last in California in June," Hannah said without looking at her friend.

"That's right. I was there training firefighters in handling search-and-rescue dogs."

Hannah curled her fingers into fists to help keep them warm. "Did something happen?"

Rose stared out at the white-and-gray landscape. "I was preoccupied with my father's death. I could have missed something. A fire that was supposed to be out sparked again. A man—an arson investigator—was trapped. No one could get to him in time, and he died. I keep thinking . . ." She turned and faced Hannah. "What if he's dead because I was so distracted by my own problems? What if a firebug's still out there because I messed up?"

"You're not a firefighter or an arson investigator."

"I understand that." She looked up at the bleak sky, her mind clearly back on that June day. "I've been such a wreck."

"What about you and Sean's partner? Nick Martini. Devin's told me about him." Hannah smiled. "He's another sexy smoke jumper, as well as a wealthy businessman."

Rose breathed out and fastened her Cameron blue eyes on Hannah. "Hannah . . . Nick and me . . . just forget whatever you're thinking, okay?"

Hannah sighed. "Your brothers will kill him dead if he took advantage of you when you were at your most vulnerable. Honestly, Rose. From what I can gather from Devin—the man's a rake."

Her friend laughed outright. "Very Jane Austen of you. Rake. Yes, Nick Martini is a total rake." Rose squatted down and opened up her arms as her wet, slobbering, eager dog returned with his stick and welcomed her affection. She was a private person, solitary despite being the youngest of four. "Now I've said too much."

"Rose, if you want to talk—"

"Thanks, Hannah. You're a good friend."

She stood up. “We all have too much tragedy on our mind.”

“It’s a new year,” Hannah said. “You haven’t been to the café in a few days. Dominique’s making her fire-breathing chili today. Why don’t you stop by for a bite?”

“Thanks. I’ll see if I can manage it,” Rose said without much enthusiasm. Her panting golden retriever flopped onto her feet. “Will Bowie be there?”

“I don’t know.”

“Do you remember the time you and I decided to try diving at the swimming hole down on the river? We were what, sixteen? We got caught in high water, and Bowie pulled us out. He was so strong—he got us both at once and hauled us out of there.”

Hannah smiled at the memory. “We yelled at him and said we weren’t in any danger, and he said we were like sisters and he was just protecting us.”

“Underneath the rock dust and muscles is a hopeless romantic. Hannah, it’s not your fault he went to jail.”

Something in Rose’s tone made Hannah’s breath catch. “You weren’t in town then. What have you heard? Rose—”

"I have nothing against Bowie. I hired him to fix my steps." Rose motioned to the snow-covered stone steps that led up the hillside to her front door, which she seldom used in winter. In summer, the steps would be flanked with flowers. "It was an easy job, but I couldn't do it by myself."

"When was this?" Hannah asked, surprised.

"November. I didn't want to ask A.J. or Elijah for help. A.J. was so busy with the lodge, and Elijah was just back home from the army. I saw for myself what he'd been through when I visited him in Germany in April." Another wind gust blew down off the mountain and whipped raindrops off her jacket into her face. She hardly seemed to notice. "I saw Bowie's van at the cemetery one day and stopped. He was checking on the culvert to order materials for that job. I asked him then, on the spur of the moment, and he agreed. He was only here a few days. I wasn't even around."

"When in November was this, Rose?"

She was pale now, scratching Ranger's head without looking at Hannah. "He was working here the week those killers went after Nora Asher and your brother."

"Who else knows? The police? Jo? Your brothers—do they know?"

"I haven't said anything to anyone. I don't see what difference it makes. I don't want to cause unnecessary trouble for Bowie any more than you do."

"Did he have a key to your house?" Hannah asked.

"I left one. To my knowledge he never used it."

"You have a phone here. What about cell-phone service?"

Rose nodded as if Hannah had asked a question. "With anyone else," she said, "we wouldn't think twice."

"Bowie isn't anyone else."

Neither spoke for a moment, only Ranger's panting and the steady drizzle breaking the silence. On a clear day, Hannah realized, with binoculars, the lodge would be visible from atop the driveway.

"Just go," Rose said, her voice strangled. She looked up, water dripping out of her tawny hair now, running off the end of her nose as she tried to smile. "I promised Ranger we'd go for a run."

Hannah nodded. "The invitation for chili stands."

Though reluctant to leave, she finally returned to her car. A few fat, sopping snowflakes mixed with the drizzle and splattered on her windshield. Mindful of the conditions, she resisted the urge to speed down the mountain road.

When she came to Harper Four Corners, she pulled into the old tavern. There was more snow mixing in the rain now.

Reverend McBane had the door open before she was halfway up the walk. "I saw you going up the road and hoped you'd stop by on your way back down."

"I went to see Rose Cameron."

"Ah. She's been keeping to herself even more than usual these days. What can I do for you?"

"She said she was here in November. Bowie O'Rourke was over in the cemetery—"

"Yes, I remember. Rose walked over to talk to him about something."

"Was that the only time you saw them together?"

He nodded, his eyes as sharp and incisive as ever. "Hannah?"

"It's nothing. Never mind. I'm not suggesting anything."

"Bowie was by earlier this morning to clean up at the crypt."

"Did you talk to him?"

"No. He was gone by the time I walked over there. Gloria hates these dreary days. She's been curled up by the fire with a book since we got up. I just had a look around. I didn't linger, I have to say. I've been inside enough crypts in my day. Not a part of the job I miss." He grinned, his lined face lighting up. "The next time I need to be in one, I'd prefer to be inside a coffin."

Hannah smiled at his gallows humor. "You weren't afraid to go over there, though."

"When you get to be my age, you're not afraid of much—certainly not ghosts. Besides, A.J. Cameron and Wes Harper have been keeping an eye out for Gloria and me. Fortunately they live on Ridge Road and drive by here often enough."

Hannah shivered. "I shouldn't keep you out here in the cold."

As she spoke, the old man's attention was drawn to something behind her. She heard a vehicle and turned, just as Elijah Cameron's truck pulled into the tavern's driveway behind her beat-up car.

Sean was behind the wheel.

Hannah's heart pounded. What was he doing back?

"He must be looking for you," Reverend McBane said, as if reading her mind.

She turned to him. "Why do you say that?"

He shrugged, tightening his sweater around his thin frame. "Gloria and I have always believed Sean would return to Black Falls to live at least part-time. We think he'd like to renovate this place."

Hannah tilted her head back. "Reverend McBane, has Sean expressed an interest in buying this property?"

The old man looked uncomfortable. "He asked us not to say anything—"

"You know he's a shark. All the Camerons are when it comes to property. Not dishonest—just sharks." She scrutinized McBane, her heart racing now. "Reverend . . . Sean's already bought this place, hasn't he?"

"He's been very generous," McBane said vaguely.

"If I looked up the deed?"

"You'd see it's in the name of a private company."

"Which Sean owns," Hannah pronounced. "I'm right?"

Lester McBane sighed. "I forget you're a lawyer."

"I haven't been admitted to the bar yet," Hannah corrected.

Gloria McBane peeked around the corner from the kitchen. "Sean suggested making us life tenants," she said. "It's worked out beautifully for all of us."

Sean was out of the truck, heading up the sanded walk. He had on his long black coat, and Hannah remembered the feel of his mouth on hers as if their kiss had happened seconds ago.

"Drew Cameron was mending fences in his last months," the old minister said quietly. "Making amends before it was too late."

Hannah shifted back to him. "Did Drew have amends to make with Sean?"

"He wanted Sean to know he was still a part of the family. Drew and Elijah had the most obviously strained relationship, but they were so similar—they understood each other. Sean . . ." Reverend McBane shrugged his thin shoulders. "His ambitions weren't easy for a man like Drew Cameron to understand."

"I've always seen them all as cut from the same cloth. Sean's as much a Cameron as the rest of them."

He was behind her now. He put one foot on the bottom step. Hannah noticed wet snowflakes splatter on the expensive leather of his boots. His eyes, almost navy against the gray, narrowed on her, but just for a moment before he shifted his gaze to Reverend McBane. "I got restless in California and decided to come back. Is everything all right here?"

Hannah relaxed slightly. Nothing had happened with Devin or Toby.

"Everything's fine," Reverend McBane said. "Gloria and I are just waiting for the rain to turn all the way to snow."

"I know the past weeks haven't been easy on you," Sean said. "If there's anything you need, don't hesitate to contact me. If you can't reach me, my brothers and sister will be glad to help."

"Hannah's good to us. So are you, Sean."

Sean grinned. "Well, don't tell her."

Reverend McBane looked at Hannah and smiled as he addressed Sean. "She's very smart, Sean. You wouldn't want to underestimate her."

"Ah. You're saying she knows."

He didn't seem concerned. Hannah found herself less and less able to contain her emotions. "Welcome back, Sean," she said, jumping down off the steps. "I have to go."

"I'll see you back in town."

But she already had her hands stuffed in her pockets as she rushed down the walk to her car. She didn't look back to see if the McBanes invited Sean inside. She drove down Cameron Mountain Road, slowing at the lane that led to the crypt and peering into the fog and mix of rain and snow.

"**Hannah, Hannah, Hannah.**"

She shuddered, more convinced than ever someone had called her name. She wished she could say for sure that it hadn't been Bowie O'Rourke.

Twenty-Four

Sean drove out to the Whittaker estate after assuring Reverend McBane he hadn't done anything wrong. Of course Hannah would drag the truth out of him. Not only had she just graduated law school with top grades, she'd been pulling information out of people since ninth grade and had raised two boys on her own. Criminals didn't stand a chance with her.

Bowie's van wasn't in the turnaround, but Sean parked there and headed up the slick walk to the stone guesthouse. As he mounted the steps to the porch, he noticed muddy footprints on the painted wood. Someone had just arrived or just left.

Vivian Whittaker pushed open the storm door and walked out onto the porch. She seemed barely aware of his presence. “Bowie only worked a short time this morning. He says he’s waiting on materials.” She blinked at Sean as if it had just dawned on her who it was standing there. “I thought you were in California. Has something happened?”

Sean heard the wind whistling in the mountains as the cold front moved in from the northwest, pushing out the fog and rain. “Nothing’s happened. I got back a little while ago.” He smiled, hoping to ease some of her tension. “Elijah thinks I was missing a real winter.”

“You and your brothers have gone your separate ways, but the bond among you is still so strong. You get along well.” Vivian glanced back toward the entry, the storm door slowly shutting on its own. “Painting isn’t going to help. I just can’t get rid of the memories of those people. Even Nora and her stepfather. I keep picturing Alex at the pond. He found it difficult to relax—” She broke off, staring out at the gloom. “If I could do it over, I wouldn't have befriended Alex. I imagine Lowell feels the same way. We ended up with Kyle Rigby and Melanie Kendall under our roof because we did. Is that heartless of me?"

"Give it some time."

She seemed to shudder with the bitter wind and hugged her arms to her chest. "I don't know where Bowie is now, if that's why you're here. I assume he's at home or on another job." Her panic seemed to have subsided. "Lowell and I both have ended up liking Bowie very much. People deserve second chances. I walked up the road past his house yesterday—it's so pretty there with the river and the stone walls. You can feel the history. Your father was interested in local history, I remember."

"How well did you know him?"

"Not well at all. He stopped by once when I was raking leaves down by the road after we first bought this place. Now that I think about it, he must have been building his cabin then. I imagine he was on his way to the north side of Cameron Mountain."

"What did you talk about?"

"He just said hello and welcomed us to Black Falls."

Lowell Whittaker came up the walk from the turnaround, in boots, not on snowshoes or skis. Sean assumed he'd taken the road down from the farmhouse. He was bundled up against the elements. He peeled a scarf off his lower face. "I do believe it's going to snow tonight," he said cheerfully. "Not a major storm, but even a dusting would freshen up the landscape. How are you, Sean? I didn't expect you back so soon."

"He's asking about Bowie," his wife said.

Sean didn't correct her. Her husband said, "I saw his van at Four Corners on my way to your sister's house after I'd run an errand in the village. I think he must have been cleaning up the mess at the crypt. Everything seemed perfectly normal."

"Why did you go to Rose's?" Sean asked.

"She's been educating me on dogs. Hannah came by not long after I arrived. She and Rose talked, but I was busy with Ranger. What a remarkable animal."

"I wouldn't want a golden retriever," Vivian said. "Too much hair, and they even look friendly."

Lowell ignored her. "What else can we do for you, Sean? Anything?"

"No, nothing," Sean said, and got out of there, the wind fierce now.

On his way back along the river, he ran into a blinding snow squall that dissipated by the time he arrived in the village. The café was closed, but all the lights were on in the dining room. He pulled into the driveway next to Hannah's car and went in through the mudroom, its door unlocked. He knocked on the kitchen door before entering.

Dominique was alone, standing by the stove. She looked up at him from the giant pot she was stirring. "You're back," she said, visibly pale. "I hope that's a good thing. Hannah's in the cellar. She was checking on Bowie's work on the leak. Scott Thorne just left."

Sean eased her spoon out of her slender hand, set it on the counter and took her by the shoulders. "Dominique," he said. "Talk to me. What's wrong?"

"Hannah found the café's petty-cash jar.

It was tucked in among the old canning jars in the cellar. Sean . . ." She blinked rapidly and took a breath, calming herself. "I don't know how much more I can take. How much more any of us can take."

"The jar?"

"There was no money in it. It's just . . . a jar." She smiled halfheartedly. "And here I am in shock over a stupid empty jar."

"You're experiencing a sense of violation. Someone came into your kitchen and took the jar and the money in order to frame an eighteen-year-old kid."

"What if it wasn't one of those killers? Sean, what if—" She pulled away from him, grabbed her spoon and stuck it back in her chili pot. "I don't even want to think what I'm thinking."

Sean could guess what it was—that Devin had stolen the money from the lodge, the café and Nora Asher's apartment, after all, and Kyle Rigby had only capitalized on what was already going on in Black Falls.

He left her and headed down the steep, dimly lit cellar stairs. He found Hannah crouched down by the shelves of old canning jars. Bowie had pulled out the old stones where water was getting in and had neatly piled them on the floor for later repointing. He'd obviously discovered more rot in a section of wall above the foundation and had cleaned it out, heaping that mess onto a sheet of plastic.

Start one repair in an old house, find more repairs to do.

"Hello again," Hannah said, her voice distant, the shock of her discovery evident. She got onto her knees, opening up the old trunk she'd moved to make room for Bowie. "Since I don't own the building or hang out in the cellar, I've never bothered checking to see what's inside—just as I never dug through all the canning jars down here."

"I talked to Dominique," Sean said. "Are you sure the jar you found is the petty-cash jar from the café kitchen?"

She nodded. "It's a slightly cracked old blue willow jar. It's pretty distinctive. Beth, Dominique and I found it in a cabinet we moved out when we were fixing up the place for the café. The mouth was narrow—it was easier to fit money in than get it out."

"Where did you find it?"

She stood up and pointed behind her at the shelves of canning jars. "Third shelf from the bottom. I started pulling out jars to check the wall behind the shelves for rot. I didn't want any more surprises, and it was something to do to help me think."

She raised the lid of the trunk and smiled, as if she had nothing else on her mind but a stash of what appeared to be old fabric. "Look, Sean. It must be swatches someone collected for a quilt. Or several quilts, maybe. It looks like men's shirts, mostly, that were cut up and stored in here."

"Are they moth-eaten?" Sean asked, reining in his impatience. He didn't care about the contents of the trunk. He wanted to know about the cash jar.

"The ones I can see look to be in good shape. Of course, I might find a mouse nest in here any second." Hannah shut the lid and latched it, her face flushed as she glanced around at the dark, dusty cellar. "Imagine what all's gone on in this house since 1835."

He didn't want to imagine anything of the sort. "Hannah, do you have any idea how the money jar got down here?"

"Yes, yes, I do." She focused now, her

hands clenched at her sides. "Kyle Rigby or Melanie Kendall, or some unnamed associate, walked into the café kitchen, grabbed it, ducked down here—possibly when I had the bulkhead open—and dumped out the money and hid the jar."

"Whoever was responsible could explain having the cash but not the jar."

"As I said, it's not that easy to dip your hand into the jar. Dominique can, and I can with some effort—but Beth can't. A man or a woman with a larger hand would have had to break the jar or dump it out to get the cash. I can imagine standing in the kitchen, thinking I was just going to snatch a handful of twenties and run and discovering the damn jar was too small—" She gulped in a breath. "Or hearing someone coming. Toby or Devin or me. Dominique. Beth. *Any* of us."

"Hannah."

She raised her gaze to him. The bruise on her cheek was faint now, just a trace of yellow against her pale skin. "We called the police. Scott Thorne came. The town police. Wes Harper showed up. It was all very fast."

"I'm sure they were thorough."

"With all the activity—with you and Bowie and Devin and me all down here in recent days, not to mention the furnace man and the plumber just since the money turned up missing in November, and the work and the dust and commotion . . ." She raked a hand through her hair. "There's really no hope of learning much of anything."

Sean took her hand and saw that the bruising on her wrist hadn't yet faded entirely. "Let's go upstairs."

"The thought of one of those killers hiding down here makes me sick to my stomach." She pulled away and sucked in a breath, or maybe it was a sob. "Bastards," she said, and ran up the stairs.

Twenty-Five

Hannah burst into O'Rourke's and pushed her way down the rough-wood bar to the stool where Bowie sat nursing a soda. She stayed on her feet. He didn't so much as glance at her. "It's Diet Coke. No booze for me until I'm off probation, and even then . . ." He sighed. "What are you all cranked up about, Hannah?"

She grabbed him by one shoulder, her fingers digging into his hard muscle as she tried to turn him to her. "Look at me."

He turned to her, voluntarily, his dark eyes narrowed into slits. "Say what you have to say."

"Did you do it? Did you steal the petty-cash jar out of the café kitchen?"

Bowie didn't respond.

"Did you grab the jar because you couldn't just grab the money?"

"Keep going," he said.

"You grabbed the jar and ducked out the back with it, thinking you could get to your van in time, but you saw someone coming. It was November. You'd have been wearing your sweatshirt or your sweatshirt and your vest. The jar wouldn't fit easily under either one. The cellar bulkhead was open. So you ran down there, dumped out the money and hid the jar."

He sipped his Coke. "How long did I stay in the cellar?"

"I don't know," she said. "How long, Bowie?"

"I guess that would depend on whether I was obsessed with you and wanted to hear your footsteps upstairs, or if I was just enjoying being down there without you knowing it. I wouldn't want to push it too far if my van was out on the street and I couldn't explain myself if I got caught. Or if you closed the bulkhead on me. Then what?"

"Don't make fun of me, Bowie. Maybe you didn't run into the bulkhead." Hannah dropped her hand from his shoulder. "Maybe you've had the jar in your van or someplace and decided to plant it among the old canning jars while you were working on the cellar."

"Why would I do that?"

"To upset me," she said.

"Why would I want to upset you?"

"Payback for your arrest." Hannah was calmer now. "Did you do it on your own, or on behalf of someone else?"

Bowie swiveled on his stool and faced the bar. Liam O'Rourke had eased in closer. "You might want to take a couple sips and head on home," Liam said, setting a glass of ice water in front of Hannah. "Bowie, you, too."

Sean materialized behind her. Liam seemed relieved. Hannah remained on her feet, focused on Bowie. "The police are going to want to talk to you," she said.

"They already did," Bowie said. "As you can see, I'm not under arrest."

"Did you see the jar when you were working down there?"

"It's blue willow, right? That's what I

heard in town." At her tight nod, he looked at her again and smiled. "I don't even know what blue willow is."

Hannah felt her shoulders slump. "You're an easy target for everyone, Bowie," she said softly. "The police, the Camerons. Me, even. Maybe you are for these killers, too."

"Don't worry about me."

"Whoever stole the jar in the first place wanted to frame Devin. Hiding the jar—"

"I think a part of you thinks it could have been Devin after all," Bowie said, "and you're wondering if those killers focused on him because they knew."

"No. Part of me doesn't think that at all. I opened up the bulkhead to air out the cellar. It could have happened then. Maybe whoever did it could explain his or her presence in the cellar."

"Kyle Rigby and Melanie Kendall couldn't."

"Melanie could have said she thought Nora was in the cellar and went down to check on her."

"Talk about the wicked stepmother," Bowie said.

Sean sat sideways on the stool, one elbow on the rough-wood bar. "The police don't believe Melanie was in Black Falls when the money was stolen."

Hannah kept her gaze on Bowie. "It wasn't Devin. I know my brother. He didn't steal that money."

"Until you hired me to fix that leak," Bowie said, "I hadn't been in that cellar since I was fifteen and helped your father on his service call."

"If you had gone down there in November and I'd seen you, I wouldn't have thought twice about it."

"A tourist interested in old houses could have sneaked down there and you wouldn't have thought twice about it. That's how you all are at the café." Bowie stood up at the bar and placed a few dollars under his glass. "You keep forgetting that not everyone has your best interests in mind."

"You learned at a young age that no one's going to step in for you."

He looked at her with his dark eyes. "You've always been smart. I'm thirty-four years old. I was away from Black Falls for a long time. I'm not the kid you grew up with, Hannah. You don't know me. Don't think that you do."

She didn't back down. "Are you afraid

you said the wrong thing and that's how Kyle Rigby and Melanie Kendall found Drew's cabin?"

"I talked stonework with Drew. I walked him through how to rebuild and preserve an old rubble foundation. It was theoretical. I didn't know he was actually doing it."

"But you had an idea he was," Hannah said.

"I thought it was none of my business." He looked at Sean. "I wish I'd asked him more questions or followed him up the mountain. I'd see him pass by my place. I knew he was headed up that way."

"When was that?" Sean asked.

"The fall before he was killed. The last time I saw him go up there was late November, I'd say. I don't think he went up much over the winter. I wasn't there in April." He shrugged. "You know where I was."

"Bowie, were you used by these killers?"

"We all were, Hannah," he said.

Bowie rose stiffly, nodded goodbye and left. Hannah spun around to Sean. "Give me a minute before you follow me."

"Half a minute."

"Sean—"

"Clock's ticking."

She sighed and ran out the door, barely aware of the dropping temperature and snow flurries as she caught up with Bowie. "You worked at Rose's house in November," she said to him.

He dug his keys out of his vest pocket.

"She hasn't told anyone else," Hannah said. "Her brothers don't know."

"It's not a secret. I just don't talk to them about my work."

"I understand that. Bowie, you know what I'm asking."

"Nah. I really don't." He grinned at her. "You're about ten times smarter than I am, Hannah. If there's something you want to know, just ask me. Remember that when you're a prosecutor."

She paused on the sidewalk. "Were you at Rose's house the day Melanie Kendall was killed?"

"Yes. That afternoon. I waited for her driveway to get plowed and went up and did some work. I was on the tail end of the job. I finished up before she came home. You and the Camerons can believe what you want."

"I make up my own mind," Hannah said.

"I don't rely on what anyone else believes or wants to believe." She followed him onto the street as he went around to the driver's side of his van. "When I look at the Camerons, I see four siblings who want to know the truth about their father's death, whatever it is."

"Define truth," Bowie said as he got into the van and shut the door.

Dismissed, Hannah jumped back to the sidewalk as Sean fell in beside her. "That was more than thirty seconds," she said.

"It's so damn cold my watch stopped."

"It's cleaning night at the café tonight," she said, her teeth chattering more from nerves, she realized, than the cold. "The police already crawled through the kitchen and dining room in November. They looked in the cellar, but the jar—it would have taken one of us to have recognized it. Dominique, Beth or me. It could have been there all along."

"Have the police talked to Devin?"

"They haven't said. He's over eighteen. They don't have to tell me."

She kept walking, but Sean easily matched her pace.

"Why did you come back here?" she

asked, without looking at him. "Why didn't you just stay in California?"

"People care about you, Hannah. They always have."

She felt a snowflake land on her cheek and melt, and she pretended not to hear him. "You came back because you and your brothers think I might be onto something that can lead you to whoever hired those killers."

"Maybe I came back because I couldn't stop thinking about kissing you."

She smiled suddenly, in spite of her tension. "Once again, I see why people call you the charming Cameron."

"Who does?"

"Your brothers."

"Ha. A chunk of granite's more charming than either of them, so that's not saying much."

"Jo and Beth Harper say so, too."

He grinned. "Then it must be so." He slipped one hand into hers and with the other brushed snowflakes off her hair. "How are you doing, Hannah?"

"Devin didn't steal that money. Neither did Bowie."

He nodded. "I know."

She leaned into him, even as she warned herself against falling for him, wanting more from him than he could give. “Thank you for coming back.”

He kissed the top of her head and squeezed her hand. “Let’s go grab some rags and get cleaning.”

Twenty-Six

January 3—Washington, D.C.

The inside of Jo Harper's ground-level Georgetown apartment was more or less what Grit had expected from the outside—small, efficient and a notch above a hotel room in personality. She was a Secret Service agent. She didn't count on staying in one place for long.

She'd had a call about Hannah Shay's discovery of the Three Sisters Café's empty petty-cash jar in the cellar. The cops were all excited, which showed Grit just how desperate everyone was getting.

Then again, who was looking for a firebug based on a tip from a genius kid?

"Your plants died," Grit said, pointing to a couple of dead-looking houseplants in the window over the sink. There were dead plants in her window box outside, too.

Jo gave the drooping former greenery a cursory glance. "They were dead before I left for Vermont in November."

"Is that a good thing or a bad thing?"

"Just a fact."

Grit turned and leaned back against the sink. He'd never been one to care much about where he was, provided he could get done what he had to do. That wasn't looking too good at the moment. Charlie's CD was filled with stuff he'd pulled off the Internet and scanned about firebugs, smoke jumpers, search-and-rescue dogs, open arson investigations and such. Charlie had added charts and his own analysis. Grit figured he'd be a hundred by the time he went through it all.

He looked at Jo. She wasn't in a cheery mood, either. "I thought I might find pictures of mountain valleys and moose on the walls," he said.

She frowned at him. "Why?"

"Reminders of home."

"What do you have on your walls, Grit?"

"Paint and a couple of flies I smooshed."

"What color paint?"

"What do you mean 'what color?' Who cares? It's paint. Beige, I think. Maybe it's white that's turned beige. It's not a great apartment." He nodded as he took in her place, its furnishings tidy and a lot more modern than anything he'd seen in her string of cabins on the lake in Vermont. "This place is in a good location."

"I pay for location in no space and no light." She pushed a palm through her copper hair. "You see Elijah here, Grit?"

"Nope."

"You could have hesitated."

"Why?"

She sighed. "To make me feel good. Everything's happened so fast with Elijah and me."

"Fast? It's been fifteen years."

"Most of which we spent apart."

"Love's not enough for you two?"

"It wasn't fifteen years ago, was it?"

"Well. Here's what I see. If you want Elijah to move to Washington, you'll need an apartment that doesn't have such low ceilings. If you two want kids, more space would be good."

She got a pained look, as if she were longing for something she believed deep down would always remain just out of reach. Grit saw the dark circles under her eyes and the strain at the corners of her mouth. “Kids, Grit,” she said. “How can I think about kids when I don’t even know where I’ll be living in a month?”

“Takes nine months to have a kid, Jo. And the kid doesn’t care where you live.”

“If I’m—”

“Jo. You’re overthinking. Vermont and Washington are both good bases for you and Elijah. Army’s not done with him yet. He just doesn’t know it. He thinks he’s ready to chop wood and pull hikers off Cameron Mountain.”

“His father . . .” Jo breathed out at the ceiling. “Drew came here right before Elijah was wounded. He asked me to go see the cherry blossoms with him. I did, and he told me he’d been having visions of the children Elijah and I would have had if we’d stayed together. They felt so real to him.”

“Maybe they were real. Maybe those kids he saw are still waiting to be born.”

Jo looked at him. “You don’t see the

world the same way other people do, Grit, do you?"

"I just see the world as I see it. Come on. Myrtle's summoned us to her house."

Jo pulled some fuzzy brown rotted leaves off a plant and dropped them in the sink. "Your leg, Grit." She spoke without looking at him. "Do you ever think about what your life would be like if you could go back in time and . . ." She shrugged. "I don't even know what I'm saying. Never mind."

"Go back in time and what, get shot in the head and die instantly?"

She made a face at him. "No. I told you—"

He interrupted her. "Yeah, actually, I do think about that. What about you, Agent Harper? Do you think about where you'd be if Charlie Neal hadn't shot you in the butt with airsoft pellets?"

"It was in the hip, Grit." She rinsed bits of the dead gunk off her fingers. "I wouldn't have been in Black Falls when Alex Bruni was killed here in D.C. and his daughter took off onto Cameron Mountain by herself."

"Elijah would have had to handle those

killers by himself, which probably he could have done, but he also wouldn't have had sex in a rickety old cabin, and that I doubt he'd have wanted to do without—"

"Grit."

He gave her an innocent look. "Am I supposed to pretend you two aren't having relations?"

She grinned at him. "Relations? Who says *relations* anymore? Myrtle?"

"Me. Speaking of Myrtle, she's waiting for us."

"All right, let's go." Jo paused and glared at him. "Bring up my sex life again, and I *will* shoot you in the head."

"I'll keep that in mind."

Something about his expression must have gotten to her, because she stopped abruptly, winced with regret. "Grit . . . I didn't mean to . . ."

"It's okay. I have good days and bad days. Today's not one of the good ones."

They went back outside and got in her car. He and Myrtle had driven it down from the frozen north. Jo had flown with Francona. She sat behind the wheel.

Grit eyed her. "Don't you need directions to Myrtle's house?"

She gave him a sideways glance. "No."

Grit settled into his seat. "You Secret Service agents know everything, don't you? Do you know where I live?"

"In a crummy apartment with beige-white walls and dead flies."

"Roaches, too." He closed his eyes. "I hate roaches."

"Rats?"

"Myrtle says probably."

"What is it with you two?"

"Kindred spirits. She's like a tough, crazy aunt. Don't tell her that."

"You didn't know her before November?"

"Nope." He opened one eye and looked over at Jo. "Is this an official interview? Should I call you Agent Harper?"

"I'm just making conversation."

She'd been in a tight, tense mood since she'd faced Charlie Neal making waffles in Vermont. The kid could fry her career. He almost had. But it was also having Elijah there and seeing him go Special Forces soldier with the vice president's son. She'd realized he wasn't the same kid she'd fallen for in high school and had the reality hit her that he had spent the past fifteen years as a highly professional soldier.

They drove up Massachusetts Avenue and onto a side street of attractive brick houses. Myrtle's had fit right in until her office had caught on fire. It was in the front of the house. She'd told Grit she'd picked that room for the view of the rhododendrons in the spring.

He truly hadn't figured out yet if she'd been kidding him about the rhodies.

Myrtle was outside inspecting the boarded-up fire damage from her plush yard when he and Jo headed up the front walk. "I could make it livable while they work on it. I just haven't bothered."

"Denial," Grit said.

She scoffed and stepped in among evergreen shrubs for a better look. "How can I deny a burned-out office? Give me a break." She pried back a prickly branch. "I look reality square in the eye every day, and what I see isn't pretty. When I arrived back in Washington, I felt as if I'd arrived home from exile. But Vermont has its charms."

"Do you want me to give you a boost up to the window?"

She gave him a cool glance over her shoulder. "No, Grit, I do not."

His cell phone trilled. He wanted to ignore it, but he had a feeling it was Charlie Neal. Mark Francona personally had the kid buttoned up, but that didn't mean anything. Grit flipped open his phone, and Charlie said, "Alex Bruni was a difficult personality."

"Like you or different?"

"Different, although he was intelligent."

Charlie, Grit realized, was just stating the facts, not bragging.

"He was more arrogant. I'm not arrogant. I know I seem arrogant to some people because—well, I just do."

"Because of the one-eighty IQ."

"That's an approximation. Regardless, Ambassador Bruni often rubbed people the wrong way, but he didn't care. He blows off Drew Cameron in April. Two weeks later, Mr. Cameron's dead. Seven months later, Ambassador Bruni's dead, too." Charlie paused for a breath. "Something about Drew Cameron's visit in April clicked with Ambassador Bruni, and he became a danger to the killers."

"You're speculating," Grit said.

"I know. Ambassador Bruni had to feel guilty for stealing his best friend's wife, don't you think?"

"Maybe it wasn't stealing. Maybe it was just one of those things."

"Then his best friend goes and falls for a much younger woman, and his daughter freaks out. Then *he's* run over." Charlie paused. "Sometimes you just have to ask the right questions."

The kid disconnected.

Jo frowned at Grit. "Do I want to know?"

"Nope."

A straight-backed, gray-haired man—medium height, medium build—got out of a dark blue sedan and headed up Myrtle's walk. He was in a khaki naval officer's uniform. Grit noticed the four silver stars on the collar, designating a high-ranking admiral.

Had to be Jenkins.

"You look fit and able, Petty Officer Taylor," the admiral said.

"Thanks, sir. Admiral Jenkins, right? That really was you calling?"

"Correct. Think there's another Admiral Jenkins?"

"Could have been a prank."

"Wasn't." Jenkins nodded to Jo and Myrtle, and Grit introduced them. The admiral was polite but kept his attention on what he'd come there to do. "I have a job at the Pentagon for you. I'm making it happen."

"I have to find a firebug for the vice president's son."

"Vice president of what?"

"U.S."

A muscle worked in Jenkins's jaw. "You in trouble, Petty Officer?"

"Not me. No, sir. Never."

He glared past him at Myrtle. "She's the one whose Russian friend was poisoned."

It wasn't a question, but Grit said, "Yes, sir."

"He was a reporter. She's a reporter. I believe in free speech but that doesn't mean I like reporters."

"I heard that," Myrtle said. She smiled at him. "I like admirals."

Jenkins ignored her. "You have forty-eight hours to clean up whatever mess you're in the middle of," he told Grit.

"Sir, I'm not out of PT yet."

"I know. I checked. Time to decide. Medically retire or come back to work."

Grit didn't explain about how he'd been assigned light duty at the hospital while undergoing treatment, until this thing with the killers. Jenkins would know.

The admiral nodded to the two women, about-faced and left.

Jo shoved her hands into her jacket pockets. "Feels good to be back in D.C. with all the reporters and military brass running around."

"Secret Service agents, too," Grit said. "That's not why you're back here, though. You're back because you have to know you didn't miss anything when Drew Cameron came to D.C. in April."

"I did miss something, Grit," Jo said. "That's why he's dead."

"He's dead because those two killers made sure he froze on Cameron Mountain."

"We all missed things," Myrtle said, ever the wet blanket. "Come on. Let's go for crab cakes and bourbon."

"We'll stop by Bruni's office in the morning," Jo said.

Neither Grit nor Myrtle argued with her.

Twenty-Seven

January 3—Black Falls, Vermont

Vivian wrapped herself in a cashmere throw and sat cross-legged in front of the fire. She'd been unsettled ever since Sean Cameron's visit. He'd seemed to look right through her and didn't give her and Lowell so much as a goodbye glance over his shoulder on his way out. The man was on a tear, and she suspected it involved Hannah Shay.

Lowell busied himself topping off the wood box. He wore thick canvas work gloves that came up to his elbows; Vivian thought they looked ridiculous. "This whole business will bite us in the end," she said, unable to feel truly warm even this close to the fire.

"What business, Vivian? The killings?" He adjusted several logs on his woodpile, as if their arrangement mattered. "It's been weeks. The Camerons are just frustrated."

"My only concern is protecting us. You and me. Our family, our finances, our reputation. They mean nothing to you and everything to me. I don't know who to trust anymore."

"Maybe that's good, Vivian. Maybe we need to be less trusting."

"What are you saying?" She barely spoke in a whisper. "No. Never mind. I can't stand the thought of all of this backfiring and hurting *us*. Please don't do anything stupid and land us in the middle of something that could ruin me and our children."

"What about me?"

"You, too. Of course. That's what I meant when I said me. I think of us as a unit."

"Ah."

"We believed Kyle Rigby was an experienced mountain rescuer. We believed Melanie Kendall was an interior decorator who was in love with Thomas Asher."

"Everyone did, Vivian."

She tightened her throw around her as she stared at the fire, obsessed with the thought of the killers in her home. Kyle Rigby and Melanie Kendall had sat here in front of the fire pretending not to know each other.

"You can go back to New York," Lowell said.

Just the sound of his voice irritated her. "I won't leave you here alone. We'll both leave soon. And how would I feel safer by myself in New York?"

"We could hire bodyguards—"

"That's ridiculous."

He peeled off his work gloves and set them on top of the wood box. "Are you warming up to the idea of having a dog?"

"No."

"You could be right. Rose Cameron's golden retriever is extraordinary, but she has the time, skill and patience to train him. I wouldn't want an adult dog—I'd want a puppy. I don't know that I could train one to turn out like Ranger."

"You couldn't." She looked up at Lowell as he dusted bits of bark off his hands. "You just like the idea of a dog. Having a golden retriever trailing behind you here in Vermont fits your image of yourself as a country gentleman."

"Ranger *is* a beautiful animal."

She returned her gaze to the fire. "What if we're a loose end for these killers? What if we know something and don't realize it?"

"It's been a long day. Come have a drink."

"What if your precious Hannah is involved?" Vivian didn't move, just drew her knees up under her chin and wrapped her throw around them. "What if she and Bowie O'Rourke are working together? She's tried to put her past behind her, but what if she can't? What if he knows something about her that she doesn't want the rest of us to know, and he's using that to manipulate her? Or vice versa. She knows something about him."

"This is all a matter for the police," Lowell said patiently. "We're not from Black Falls. We weren't close to Drew Cameron or even to Alex Bruni and the Ashers, for that matter. We certainly weren't close to Melanie Kendall or Kyle Rigby. We were just being hospitable."

Vivian hardly heard her husband's words. He just wasn't a fighter. "Sean Cameron will take care of Hannah. I have no one who will take care of me."

"We're out of coffee and we need milk," Lowell said.

Of course he wouldn't reassure her. She watched red-hot coals fall from a burning log. "Lock the door on your way out."

As he drove down the winding road along the river, Lowell turned up the heat full blast and flipped on the seat warmer. The snow squalls had covered the road with an inch of fresh powder, but the sanders had been out. His car's headlights were all that penetrated the darkness. There was no moon. The dark mountains loomed around him, and somehow the stars seemed farther away than they did in New York—when they could be seen at all—but they were also brighter, sharper against the black night sky. He and Vivian had talked about taking a class in astronomy and learning the constellations.

More lights appeared as he came to the village. Christmas lights still lit up the town green. He pulled into a space in front of the library and looked across Main Street to Sean Cameron's brick house and the café.

The café was lit up, and he could see Zack Harper, Beth Harper, Scott Thorne, Dominique Belair—he whispered their names as if they were his friends. He was only forty-eight, but he suddenly felt old. Vivian would say she wanted to meet people in Black Falls and be involved in the community, but she also recognized that they were destined to remain apart from them. "They'll never let us in," she'd say, "and that's not what we want, anyway."

Yet Lowell longed to walk over to the café and be a part of relationships formed in childhood. He and Vivian and their children and friends lived in a bigger, more open world than this one small, insular Vermont town. He didn't romanticize Black Falls. He knew its shortcomings. He didn't care—he wanted this simple life made up not of people scattered across the country, even the globe, but who lived nearby, who had to deal with each other because who else was there?

His heart jumped when Hannah came

into the front window. She was smiling, laughing. She was so delicate, so vulnerable—and she had fire and grit. She knew from experience that being passive and hoping for the best never worked.

He shuddered as the heat went out of his car. There were those he'd hired and who'd hired him over the past fifteen months who would be anything but passive. They weren't ones who hoped for the best. They made it happen, and they'd deal with him should he fail.

He'd covered his tracks well, but it would only take one person, one mistake, to undo him.

He had to make certain that didn't happen.

Then Sean Cameron slipped in next to Hannah in such a proprietary way that Lowell cringed, his stomach twisting in real, not just emotional, pain. Vivian would be disgusted with him and remind him how incompetent he was compared to any of the Cameron brothers.

If she could lust after them, why couldn't he lust after Hannah?

It was more than lust, Lowell thought

as he started his car again. His feelings for Hannah Shay were as pure as any he'd ever known.

They didn't mean he couldn't do what he knew he had to do. He understood when a situation demanded caution and restraint, and when one demanded boldness and action.

He headed down Main Street. He would drive up Cameron Mountain Road to the ridge. If anyone saw him, he would say he was looking at the stars. But he wasn't worried.

No one would see him.

Twenty-Eight

Sean took a bucket of dirty cleaning water from Hannah and dumped it into the utility sink in the back storage room. "The work helps clear my head," she said as he set the bucket in the sink. She turned on the faucet and filled it with fresh hot water, the steam helping to return some color to her cheeks. "Bowie didn't stash that money jar. He's not that subtle. He'd just have smashed it and grabbed the cash."

"Why didn't you tell me about the leak in the cellar sooner?"

"I didn't think it was that bad."

She didn't protest when he lifted the

bucket out of the sink and carried it to the dining room. "Where did everyone go?"

"Home." He set the bucket on the floor by a back table. "The place is clean. You can dump out this water and—"

"I might as well wipe down these windowsills," she said, pointing to the riverside windows.

"Does Rose ever join you on cleaning night?" Sean asked.

Hannah shook her head as she grabbed a steaming cleaning rag out of the bucket and suspended it in midair, letting it drip into the water.

"A.J. and Lauren are concerned she's spending too much time alone."

"She was upset about your father as it was. Then came that mess in November. It's a lot."

"She'll work her way through it," Sean said.

"She's strong, yes. A true Cameron. Granite spines." Hannah gently squeezed excess water from the rag. She wasn't wearing gloves. "There could be a man, too, you know."

He reached for a sponge floating in the bucket. "Do you know something, Hannah?"

She smiled at him. "I know that men can be a problem."

"Women can't?"

"Romance, then. Romance can be a problem."

"Are we talking about Rose, or are we talking about you? If you and Bowie—"

"Bowie's covered in plaster and cement dust half the time, and he's more like family than anything else." She slapped her rag onto a windowsill, scrubbing nonexistent grime. "I'm not falling for Bowie, Sean, and he's not falling for me. After my mother died, he was security. He helped out. He has his demons. That's why he stayed away for as long as he did."

"Maybe he's back because of you."

"He's back because he loves it out on the river, and his place there is the one thing he owns in this world. It'd be hard to sell. He wouldn't get anything for it—and he doesn't want to sell it. The hollow wasn't his problem." She moved to another windowsill, attacking it with as much fervor. "Scott called Devin and Toby and asked them both about the money jar."

"Were they any help?"

She shook her head. "They're just as

creeped out by the idea of a killer walking in here under our noses as I am."

Sean said nothing, just took his sponge and wiped up the drips from Hannah's rag.

"Devin's as fascinated as ever by your work as a firefighter," she said. "He mentions it whenever we talk, even tonight. Your friend Nick's been telling him what he needs to do to become a smoke jumper."

"It takes a lot of work," Sean said. "He's in good shape from humping up and down Vermont mountains. He can do it. He'll have to get experience before he can try out. He'll know."

"What if he fails?"

"He'll have learned a lot about himself as well as have developed some solid skills along the way. We all fail, Hannah. We all make mistakes."

She glanced back at him, her cheeks rosy from the steam of the hot water and the exertion of her manic cleaning. "Do you think I baby my brothers?"

Sean shrugged, standing up with his sponge. "You're protective of them. It's understandable."

"Why, because they're orphans? Because I'm—"

"Hannah. Hell." He grinned at her. "Stop already."

She smiled. "I'm sorry. It's a sore spot with me, obviously. I guess there's a fine line between providing helpful encouragement and support and being overprotective. I just want to be there for them."

"Has anyone ever been there for you?"

"Yes, but that's not the point."

"You're so serious," he said. "When's the last time you really laughed?"

She tossed her wet rag at him. He caught it and laughed, and next thing, he had her over his shoulder and was carrying her into the center hall and up the curving stairs to her apartment. The bucket, the wet sponge, the wet rag—they all could wait right where they were.

He carried her all the way back to her bedroom without so much as a peep from her.

"Thank God your brothers are in California," he said, laying her on the bed, coming up off her. "Hannah, kick me out if you have to, but at least let me kiss you first."

She was already draping her arms over his shoulders, pulling his mouth to hers. "Those men last spring." She spoke between light kisses, obviously determined to get the words out. "What they said about me wasn't true."

"Nothing they said matters."

"No, Sean. It does matter. What they said wasn't true."

"I know," he whispered, her hands cold on his as she caught his fingertips into hers. An urgency he'd never experienced surged through him. He had to have her. Now. "Hannah, if you want me to go . . ." But he freed his hands from hers and skimmed his palms over her, through her clothes, her soft shirt, her jeans, and he heard her moan, felt her sink deeper into the layers of blankets. He said, finally, "I'll go."

"Don't go."

It was a whisper between kisses, and when she slipped her hands under his shirt, they weren't cold anymore. He smiled. "Now that I know you won't freeze, I feel free to tear off your clothes."

"I was hoping that's what you were thinking." Her hands drifted lower, easing between his jeans and the hot, bare skin of his hips. "You're very warm yourself."

"About to get warmer," he muttered, lifting her shirt, trying to be patient, even gentle.

But he was aching, the feel of her smooth skin, the sight of her breasts in her filmy slip of a bra almost more than he could handle. He took a moment to get his jeans off, and when he came back to her, he'd lost all patience for tiny clasps and delicate fabrics. "I'll buy you a new one," he said, snapping the bra, whisking it off her.

Her nipples were pink and pebbly, and he heard her gasp, knew she was self-conscious. He responded by taking one nipple between his lips, tonguing it as he eased her pants down her hips. She moaned, parting her thighs as he slid his fingers between her legs, found the heat and wetness of her. As much as he wanted to drive into her now, without waiting, without thinking—just give in to the pounding ache—he wanted even more to satisfy her. To feel her urgency, to feel her in release.

He scraped her nipple with his teeth as he eased his fingers into her, thrusting as she went very still. She seemed almost to stop breathing. He didn't relent. He trailed his tongue down her abdomen, over her hips, then followed where his fingers had been.

He was on fire now. Heat and desire poured out of her, and she cried out as he drove into her, clawing at him in a frenzy of wanting, matching his pace with a want and urgency of her own. She held him, quaking in his arms as she came, and it was all he needed before he let himself go.

It was a long time before they needed to crawl under the blankets.

"Sean . . ." She felt warm next to him. "I don't think you need to worry about the furnace this winter."

He laughed and held her close, knowing there was no going back now. Elijah's truck was parked outside. It'd be parked out there in the morning. By dawn, word would be out that he'd spent the night with Hannah Shay.

Twenty-Nine

January 4—Black Falls, Vermont

Hannah had showered, dressed and was on her way down to the café before sunup, leaving Sean warm under the covers in her bed. She didn't know whether he was asleep or wide-awake, contemplating finding himself in her bed. Would he get out of there before either of her "sisters" arrived, or would he join them for coffee and scones as they did their morning routines?

He'd been about five minutes behind her, and when she'd seen him in the light in the café dining room, dressed and fully awake, she'd had to stifle a wave of the stubborn self-consciousness that had plagued her for so long. He'd caught her around the waist and kissed her, lifting her off her feet. Dominique or Beth or anyone could have walked in, and it pleased Hannah that he didn't seem to care. He'd gone off to collect Elijah to see their sister and take another look at the crypt.

She hadn't had any nightmares last night.

Now, ten minutes after Sean had left out the back, she pulled a stool over to the counter to do paperwork ahead of a visit from a supplier later that morning, but she couldn't concentrate and closed her notebook and laptop. Beth and Dominique had the routines at the café under control. They hadn't mentioned finding a cold cleaning bucket in the dining room. Hannah figured they could draw their own conclusions. She could feel Sean warm next to her in her bed and suddenly she realized she didn't care who knew he'd spent the night in her apartment or what anyone thought of it.

Beth sprayed hot water into a sink full of baking pans. She shut off the faucet and wiped her wet hands on her apron. "I hate doing dishes. Have I ever mentioned that?"

Hannah smiled. "Every day."

"Ah. Every day I forget how much I hate doing dishes. Especially pots and pans." She leaned back against the sink. "Plans for the day?"

"I can finish up here. After that I don't know."

Judge Robinson appeared in the back doorway to the kitchen and invited Hannah to join him out in the café. "If you have time," he said.

Beth turned back to the sink and said cheerfully, "That's the judge's 'make time' voice. I'm fine here. Back to sink duty. You two go talk Thomas Jefferson and John Adams."

Hannah joined the judge at his favorite table in the corner by the side porch that faced Elm Street. "I crave sugar and caffeine," he said cheerfully, a warm scone and mug of coffee in front of him. "I wonder if it's winter."

"In August you wondered if it was summer."

"I always said you have a mind for detail." He leaned back in his chair. "It's also a mind that's not focused right now on getting ready to study for a bar exam." He smiled at her. “I’m an experienced jurist. I can tell.”

Hannah didn’t argue. “I’ve been thinking about Drew and Bowie in the months before Drew’s death. I knew Bowie was working in Black Falls. I thought I had Drew all figured out as a hard-bitten, unforgiving man—decent, but once you’d crossed him, you were done.”

“But he gave Bowie another chance and recommended him for a job at the Four Corners church,” Everett said.

“What if it was a mistake that cost him his life? What if Bowie knew about Drew’s cabin and told Melanie Kendall or Kyle Rigby—”

“Inadvertently, Hannah, or deliberately?”

She looked out at the street, quiet on the cold morning. “Bowie’s an expert on historic stonework.”

“Yes, he is,” the judge said. “It’s an interest of mine—of a lot of people in this area.”

Hannah turned from the window. “I’m going out to talk to him.”

“He’s working at the Whittaker place, isn’t he? He might appreciate the company. Vivian isn’t an easy person. She can be belittling and controlling. Lowell doesn't say anything, but he must notice. People order their lives in different ways, but when a couple relies on that kind of communication style . . . it doesn't make them easy to be around."

"Communication style?"

"All right." He shrugged, grinning. "So I'd smother her with a pillow if I were married to her."

"Then you'd come before a judge in the state of Vermont and off you'd go to prison. You can't take the law into your own hands."

"That doesn't mean one can't fantasize." He sighed, sitting back, his scone barely touched. "You're under a lot of strain, Hannah. Everyone in town is. We're all struggling to get back to normal, but until we have answers, it'll be difficult."

"What's on your mind, Judge?"

"Crime and punishment."

"Are you talking about Bowie or my father?"

"Neither. I'm talking about you."

"I learned a love of the woods and New England history from my father. I'm not making excuses for Bowie, if that's what you're worried about. If he's involved with these killers—wittingly or unwittingly . . ." She felt a tightness in her throat. "I was rough on him last night. He's had a chance to think, and so have I."

"Hannah—"

She smiled at him as she got to her feet. "I'll take my cell phone and call you if we get into a snowball fight."

She left him at his table and went into the center hall and back to the mudroom. She grabbed her coat, hat and gloves and slipped on the boots she'd worn when she'd snowshoed up Cameron Mountain to find Drew's cabin.

It was below zero, the coldest morning yet of the winter. She got in her car and gave it a minute to warm up before she headed out past the common and up along the river.

She pulled in next to Bowie's van in the turnaround at the guesthouse and parked tight next to a snowbank. Even with her hat yanked down over her ears and forehead and her jacket zipped up to her chin, she could feel the brutal cold as she made her way along the walk. It had been shoveled since this last snowfall, but not sanded or salted.

She quickly mounted the porch steps and noticed the storm door was ajar. She knocked on the doorjamb and called Bowie, but he didn't come.

A dog barked behind her, and she went back down the steps. The wind stirred up the fresh snow, whipping it into her face. She spotted Poe wandering by himself under the weeping willows down by the frozen, white-blanketed duck pond.

Where was Bowie?

Hannah saw only the black lab's prints in the snow. The ski tracks on the slope down from the Whittakers' farmhouse were dusted over with undisturbed fresh snow. With the brutal windchill, she doubted either Vivian or Lowell would be out for a recreational spin across the meadow anytime soon.

"Come on, Poe," Hannah said. "Let's get you warm and go find your master."

She couldn't stifle a prickly feeling as she stepped into the knee-deep snow.

Thirty

Sean had collected Elijah out at his house on the lake just as the sunrise consumed the sky in shades of red, orange and lavender, which made his life in Southern California seem very far away. His brother wasn't in a good mood as they drove up Cameron Mountain Road to their sister's house. "Hannah's got to live in Black Falls after you go back to Beverly Hills," Elijah said.

"Who's to say I didn't sleep on her couch?"

"I'm just saying. Be careful."

"Elijah—"

"She doesn't have to explain herself to me, and neither do you. People in town know her better than she gives us credit for, or better than she realizes. That bar fight in March changed things for her. She's been off balance, wondering if people think those bastards were telling the truth about her."

"I wish I'd shut them up sooner."

"Yeah. A.J. and I do, too. Instead we let Bowie tear their damn heads off. All in all, I think he was restrained. Doesn't mean he should have done it."

Or, Sean knew, that any of them should have, either. Hannah lived in Black Falls, and she'd just slept with a Cameron. People liked to talk about her. Last night they'd given them fodder.

"Hannah's a private person," Elijah said.

"I got out of there as early as I could. Maybe I made a mistake staying last night, but I wasn't leaving her there alone."

His brother gave him an unwavering look. "What's between you two is your business. You're old enough to take care of yourself." He grinned. "Hannah can take care of you, too. I don't worry about her."

"She has more friends in this town than I do."

"Than any of us. She's got backbone, she's a hard worker and she's a gentle soul."

"I don't intend to break her heart."

Elijah was silent a moment. "I didn't intend to break Jo's heart."

"Have you heard from her?"

"Nope."

They climbed out of the truck into the dry, heart-stopping cold of January in northern New England. The front had blown in overnight. It was Sean's favorite kind of winter day. Why hadn't he just grabbed Hannah and pulled her back under the blankets?

Elijah looked at his younger brother as they walked across their sister's frozen driveway. "This is your show."

Sean nodded without argument. "What if she's not up?"

"Then we get her up," Elijah said.

They found Rose already out in the snow with Ranger. Sean saw from her expression that she knew they weren't there to help her fill her wood box or sand her walks. He didn't give her a chance to adjust. “A California arson investigator named Jasper Vanderhorn was killed in a fire last June. How well did you know him?”

She glanced at Elijah, then looked out at her dog pawing in a snowbank. “Not well. I know what you’re asking. Yes, I’m just afraid my distractions helped cause his death.”

Sean shook his head. “There’s no evidence of that. The fire was still hot. It shouldn’t have been. That’s not your area of expertise.”

“Does Jo suspect Jasper’s a potential victim of these killers? Or do you?”

Sean didn’t back down. “What happened in California?”

“Nothing that matters. Please don’t ask me anything else, Sean. If the police have questions for me, they can ask them. Pop’s gone, but you and Elijah and A.J. aren’t his replacements. You’re my brothers.”

“You weren’t in town in November,” Elijah said.

She was silent.

Sean steadied himself against the bitter cold.

“I hired Bowie,” Rose said. “It’s not a secret. It’s just none of your business.”

Elijah stabbed a toe into a snowbank. If he was patient with Hannah, he wasn't with his sister. "He'd just gotten out of jail. He's on probation—"

"I know. He also fixed my stone wall."

Sean nodded to the fading sunrise. "Nice view of the lodge from here."

Rose wasn't as combative now. "I think Hannah noticed, too. Other people have been up here. Judge Robinson, the McBanes, Lowell Whittaker. Dozens of people could have inadvertently mentioned the view to the wrong person. We don't even know the bomb was triggered here."

"We're done," Elijah said, turning to his sister. "You're not staying here alone."

"My house isn't the only point on this road the killer could have used."

Elijah ignored her. "The lake, A.J.'s, the lodge. Pick one. Pack. Let's go."

Ranger sat on Rose's foot, as if he wanted to get as close to her as possible. She didn't back down. "Maybe I'll fly to California and stay at Sean's house and swim in his heated pool."

Elijah didn't back down, either. "That'd work."

Sean noticed the barest flicker of pain

in his sister's eyes as she shook her head. "No, it wouldn't work. Elijah, I'll stay with you. I know it must be lonely for you without Jo." She immediately gasped and said, "I'm sorry. That was a low blow."

Elijah grinned at her. "Nah. You just stated a fact. It *is* lonely without her."

"You and Jo were by Melanie Kendall's car that day. You'd just grabbed Nora out of the front seat. She's an innocent teenager. She could have been blown up. You and Jo . . ." Rose inhaled. "If whoever set off that bomb did it here . . . I don't care if he was used or paid off, if Bowie was involved—"

"First things first," Elijah said. "Get your dog biscuits or whatever you need. Sean and I will drop you off at the lodge with A.J."

Five minutes later, they were on their way. Rose drove her own car, and Elijah and Sean followed her out Ridge Road. Sean called Hannah, but she didn't answer her cell phone. He tried the café, but she wasn't there.

A.J., Lauren and their two young children were just arriving at the lodge. Sean saw Elijah's tight expression and knew his brother shared his fear. “A.J. didn’t bargain for killers turning up in his backyard,” Elijah said.

“You can stay, and I’ll go on,” Sean said. “I’ll be fine.”

Elijah shook his head. “A.J. and Lauren know what to do. Rose’s head’s not screwed on straight. It hasn’t been for a while. Even if she knows what to do to protect herself, it doesn’t mean she’ll do it. Sometimes,” Elijah added, “people just get reckless.”

Sean didn’t argue. They gave A.J. a brief update, and as Rose got out of her car with Ranger, Sean saw that their baby sister was as pale and withdrawn as he’d ever seen her. He tried to speak to her, but she just muttered about needing to walk Ranger. A.J. fell in next to her as she and her golden retriever headed off into the snow by the stone terrace.

When Sean and Elijah were back on Ridge Road, Elijah dug out his cell phone and made a call. “Do you and your pals in law enforcement have Rose’s place down as a spot where whoever triggered that bomb could have seen Melanie Kendall get in her car?” He listened to her answer.

"Get off this task force, Jo." He disconnected and dropped the phone back in his pocket.

"What did she say?" Sean asked.

"She told me to go throw a log on my woodstove."

"When you suggested she get off the task force—"

"It wasn't a suggestion," Elijah said, then shrugged, unperturbed. "She hung up."

"I would have, too," Sean said. "Let's have another look at the crypt."

"We're on the same wavelength," Elijah said. "Melanie Kendall's car was parked at the lodge most of that day. Someone could have placed the bomb in it while it was there."

"Then went up to Rose's and triggered it."

"Not a stranger. A.J. was on high alert while Jo and I were on the mountain. He'd have noticed strangers." Elijah glanced over at his brother. "The bomb had to have been made somewhere. The black powder, the gunpowder, the copper wire—they had to be stored somewhere, or maybe in several places so as not to draw suspicion. That's what I'd do."

When they stopped at the cemetery, Sean knew they were both thinking about Bowie. They headed down the lane. Theirs were the first prints in the fresh snow.

Elijah knocked the stick out of the latch and entered the crypt.

It wasn't empty this time.

Sean went inside with his brother. A bright ray of the cold winter light struck a roll of thin copper wire. Next to it were number-ten cans. Elijah peeled back lids, revealing several inches of gunpowder and black powder.

"Our guy's back at it," Elijah said.

Sean nodded. "It doesn't matter if he planted this stuff for us or if he's arrogant enough to think we wouldn't come back here."

Elijah headed out of the crypt. Sean fell in next to him as they headed back down the lane to the truck. "You can wait here for the police," Sean said. "I'm going after Hannah."

"I'm going with you." Elijah climbed in behind the wheel and glanced over at Sean. "We'll get to her in time, brother."

"It's obvious?"

"Since Thanksgiving for me." Elijah

stuck the key in the ignition, his hand steady. "Jo saw it earlier. She's tuned in to these things now, but don't tell her I said so." He nodded to his brother. "Call A.J. Have him get in touch with the police. If we call them . . ."

"They'll have us wait here, which will waste time. Jo?"

"She's a federal agent, Sean. We don't want to disobey a direct order from her, either." Elijah threw the truck into gear. "A.J. can call her, too."

Thirty-One

January 4—Washington, D.C.

Grit met Jo in the lobby of Alex Bruni's building a few blocks from the White House. Her badge got them into the elevator. On the way up to the fourth floor, she told him about the goings-on in Vermont. Elijah hadn't called and updated her, Grit had noted. Trooper Thorne had. She didn't seem mad—more like she'd expected it and would have done the same in Elijah's place.

"The crypt's a good choice to assemble a bomb," Grit said. "Last place I'd look."

"If you were caught—"

"You'd want to be someone who could

explain being in a Vermont cemetery on a cold winter day." He glanced at her. "Please tell me that's not everyone in Black Falls."

She ignored him. "There was nothing in the crypt after Bowie and Hannah were hurt," she said. "I should have thought to test for gunpowder and black powder traces."

"Elijah has a point. Maybe our bomber tucked supplies in different spots all over your cute Vermont town. He might not have had explosives in the crypt until now, or he might not have assembled the bomb in there."

"So, what happened with Bowie and Hannah out there last week? The voice, the falling rock—"

"O'Rourke didn't start work on the culvert until after Rigby and Kendall were killed. Our guy could have left something behind at the crypt and went back to get it. Maybe it was the first real chance he had. O'Rourke turns up, then Hannah. Our guy knocks over the rock and escapes."

"Why call Hannah's name?"

Grit raised his eyebrows. "Wouldn't you? Cemetery. Dusk. Cold. Relentless woman about to discover you. You whisper her name and figure she'll beat a path out of there."

"Not Hannah," Jo said.

"Then later, when our guy figures he's got to take action again, he thinks what the hell, I've got to blow something else up, might as well go back up to the crypt, assemble the bomb and implicate Bowie O'Rourke while I'm at it."

"That's devious thinking. Most criminals aren't that complicated."

Grit shrugged. "We're not talking about most criminals."

She tensed visibly. "Blow 'something' up means blow 'someone' up, Grit." She sighed. "I don't know anything anymore."

"Anymore? Who says any of us ever know anything to begin with?"

She gave him a curt smile. "True." She sighed again. "This is one damn slow elevator. What'd you do last night?"

"De-roached my apartment. Leave and they take over. You?"

"Cleaned."

"Sleep?"

Her tight shake of the head was her only answer.

"Myrtle's meeting with carpenters this

morning," Grit said cheerfully. "She's thinking about selling her place after people forget it was set on fire. I think it's safe to say she won't be moving to Vermont."

"She likes her independence." The elevator dinged when it came to the fourth floor, and in that split second before the doors opened, Jo said, "So does Elijah. All the Camerons are that way. They do their own thing and you can follow or not."

"Aren't you doing your own thing?"

"Elijah isn't law enforcement, Grit."

"You barely are."

She held the elevator door open with one hand and turned her turquoise eyes to him. "Are you going to keep rubbing salt into my wounds?"

"What?" He was mystified.

"I'm breaking the rules coming here alone—having you here—"

"Did you tell Deputy Special Agent in Charge Mark Francona?"

She stepped out of the elevator into a carpeted hall. "No."

"Relax, Agent Harper. Ambassador Bruni's secretary likes me."

"You've met?"

"No, we haven't met. Not yet."

Jo didn't say anything as they entered the elegant office. The secretary did like him, but she was also married. Young and pretty, she was packing boxes to close up the office now that the police had finished with it. "The ambassador's wife and step-daughter are stopping by later this week," she said, all professional. "I told the police everything I know." She was obviously still shaken even after more than a month. "I'm just closing up his office now. My last day is in two weeks. Then I'm taking a vacation and trying to forget."

"Did you listen at keyholes when the ambassador was alive?" Grit asked.

Jo's eyebrows went up, but she kept quiet. The secretary got huffy. "Of course not."

"He was a prickly guy," Grit said. "I wouldn't have been able to resist. Did he unload on you? You know, did you sit here after hours with a bottle of wine—"

"Ambassador Bruni was loyal to his wife."

"That doesn't mean he can't have a glass or two of wine with his secretary, does it?"

"Sometimes . . ." She sniffed. "*Twice.*

He worked late and had to go to a dinner, and in between—it was never more than one glass of wine."

"You'd talk?"

"Some. About my goals and policy opinions. I love all that. He hated talking about work unless he had to."

"What else did you talk about over your one glass of wine?"

"His frustrations with Nora. His stepdaughter. Normal stuff—he really tried to do right by her. He knew she was angry at him and her mother for what they did to her father. That's how she saw it."

Grit realized Jo was letting him loose, but he avoided her eye just in case she changed her mind. "He looked to you for advice because you're young and female?"

"Ambassador Bruni wasn't a man who looked to anyone for advice. He was just venting over a glass of wine. He wanted to do right by Nora. Really, he did."

"What about his visit from Drew Cameron in April?"

"He was murdered, too. I can't believe . . ."

"Ambassador Bruni didn't know Drew

had been murdered before he himself was killed," Jo said.

"I think . . . at the end . . ." The young secretary fidgeted. "I think the ambassador was getting suspicious about something. I remember the day Mr. Cameron was here. The ambassador was especially frustrated with Nora. She was a high school senior. You know how that can be. All the angst and drama. She was here, too, and he bit Mr. Cameron's head off."

Grit nodded sympathetically. "It's tough being a stepdad."

"Yes, that's right," she said, warming up again, less fidgety. "Right before he was killed in November, he said he wished he'd been nicer and listened, because he thought Drew—that's what he called him—was onto something in Black Falls. They both loved Black Falls. Ambassador Bruni said it was the one place he could truly relax and be himself, not such a bastard. He'd been going up there for several years. He stayed at the Cameron family's lodge."

"He and the Whittakers became friends after they bought their place in Black Falls," Jo said. "He stayed with them a few times."

"I almost forgot, but yes, that's right."

"What did he say about the Whittakers?" Grit asked.

"Not much. Nora was living in their guesthouse. Ambassador Bruni remembered that Drew Cameron had asked about them."

"Asked what?"

The secretary looked awkward and blushed.

"Ha," Grit said. "You did listen at the keyhole."

"I did *not.* I just—I just didn't remember when the police asked me. I don't want them to think I'm holding back."

"Just tell us what you remember now," Jo said.

"Ambassador Bruni was drinking wine, sitting here on the corner of his desk. It was as if I wasn't here. I think that's why I didn't think of it—it seemed so in passing. He was just thinking out loud. Mr. Cameron had come in here specifically to ask him what he thought of Lowell and Vivian Whittaker and Thomas Asher. 'Who are these people?' he'd asked."

It was Jo who asked the next question. "Did Drew say why he wanted to know?"

"Not really."

"What do you mean, 'not really'?"

The secretary scrunched up her face, remembering. "Mr. Whittaker had helped him or he had helped Mr. Whittaker. I don't remember which."

"Something about stonework?" Grit asked. "An old foundation, maybe?"

"An old cellar hole," Jo said.

"That's it. An old cellar hole." The young woman was clearly pleased with herself. "It's not a phrase I use. He was interested in old cellar holes in the area. Old stonework. Mr. Whittaker was, too. Mr. Cameron had a project—it was a few months earlier. We're talking more than a year ago. It can't be relevant, can it?"

"We'll find out," Jo said. "Thank you."

"No problem. Is that all?"

"For now."

Jo walked out into the hall with Grit. "Drew had his doubts about Lowell Whittaker. Not enough for the police or to tell Rose and the boys."

"Maybe Lowell didn't want the scrutiny and knew Drew would keep digging. He was like that, wasn't he?"

"A Cameron. Lowell nipped his questions in the bud. Bruni's, too."

"Yeah," Grit said, pressing the elevator button. "You call Elijah a boy? Really?"

"Grit . . ."

His comment sparked a smile in her, and that was good. When they got downstairs, Myrtle was out front. She'd come on her own. "I talked to a window washer who remembers Drew from April," she said. "Useless."

"Sometimes there are no worms under the rocks we turn over," Grit said philosophically.

Jo was pensive. "I knew Drew had stuff on his mind in the weeks before he died. Elijah. The two of us. But there was more, and we saw the cherry blossoms together and he never told me."

Grit shrugged. "He didn't know what he had would get him killed. He'd stepped on a land mine. It just hadn't gone off yet."

Jo was dialing Black Falls. "Sean and Elijah can't be freelancing," she said. "They need to get the police in there."

"They armed?"

"Grit. It doesn't matter. It's not a war zone."

He and Myrtle looked at each other, but neither said anything.

Thirty-Two

January 4—Black Falls, Vermont

Bowie's van was unlocked. Hannah had led Poe by the collar up from the pond, and he looked eager to get into the van. She opened up the side door. "In you go, Poe. I'll see if I can find your master."

When she turned around, Lowell Whittaker was there, in a parka, hat, gloves and boots. He must have walked down from the farmhouse on the road, or he'd been in the guesthouse and hadn't heard her knock.

He smiled at her. "I didn't mean to startle you."

"Have you seen Bowie?" she asked him.

"It's not like him to leave Poe wandering around by himself."

Lowell gestured back toward the house. "He's taking a look at the chimney in the farmhouse. Vivian thinks there might be a leak. He must have left Poe here."

"We'll be lucky it if gets above zero today. Are you heading back up there? I can give you a ride—"

"I don't mind walking. I'm prepared for the cold." He gestured back toward the guesthouse. "I want to take another look at the color Vivian chose for the kitchen in Nora's old apartment."

"If you see Bowie before I do, will you let him know I'm here and collected Poe?"

"Of course. You're welcome to stop by the house yourself." Lowell tilted his head back, frowning. "You don't seem yourself, Hannah. Nothing's wrong, is there?"

"Just snow in my boots."

"Bowie makes Vivian nervous."

"I'm not afraid of him, if that's what you're wondering."

"Quite understandable, given your history together. Loyalty is admirable but it can also be a weakness." Lowell suddenly seemed awkward. "We saw Sean Cameron yesterday. I'm surprised he's let you out of his sight."

Hannah felt her cheeks burn despite the cold. "I won't keep you."

She noticed Poe had collapsed in the van and gone to sleep and left Lowell standing in the snow as she headed to her car. Every bit of heat had gone out of it. She kept her gloves on as she put the key in the ignition.

She noticed an odd smell and looked over her shoulder into the backseat. Her car blanket was pulled up over something. She hadn't seen it earlier. Had Dominique or Beth left goodies for her to take to the McBanes?

The smell wasn't shepherd's pie or brownies—or any kind of food.

Lowell.

He'd been in the guesthouse when she arrived. He'd let Poe out, or Poe had slipped out on his own.

She hadn't locked her car. Lowell would have had time while she was tramping through the snow after Poe to set whatever it was on her backseat and toss the blanket over it.

A bomb.

Hannah recognized the smell now. Gunpowder. Black powder.

The lingering odor of Lowell's sweat.

She reacted instantly, pushing open her door and leaping out onto the snowbank. She landed on her stomach and hurled herself over the bank and down the hill, into the soft snow under the branches of a white pine.

Her car exploded above her, the concussive impact of the blast sucking the air out of her, propelling her farther down the hill. She heard metal ripping apart, smelled the fire—felt it—as she landed hard on her side, striking a boulder that jutted up out of the snow.

Stifling a moan, she rolled back up onto to her feet. She'd lost her gloves in the snow, but grabbed them even as she reached for her cell phone.

With a jolt of panic, she realized her phone was still in her burning car.

She couldn't call for help.

Was Lowell telling the truth and Bowie was at the farmhouse? Was Bowie with Vivian? Had they heard the blast?

Hannah pushed back the assault of questions and, aching with the cold, with fear, headed through the woods along the far edge of the duck pond, toward the river and the Whittakers' farmhouse.

Her first job was to keep Lowell from seeing her. He couldn't know she'd escaped the blast.

She started to put on her gloves but they'd filled with snow. She shoved them into her jacket pockets and glanced back through the trees, wincing at her trail of boot prints. If Lowell saw them, he'd know she was still alive. He'd be able to follow her.

Was he inspecting her burning car even now, discovering where she'd leaped free of the explosion into the snow?

She moved as fast as she could through the knee-deep snow, every step torture. Her head throbbed, and she could smell the smoke from her burning car and glanced back, seeing it rising in the air.

Where's Lowell?

She couldn't see him through the trees. How long had he been planning to frame Bowie? Days, weeks—months? Lowell had been to Rose's house several times and would have known Black Falls Lodge was visible from her driveway. He'd just needed binoculars to see Melanie Kendall get in her car at the lodge and a cell phone to trigger the bomb.

Had he planned, even then, to blame Bowie?

Hannah didn't slacken her pace. She had to get to Bowie. She needed him as an ally.

And she needed to warn him that Lowell Whittaker meant to frame him as an accomplice—even a mastermind—to murder.

Thirty-Three

Lowell tried to stay close to the old stone wall that ran along the edge of the road that led down from the farmhouse and, ultimately, to Bowie's place on the river—and the old logging road at the base of Cameron Mountain. A line of Scotch pines a previous owner had planted grew along the wall. The pines were gnarled and overgrown, but they helped block the wind.

He fought tears, stumbling as he made his way up the road, clutching the cell phone in his bare right hand. His ears were ringing from the blast. He could smell the acrid smoke of the fire but refused to look back to see it, to check if the flames had spread—if Hannah had died instantly.

Was she in the burning, twisted metal now, fighting for her life?

He sobbed, his heart pounding. *No.* She was dead. He would no longer see her lovely face at the café.

He had no desire to see the results of the simple dialing of a number on a cell phone. He had to make his next move. There was no time to waste. Sean Cameron was besotted with Hannah. How far behind her could he be?

Lowell choked back more useless emotion. He'd had no choice but to kill Hannah. He didn't have the base, violent impulses of a Kyle Rigby or a Melanie Kendall. Drew Cameron and Alex Bruni—even Melanie—would be alive now but for the threat they'd posed. Lowell hadn't killed them out of any deep yearning to commit violence. He'd hoped with each of their deaths that he could avoid the situation he was in now, with his exposure imminent if he didn't act.

He was prepared. His plan was airtight. It would confirm everyone's suspicions about Bowie O'Rourke. The bar fight.

Bowie's combustible anger. His troubled past. He'd been ripe for recruitment by Melanie and Kyle, and after their deaths, he'd gone solo and carried out his own plans in an attempt to exact revenge on those who'd wronged him. His simmering resentment of Hannah Shay and the role she'd played in his arrest, her obvious love for Sean Cameron and her suspicions of his actions in November had all led Bowie to place a bomb in the backseat of her car.

Bowie was a stonemason and an ex-con. Police would have no trouble believing he was capable of assembling the materials for a bomb and figuring out how to build one. Lowell breathed deeply, not as panicked. Jo Harper and her task force would have their network: Melanie, Kyle and Bowie. There was no mastermind. There were just two professional, clever killers and the local thug they'd recruited. Bowie couldn't stand the scrutiny of the Camerons and investigators, and he'd realized the New Yorkers who'd hired him—who'd given him a chance—had figured out that he'd helped Melanie and Kyle find Drew Cameron in April. His cabin. The stonework. All of it.

Sean Cameron would be miserable now that Hannah was dead. Lowell felt a rush of pleasure, but he didn't indulge it.

He had another number to dial.

Bowie would still be upstairs in the farmhouse checking the chimney with Vivian. The man radiated raw masculinity and a palpable, if bridled, capacity for violence. Lowell had noticed how his wife had stood obnoxiously close to the stonemason while he'd explained brick saturation levels and how old brick, if not properly sealed, couldn't absorb moisture properly and water would just spill out.

Lowell held his cell phone tight in one hand. He had one more bomb to trigger. He'd placed it carefully early that morning, while Vivian drank tea and read a book in the kitchen.

She would be dead soon, too. The police would blame Bowie.

He was surprised at how little emotion he felt. No anger, no fear, no regret. Their children would be grief-stricken, but they'd still have him. They'd turn to him now. They'd see him as he was, not just as Vivian painted him.

Once the bomb was triggered, he'd

have to get rid of the cell phone. He could toss it into the fire. The police would believe that Bowie either killed himself or triggered the bomb prematurely and was caught in the blast.

It'll work.

Then, when it was over, Lowell would rebuild the farmhouse and plant a beautiful flower garden in Vivian's memory. He'd sell their house in New York and live in Vermont full-time. He didn't have to continue to arrange killings. He could live here and spend his days chopping wood, walking along the river, watching the snow fall.

He'd be at peace.

Vivian jumped back from the chimney in the upstairs hall and gripped her chest, her heart racing. "What was that?"

"An explosion." Bowie was already at the end of the hall, looking out the window. It provided a view of the backyard and the river, just beyond a line of trees. "Where's your husband?"

Vivian gasped. "He went down to the guesthouse. He can't— You didn't . . ." She couldn't breathe. "You didn't just kill him, did you?"

"No, I didn't. The bomb in Melanie Kendall's car was triggered by a cell phone. Did you see me make a call?"

"Bowie." Vivian hardly breathed now. "What are you saying?"

"Spare me." He gazed back out the window. "You'd better hope no one's hurt."

She edged toward the stairs. She had to get out of there. She had to run. "I don't know what you're talking about," she said in a half whisper.

"Yeah, you do." He was calm, steady, but his eyes were narrowed and menacing when he turned back to her. "When did you figure out your husband was behind all these killings?"

"You're insane." Her tone was icy, bitter. She wouldn't give in to this man. She'd stand her ground. "I'm calling the police."

He looked back at her again, his expression tight, angry. "Do that. Where was your husband when Melanie Kendall was killed?"

Vivian didn't answer. The question had been plaguing her for days, but she'd kept repressing it until she couldn't any longer. She'd lain awake last night, as still as a corpse next to her husband. Pieces—

scraps of information, memories of looks, scraped knuckles, odd smells—had flown at her, and she'd realized the clues had been there all along for her to see. She'd simply refused to see them. She'd buried her suspicions deep, protecting herself, her children—denying that the passive, cerebral man she'd married was capable of organizing and operating a network of paid killers. She'd become even more determined to see him as not the sort of man who could engage in such acts. To treat him as such.

Bowie dropped the curtain back in place. "He wasn't here, was he? He was off blowing up one of his hired killers, trying to cover his own tracks."

"Stop," Vivian whispered, taking another step toward the stairs. "Just stop."

Bowie shook his head at her. "You two are a piece of work. He gets on your nerves or you start feeling anxious, and you lace into him."

"No—"

"It's been going on for years, hasn't it? Now you find out he's a killer."

Her lips thinned. "You think you're so superior."

"You don't want him discovered. You'd rather see an innocent man blamed than have people know about your husband's little side business."

Vivian felt sick to her stomach as she experienced an incomparable sadness at what her life had become. Bowie was right. She'd decided that morning. She'd let Lowell get them out of this mess. She'd let him enact whatever plan he had in mind to give the authorities their killer mastermind and take any hint of suspicion off them once and for all. What other choice did she have?

"He wasn't here when Melanie Kendall was killed." Vivian was at the top edge of the stairs now. Her words seemed to be coming from someone else. "He took the car and left. I don't know where he went. I was raking leaves, mulching the gardens."

"When did you know?"

"For sure? This morning." She placed a hand on the railing. What did Lowell have in mind for Bowie? Did he need her to keep the stonemason up here, talking? She continued, her voice less strangled. "I remembered how calm he was in November when he came back."

Bowie's eyes remained almost closed. She felt him zeroing in on her, trying to penetrate some hard outer shell to get inside her, to what she really knew, really believed.

"What else?" he asked.

Vivian felt chilled now. "I went into the woodshed out back."

"What did you find?"

She raised her eyes to him. "You already know."

"Bomb-making materials." He added, his tone certain, "A bomb."

"Two. There were two bombs."

She knew what Lowell meant to do. Her husband. The man she'd married and had loved planned to kill Bowie O'Rourke. Just as he'd killed Melanie Kendall.

Bowie remained calm, clear-eyed. "We need to get out of here. One of those bombs is meant for us."

"Not *me*—"

"Yeah, you, too. Lowell's going to kill us both. You're an abusive bitch who belittles him night and day. You don't think he wants you dead?"

"I'm not an abuser."

Panic welled up in her. She pictured

Lowell up here in the hall just before Bowie had arrived to investigate the potential leak. Lowell had sent them both upstairs while he went outside.

Bowie hadn't found any trace of a leak upstairs.

Vivian froze. She couldn't run. She couldn't speak. It couldn't be true. Lowell couldn't be willing to kill *her*.

"I have to get out . . ."

Bowie was already lunging for her. He scooped her onto his broad shoulders as if she were a ragdoll and ran with her down the stairs. For a moment, she wanted to go limp and just let this strong, competent man rescue her and save himself. She could deny everything she'd just told him. She could exonerate her husband. The police would believe her.

It was too big a risk. She'd lose *everything* if authorities could prove that Lowell was responsible for the murders of Drew Cameron, Alex Bruni and Melanie Kendall.

That he'd arranged other murders.

She couldn't let that happen. Lowell's plan had to work. Bowie O'Rourke had to take the blame.

He had to die in the explosion.

Thirty-Four

Hannah sank to her knees in the snow. She was relieved, exhausted. She didn't think she could take another step, but it was okay.

Bowie had to have seen her.

Thank God.

She'd spotted him in the second-floor window and had waved to him from the trees.

He knew she hadn't been killed in the blast. He knew she was trying to avoid Lowell.

She'd motioned for him to get out of there. He was next.

She'd done all she could to warn him.

Her entire body ached from the blast, from running through the snow, from the cold. She was gasping, choking with emotion and pain, aware she was still a little disoriented and in shock.

Snow melted through her pants and froze her knees. It had already filled her boots. Her feet were frozen. She was too weak to stand up, but she knew she had to summon the energy, the will to move—to hide. Lowell couldn't find her. He couldn't know she was still alive.

She heard something—someone moving by the shed.

Lowell?

She leaped up, her legs heavy, and pushed her way through the snow, toward the trees along the river. She'd get to the old cellar hole where she and Drew Cameron had found Bowie back in March. She could hide there. She'd be safe, at least somewhat protected from the elements.

"Hannah!"

She recognized Sean's voice. Her feet went out from under her, but before she could fall face-first into the soft snow, he was there, his arms around her. "I'm here, baby. Elijah's right behind me. We're here for you. We saw your car. . . ."

She stood back from him, his arms still around her as she saw the fear in his eyes, and she realized he'd thought he'd lost her. Her heart jumped. "Sean . . ." She touched his cheek, her bare hands red and frozen. She forced herself to focus. "It's Lowell."

"I know."

"We have to find him. He doesn't know I got out before my car exploded. I don't care how he deludes himself, I was no more than a spider he had to clear out of the bathroom sink."

Hannah saw Elijah now, behind Sean in the snow, standing next to a bare, gray-barked sapling. He had a gun in one hand, everything about him alert, serious, even as he winked at her. "It's about time someone blew up that car of yours."

Sean slipped an arm around her waist and lifted her off her feet and out of the snow. She already felt warmer. "I think he planted a second bomb," Hannah said. "He's going to kill Bowie and let him take the blame for everything. I warned Bowie, but we have to find Lowell before he—"

"Not we," Elijah said. He looked back

toward the shed and the farmhouse. "I'll go. You two . . . The police and firefighters are on the way. Wait for them."

Another explosion ripped through the quiet, echoing along the ice-bound river.

Hannah tensed, her heart pounding, but Sean continued to hold her close.

She could hear Lowell screaming, "Fire!" He appeared by the shed, frantically waving his hands. "Sean, Elijah. My wife! Help! The house is on fire!"

Elijah raised his weapon. Hannah eased herself back down into the snow. Sean kept one hand on her hip. "Stay close. Take cover if you have to." His eyes were a dark navy, intense. "Elijah and I won't let him near you."

Lowell was panting as he pointed back toward the house. "Bowie—we opened up our home to him. We gave him a chance, but he hates us. All of us. You, even, Hannah. I had no idea."

His wife staggered through the snow, coming up behind her husband. Her face was smeared with soot, her eyes red-rimmed. Her hair hung limply in her face. She seemed to be at least partially in shock. "I was on the stairs . . . Bowie was right behind me. He . . . he couldn't . . ." She was shaking, her voice hollow. "He didn't get out in time."

Hannah forced herself not to react. Up ahead, smoke and flames were already visible in the upper-story windows of the farmhouse.

"Where did you last see him?" Sean asked.

"In the upstairs hall. He'd been at the guesthouse." Vivian blinked back tears. "We were checking on a leak in the chimney."

Lowell turned to Sean and Elijah. "Bowie must have seen Hannah arrive and put a bomb in her car, then triggered it somehow. I thought he was already up here checking on the chimney leak."

Vivian shuddered. "He came here to kill us. I think he saw Hannah from the hall window. He knew she'd survived. He decided not to wait for Lowell. He . . ." She started to sob. "He didn't expect to die himself. He thought he'd get out alive. I saw it in his eyes."

Hannah grabbed Sean's hand into hers, but kept her gaze on Vivian Whittaker. "They're both lying. Bowie's in there. I'm going after him—"

Sean squeezed her hand, and Elijah stepped in close to her, both brothers obviously ready to stop her if she tried to make a break for the burning farmhouse. "Easy, Hannah," Elijah said. "You're hurt, and this is what Sean knows how to do."

"You can put that gun away, Elijah," Lowell said.

Elijah shook his head. "Nope. Can't."

Vivian sniffed at him. "You have your killer."

"Yes, we do," Elijah said stonily, then turned to Sean. "Do your firefighter thing, brother. Let's hope these two failed and Bowie is still alive."

Sean ran into the house through the back door, covering his head with his coat to protect himself as much as possible against the smoke and flames. Right now the fire was contained to the second floor, but it would spread quickly in the farmhouse, with its old, tinder-dry beams. Every firefighter he knew in Vermont hated old-house fires.

Doing his "firefighter thing" amounted to getting in and out of there fast.

Preferably with Bowie alive.

Staying low, Sean raced through the kitchen and down a short hall to the living room. He could hear the rush of the fire on the second floor.

He found Bowie sprawled facedown at the bottom of the stairs, semiconscious but alive. He was deadweight as Sean got hold of him. "You're too damn big, O'Rourke. Up on your feet. Let's get out of here."

"I saved her life and the bitch left me here to die. The blast knocked me off balance on the stairs." He was disoriented, struggling to breathe. "I was carrying her—"

"She's got Hannah and Elijah to deal with now. Come on. We don't know how many bombs this bastard planted in here. He doesn't need to call them in to trigger them. A spark—"

"Right," Bowie said, more alert.

With Bowie leaning against him, Sean moved back to the hall and the kitchen. Firefighters in full gear entered the same door he had. Zack Harper, in the lead, got hold of Bowie. Sean warned him about the possibility of more bombs. Another firefighter reached for Sean, but he shot out the door, past more firefighters.

He sucked in the cold, clean air and put his coat back on.

A visibly shaken Beth Harper was there with the rest of her ambulance crew. “You and Elijah are idiots,” she said to Sean. “Wait until Jo gets back from D.C. In the meantime, let’s get some oxygen on you.”

“I don’t need oxygen.”

Beth started to argue with him, but Sean zeroed in on Hannah by the woodshed with Elijah. She was standing with her arms crossed in front of her, and all he could think of was the agony he’d felt when he’d seen her burning car, the relief when he and Elijah had spotted her prints in the snow.

Beth gave a resigned sigh behind him, but he didn’t need her permission. He was already running, focused only on getting to Hannah.

He scooped her into his arms. “Bowie’s safe,” he said, kissing her, “and I love you, Hannah. I love you.”

Elijah grunted. “Finally,” his brother said.

Hannah pressed her forehead onto Sean’s chest and he thought he heard her sniffle, but when she raised her eyes to him, she was smiling. She was so self-contained, so reserved, he thought. Half the damn town was arriving—state and local cops, firefighters, the feds on the task force—but this time, she didn't seem to care who might see her.

"I love you, too," she whispered.

Sean winked at her. "More to come," he said.

They turned to Lowell and Vivian Whittaker, standing side by side, not touching, under Elijah's watchful eye. Hannah spoke first, addressing Lowell. "Bowie didn't find Drew's cabin and tell those killers," she said. "It was you. You followed his trail up the mountain and found the cabin and told Kyle Rigby and Melanie Kendall."

Lowell met her gaze dead on.

"And it was you at the crypt," Hannah said, undeterred, "knocking the rock onto Bowie, calling my name."

"You're wrong," Lowell said coldly. "You local people always stick together against the outsider. It was all Bowie. Those two killers hired him as their local contact. He helped them. He has his own scores to settle here. He knew Vivian and I were on the verge of figuring out he was involved with these killings."

Hannah tightened her hands into fists. Sean remembered her at the bar fight back in March and thought she might jump Lowell, but she just glared at him. "You went to the crypt in daylight because it'd be easier to explain your presence. You could say you were up there indulging your passion for Vermont history and old tombstones."

Lowell sniffed at her. "Your lower-class roots are strong, aren't they, Hannah? You'll never escape your past. I'm disappointed in you."

"What did you do, sneak into the crypt to make the bomb that killed Melanie Kendall? Did you leave behind some of your materials? You wouldn't risk going back there when the police were combing the area for clues. You waited." Her voice was steady, the budding prosecutor at work. "You tried to get rid of Bowie. He was both a threat and a perfect fall guy."

"I don't know what you're talking about. You people are so clannish. You can't see through your ties to one another to the truth."

Elijah looked at Sean. “Do you want to shoot him, or shall I?”

Lowell paled, clearly not knowing that Elijah wouldn’t shoot unless in self-defense.

Vivian was shivering uncontrollably. “Our beautiful house on the river is in flames, and you heartless people dare to accuse us. . . .” She sobbed and brushed a tear out of the corner of her eye. “I’ll never come back here.”

Sean slipped his arm around Hannah and focused on Lowell Whittaker. “Who taught you how to build a bomb? Who told you what materials you’d need?”

Elijah kept his gun steady. “Did one of your hired killers give you instructions?”

Lowell didn’t answer. His wife was silent now, staring at the man she’d married as if seeing him for the first time. But it was an act, Sean thought. Whatever the police could prove or couldn’t prove, Vivian Whittaker had figured out her husband was a murderer. She’d done what she could to keep Bowie from getting out of the fire alive.

Elijah lowered his weapon, and Sean felt Hannah’s arm come around his waist and hold him as he and his brother watched

Scott Thorne place the man who'd ordered their father's death under arrest.

No one stopped Hannah as she made her way to Bowie, who sat on the side of a stretcher under Beth Harper's watchful eye. She stepped back, giving them a moment. He pulled off his oxygen mask. "Sean's been a damn fool."

"You, too, Bowie." Hannah shook her head and tried to smile. "As strong as you are from all your years hauling rock, and look at you now."

He grinned at her. "Who just jumped from an exploding car?"

"I jumped *before* it exploded."

But there was no humor in his dark eyes as he blinked up at her. "A good thing."

"I've been a damn fool, too," she whispered.

"This was a close one for both of us." He nodded back to the farmhouse, firefighters working hard to put out the flames and save the structure. "Thanks for the warning. I'd never have gotten out of there if I hadn't spotted you down here. You could have stayed hidden, not taken any chances—"

"No, I couldn't have."

"I knew . . ." He sighed heavily. "I knew that first bomb was meant for you."

"I never suspected you, Bowie. Not even for a split second."

"Poe?"

"He's curled up in the blankets in the back of your van. We'll make sure he stays warm."

"I came up here to check on the chimney. It was all a setup." He looked down at his callused hands holding the oxygen mask in his lap. "Vivian took advantage when I stumbled on the stairs while I was carrying her butt to safety." He shrugged his big shoulders. "No good deed goes unpunished."

"Sean, Elijah and I all heard her lie about what happened."

"She grabbed the rail and kicked me from behind. I was already off balance, and I fell down the stairs, hit my head. Next thing I know, Sean's helping me up." He winced, the fading bruises of his earlier encounter with Lowell Whittaker visible in his pale face. "She threw her lot in with her husband in the end. With me dead, she could tell her version of events."

"I'm sorry, Bowie."

"Not your fault." He looked back toward the woods and the river, the sky cloudless against the white landscape. "I'd like to build a place on that old cellar hole on the river and live as a hermit."

"I don't blame you. Right now just do as the paramedics say and take care of yourself. Then we'll see."

"I'd have helped Drew with his cabin if he'd asked." Bowie stared down at the oxygen mask in his hands, his mind obviously drifting. "Vivian's rough on Lowell. She belittled him about you and Sean. She was constantly comparing him to the Camerons."

"She's a controlling, abusive woman," Hannah said.

"Why'd she take Lowell's side in the end?"

"She couldn't let anyone find out about his role in the killings. That by itself represented an existential threat to her."

Bowie grinned through his pain. "Existential threat, Hannah?"

She smiled at him. "Put your oxygen back on."

He didn't. Instead, he said, "I think every time he arranges a killing, he thinks of her. He just doesn't have the guts to stand up to her."

"Does she know he hates her?"

"What do you think?"

"She knows."

Thirty-Five

It was dusk by the time the police finished with them, but dusk came early to northern New England in January. Hannah had just finished reporting the events of the day to Devin and Toby when the Cameron brothers arrived at the café and gathered at the big table overlooking the river.

"Here, Hannah," A.J. said. "Have a seat."

She pulled out a chair between him and Sean. She ached all over, but she was warm. Jo, Grit and Myrtle were en route from Washington. They all planned to meet up the street at O'Rourke's before it closed.

"Why did Lowell do it?" A.J. asked.

"It made him feel powerful," Hannah said. "He was passive and cerebral in person, especially with his wife, but he was cold, calculating and bold in his work pairing his clients and his killers. He really was afraid Bowie was working against him."

Elijah nodded. "He was in bed with some ruthless people."

"The thought of Lowell hiding in the cellar with the money jar—fixated on me—gives me the creeps." Hannah winced, surprised at how calm she was. "He must have grabbed it and run, then panicked and ditched the jar in the cellar."

Sean leaned in closer to Hannah. "I'm guessing Kyle Rigby and Melanie Kendall didn't know Lowell was their middleman, the guy who paid them and gave them assignments. Lowell hired them on his own behalf to kill Pop and then Ambassador Bruni, because they were getting too close to him. Then he had them go after Nora and Devin. He killed Melanie himself. He'd have killed Kyle, too, if he'd had to."

"It wasn't another of his contract killers," A.J. said. "Lowell made the mess he was in into a bigger mess. He was afraid of what Bowie and Hannah knew."

"How many killers do you suppose he had on his payroll?" Hannah asked.

"Law enforcement has his computer," Elijah said. "They'll find out."

Hannah saw Judge Robinson enter the warm café. He was pale and obviously shaken by the day's events as he walked behind the glass case and helped himself to a mug of coffee. "Just when I think I've seen everything in my long career," he said, shaking his head in dismay as he joined them at the table with his coffee, "along come Lowell Whittaker and his faithful wife, Vivian. Dear heavens. Lowell thought he could put killers together with people who wanted killing done and not engage in any violence himself, but he certainly took advantage of the opportunity once presented, didn't he?"

A.J. sat back. "He won't be back here playing the gentleman farmer again anytime soon."

In the ensuing silence, Hannah decided what she had to do. No more dancing around the subject. No more waiting. She was who she was. Abruptly, without looking at the men seated at the table with her, she said, "For those of you who don't know, my father spent five years on and off in state prison. It's not a secret, but it's not something I talk about. I don't want to wonder who knows and who doesn't know, or tiptoe around the subject. I'm not proud of anything he did wrong, but I did love him. My brothers did as babies, too." She paused, picturing her father with Devin in one arm and Toby in the other, all of them laughing on a rock above the river. She smiled at the memory and promised herself she'd share it with her brother. "I remember."

No one spoke. She got up and headed out of the café and into the center hall, then back to the mudroom. She grabbed a coat and burst outside, through the snow to the riverbank.

She heard the back door creak open and thud shut and knew it was Sean.

He slipped an arm around her waist. "You miss your folks," he said, kissing the top of her head. "I miss mine, too."

She didn't respond, just leaned into him and stared down at the frozen river.

"I have a feeling," Rose said, "that you won't be doing any quilting by the fire this winter."

After everyone had left the café, she and Hannah had dragged the old trunk up the stairs and stacked the swatches into piles: definite potential, maybe with some work, trash. Sean had gone up to the lodge with his brothers. Rose had stayed behind.

"Bowie wasn't just protecting me in that bar fight," Hannah said, "and he wasn't completely out of control."

"I know. Hannah . . ." Clearly pained, Rose didn't continue.

"Those men were drunk. Derek Cutshaw, especially."

Rose stared at the fabric sorted on the worktable. "I was in a bad place last winter and fell for the wrong man."

"Derek?"

Rose hesitated, then nodded. "I haven't wanted anyone to know. I was so stupid. He's manipulative and possessive. I dumped him in March, and he didn't like it."

"Bowie knew about the two of you?"

"Derek told him, bragged to him. Bowie tried to warn me that things could get ugly. I didn't listen. He probably saved my brothers from getting arrested that night by taking matters into his own hands. I've been in a very dark place, Hannah."

"Don't be so hard on yourself."

"Derek and me . . . the insults . . . the bar fight—he was also talking about me that night. Not just you."

Hannah could feel her friend's pain and embarrassment. "Rose, don't judge yourself—"

"I pride myself on my good judgment, but I let Derek Cutshaw into my life. Then I didn't tell you that his insults weren't about you. I didn't tell anyone else."

"It doesn't matter who they were about or if they were true or false. He was in the wrong."

Rose looked pained. "What he said—it's not something you live down in a small town. No one really ever believed you . . ."

Hannah smiled through her own discomfort. "Why, because I can't make that kind of mistake?"

Rose managed a smile back. "No, because everyone knows everything about you. You live right in town and run the café, and people have been looking out for you for years. Hannah . . ." Tears shone in Rose's eyes. "I'm not proud of myself. I'm sorry you had to go through this. It's all because of me."

"Derek is a jerk and a heel and I hope he never bothers either of us again."

"I never thought I'd be in this position," Rose said, her voice quiet now. "I was recovering from a series of tough missions. Derek is cocky, good-looking. A mean drunk, though. And here we are. My brothers can't know, Hannah. I couldn't stand it if they did."

"Do you think your father knew?"

"Whatever he knew, he kept to himself. It wouldn't be that way with A.J., Elijah and Sean." She gave a small laugh. "They need another forty years to mellow."

Hannah grinned. "I wouldn't have called your father 'mellow' even at seventy-seven."

Pensive again, Rose ran her fingertips over her fabric. "I haven't heard from Derek since the fight at O'Rourke's in March."

"Bowie kept him from saying your name that night. Maybe Derek got the message and decided to be smart and stay away from you." Hannah deliberated a moment, but decided she had to say the rest. "Rose, do you need to report Derek to the police for what he did to you?"

"No. What he did to me wouldn't put him in jail. My brothers were at O'Rourke's that night. Derek was nasty and out of control, and it would have been easy for things to get seriously out of hand. Bowie shouldn't have done what he did, but maybe it would have been even worse if he hadn't."

"What's done is done. Nick Martini?"

"A sexier mistake."

"One you'd make again?" Hannah asked.

"I'm not a good judge of men. You understand you can't tell my brothers, don't you?"

"Maybe you should give them a chance."

"They've gone through enough. Promise me."

"I think Sean's guessed."

"Yes, well—" But Rose broke off and smiled. "I noticed you didn't argue when I said you wouldn't be doing any quilting by the fire this winter."

Thirty-Six

Grit, Jo and Myrtle arrived back in Vermont and took a table at O'Rourke's. Grit knew the call coming in on his cell phone—although the screen didn't say so—was from the son of the vice president of the United States. Charlie Neal was supposed to be back under the thumb of an ever-watchful Mark Francona, who'd told Grit he would personally arrest him if he had anything more to do with any of the vice president's offspring.

Grit answered anyway. "I'm right," Charlie said. "There's a firebug out there."

"Lots of firebugs."

"It looks as if Kyle Rigby and Melanie Kendall were responsible for the bulk of the hits Lowell Whittaker arranged. Lowell hired them to kill Myrtle Smith's Russian friend, Andrei Petrov, on behalf of a former KGB agent. Did you know that?"

Grit was aware of Jo Harper frowning at him in that Secret Service–agent way of hers. He chose his words carefully. "Just heard." In fact, he thought, Jo had been the one to tell him. He said, "I have to go."

Charlie sighed. "Agent Harper's there, isn't she? Okay. Just listen, then. The KGB agent could have done the job himself but he didn't want to take the chance. Have someone poison Petrov's toothpaste. Keep things simple."

"Sometimes simple works. Sometimes it doesn't."

"Only no one expected Myrtle. Ms. Smith, I mean," Charlie said. "She was closing in on the assassins' network. Lowell had our firebug torch her office to destroy her notes."

Grit didn't argue. "Okay, fine."

"The police can't pin the fire on Kyle Rigby or Melanie Kendall because they weren't responsible for it."

"Right."

"Jasper Vanderhorn was killed by this firebug." Charlie paused to take a breath. "I'm serious. It won't matter that this network's been shut down. Firebugs don't like to stop. They prefer to work alone."

"Where are you now?" Grit asked him.

"Conor and I are setting up for another airsoft game. Dad's letting us play again. He thinks it'll keep us out of trouble if we have something to focus on."

"Will it?"

"This firebug is a murderer, Petty Officer Taylor."

"So when you get the wrong answer on a test, do you argue with your teacher until she proves you wrong?"

"Only if I know I'm not wrong. Want to come play airsoft with me sometime?"

Grit heard a sudden tentativeness in the kid's voice and realized the invitation was sincere. "Yeah, sure. Be good in the meantime."

"Always."

After Charlie disconnected, Grit set his phone back on the table. Jo was eyeing him as if she were a split second from whipping out handcuffs and arresting him. He said, "I meant lightning bugs. I don't know why I said firebugs. Lots of lightning bugs out there in the Vermont wilderness."

"Not in January, Grit."

"Buy you a beer, Agent Harper?"

She relaxed some. "I'm not conflicted," she said quietly.

He knew what she meant. "Okay."

"Elijah and I will figure out what's next. Together. Lives, careers, families. Half the fun is the complexity of it all."

"You weren't even tempted to move back to your low ceilings and dead plants and forget him? Hit the reset button on your life?"

"No."

"You thought about it, though."

"I'll take that beer, Petty Officer."

Grit noticed he had another message from Admiral Jenkins suggesting he report for duty at the Pentagon in three days. A suggestion from a four-star admiral was another way to say "order." Grit texted him back: Aye-aye. He hit Send, then texted him again: Sir.

If he were about to start work at the Pentagon, some things had to get straightened out right from the start. He wasn't the same Navy SEAL he'd been a year ago. It wasn't a question of better or worse. Just different.

Myrtle joined him and Jo at their table. Myrtle had on leather gloves the color of her eyes and was bitching about the cold.

"Seriously, Myrtle," Grit said, "I've got to get you to the Florida Panhandle and introduce you to tupelo honey."

Sean, Elijah, A.J. and his wife, Lauren, and Beth and Zack Harper all turned up, dragging chairs over so that they all could sit at the same table. A few minutes later, Hannah arrived on her own. Sean rose immediately and pulled a chair up to their table for her. She thanked him. She was reserved and quiet but not as self-conscious as Grit had seen her since he'd first arrived in Black Falls. She just, he thought, wasn't sure she belonged there with the Camerons and Harpers.

"My father told me about your father," Jo said, less combative. "I didn't look him up. He also said your dad's death was an accident."

Her comment seemed to come out of the blue, but not, as far as Grit could see, to

Hannah. It was something she seemed to need to hear and Jo seemed to need to tell her. "Your father, Jo—"

"He was the first law enforcement officer on scene after the accident. Your dad wasn't in any trouble and hadn't been since your brothers were born. I know you know that," Jo added. "I just want you to know that I do, too."

Liam O'Rourke delivered a round of drinks on the house. "Your dad was the love of your mom's life, Hannah. She missed him, but she carried on without him."

Hannah finally spoke. "My mother, Devin, Toby and I all had some good times together." She seemed to consider whether she should reveal this much of herself. "Before she died, she asked us to remember her and love her always but to have good times again. We have, too. We've had some great times."

Grit understood what she was saying, and he thought everyone at the table did, too. The people who'd known and loved Drew Cameron best, especially his four children, would miss him, but they'd have good times again.

Liam set the glasses on the table and

addressed Hannah. "I remember you out on the common with Devin and Toby when you were first trying to get them under control. You had the snowball fight from hell. They had you outnumbered, and they were sneaky little rascals, but you didn't back down."

Elijah raised his glass and grinned. "That's our Hannah."

She said nothing, just smiled as she sat close to Sean, his two older brothers right there.

Jo glanced at Grit, then grinned at the three Cameron brothers. "Speaking of snowball fights . . ." she said, taking a sip of her beer and rising. "Who's game?"

Elijah was the first to his feet and led the way, all of them ending up on the town common, across from Three Sisters Café.

Snow was falling, just wet enough to hold together.

Grit knew who threw the first snowball, but he was an outsider and didn't say. Even Myrtle joined in with her purple gloves.

Rose arrived a few minutes after the snowball fight started and walked across the common with her golden retriever. She didn't say a word, just scooped up a handful of snow, fashioned it into a fist-size snowball and hurled it, striking Sean in the shoulder. He pivoted and nailed her with a snowball of his own.

Ranger obviously loved snow and dived into the fun.

Grit didn't love snow, but when he got beaned by an unrepentant Jo Harper, he made his first snowball.

When he threw it at her, he realized they both were laughing.

Bowie entered O'Rourke's. Sean had spotted him after the snowball fight had broken up, with no clear winners, and come over by himself. It was late, and he was tired. Hannah had gone home to take a hot shower, complaining—teasing—because her apartment didn't have a bathtub.

Liam tapped a thick finger on the bar. "Any punches thrown in here will be mine. Understood?" He turned back to his work before either Sean or Bowie responded.

Bowie sat on the stool next to Sean. "You're thickheaded, Cameron, but you and your brothers didn't do anything stupid that night."

"None of us would have let Hannah get hurt."

"Or hurt anyone," Bowie said dryly. "Thanks for saving my life today."

"I like to think you'd have done the same for me."

"Yeah." Bowie grinned at Sean. "Probably."

"My father didn't come to any of us with his concerns. My brothers, Rose, me. You. I wish he had. He was in Washington talking to Ambassador Bruni and never said a word to Jo, just had her go with him to see the cherry blossoms."

"What could any of you have done?"

"Hiked up the mountain with him in April. Been there when those two came after him. Stopped them."

"Yeah," Bowie said. "You could have done that. Me, too."

Sean hesitated, knowing he was on difficult ground now. "I need to ask you, if my sister were in danger, would you tell me?"

"In a heartbeat."

"Those cretins that night weren't just talking about Hannah, were they?"

"I don't give a damn who they were talking about."

Sean decided to leave it there. "So why am I 'thickheaded'?"

"Hannah. You've been out of reach for her since you were kids. She only had to prove herself to herself. The rest of us know she's too damn good for you."

"It's true."

"You may have left Black Falls, but it's never left you. I figure you had some proving to do. I also figure you made all that money for a reason."

"And that would be?"

Bowie grinned. "To spoil Hannah Shay."

Thirty-Seven

January 8—Black Falls, Vermont

Hannah delivered warm shepherd's pie to the McBanes, then walked across the road to the cemetery. Sean had once again returned to California. She could have gone with him, but in light of everything that had happened, she wanted him to have a chance to get his head clear back in the place he'd lived since college. She ached to see him again, and she was downright desperate to see her brothers, but the practicalities of her own life had swarmed over her.

She needed to hire help at the café, and she needed to start some serious studying for the bar.

There was also that to-do list of house repairs to tackle.

She found Bowie collecting the last of his stuff from outside the crypt. “Need any help?” she asked him.

“Sure, Hannah. Pick up that hundred pounds of granite over there and carry it to my van, will you?”

“Funny, Bowie.”

He grinned at her. “Grit Taylor was up here, and he and Reverend McBane and I were talking, and we figured out that some women are like sisters. It’s just the way it is. Some aren’t.” He looked at Hannah and winked. “You and Rose? For me? Sisters.”

“So who would be under ‘not sisters’?”

He sidestepped her question with another grin. “Judge Robinson thinks Southern California could be a good place for you to study.”

“Do you know everything that happens in this town?”

“I didn’t know we still had killers on the loose, but everything else? Yeah.”

When Hannah arrived back at the café, Rose, Dominique, Beth and even Jo were gathered in the kitchen. Rose grabbed a folder and opened it up on the worktable. “I have airline points. I know you don’t do tips here, but people insisted. Liam O’Rourke even got in on it with tips from his place. Anyway, we’ve pooled our resources, and we’ve made our decision. We’re sending you to Los Angeles.”

“You leave tomorrow,” Beth said.

Hannah was overcome. “Thank you. You’re all too generous.”

“None of us wants to go to Los Angeles,” Rose said, then added quickly, “Sean would arrange for a private plane for you—”

“This is perfect,” Hannah said.

Dominique produced an envelope. “And here’s cash for a shopping spree on Rodeo Drive. We expect receipts. No sneaking off to a discount store—and no spending it on your brothers.”

“It’ll be a minor shopping spree compared to some Rodeo Drive has witnessed,” Beth said. “But have fun. We’ll handle the café. It’s been quiet.”

“Thank you again.”

“I can help stand in for Hannah here at the café,” Jo said. “Beth and I really are sisters, so we’ll uphold the name.”

"No." Beth was horrified. "We'd kill each other. Back to D.C. with you before the Secret Service fires you. You're not done, and neither is Elijah. Vermont is here. Lake, home, cabins, land. None of it's going anywhere."

Rose said, "Myrtle Smith suggests the two of us switch off subbing as the third sister."

Dominique pointed her knife to the cash. "She contributed to the shopping spree and included a note on stores she recommends."

Leave it to Myrtle, Hannah thought, amused. Myrtle had surprised everyone by not returning immediately to Washington. Grit Taylor was gone, at least for the moment, rumored to be assigned to the Pentagon.

There was even a note in Rose's folder from Everett Robinson telling Hannah she could e-mail him with study questions, unless she decided to do something else with her life. "Want what *you* want, Hannah," he wrote, "not what you think you should want, or what someone else wants. Including me."

What she wanted right now, more than anything else in the world, was to be in Southern California with her brothers—and, she thought, a certain smoke jumper turned multimillionaire.

Thirty-Eight

January 10—Beverly Hills, California

"This isn't the right hotel," Hannah said.

"Yes, it is." Nick Martini stopped at the front door of the Beverly Hilton, a sprawling hotel built in 1955, its "retro chic" decor calling up glamorous images of Humphrey Bogart and Lauren Bacall. "The one you picked out is a fleabag."

She'd insisted on booking a motel for herself. She wasn't entirely sure of the effects of being back in California on Sean, if he felt the same way about her. She didn't want to box him in. Or herself.

"I don't care," she told his fellow smoke jumper, who was, she'd duly noted, in his own way as irresistibly sexy as Sean was. No wonder Rose was doomed.

Martini ignored her and typed on his iPhone.

"Who are you texting?"

"Sean," Nick said. "I'm telling him your coach is about to turn back into a pumpkin and I'm out of here. You're from the sticks. You like pumpkins, don't you?"

Hannah wasn't succumbing to his charms and said, nonchalant, "Rose says hello."

"No, she doesn't."

"You're right. She doesn't."

Nick kept typing.

"Her brothers don't know about you two," Hannah said. "Sean included."

"Blackmailing me?"

She sat up straight. "Wait. Maybe *I* don't know."

He grinned at her. "Some kind of hanging judge you'll make."

"Rose is one of my best friends. She doesn't tell me everything, but enough. I just want to say her brothers wouldn't be pleased if someone took advantage of their grieving sister."

"By 'wouldn't be pleased' you mean 'kill dead.' How is Rose?"

His dark eyes had softened. Whatever had gone on between Rose and Nick, he was worried about her now. Or doing a decent job of pretending to be. “I don't know,” Hannah said. “She keeps to herself a lot these days.”

“I would, too, with three older brothers and all that's happened this past year. All set. Climb out. Enjoy yourself.”

“I can't afford to stay in this place for two hours, never mind one night.”

Martini grinned at her. “No, you can't.”

Hannah realized her mistake. “I've been set up, haven't I?”

“Nice to meet you, Hannah. I hope you never have to prosecute me for so much as a speeding ticket in Vermont. How cold is it there?”

“Seven degrees when I left.”

He grinned at her. “You're going to love Southern California. Welcome.”

Hannah got out and grabbed her suitcase from the back. A sign in the elegant lobby indicated that many of the well-dressed people streaming out of the hotel had just attended a fund-raising dinner for volunteer firefighters.

Sean appeared behind an older couple.

Her breath caught at the sight of him in his tuxedo. This was another Sean Cameron from the one she knew. He smiled at her. "Am I seeing things, or is that Hannah Shay?"

"Hello, Sean."

He picked up her suitcase. "You're staying with me." When she started to protest, he shook his head. "No argument. I'm irritable enough being in this damn tux. Let's go."

"Sean, I appreciate the gesture—"

"Let's go."

She grinned at him. "Ah, yes. I know these Camerons when they get that stubborn set to their jaws. No point arguing."

Sean softened his expression. "I'm trying to be hospitable."

"Hospitable is 'Hannah, I'd love to invite you to stay at my house.' "

"Hannah," Sean said, repressing a smile, "I'd love to invite you to stay at my house. I have plenty of room, and it'd be a pleasure."

She laughed. "That's better, but I can't—"

"You can," Sean said.

"For Devin's sake, then. I think he's a little homesick."

"He's gone mountain biking with Toby for a few days."

Hannah smiled in amused disbelief. "Okay. So he's not even a little homesick."

"Nick and I encouraged him to see some of California and get in shape if he wants to be a smoke jumper. Toby doesn't want to admit how excited he is to have you here for his upcoming race."

"I'm excited, too."

The valet brought Sean's car, and he opened the front passenger door for Hannah. She hesitated, but he put his arm on her shoulder and she got in. A woman who obviously knew him waved from the walk as she switched from her high heels to a pair of running shoes. "That's the way to do heels." Hannah looked over at Sean. "You fit right in with that tux."

"Different uniforms for different occasions."

"I don't have that many excuses to dress up. It's fun sometimes. We're having a Valentine's Day celebration at the café. I'll dress up for that." Her eyes sparked with sudden humor. "I might even buy a pair of ruby-red high heels on Rodeo Drive and wear them."

"It's not helpful for my driving," Sean muttered, "picturing you in red high heels."

"Beth and Dominique want us to wear red aprons. Red aprons and red high heels. Kind of sexy, don't you think?"

Sean cleared his throat and kept driving.

Devin had described Sean's house in detail, and Hannah was prepared. He showed her to a quiet room on the first floor, and she set her suitcase in the middle of the floor and looked restless. "If you packed a swimsuit," Sean said, "feel free to make use of the pool. It's heated."

Sean waited, restless, by the pool. Finally Hannah walked out onto the terrace in an oversize T-shirt, with her slim, pale white New England winter legs. It was a warm night for Los Angeles in January but still relatively cool. She didn't seem to notice as she dipped a toe in the pool. Her toenails were painted watermelon-pink.

Sean smiled. "You knew what you were getting into coming out here."

"So I did."

Without a second's hesitation or a hint of self-consciousness, she dove into the still, blue water. Sean watched her breaststroke underwater, her movements strong and sure. She surfaced, splashing him, laughing.

"You're going to ruin my tux," he said.

"Then maybe you should take it off."

He needed no more encouragement and was out of it in seconds and into the water, swimming to her, his mouth finding hers. "Don't say anything," he whispered.

She eased her arms around him. "I have to say this one thing." Her eyes held his as she continued. "I'd never have made it these past seven years without the support I received from so many people. Sean . . ." She kissed him lightly. "I often thought I was alone, but I never was."

He couldn't breathe. "Hannah . . ."

"I love you," she said. "In some ways, I always have."

He smiled. "I know what you mean. Latin class . . ." He was aware of her slipping off her swimsuit and was glad they were in five feet of water and not ten, or he was sure he'd have drowned. "I love you, Hannah. I want to be with you. Here, Vermont—wherever you are."

"Home is Vermont," she said, "but this is

good. The pool, the bougainvillea, the sunshine. *You.*" Her swimsuit was gone now, and she wrapped her legs around his hips and sank onto him. "This is very good."

"It is," Sean said, knowing there was nowhere he'd rather be at that moment than right where he was, with Hannah Shay in his arms.

Dear Readers,

Thank you for reading COLD RIVER! I hope you enjoyed the story and are wondering what's next for the Camerons, the Harpers, the Shays, their friends . . . *and* their enemies. Rose Cameron and her golden retriever, Ranger, a search-and-rescue dog, take center stage in COLD DAWN, my next Black Falls novel, due out in late 2010. As private and competent as her three brothers, Rose is coming off a tough year, and big challenges await her.

We'll also get to see A.J., Elijah and Sean Cameron in COLD DAWN, as well as learn more about Navy SEAL Ryan "Grit" Taylor and Charlie Neal, the genius, incorrigible son of the vice president of the United States. Look for the return of Secret Service agent Jo Harper and the "sisters" of Three Sisters Café, too. Jo and Elijah Cameron, of course, played a central role in COLD PURSUIT, the first Black Falls novel, which introduces this fictional small town in my home state of Vermont.

Also in 2010, the paperback edition of

my *New York Times* bestseller THE MIST will be out in June. The book features Lizzie Rush, a hotelier whose spy father taught her everything he knows, as she goes after a missing billionaire out for violent revenge . . . and takes on mysterious Will Davenport, who lives by his own personal code and answers to no one.

As I write this note, I'm working on THE WHISPER, the follow-up to THE MIST, and loving being back in this "world" of Boston detectives, FBI agents, Irish folklorists, eccentric hoteliers and spies. If you're new to this series, the first two books, THE WIDOW and THE ANGEL, are both out in paperback now.

Finally, I'm thrilled to see ON FIRE returning to print in February, with a gorgeous new cover. Set on the coast of Maine—one of my favorite places—the story pits oceanographer Riley St. Joe and FBI agent John Straker against a very clever and dangerous killer.

Thank you again, and I hope you enjoy escaping into these "worlds" I've created!

Happy reading,
Carla

For all my latest news and to enter my monthly contest, please visit my Web site at www.CarlaNeggers.com. If you wish to write me by mail, please address any correspondence to: PO Box 826, Quechee VT 05059